CW00767182

THE HAPPY THISTLE

The Curious Case of the Katenapped Girl

A Verbal Animation

em.thompson

Sir Frederick Prendergast (born 24 March 1962) is a British entrepreneur, businessman and merchant banker. The Sunday Times Rich List estimates his fortune at £1.15bn, ranking him as the 95th richest-person in the UK. Knighted in 1998 for services to prophylactics, he is CEO of the Lucky Latex rubber empire and a founder member of The Chelsea Jockey Club. Upon marriage to Lady Rose Trevelyan, an heiress to the Trevelyan banking dynasty, he was appointed Chairman of Midshires Merchant Bank. Following Lady Rose's untimely demise he married former catwalk model and French film actress, Fifi Clark, better known by her stage name of Fou-Fou LaPorte. They live in Kensington with Fifi's daughter from a previous marriage to Las Vegas hot air tycoon, Basil Clark.

i

Heather Prendergast slung her cap on a hook by the door, hung her tunic in the wardrobe and stowed her workboots under the sink. Exhausted after another ten-hour shift, she unknotted her tie, slackened her belt, flopped down on the futon and pummelled the cushions in a fit of pique. She had been *so* looking forward to spending her annual leave holidaying with the love of her life, Detective Simon Robinson of the North Huddshire Covert Operations Unit, or Naff as he was known for reasons that were fast becoming clear. But when she returned to her studio flat that afternoon, she found a note on the kitchenette table. If he was to be believed - a very big if – it seemed that he had been seconded to the serious crime squad to undertake a top-secret undercover mission. 'Bet you have,' Heather grumbled under her breath. Undercover could mean all sorts of things in Naffspeak, most of them *unspeakable*. The man was impossible. But she supposed that if anyone was to blame for their stopgo relationship, it was her for falling head over heels in love with a man who was already madly in love with someone else - himself.

But looking on the bright side - as she went to great pains to do - she had at last taken the first few steps towards fulfilling a lifeheld ambition. Having applied her remarkable deductive talents and keen forensic powers of obfuscation to cracking *The Curious Case of The Throatslit*

Man, she had been promoted from Hornsey Road Police Station to New Scotland Yard, or to be more precise, she had been seconded to the Metropolitan Police Operational Feeding Arm.

She was quite literally over the moon when, after a gruelling interview, she was assigned to undercover duties in the New Scotland Yard staff canteen to investigate suspected cookery crookery. Ever willing, she set about her cloak and dagger duties - her pinny and skillet duties as Naff scoffingly dismissed them - with the alacrity for which she was – or would one day be - renowned. Issued with a pinafore, a pair of rubber gloves and a hair net, she was instructed to keep an eagle eye out for lightfingered tealeafs pilfering teaspoons, sugar lumps and the like. In the event, this proved easier said than done, as she spent more time peeling potatoes than keeping her eyes peeled. Indeed, as the weeks wore on, she began to suspect that her undercover mission was largely, if not entirely, a means to bolster the depleted ranks of kitchenary skivvies; Chef Dibley's reputation for cracking the whisk and flying off the mangle at the drop of a toque-blanche made it difficult, if not impossible, to recruit – or more to the point, to retain – menial millennials. A step up the police ladder, it was not.

Needless to say, it was demanding work - demanding and exhausting. Granted, catering for a swarm of ravenous police locusts was hardly a thrill a minute, but it had its challenges. Heather was to learn that there was more to baking a bean than met the eye. But stoic as ever, she stiffed her upper lip and reminded herself that she was now an apron string closer to the throbbing gristle of police action. Indeed, she had high hopes that if she kept a steady hand on the skillet and did not spread her talents too thinly, she might secure promotion to the prestigious Salmonella Squad. What mattered was that she now had one boot wedged firmly in the door of criminal investigation. It was surely only a matter of time before she would be called upon to assist with more serious felonies than misrepresenting catfish as cod or counterfeiting gnocchi. She was confident of a glittering career tangling with blackmailers rather than black puddings . . . clearing up unsolved homicides, not leftover hummus. Until then, she resolved to look, listen and learn as she wheeled her tea-trolley around the clatterous corridors of New Scotland Yard. As she proudly boasted to Aunt Elizabeth, now that she had joined the ranks of CID, she was a police-force to be reckoned with. What she failed to say was that in her case, CID stood for Catering Induction Detail, but when all is said and done, who gives a tuppenny fig about semantics? In that PC Prendergast of New Scotland Yard Staff Canteen didn't quite cut the mustard, Prendergast of The Yard it was beyond the yellowed portals of the cafeteria kitchen.

To be honest, in her heart of hearts Heather harboured doubts whether she was really cut out for slicing bread and peeling potatoes. To be perfectly frank, all was not going well. Today had been a case in point. After receiving a dressing down from Chef Dibley for mistakenly using syrup of figs instead of vinegar in the salad dressing and erroneously topping the rice puddings with black pepper in the belief that it was nutmeg, she tripped over a bootlace and emptied a jug of piping hot custard into Chief Inspector Wheeler's lap. Embarrassing though this was, what most punctured her pride was that the episode had been witnessed by her hero, Detective Inspector Isaac Obafemi.

To Heather's way of thinking, Obafemi was a latterday Sherlock Holmes. He was an old school master of the deductive arts with a legendary reputation for solving the most intractable cases. More often than not, she dozed off at night dreaming of working alongside him as the saucerer's apprentice. Having craved to attract his attention from the moment she arrived, she had finally succeeded. Unfortunately. His good-natured chuckles still rang in her ears like a death knell for her fractured ambitions.

Having consigned her deflated pride to the cringebin of past blushes, Heather was pondering how to spend her leave in Naff's absence - stay with Aunt Elizabeth on her ancestral estate in St. Mary Nook perhaps or maybe write those blockbusting detective novels she had been plotting ever since being asked to leave finishing school - when the phone rang. Putting thoughts of PC Bruyère 'Kitten' Galore - the glamorous redheaded heroine of her pending bestsellers - to one side, she took the call. She naturally assumed that it would be her boyfriend. After all, apart from Aunt Elizabeth, she had only entrusted

4

her cellphone number to the odd friend, or to be precise, to Naff. And were it not for the fact that he just had, she was sorely tempted to tell him to pack his bags and leave. Whatever had possessed her to invite the *insufferable* scally to move into her cosy bachelorette pad in Crouch End, she asked herself as she cast an eye about the pokey bedsit. It was cluttered with shaving tools, blokey magazines and *unmentionable*s of a decidedly masculine gender. She had no idea what she could possibly have seen in the man. He was loud, arrogant, messy, unreliable, egotistical, vain, mouthy and had the libido of a rutting stallion. But his spaghetti bolognaise was to die for. Her mind's-eye salivated as it pictured his seductive smile and rippling pecs as he grated a slab of fresh Parmesan cheese onto a steaming dish of home-made pasta. She slurped her lips . . . yum, yum – if food be the music of love, munch on.

With thoughts of his Penne Arribiata in mind, she donned a mischievous smirk, lounged back on the sofabed, closed her eyes, held the cellphone to her lips and whispered a husky, 'hello, sexy. Guess what - I'm lying naked on the rug with a photograph of you in one hand and . . .'

'Heather,' a fruity Beaujolais voice boomed. 'Great Scott, pull yourself together, girl.'

'Oh, my gosh - daddy.' Heather scrambled to her feet and stood to attention. 'How did you get my number?'

'Never you mind.'

'Aunt Elizabeth gave it to you, didn't she?' Stung by the ultimate betrayal, Heather clenched her jaw and narrowed her eyes. Her aunt had promised faithfully not to breathe a word of her current whereabouts to her estranged father.

'Indeed. She was reluctant, but I insisted.' Sir Freddie cleared an awkward frog from his throat. 'She tells me that you have been promoted to CID. New Scotland Yard, no less. Rose would have been proud of you.'

At mention of her mother, Heather's knees buckled like a shoe and she slumped down on the sofabed. 'You sound upset, daddy. Are you alright?' she asked, praying that the answer would be no. It was years since they last spoke. If she remembered right, it was his terse farewell when he parked her with Aunt Elizabeth after she had been declared persona tres, tres, *tres* non grata at the family home by her new stepmother.

It was all that Heather could do not to gag as a picture of Fifi Clark-Prendergast chundered to mind. It wasn't so much that she disliked the woman, but rather that she hated the gold-digging witch with every fibre of her fibre. So, what if it had been a mistake to make her feelings known over the public address system at the wedding reception? Instead of cutting her out of his life like a rancorous tumour, her father should have applauded her honesty. Because the fact was that Fifi was obese. And she did stink of garlic. And she did have the manners of une femelle du porc. To put it in a nutkernel, she was gross, manipulative, idle, stupid, self-centred and French. Apart from that, she seemed pleasant enough – a barrel of laughs some might say . . . if they were drunk. It was her spoiled brat of a daughter that really set Heather's teeth on edge, in no small part because Sir Freddie doted on her. Katerina Clark? Bratty Upchuck, more like.

'A problem has arisen,' Sir Freddie announced. 'And I am in urgent need of your assistance.'

'Has the dishwasher broken?' Heather asked with all the irony of an ironing board.

'No idea. That is Missus Beaten's department.'

'Eggy still works for you?'

'Always has, always will. Best housekeeper and cook I have ever had. And Smothers is still with me, after a fashion. Now, when you are suitably attired, I wish to call upon your services.'

Heather held the cellphone at arm's length and gave her head a slap. The only time that her father had ever asked her for a favour was when he requested that she leave home . . . for good.

'A criminal matter has arisen,' Sir Freddie continued. 'I am in urgent need of professional advice but am under strict instructions not to contact the constabulary.'

'What do you mean . . . a criminal matter?' Heather asked, heartened by the note of desperation in her father's voice.

'Your stepmother and I have fallen victim to an unscrupulous gang of brigands.' Sir Freddie announced. 'I cannot discuss the matter on the telephone. I will explain when I see you. And whatever you do, wear something respectable. We must pretend that this is a family reunion. If the felons see a uniformed police officer enter the house, there will be consequences. Need I say more?' He paused for a moment, then requested, nay demanded, 'I will expect you within the hour. Pack a nightdress and a suitable change of clothing. Oh, and Heather . . .' He took a deep breath. 'I am relying upon your discretion. If news of this leaks out, the consequences will be grave,' he said, then added an ominous, 'in every meaningful sense of the word.'

ii

A caber's toss from the North Circular Road in the insalubrious North London borough of Willesden stands The Happy Thistle restaurant. Intended as the first in a nationwide chain of Highland themed eateries, no expense has been spared to convert the servery of a rambling disused Victorian bakery into a faithful reproduction of a Scottish bothy complete with peat burning griddle, stag's head and tartan tablecloths.

The kilted chef is a bumptious Scotsman who goes by the name of Groaty McTavish. His specialties include gastronomical twists on traditional Caledonian recipes such as Bannockbuns, Pickled Seaweed, Malty McOatshakes, Nutty McFruitcake, Loganberry Trifle and a variety of similarly mouthtempting delicacies. But all is not what it seems. The fact is that the fastfoodery is merely a front. The true purpose is to provide a lucrative income stream to fund the construction of a state-of-the-science laboratory in the cavernous basement. For behind the Highlandish façade lies a labyrinthine warren of corridors leading to a sinister world of scientific malady.

The brainiac behind the operation is an enigmatic shadow who jealously guards his identity. The Professor, as he is known to those who profess to know him, has devoted his extraordinary genius to solving the greatest astrophysical challenge of the age - the creation of dark matter. As every schoolnerd knows, dark matter is the key to unlocking the secrets of the space-time continuum and by this means, enslaving the world. In the furtherance of his malicious ambitions, the Professor ploughed his life's ill-gotten gains into the purchase of the derelict bread factory and enlisted the services of McTavish to provide a veneer of Highland respectability.

A creature of ruthless logic, the Professor is not a man to be trifled with. Nor is he a man to chance his arm. Rather, he seeks to eliminate ambiguity by reducing every parameter of uncertainty to quadratic equations, or to put it another way, to employ the methodology of empiricism for the avoidance of temporal doubt. Mathematical determinism, he maintains, governs the vagaries of life. To put it at its simplest - as he is loath to do - if $a + b + c = x$, should the value of a or b vary, by amending the value of c, x will remain constant.

And so it was with the bakery; a represented the cost of acquiring the derelict building, b the cost of renovation, c the cost of equipping the laboratory and x the available funds. Should any of the parameters change, the Professor could amend the others accordingly, thereby ensuring that the immovable constant - x - remained unchanged.

All well and good I hear you say, but to the Professor's bamboozlement, all did not go entirely to plan. After months of sleepless nights puzzling why this should be so, he realised that he had failed to account for Value Added Tax and more to the point, the ineptitude of the firm of builders he had employed to realise his architectural ambitions. In their defence, it is only fair to point out that when he instructed them that the basement should be bombproof, he made no mention of nuclear devices. Lowering the floor by eight feet and cladding the walls with several metres of reinforced concrete doubled the building costs. To cut to the chase, $a + b + c$ now equalled far more bitcoin than he could readily afford.

As the building costs spiralled, the Professor was left with no alternative but to borrow up to and beyond the hilt. Having no truck with banks nor they with him, in desperation he turned to the Proust Mob, a notorious East End firm of pawnbrokers and loan sharks. He had no choice. Without a laboratory he could not manufacture dark matter and thus enrich his coffers beyond imagination, but he could not fund the building work without borrowing eyewatering amounts of cash. As security, the Prousts demanded the deeds to the old bakery, four ColdFusion nuclear centrifuges and a treasured domestic Hadronette Collider that he held in storage pending their installation in the new laboratory.

Doubts set in shortly after the restaurant opened when, after a slow start, trade hit a brick wall. No matter what McTavish tried – two Bannockbuns for the price of one . . . three for the price of one . . . ten for the price of one – the fastfoodery failed to titillate the tastebuds of the locals. It did not help that the competition was stiff. The area boasted every manner of cafes, trattorias and restaurants. Indeed, that was the very reason the Professor had been convinced that The Happy Thistle would be a rip-roaring success; he was confident that he had spotted a gap in the market. With so many exotic culinaries in the vicinity, a Highland themed restaurant was bound to pack them in. After all, are not condiments the spice of life? Well, it seemed that Rabbie Burns was right – the best laid plans of mice and men gae aft awry. The Professor's certainly had.

And now, unreasonably, in his opinion, the Prousts were demanding their money back with three hundred per cent interest. Solly Proust made brutally clear that unless the Professor stumped up five million cash pound notes by the end of the month, the Proust Syndicate would have no qualms about foreclosing on the loan, auctioning the bakery, selling the nuclear centrifuges to a contact in Iran and taking one hundred and sixty pounds of flesh in grizzly interest. Nothing personal, Solly maintained, but business is business. He felt duty bound to make an example of the Professor to show others the terminal consequences of defaulting on a loan.

Not one to ever admit to having made a mistake, in no small part because so far as he was aware, he never had, the Professor blamed the banks and more to the point, the alien lizards who controlled them. He was determined to make them pay by nook or by cranny, a sentiment not shared by his Scottish henchman.

'It's nae on, Chief. It's nae on at all,' McTavish protested. 'Kidnapping an innocent wee lassie is nae in ma job description.'

The Professor sat at the recreationary table in the staff quarters of The Happy Thistle simmering like malignant gruel. 'Kidnap?' he snarled. 'Humbug. We are merely borrowing Miss Clark pending a modest gratuity from her besotted stepfather in acknowledgement of our good intent. No harm will come of her as long as Sir Freddie does my bidding.'

'But just look at the bonnie wee bairn.' McTavish double-clicked The Eastminster Academy for Young Gentleladies website on his Mc-ayePhone and scrolled down to a photograph of the school hockey team. He pointed to a small pigtailed girl in the front row. 'Hardly able tae tie her aen shoelaces by the looks of her,' he said. 'I bet ye a muckle tae a mickle she's nae even alloowed oot on her own after dark.'

The Professor gave the picture a cursory glance. If truth be told - not his strongest suit - he was minded to acknowledge that his Highland accomplice had a point. Sir Freddie Prendergast's stepdaughter, Katy Clark, looked the epitome of innocence - cherubic, it might perhaps be said - with her bunched blond hair, gap teeth, cheeky grin, pleated gymslip, bobby socks and sandals. 'Clever girl,' he muttered as he read the accompanying caption. 'Top of her class and winner of Eastminster Academy's annual prize for initiative, no less. I can see why her stepfather dotes on her . . . fool.' Loath though he was to admit it, he too harboured reservations but what alternative did he have? He needed an abundance of money in an abundant hurry and unless he won the lottery - unlikely in the extreme bearing in mind odds of one in forty-five million, fifty-seven thousand, four hundred and seventy-four to one - kidnapping the daughter of a billionaire banker was his only option.

Although sympathetic to the Professor's predicament, McTavish was reluctant. The fact was that he had not signed up for such depraved skullduggeries. The situations vacant advertisement in the Pest Control Times had been vague . . . *Ruthless chef required for new Highland themed restaurant. Bed and board provided.* In desperate need of a job, he submitted a CV and to his delight his application was accepted by return. That night he packed a bin liner, borrowed a stolen bicycle from a squat mate and set off for the bright lights of London, blissfully unaware of the rocky road ahead . . . in every sense of the word. Or words.

Nothing if not pragmatic, McTavish accepted that having made his own sleeping bag he would just have to lie in it. To cut a long ramble short, after debating the pros and cons, the ins and outs and the rights and wrongs of the matter, he was won over by the Professor's reasoned argument. After all, he had an anatomical desire to keep his kneecaps intact. And let's face it, a job is a job.

The very next afternoon, the Professor hacked into traffic control and disabled the Pelican lights in Eastminster High Street. With Sir Freddie's Rolls Royce clogjammed in trafficary mayhem, McTavish parked a stolen getaway car in a quiet cul-de-sac around the corner from the Eastminster Academy for Young Gentleladies. After donning a false beard, a white wig and an ankle-length McGabardine, he allowed himself a smug smile, confident that nobody would recognise him. Indeed, were it not for the distinctive strawberry birthmark on the dark side of his neck, he might not have recognised himself. He could be anyone he thought. And if truth be told, he was.

McTavish waited nervously for the telltale knell of the school bell that would spell the end of term and, quite possibly, the beginning of the end of time. As the clock struck four, he readjusted his beard, leant on his cromach and studied the jabbering crocodile of excited schoolgirls exiting the exclusive private school for young gentleladies. Adopting his most convincing smile, he accosted a small girl in a pleated gymskirt and an aquamaroon blazer tagged onto a crocodile of pigtailed schoolclones pavementing the gates. 'Hello, lassie,' he muffled through his false beard and offered her a fruity lollysuck. When she shrank back, he added a reassuring, 'Freddie sent me tae fetch ye.'

'Fred sent . . . you?' Katy turned up her button nose and looked at him with an expression of derisory scorn.

'Aye, he's been called away on business,' McTavish bluffed, then relaxed when Katy shrugged, hooklined and sinkered by his convincing cuddlyuncle act. He pointed round a nearby corner and said, 'I parked the motor down yon alley.'

Casting prudence to the wind, Katy took McTavish's hand and followed him to a battered Ford. 'Got top marks for all me exams,' she jabbered as she skipped along beside him swinging her satchel, 'and a scholarship for initiative. Mam will be dead chuffed that head-teach kept her word.' When they rounded the corner, she slowed down, looked around, frowned and asked, 'so where's dad's Roller?'

'In the menders having the dashboard waxed,' McTavish said as he opened the hot-jalopy's boot. 'But look – Freddie sent ye a present.'

'A pressy? For me? Oh goody. I love surprises.' Katy clapped her hands, peered into the trunk and scratched her head. 'What is it?'

'Chloroform,' McTavish growled and clamped a rag over Katy's mouth. After an obligatory struggle, she slumped into his arms like a raggedy doll, out for the foreseeable count.

McTavish cast a wary eye or two around the deserted street, bundled Katy's limp body into the trunk and rubbed his hands. 'Time tae teck a wee trip, bonnie lass,' he gloated. The trap was sprung; the spider had his fly. The tricky part was over. From here-on in, everything would be plain sailing. With a triumphant smirk, he scrambled into the driver's seat, ignitioned the engine, engaged the gears, put his foot down on the gas and . . . nothing. Nonplussed, he brushed his bushy eyebrows out of his eyes and squinted at the petrol gauge. 'Hoots mon, I dinnae believe it,' he groaned and slumped over the steering wheel with his head in his hands.

iii

Heather Prendergast had made herself a faithful promise that she would not return to her former family home until she or her stepmother died, whichever was the sooner. Yet here she was, bound by a sense of duty to her least, least, *least* favourite person in the whole wide world – her despicable apology for a father.

As far as she could see – and if she stood on tiptoe she could almost see from one end to the other - the gated street was much as she remembered . . . grandiose four storeyed houses with basement servants' quarters accessed by steep pavemented steps. A pride of Rolls Royces, Bentleys and upmarket Mercedes were parked in the drives, each intimidating the next in ascending order of social pretension. An old-fashioned pillar box stood at one end of the street and a red telephone box at the other, reminders of a bygone age of lickstickered stamps and penny payphones. Halfway along stood Trevelyan House. No longer elegant and sedate - the architectural jewel in the terraced crown - it bore the telltale signs of Fifi Clark-Prendergast's colour-discoordinated lack of taste.

Heather winced as she ran an eye over the gooseberry stucco, shocking pink shutters and harlequinned front door. My goodness, she thought - it looks like a Wendy House. She had no doubt that her grandfather, Lord Jinx Trevelyan, would be turning in his grave had the authorities ever found his body. Still, as Aunt Elizabeth would say, needs be as needs must when duty calls, so she stiffed her upper lip and put her best kitten-heel forward.

Thankful that she could see no snooty neighbours peeking through their chintz curtains, she breathed a quiet sigh of relief. To her way of mind, she looked *unsufferably* stuffy. She tugged the hem of her herringbone skirt - her knees were not her best feature – buttoned up her dowager jacket, reknotted her silk scarf and tidied a few stray hairs into her bun. Plainclothes disguises don't come much plainer than this she thought with a sartorial scowl as she unscrewtopped her Maxfactor and unhandbagged her powderpuff to touch up her makeup.

Confident that she would measure up to her father's definition of respectable, Heather rested her overnight case on the doorstep and rang the bell. Nauseous at the prospect of seeing Sir Freddie again, she asked herself, what am I doing here? Quick as a flash, the answer came – you must be out of your frolicking mind.

The tarte truth was that Heather owed her father no favours. Far from it. She had been about to fling her cellphone on the floor and stamp on it when he mentioned Missus Beaten and dear old Smothers. At thoughts of the eccentric domestics, she broke into a smushy smile. She could not help it. They were the closest things that she had had to a family during her mother's long illness - things being the operative word. Her father on the other hand, ranked lower on her scale of unmentionables than toothache, haemorrhoids or those *ghastly* oiks who swanned around the police canteen making lewd remarks about her buns.

As she waited to be ushered into the Georgian townhouse where she had been born and partially bred, a flood of memories flushed between her ears, some good, most not. She could only hope that when volume one of the Official Biography of Prendergast of The Yard came to be written, the distinguished author would dismiss her early years in a few brief words, along the lines of . . .

Born of ordinary commonfolk stock, after an uneventful upbringing Prendergast joined the Metropolitan Police at the age of twenty. What follows is the remarkable story of how this humble, unassuming woman of the people rose from modest roots to become the most illustrious crimefighter in the history of New Scotland Yard.

Alright, so what if that might be bending the truth a tad or perhaps a smidgeon more? As Aunt Elizabeth would say, history is merely myth dressed up as fact to titillate the palate of the hoi polloi.

The fact of the matter was that Heather harboured a dark secret that she dared not reveal to her colleagues in the Metropolitan Police staff canteen. For unbeknownst to Chef Dibley's cookie crew, her life had been blighted from the outset by a privileged upbringing.

A more candid account of Heather Prendergast's early years might read as follows . . .

Born rich – the sole heir to the Lucky Latex rubber empire – Heather's father, Sir Freddie Prendergast, had an uncanny knack of accumulating debt much as a pavement attracts spittle. Miserly, self-centred and ill-tempered, he had few friends other than bookmakers and bartenders, his penchant for a tipple only being trumped by a fondness for a flutter on the nags. These two Achilles heels almost proved his undoing when, acting upon a tip from an acquaintance at his gentleman's club, he bet the family fortune on a rank outsider in The Cheltenham Gold Cup. Despite the nag's advanced age, failing eyesight - it had no need of blinkers - and abysmally dismal track record, Sir Freddie was reliably assured that it was a sure thing. 'Trust me, old boy, it's in the bag. A dead cert,' his acquaintance told him with a nudge, a nod and a wink. However, Sir Freddie's trust - and his bet - proved sorrily misplaced when, upon hearing the starter's gun, the horse suffered a massive coronary. It might not have been a cert but it was most certainly dead and destined for a bag - according to the post-mortem the result of a toxic intravenous cocktail of etorphine, caffeine and diamorphine.

Faced with losing his shirt, braces, plus fours and brogues, Sir Freddie did the only thing he could to stave off bankruptcy . . . he married money. Eyebrows were raised in aristocratic circles when the Times carried an announcement that Sir Freddie Prendergast and the beautiful Lady Rose Trevelyan were betrothed. The most eligible debutante on the society circuit, Lady Rose was the eldest daughter of Sir Freddie's old school chum, Lord

Jameson 'Jinx' Trevelyan, owner of Midshires Merchant Bank and another inveterate drunkard.

A generation younger than Sir Freddie, Lady Rose had inherited half her father's vast fortune after he lost his way home from the casino one night and stumbled into Regent's Canal. With both eyes on the main chance, Sir Freddie took the emotionally vulnerable teenager under his wing, offered her a shoulder to cry on, popped the question and threatened to slit his wrists - and hers - if she said no.

From the outset, the marriage proved an unhappy union. This being the case, more than a few more eyebrows were raised when Rose fell pregnant. Heads nodded wryly when word leaked that Sir Freddie had bet a sizeable chunk of his new wife's fortune that he would father a son and heir within a calendar year. It goes without much saying that he was distraught when she gave birth to a daughter, Heather. He never forgave her; he was not a man to readily forgive or forget. 'Do you have any idea how much your damn negligence has cost me?' he railed at his tearful young bride. 'Now I am going to have to do some ruddy work for a change.' And that, by all accounts, was the last meaningful conversation the two ever had.

As we all know, even mismanaged banks make obscene amounts of money and when condom sales skyrocketed during the AIDS pandemic, Lucky Latex's patented Durafix Fruity Rubbers were gobbled up by the boxful by randy clubbers. And so it was that despite his spendthrift ways and legendary indolence, Sir Freddie became incalculably rich by default.

Heather looked back upon her early girlhood with fondness. From what she could remember, she had been a happy if somewhat solitary child with an over-fertile imagination who doted on a mother who doted upon her. So, when Lady Rose succumbed to breast cancer at the tender age of twenty-nine, Heather was beside herself. Not merely did her father ignore her – dismissing his daughter as an ill-conceived wager gone disastrously wrong – he acted as though she didn't exist. Or rather he acted as if he wished that she didn't exist.

Heather was ten when Sir Freddie was ensnared by former *fille de choeur* and fuller-figure catalogue model, Fifi Clark, a serial divorcee he met on what he euphemistically described as a business trip to Hippadrome de Longchamps near Paris. It was a whirlwind romance and they were engaged before the month was out. In that Fifi brought a prepacked family to the dining table in the gangly shape of six-year-old Katerina, her child by her third marriage to Las Vegas business mogul Basil Clark, little Heather was relegated to the outer fringes of the family shrub.

When Heather's meticulously scripted impromptu speech at the wedding reception met with an embarrassed silence from the assembled guests - apart from Rose's younger sister, Lady Elizabeth Trevelyan, who roared with laughter - she was banished from the fold. Taken in by Lady Elizabeth, the other shareholder of Midshires

Merchant Bank, she spent her teenage years at boarding school and after a truncated spell at a swish Swiss finishing school, scraped into Merton Police College, determined to pursue a burning ambition to become the world's most renowned detective - Prendergast of The Yard.

Heather was jolted back to the present by the sound of footsteps shuffling to the door. After an age, the lock clunked and a greyfrosted face peered out, precariously attached by folds of wrinkly skin to a human skeleton dressed in an old-fangled butler's uniform – oversized black tailcoat and undersized bow tie, starchywhite crumpled shirt, shabby orange waistcoat, saggy pincreased trousers and softshoeshuffle slippers. He handed Heather a bag of potato peelings, said, 'not today, young lady,' and was about to close the door when she clapped her hands and squealed, 'it's me, Smothers. Don't you recognise me?'

'Goodness gracious, if it isn't Lady Trevelyan.' Smothers' lips creased into a tortuous smile. 'I do believe that I haven't seen you since your funeral.'

'Oh, Smothers, you haven't changed a bit. I'm Heather. Rose died eleven years ago. Remember?'

'Well, well, well, if you are not the very image of your mother. A little younger, perhaps, but that is only to be expected. Come this way. M'lud and his fancy bit of French stuff are expecting you.' Smothers picked up Heather's overnight case, took a few steps, stumbled to a halt, wheezed, put it down, felt his back and mopped his brow. 'Goodness me, Miss Heather. What do you have in

24

there - lead?'

'A jumper, a blouse and a pair of jeans. Here, let me . . .'

Leaving Heather to carry her case, Smothers led the way to the sitting room at a sloeworm's pace. 'I will let Missus Beaten know that you are here,' he told her. 'When she heard that you were coming, she boiled you a special treat.' He opened a door and stood aside to show her in. 'Goodness,' he said as he squinted into the broom closet. 'They have moved the sitting room again.'

'Don't bother, really. I know the way.' Leaving Smothers to scratch his head and blink, Heather hurried down the hallway to a starspangled door between the stairwell to the servant's quarters and the walkway to the scullery. She patted her bun, straightened her skirt, dewrinkled her blouse, gathered her pluck in both hands and walked in.

Aghast, she stopped in her tracks and caught her breath believing that she had unwittingly stumbled into an hallucinatory Barbieworld. For in place of the staid trappings she remembered from her childhood, she was confronted - affronted might be a more appropriate word - by a veritable vision of vulgarity. From the deep-pile nylon carpet, velveteen windowdrapes and plastic candelabras to the ersatz furniture, everything was a garish shade of shocking pink. Even her mother's treasured Steinway had been relaquered cottoncandy with sugarplum-fairy motifs and blue and yellow keys. It was, Heather thought, as if the very fabric of the room blushed with embarrassment.

Covering the walls were mementos of her stepmother's putative brush with stardom in her misbegotten sex-pussy days when, as Fou-Fou LaPorte, she enjoyed a short-lived moviestar career. In pride of place above the marble fireplace was a glitterframed poster of her starring as Marie Antoinette in a long forgotten bollock-busting movie. Pouting provocatively like a trout on heat, her rotund face was peeking coquettishly out of a mountainous white wig festooned with pink ribbons. Her ample curves were shoehorned into a bodice-busting corset and a translucent pink chemise. A caption splashed across her heavy hips read . . .

Laissez-les manger du mon gateau.

Avec 'La Reine de la Passion' bombe blonde Fou-Fou LaPorte dans le rôle de Marie Antoinette

Relaxing in a magenta armchair by the fireplace with his nose in The Tipster's Times was a hoary gentleman in a pinstripe suit. His shrinking hairline, walrus moustache, flabby double chin and droopy jowls gave him the appearance of a beached walrus. He looked up when he heard Heather enter and snapped, 'no one teach you to knock before you barge into a room, young lady?' Sir Freddie – for it was he - put aside his newspaper, stubbed out his cigar and glowered over the rim of his monocle. 'Born in a barn, were you, Helen? And I thought I told you to wear something respectable.'

'I'll close the door on my way out. Oh, and by the way my name is Heather, spelt s-c-r-e-w-u,' Heather said as she turned to leave.

'Less of your lip, young lady. If you value your career, you will watch your tongue. The Commissioner of Police is member of my Lodge. I am sure that Sir Toby would take a dim view of one of his officers behaving like a common-or-garden washerwoman. Now take a seat.' Sir Freddie flicked a wrist at a bright pink vinylpadded sofa. 'We have something to discuss. It would not be over-egging the pudding to say that it is a matter of life and death.'

Hardly had Sir Freddie finished speaking than an animal howl rent the air. 'Mon pauvre, pauvre petit bébé,' a shrill voice wailed. 'I am in despairs.'

Sir Freddie leapt up from his armchair and hurried to the chaise-lounge. Having tried and failed to shuffle Fifi's stout frame aside, he knelt down and petted her hand. 'There, there, my precious,' he said. 'I am sure that this is just a mischievous hoax perpetrated by a deranged prankster. To be on the safe side, I have enlisted one of the foremost detectives in the land to assist.' He scowled at Heather from the corner of an eye. 'You remember Rose's girl, don't you?

'Sacre bleu . . .' Fifi clapped a hand to her brow. 'Do not mention that vile woman in my presence. I will have a fit of the faints.' She closed her eyes and feigned a swoon. 'Quick, mon cher. My smelly salts.'

Well, that brought back memories, Heather thought.

Had she been called upon to describe her stepmother – which thankfully she was not – she would have refused. The fact was that she would not have needed to. When not singing the praises of her daughter, Fifi's sole and constant topic of conversation was herself. Heather knew the patter off by heart. After all, she had heard it often enough. But although Fifi Clark-Prendergast boasted an illustrious career as a ballet dancer, catwalk model and motion picture actress, Heather knew better.

As co-owner of Midshires Bank, Heather's aunt, Lady Elizabeth Trevelyan, had hired a private detective to investigate her former brother-in-law's proposed spouse when the engagement was announced. Shocked but not unduly surprised, she learned an altogether different truth.

It transpired that in her youth, Fifi LeBoeuf - to use her birthname - had been employed as a chorus girl at the Folies Bergère. Renowned for her buxom figure and elephantine thighs, she was talent-bedded by the famous French film director, Luc Bassoon, and enjoyed a short-lived career as Fou-Fou LaPorte, France's answer to Diana Dors. Her trademark bottle-blonde perm, atomic breasts and ballistic derriere soon fell out of favour with movie-going audiences and her star burnt out as quickly as it had ignited. After binge-eating her way through a succession of failed marriages, she was reduced to modelling casualwear for *dames bien construites*, size eighteen and above. Overnight, her fortunes changed when she was rescued from the twilight zone of her twilight years by a chance encounter with an inebriated Sir Freddie Prendergast in a Montmartre bordello. Animal attraction trumped morning-after sobriety and following a weekend of impassioned rumpy-pumpy, they returned to England and tied the knot.

Seeing Fifi lounging on the chaise-lounge in a frilly pink organza negligee embroidered with lucent satin cherries and crepe de chine bananas, Heather was reminded of why she had retreated to her attic bedroom to bawl her eyes out after being introduced to her future stepmother. How could her father have fallen for such a grotesque folly of narcissism, she demanded of the Gods of Blind Cupidity? She could only assume that Fifi must possess some kind of mysterious hold over him. And as for her new stepsister, Katerina, or Katy as she was commonly known . . . enough said. More than enough.

'See what you have done?' Sir Freddie reached for his top pocket handkerchief to mop Fifi's blubbery eyes. 'You have upset your stepmother.'

'Pardon me for breathing,' Heather said. 'Anyway, what's this about? Surely you didn't ask me here just to show off that lump of slobbering lard.' She pointed to Fifi.

Sir Freddie's wing collars twitched like agitated ailerons and his blotchy nose went a staphylococcal shade of purple. 'How dare you?' he fumed. 'Young lady, in any other circumstances I would demand that you leave.' He took a few deep breaths to fumigate his apoplexy. 'Be that is it may, your frightful aunt tells me you are now a

CID officer. Extremely well thought of at The Yard by all accounts.'

'Oh, I'm not sure I would go that far,' Heather said with a modest smile, fingers tightly crossed behind her back.

'Think New Scotland Yard can manage without you for a few days?' Sir Freddie asked in such a way as to suggest that an officer of Heather's calibre should be free to come and go as she pleased.

'As it happens, I'm currently on leave. Goodness only knows how CID will cope without me,' Heather sighed, remembering the stack of dirty saucepans awaiting her in the canteen scrubbery. 'Why?'

'Darling Katy has been kidnapped. I require the services of a top-notch detective to rescue her from the clutches of a ruthless gang of villains.'

Heather sat bolt upright and gasped, 'golly . . . did I hear you right? Bratty has been kidnapped? Who in their right mind would do a thing like that?'

'That is for you to determine.' Sir Freddie showed Heather a piece of parchment upon which was pasted a missive made up of words snipped from a miscellany of newspapers . . . *We got your stepdaughter. If you want to see her alive again, log onto Ransom.com at eight o'clock tonight and you will receive our instructions. Your movements are being monitored round the clock. Do not contact the police, I repeat again, under no circumstances at all contact the police unless you want Katy to be returned in tiny pieces.*

'Gosh, how awful,' Heather said, hardly able to believe her eyes; the *appalling* syntax boggled her imagination.

'I am relying upon you to rescue your stepsister and apprehend the villains responsible for her abduction.' A hint of desperation replaced the default note of contempt in Sir Freddie's voice. 'But you must swear upon your late mother's grave not to breathe a word to a living soul. Should anyone ask, say that Katy is visiting her father in America. Do I make myself clear?'

Heather sat smartly to attention. 'Mum's the word, sir,' she said. A tingle of excitement squirrelled up her spine. She knew that if she cracked *The Curious Case of the Katenapped Girl*, it went without saying that her father's chum, the Commissioner of Police, would elevate her to Prendergast of The Yard. And if she failed? Katerina Clark would be a gonner.

It was a win-win scenario if ever there was one.

iv

The Professor thundered, 'you are late,' as Groaty McTavish crept through the door like a timorous wee beastie. 'Have you been drinking? Your breath reeks of Glasgow aftershave.'

'It's petrol, Chief,' McTavish said. 'Ran oot so had tae siphon some oot of a handy Lada.'

'Diabolis give me strength . . .' Tall, lean and wiry with a bulbous cranium befitting one of the greatest criminal meglaminds the world might ever see, the Napoleon of Crime jabbed a spindly finger in McTavish's face. 'Here am I, about to take over the universe, and you risk everything for the want of refined petroleum.'

McTavish hung his head and mumbled, 'sorry, Chief. I'm nae Einstein.'

'That, my dimwitted Groat, is clear for all to see, but I suppose I must be thankful for small mercies.' The Professor unbuttoned his frockcoat, loosened his britches, sat down on a bothystool and tossed his top hat on the table. 'Einstein was an imbecile,' he said. 'He mistakenly assumed the dark energy equation of the state parameter to be $w\Phi:=p\Phi$. But as any retarded chimpanzee with half a brain knows, $\Phi+3H\dot{\Phi}+dVd\Phi=Q\dot{}\Phi$. You see, the moron failed to account for latent radiation so ignored the fact that $\rho b=-3H\rho b$, $H=-\kappa22\rho c+\rho b+\dot{}\Phi2$. Can you believe it?

And the lizards say that I am demented,' he said with a hollow laugh. 'Compared to Einstein, I am a paragon of sanity. You see, were he to have defined an effective equation for the dark components which describe the equivalent uncoupled model in the background, the secrets of the time space continuum would have stared him in the face.'

'What a glaikit.' McTavish shook his unkempt mop of ginger hair. 'So what ye saying exactly, Chief? That this Einstein eejit disnae know his arse frae his elbow?'

'What I am saying, my ignoble Groat, is that $\rho c+3H(1+wc,eff)\rho c=0, \rho\Phi+3H(1+w\Phi,eff)\rho\Phi=0.$ Pretty damn obvious, I would have thought.'

McTavish's nod suggested that a mickle had just dropped, needless to say a pecuniary illusion. The truth was that for all his innate tenement-savvy, he was quadratically challenged. 'Aye, with ye the noo, Chief,' he bluffed, keen not to show his astrophysical ignorance. 'So, this Einstein glaikit gan and put the decimal point in the wrong place. What an eejit.'

'Decimal point, you say? Decimal point?' The Professor sat bolt upright and glared McTavish in the eye. 'What did they teach you at school, dolt?' he railed, shocked by his Highland henchman's rank ignorance. 'Had you been listening, you would realise that Einstein's theory of relativity has a fundamental flaw. He failed to account for the negative gravitation pull of dark matter.'

'So the laddie was constipated?'

'That is by the bye. Dark matter, my mentally challenged minion, is the basic building block of the universe. It is all around us. Follow me to my laboratory and I will prove it.' The Professor led the way down a double-decker stairway to the bowels of the old bakery, pushed open a steel-clad door and shuffled in. He swatted a hand at a naked filamental element dangling from the ceiling by a tangled wire and said, 'now, turn off the light and tell me what you see.'

McTavish flicked a switch and looked around. 'Nothing, Chief,' he said as he peered into the abyss. 'It's pitch black.'

'Precisely. That is because we are surrounded by dark matter.'

'I dinnae understand.'

'Of course you don't. Nobody does,' The Professor said. 'The greatest minds of this and every other age have failed to solve the ultimate puzzle of physics. Fools. The answer has been there for all to see since before the dawn of time. Take a look at this . . .'

'What?'

'Turn on the light, you dolt. Now, what do you see?'

'You mean that deepfreeze with a funnel bolted on top?'

34

'A deepfreeze? A deepfreeze, you say?'

'With a funnel on top.'

'That, my dimwitted henchman, is a Dark Matter Time Projection Chamber. The only one of its kind in existence. My life's work. It can condense atomic molecules into dark matter briquettes.' The Professor broke into a calculating smirk, knotted his fingers and clacked his bony knuckles. 'In simple layman's terms, it will enable me to create synthetic black holes infinitesimally smaller than a pinprick but with the mass of a star. It is the Holy Grail of physics. Whoever controls dark matter will rule the world.'

'And that'll be us, Chief?'

'That, my annoying ginger friend, will be me. Master of the Universe and all beyond. I and only I hold the key to producing sufficient energy to fuel the process. See that?' The Professor pointed a spindly finger at a wall-to-wall bank of floor-to-ceiling pipes, dials, meters, thermostats and rheostats. 'All very mundane, I hear you say. Typical of what one might find in any run of the mill domestic nuclear fission laboratory. But as you are no doubt aware, even a modest nuclear reaction capable of generating sufficient energy to power a time projection chamber requires immense pressure and will generate temperatures of millions of degrees. Enough to reduce North London to a toxic wasteland.'

'What - yae mean worse than it is the noo? Yaer

kidding.' McTavish masked his scepticism behind a semi-toothless smile. 'Gie me the nod afore ye turns on them nuclear jibby-jobbies and I'll meck mesself scarce.'

'Have no fear, my tartan terror. You see, I have solved the holy grail of cold fusion. Did it at nursery school, actually, but nobody took me seriously.' The Professor shuffled over to the time projection chamber and tapped an aperture above the subliminal velocity display. 'This is where you will insert the Queridium while I watch on from a safe distance. Coventry, perhaps, or Manchester.'

'Queridium?' McTavish asked casually, not wanting to display more rank ignorance than needs be.

The Professor's eyes glazed over and he stared unseeing into the mists of time. 'Indeed,' he said. 'Queridium is the rarest element in the galaxy. When cooled to a temperature of absolute zero and ionised in a bank of negative-gravity ColdFusion centrifuges, it produces unadulterated pure energy without harmful side-effects such as lethal radiation, gamma rays or noxious smells.'

McTavish nodded in a show of understanding, not that he did. Understanding was not much in his nature. 'Want me tae lift some, Chief? Tell me where it's stashed and I'll gan on the case.'

The man known as The Coffinary Boffin to those who called him that prodded a spindly finger in McTavish's chest. 'Dolt,' he snorted. 'There is but one source and one source only. A meteorite of pure Queridium fell to earth six years ago and is on display in the National Science Museum. Or it was.' He broke into a maniacal cackle and rubbed his hands together needlessly. 'Cunningly disguised as a cat burglar, I disabled the security alarms with an algorithm I cobbled together on the way over, climbed through a skylight, dangled from the ceiling by my hind legs, cut a hole in the display case with a laser, removed the Queridium with a pair of asparagus tongs, hailed a Hackney Cab and was home before the guards knew that anything was amiss. Imbeciles.'

Groaty McTavish masked his incomprehension behind a cautious smile. 'So yae tested this time projection jibby-job?' he asked.

'Pah. I have done the math so why waste valuable time I don't yet have?' The Professor's intemperate flick of a wrist suggested that McTavish might as well ask how anyone could know that the sun would rise in the morning without first experimenting to prove what was, in fact, a matter of fact. 'Whilst under lock and key for threatening to alert mankind to the pestilence of alien lizards governing our nation state, I calculated every possible variable to an infinitesimal degree.'

'Hoots mon - lizards are running the country?' McTavish gave the Professor an alarmed look to end all alarmed looks.

'Shhhh . . .' The Professor pressed a finger to his lips, looked over both shoulders and glanced nervously at the door. 'Walls have tympanums,' he whispered. After peering into all four corners of the gloom, he mopped his brow and cleared his throat. 'Take my word, my hairy Highlander,' he said. 'My time projection chamber cannot fail. The idea is unthinkable.' He gave McTavish a confident sneer. 'But enough of this puerile banter,' he said. 'Did you imprison our angelic little turtle dove as I instructed?'

'Aye. Trussed up like a haggis in the auld grainstore. Tied her tae the barleycot like ye said. She will nae have a clue where she is when she comes tae her senses.'

'You are quite sure that she did not get a good look at your face?'

'Ye kidding? Didnae even recognise messell with this wig and beard.'

'Excellent.' The Perverse Purveyor of Putrefaction as his dismembered psychiatrist used to call him, took an envelope from his frockcoat pocket and thrust it into McTavish's hand. 'Deliver this missive to Sir Freddie Prendergast's townhouse post haste. There is a postman's uniform in the cupboard under the stairs with your sleeping bag. And be sure to wear gloves.'

'Expecting snow?'

'Fingerprints, you moron. DNA.'

'Dinnae what?'

The Professor rolled his bulging eyes. 'So help me. Here am I, with a brain the size of Uranus, trying to explain simple quantum mechanics to a dim-witted Glaswegian with a tattoo of a spider on his neck.'

'It's nae a tattoo,' McTavish said with an injured look on his pockmarked face. 'It's a birthmark.'

'Do not give me that,' the Professor said. 'You were not born, you were quarried. Now off with you. I have important matters to attend to. This evening our little chickadee will star in her very own television show – to an audience of one. And then . . .' He rubbed his hands and cackled as was his wont when so mooded. 'I will deposit five million pounds in Solly Proust's thieving hands, retrieve my ColdFusion centrifuges and an endless night of reckoning will be visited upon this and every other land.'

v

Heather Prendergast drew back the bedroom curtains and gazed down at the garden. She sighed and sighed again as she remembered playing hide-and-seek with the elves in the rhododendrons – they always won – and dancing with the faeries in the buddleia behind the sandpit. And then she winced as she recalled being ticked off by Missus Beaten for squelching through the cultivated paddy field that had once been an ornamental pond when playing Swallows and Amazons. Tears trickled down her freckled cheeks as she was visited by a flashback to that balmy summer's day when she sat upon her mother's lap with buttercups plaited in her tumbling red hair - my precious little pre-Raphaelite angel, Rose used to call her. She wriggled on her mother's knee plucking petals from the stalky stamen of a dog daisy with her delicate little fingers . . . *she loves me, she loves me not* . . . and cast them to the forewinds of future fortune.

'Don't be silly, Spriggy,' her mother said with an ever-loving cuddle of a smile. 'I will love you to my dying day.'

To my dying day . . . a lump formed in Heather's throat as she remembered how her aunt had comforted her as best she could at her mother's funeral. 'Rose is in Heaven, Spriggy,' Aunt Elizabeth told her with a tempered fondness of surrogate affection. 'Now put on a brave face. She wouldn't want your father to see you cry, would she?'

'Then tell him to go away.'

'Really, sweetheart. Where is the Trevelyan stiff upper lip?' Aunt Elizabeth said with the best of upper-lip intentions. And that was when and why little Heather ran out of Eastminster Cathedral in floods of tears. She carried on running until her lungs were heaving fit to burst. Distraught, she slumped down on a park bench, wretched to the pith of her ten-year-old stomach and cried and cried and cried until her tears ran dry. And so she lay there wishing she could die for longer than she cared to dare until she felt a hand upon her shoulder.

'Are you alright, miss?' the policeman asked. He helped her to her feet and draped his tunic over her goose-pimpled shoulders. And then the most extraordinary thing happened . . . he offered her a jelly baby.

To this day, PC Heather Prendergast made sure that she was always, always, *always* armed with a fully loaded packet of jelly babies when she went out on the beat. It was a totem of the day that she decided to join the Metropolitan Police and an everloving reminder of her mother's gentle smile. How she missed her. How she would always miss her . . . to her dying day.

Heather was convinced that Rose watched over her every second of every minute of every hour of every day. Indeed, that was one reason she made sure to wash behind her ears last thing at night. She was determined to make her mother proud by making something of her life. And if, or rather *when*, she cracked this Katenapping case, her father would have to take her copperly credentials seriously. Maybe then he would grant her the paternal respect she so deserved. If that meant flying solo and rescuing Katy by her very own solitary sleuth, so be it.

Her college tutors might have been adamant that the foremost principle of policework is to never under any circumstances whatsoever embark upon a felonous investigation without backup - ever - but hey . . . what did they know? As Aunt Elizabeth would say, those who can, do, those who can't, teach, and those who can't do didley-squat go into politics. Had her hero, the legendary Detective Inspector Isaac Obafemi, not forged his reputation by single-handedly bringing the notorious Breakfast Serial Killer to book in the library where she worked? She couldn't imagine him shouting, 'stop daydreaming at the back there, you moron,' and flinging a piece of chalk at her. He would not have needed to. Had Isaac Obafemi been her mentor, she would have always been one bootstrap ahead of the rest of the *ghastly* swots in her class.

Of course, she knew that she would have to exercise the utmost discretion . . . although on second thoughts, not too much. After all, what most mattered was not to succeed but to be seen to succeed. If good old Doctor Watson had not been on hand to chronicle Sherlock's achievements, civilisation would have been none the wiser about the great detective's genius. If only she could enlist her own Watson to record her every step. Smothers maybe? Maybe not. He could hardly hold a thought, let alone a pen. What about Missus Beaten? Prendergast and Beaten . . . hmmm. Not quite Holmes and Watson. No, she would just have to record her heroic exploits with her own fair hand. Mind set, she determined to diarise events for future posterity. Needless to say, she would be brutally honest - freckles and all.

She derummaged a notepad from her shoulder bag and scribed *Prendergast of The Yard– The Curious Case of the Katenapped Girl* on the cover in italic script. Then she turned the page and wrote . . .

It is fair to say that the fate of the British Empire hung in the balance. The Commissioner knew that I was the only officer he could call upon with the deductive acumen, the forensic attention to detail and the psychological insight required to crack the case. Although indispensable to the running of the staff canteen . . .

She paused, nibbled the end of her pencil, crossed out the last line and replaced it with . . .

Leaving my assistant, Chef Dibley, in charge of my team at The Yard, I went undercover at daddy's house in Kensington disguised as a civilian. He was overjoyed to see me and honoured that New Scotland Yard had seen fit to entrust their most promising probationary officer to the case.

Satisfied that Chapter One was ready to go - bar the editing - she packed away her notepad and flopped down on the bed. It had been a long and emotionally challenging day, and it was not yet over. Head spinning with a cocktail of excitement, apprehension and exhaustion, her eyelids drooped. Before she could prise them open again, she drifted into a deep, deep sleep.

Groaty McTavish leant against the neon Nessie frontaging The Happy Thistle restaurant and watched the traffic crawl by. As the starstruck pipistrelle of night cloaked its wings across the milkywayed horizon to presage the passage of another customerless day, he shuttered the reproduction barn doors and snuffed out the lights. To say that he was feeling glum would not be over-scotchegging the pudding.

Why, he wondered, did no one stop for a takeaway temptation or pop in for a bracing jug of Thistle Tea and a crunchy Oaty Mctoasty? Was it the Gaelic menu, the jolly thistleman in sporran, kilt and tam o'shanter grafittied on the front door, the kerbside bollards, double yellow lines and no parking signs outside the entrance, the tartan colour scheme, the bagpiped muzak, the prices . . .? He had turned his brain inside out and back again to no avail. To conjoin a word, it was unfathomless.

Weary after another do-nothing day, he withdrew to the recreationary to watch the Professor pit his legendary wits against his laptop computer in a game of three-dimensional chess. Awestricken, he said, 'I dinnae ken how ye can do that, Chief.'

The pending Master of the Omniverse rocked back in his chair and clacked his bony knuckles. 'Simple, my dear

Groaty. It is merely a matter of mind over matter. You see, to a run-of-the-mill genius like me, the perpendicular and the horizontal are one and the same. Granted, they enjoy a right-angular relationship but other than that they are identical.' He placed a bumper pack of cut price Handy-Pandy Brainwipes on the table. 'Horizontal. And now . . .' He flipped the packet on its end. 'Perpendicular.' He leant across the table and fixed McTavish in the eye. 'If you had the wit to see beyond the end of your broken nose, you would understand that the horizontal and the perpendicular are dimensional siblings. To put it another way, spatial status is merely an anomaly of perception. A point of view, if you will.' He chuckled when McTavish nodded in bemused incomprehension. 'There you are. Without knowing, you have unwittingly proved my point.'

'I have?'

'Indeed you have, my good Groat. You see, to all intents and purposes, a nod is merely an inverted headshake. The difference is purely dimensional.' The Professor pointed to a stream of complex code darting across the screen of his fliptop. 'You must understand that computers have an inherent flaw. Artificial Intelligence is incapable of thinking outside the box, whereas I possess an infinity of mental algorithms I can employ to unravel indeterminate problematic complications no matter how incomprehensible.'

'So how we ganna drum up trade for The Happy

Thistle?' McTavish asked. 'We got maer puddings than I ken what tae do with.'

'Pah - think I care about petty trifles?' The Professor scoffed.

'But Chief, the 'lecky's ganna get cut off any day the noo if we dinnae pay the thieving bastards.'

'Well, place an advertisement in the parish magazine offering two bites of the loganberry for the price of one or somesuch. Use your imagination.' The Professor gave McTavish a hardlong look and shook his head. 'Maybe not,' he muttered with a despairing sigh. 'Just deal with it, will you? I have bigger fish to fry.' He cocked a thumb at the wallclock and broke into a sinister smile. 'In exactly one hour, I will stream an online message to Sir Freddie Prendergast making clear that unless he accedes to my demands, his precious stepdaughter will suffer a slow and agonising death.'

'Ye winded up the clock, then?' McTavish asked, impressed by the Professor's extracurricular dexterity. 'Like I told you, it runs slow when the spring gans slack.'

'Streuth . . . I knew there was something I meant to do.' The Fount of Mellifluous Malice checked his pocket watch and shuffled up from his chair. 'Make haste, my stout friend. We are due on air in five minutes. Did you purloin a suitable camera?' When McTavish nodded, he patted his heart and let out a steep breath of relief. 'That feeble flea-brain, Albert so-called Einstein, may claim that time is just a sequence of events,' he said as he tucked his floptop under an arm and shuffled to the door, 'but take it from me, a minute here or there can make a parallel dimension of difference.'

McTavish unlocked the humid grainstore and turned on the light. His heart missed a flutter when he saw little Katy strapped to the barleycot with her arms and legs splayed like a bizarre human starfish. He was already having second thoughts about the kidnap-hostage scheme but bearing in mind the Professor's parlous predicament and unhinged temper, he could see no visible alternative.

When the Professor of Doom shuffled into the dank grainstore looking for all the world like a malevolent undertaker in a shabby black frockcoat, battered top hat, rimless glasses and spats, Katy Clark's eyes opened wide. Terrified, she thrashed about like a pinioned penguin trying to scream through the muffletape gagging her mouth. Her every gap-toothed sob, her every thrash, her every flail was captured by a flimsy plastic video camera mounted on makeshift broomstick tripod.

The Professor turned to McTavish with a fiercesome scowl. 'Was that the best you could do, harebrain?'

McTavish hung his head and mumbled, 'sorry Chief. Went thieving in Cricklewood, nae Hollywood.'

'Here am I, all but omnipotent, forced to make do with a plastic video camera pilfered by a ginger-headed moron with an unsightly spider birthmark on his neck.'

Aware that the sands of time were trickling inexorably by, The Professor plugged the Peking Economy Gaming Camera into his laptop, logged onto Ransom.com and donned a sinister Micky Mouse mask. 'Pretend that you are frightened, my little cocksparrow,' he instructed Katy as she writhed about in uncontrollable fits of inconsolable tears. As the hands of his pocket-watch nudged eight, he took up position at the end of the barleycot with his arms upstretched like an Angel of Gloom.

'How good of you to join us, Sir Freddie,' The Professor said to camera in a deathly deadpan voice. 'As you can see, I have lined up a few minutes of wholesome family entertainment for your delectation.' He stepped aside to grant Sir Freddie an unfettered view of his sobbing stepdaughter. 'Please do not be alarmed. Little Katy will be quite safe as long as you follow my instructions.' He broke into a crooked Micky Mouse grin and waved a spindly hand at his terrified hostage. 'Do not go the authorities. Do not inform the police. Do not leave the house. We are watching you every second of the day. Tune in to this channel at midday tomorrow and I will instruct you how to proceed. Until then, I bid you farewell . . . for now.' With that, the camera focused on Katy's tearbrimmed face, and the picture faded to black.

His demonic duty duly done, The Star of Television Screams ripped off his mask, turned to McTavish and clapped his hands. 'The lighting could have been better, but all in all I thought it went rather well,' he said modestly.

'Aye, Chief. Storming. A star is born.'

'Let us see what our little magpie has to say.' The Professor loomed over Katy flexing his fists. 'As long as you behave, my precious peafowl, you have nothing to fear,' he told her with a chilling insincerity in his voice. 'It is in my interests to keep you as alive as possible. But please forgive me, you must be feeling peckish.' He clicked his fingers. 'Groaty, a little nourishment for our guest, if you will.'

McTavish took a packet of Highland McOatcakes from his sporran, ripped off Katy's gag and forced a McOatie to her trembling lips.

'Fuck off, spiderface. I in't eating that foreign muck.' Katy bit off the tip of McTavish's finger and spat it his face. As he staggered back clutching his hand at arm's length, she licked the blood off her lips, turned to the startled Professor, narrowed her baby blue eyes and hissed, 'you're dead, you are, when my mam finds out where you live. And she will.'

vii

Heather Prendergast surfaced from her powernap – a word that was to pepper the pages of her case notes – and gazed around the bedroom. The sloping eaves, Snow White curtains and Cinderella bedspread were much as they had been on that fateful day when she left home and moved into her aunt's modest Tudor manor house in County Kent. Like a shrine to the departed, her kiddie clothes were neatly folded in the chest of drawers – flannelette knickers, cotton socks and nighties. A distant smile settled on her lips when she saw a sprig of heather vased on the bedside table. Her father might have blottered her from his copybook, but it seemed that somebody still cared.

Heather was deeply madly truly touched by the loving tend of Missus Beaten's feather duster, particularly as the rest of the house had changed beyond recognition. She was incensed that her father should have had the *brazen gall* to let Fifi convert the grade-one listed building into what she could only describe as a Disneyland Versailles. She imagined that Thomas Leverton would be turning in his mausoleum if he knew that his architectural masterpiece had been gutterised into what Aunt Elizabeth snootily dismissed as the Pits of Glitz. And Aunt Elizabeth had every right to vent her contempt. Trevelyan House had been her ancestral home. Sir Freddie had grown up in a condom-inium in Pinner sandwiched between a dog track and the Lucky Latex factory.

Aware of where she was and why, Heather squeezed into a new pair of blue jeans, a demure plain collared blouse and a lamb's-hair sweater and slipped on a pair of training shoes. She hung her tweed twinset in the wardrobe alongside her mothballed teeny sailor suit, her old school uniform and her Brownie outfit, reminders of a more innocent age . . . in every sense of the tense. My, she thought, how tall I was when I was ten; almost as tall as I am now. Since then she had hardly grown an inch. Of course, she had filled out a little although not as much as she would have liked. If truth be told, her figure was more stickyinsect than hourglass, but as Aunt Elizabeth would say, better flat chested than flab chested. Hmmm . . . moot point.

Nothing if not diligent, last but by no particular means least, she unpacked the tools of her deductive trade. Taking care to take the greatest care, she arranged her magnifying and spyglasses on the chest of drawers beside her well-thumbed bible, The Illustrated Sherlock Holmes Omnibus. She never went anywhere without it. Does anyone, she wondered? She tried not to chuckle as she leafed through the dogeared pages. After all, she had read the sacred tome so often that she knew every chapter, verse, line, comma and full stop as if by wrote. She winced as she recalled her punctured pride when her college tutors swathed her essays in red ink claiming that she had regurgitated the great detective's words verbatim. Nonsense, she used to say, it was just that great minds think alike. The fact was that she had not realised what she was doing. Sherlock's wisdoms were so ingrained into her psyche that she no longer knew which were his deductive theorems and which were hers. Not that she gave a tuppenny fig. She was confident that one day Holmes and Prendergast would bookend the pantheon of legendary crime busting sleuths. It was, was it not, chiselled in the stars?

Having arranged her disguises in subterfugical order - false moustaches, false eyelashes, panstick, foundation, blusher-brushes, a variety of wigs, dearstalker and porkpie hats, eyepatches, binoculars and sunglasses - she stowed her spare undergarments and emergency chocolate in a convenient drawer. Tingling from spine to toe with anticipation, she pocketed her off-duty pocketbook and Wangchung patent-applied-for miniature spy recorder and hurried downstairs to join Sir Freddie in the former Smoking Room - the Deja View Room as it was now called. Halfway down the winding staircase, she stumbled across Smothers wheezing up the other way. Sludging along behind him was a recalcitrant bloodhound, a saggy doggiebag of flabby flesh with droopy ears and a balding muzzle - the canine familiar of his master.

'Good evening, Miss Heather.' Smothers docked his balding forelock. 'Me Lud requests that you join him at seven-thirty.'

Heather checked her watch and frowned. 'But it's quarter to eight.'

'It is all these stairs, Miss Heather. I am not as young as I ought to be.'

'Oh, poor Smothers. Have you thought of retiring?'

'I have thought of little else for the past forty years, Miss Heather. Oh look, Baskerville remembers you,' he said with a gummy smile as the grizzled bloodhound bared its remaining fang and growled. 'Might I suggest that you don't flaunt your ankles when he is in one of his moods?'

'How many moods does he have?' Heather asked as she inched past the snarling mutt.

'Three, Miss Heather. Miserable, depressed and suicidal. Don't we all?' Smothers gripped the banister, cast his eyes atticwards, mopped his brow, took a deep breath and set off for the attic.

'Smothers,' Heather called after him. 'You don't need to. I'm not there.'

'I had better check to be on the safe side, Miss Heather. In any event, the exercise will do Baskerville good. I haven't taken him for his daily constitutional for months,' Smothers said as he groaned on up half a step at a time dragging the reluctant hound behind him.

In next to no time, Heather found herself outside the Deja View Room. She was hiving with excitement. Was she really about to unriddle a real life or death kidnapping case? Of course, she knew that it would be a dangerous assignment, quite possibly the most dangerous of her probationary career. She feared that if she made the slightest slip, came out with the tiniest unguarded comment or mis-stepped by as much as a varnished toenail, she might never see her stepsister again. Hey-ho . . . such is life, she told herself. After all, as Aunt Elizabeth would say, we all have to end somewhere.

Primed to take command of the moment, Heather pushed through the door, stumbled to a stop and rubbed her eyes. Had she known no different – which she did – she might have thought that she had unwitting ventured into a Soho pornodrome. Dimlit by sunken ceiling lights with tiers of fold-up seats, what had once been a sedate mancave had been given a cinematographic makeover. Playing on the floor-to-ceiling screen was a Technicolour movie of the young Fifi's buxom alter-ego, Fou-Fou LaPorte. Wearing more makeup than Coco Chanel and Coco the Clown combined – perish the thought – she was sporting an unconvincing Cleopatra wig and a translucent off-both-shoulders mini-toga. Lips aquiver, she was being ravished by a brawny centurion who for no transparent reason was wearing a gold lamé loincloth and a leather dog collar. Surrounded by gothic columns, cupid statues, dusky scantily clad handmaidens and hunky jockstrapped handymen, they were writhing on a bed of rose petals to a rumpy-pumping soundtrack of horny trumpets, wheezy woodwind and climactic strings. Nothing – absolument rien – was left to the voyeur's imagination.

'Je t'aime de tout mon cœur, mon petit chaton,' the

centurion grunted between French kisses.

'Moi aussi,' said the busty Cleopatra. She turned to the camera, pouted her lips suggestively and fluttered her lashes. As the semi-naked stallion mounted her, she arched her back, closed her eyes, clapped a hand to her brow, groaned, 'fais-moi plaisir mon brave,' and feigned a swoon. And so it went . . . on and on. And on.

Nauseous to the pit of her stomach - disgusted was hardly the word - Heather pulled the plug on the video projector and turned up the houselights. It would hardly be over egging the nookie to say that she was scandalised to see a popcorn machine in one corner, an ice cream kiosk in another and a prophylactic vending machine in a third. Framed photographs of Fou-Fou LaPorte in a variety of poses disgraced the walls – a scantily clad Fou-Fou LaPorte in the arms of a muscular mustachio with Brylcreemed chest hair, Fou-Fou LaPorte in a skimpy bathing costume suggestively licking a phallic lolly, Fou-Fou LaPorte in a Bunny costume sitting on Hugh Hefner's knee brandishing a cat o'nine tails, an ostrich-feathered Fou-Fou LaPorte flanked by a high stepping chorus line at the Moulin Rouge and Fou-Fou LaPorte sheathed in a seam-busting tutu held aloft by a musclebound weightlifter in an ill-fitting singlet and obscenely tight tights.

It was, Heather thought, a house of unimaginable horrors.

Sir Freddie was huddled in the front row of the stalls

with his knees pressed together smoking a cigar. When the screen went blank, he put down his opera glasses, turned and glared at Heather. 'I say, young lady, what's your game?' he thundered. He scowled at her as if she was a cat-scat and turned up his nose. 'You look like something Baskerville dragged in,' he said. 'Just as well your stepmother isn't here to see you dressed like a tramp. She would have a fainting fit. She has a fragile constitution.'

'So I see.' Heather planted her hands on her hips and nodded at the screen.

'Do not be so uppity, young lady,' Sir Freddie snapped. 'Can't you recognise great art when you see it? Must say I'm not surprised. Your side of the family have always been uncultured louts.'

'Uncultured?' Heather gasped, barely able to credit her hearing. 'I will have you know that Aunt Elizabeth performed with the Bolshoi Ballet when she was fourteen. And she gave a solo cello recital at the Royal Albert Hall a few years ago.'

'Didn't we all,' Sir Freddie scoffed. 'Let me tell you, by the time she was your age, your stepmother had been awarded a Hot d'Or at the Cannes Adult Film Festival and a Pinky Ribbon at the Tokyo Festival of Alternative Entertainment.' He was about to list some of the young Fifi's other glittering prizes - Totty of the Month in Nature Lover's Magazine and Tit of the Year in Hustler - when the Ransom.com logo flashed onscreen. Still scowling, he sat back, stubbed out his cigar, straightened his bow tie, adjusted his monocle and said, 'now pay attention. You are here to work, not bandy words with your elders and betters.'

Heather plugged in her Wangchung digiblah recorder and logged onto the Deja View rudderless Wi-Fi. All set, she made herself comfortable on a flipflop seat, balanced her pocketbook on her book thigh, tiplicked her pencil and prepared to take notes. But behind a calm, cool, collected façade, she was tingling with excitement. How would the legendary Detective Inspector Isaac Obafemi of The Yard handle such a delicate assignment, she wondered? Delicately, she decided. She suspected that he would position himself as the prime interlocutor, win the hostageers' trust and, once their guard was down, pounce like a stegosaurus, free the hostage and bang the perps to rights. And that was precisely what she intended to do. Eyes glued to the screen, she held her breath as the logo faded to be replaced by a sinister man wearing a Micky Mouse mask.

'How good of you to join us, Sir Freddie,' the Master of Criminal Ceremonies announced. 'As you can see, I have lined up a few minutes of wholesome family entertainment for your delectation. Please do not be alarmed. Little Katy will be quite safe as long as you follow my instructions. Lest you be in any doubt,' he snarled, 'let me assure you that I am deadly serious. Do not go the authorities. Do not inform the police. Do not leave the house. We are watching you every second of the day. Tune in to this channel at midday tomorrow and I will instruct you how to proceed. Until then, I bid you farewell - for now.' With that, the camera zoomed in on Katy's tearstained face and the picture faded to a fuzzy blip.

Heather's notepad flew out of her lap as she leapt to her feet. 'Jeepers creepers - who is that scary man?' she gasped.

'More to the point, who the dickens is the gal?' Sir Freddie fingered his walrus moustache and announced, 'never seen the filly in me life.'

xiii

Groaty McTavish cowered on the naughty step of the recreationary shielding his head in his hands. 'It wasnae ma fault, Chief,' he pleaded in mitigation. 'I was busy in the surgical cubicle.'

'Busy, you say? Busy? Pah. You would not know the meaning of the verb,' The Professor railed, a scant hare's breath from losing his legendary incendiary temper. 'The moment I turn my back, you let our hostage flee her cage like a gilded bird.'

'She chomped through the ropes.' McTavish fingered his bandage and winced. 'Then she made a bolt for the door while I was off gluing ma fingernail back on and picked the lock with a hairpin. Sorry, Chief.'

'Sorry? Is that all you have to say for yourself? You might at least apologise.' The man occasionally known as The Manic Machinator of Misanthropy propped his elbows on the table and buried his bulbous brow in his hands. 'Hostage negotiations are due to resume at midday tomorrow. There is every chance that Sir Freddie's suspicions might be aroused if I inform him that his stepdaughter has popped out for a breath of fresh air.' He glared red-hot thunders at his co-conspirator in crime. 'This is another fine mess you have landed me in, dolt.'

Keen to make amends for his unintended slip of the

knot, McTavish furrowed his brow and lapsed into thinking mode. After an inordinately long pause for thought, a rare idea snuck up on him. 'How's aboot I pretend tae be the wee bairn?'

'Unless my ocular senses deceive me,' The Professor said, 'you are twice Miss Clark's size and have ginger hair, sideburns and rotten teeth.' He shook his head, muttered, 'and the doctors say that I am unhinged . . .' He set his jaw, reminded of how maliciously maligned he was by a conspiracy of alien lizards masquerading as psychiatrists. 'Compared to you, my hirsute Highlander,' he told McTavish with a snarl in his voice, 'I am as sane as a doorpost. In any event, I very much doubt that Sir Freddie would be taken in by the ruse. It could backfire.'

Not to be dissuaded by petty persnicketies, McTavish had a second thought, so to speak. 'Well, how's aboot ye keep the light off while yaer filming? I can bounce aboot on the bed and squeal like a lassie whenever ye threaten tae chop me intae little pieces.'

'Hmmm, now there is a thought.' The Professor stroked his jutty jaw. 'Might work. Let me think about it,' he said, not entirely - that is to say, not in the least - convinced. 'Alternatively, I could just have done with the matter and live out my days in Stoke-on-Trent. It is a fate worse than death, I gather.' He raised a don't-go-there finger as McTavish's eyes lit up. 'Where is the little fly-by-night, anyway?'

'Barricaded hesself in yon oatstore.' McTavish pointed

to a steel-clad door on the far side of the recreationary.

Making sure not to dislodge his top hat, the Professor threw back his head and cackled out loud. 'Fool,' he scoffed. 'Does the little gannet not realise that we will starve her out?'

'Ye reckon?' McTavish raised a ginger eyebrow. 'Last time I checked there was enough takeaway trifles and cans of fizzy back there tae last a month. Maer judging by the size of the wee bairn. So what we ganna do, Chief?'

In an unusual display of indecision, the Professor scratched his cerebrum and frowned. 'Without my flighty bargaining chip, I do not have a limb to stand on. She is my ten-million-pound stake in a deathly game of apocalyptic chance.'

Hardly had the Professor ceased pontificating than the oatstore door slammed open and a gymslipped figure swaggered out. 'Did I hear you right – a measly ten mill?' HostageKaty lounged against the wall with a can of Scotchpop in one hand and a family pack of thistleberry trifle in the other. 'Hardly worth getting kidnapped for.'

The professor swung around and glared at the pigtailed teen with a look of utter obfuscation upon his face. 'Be gone with you,' he roared. 'It is a hostage's solemn duty to be neither seen nor heard.'

'Stuff that for a game of soldiers,' HostageKaty said with a toss of her pigtails. 'I'm worth loads more than that. Fred's minted and mam'll chew his bollocks off if he don't cough up.' She skipped over to the table, arranged six cushions on a chair and hopped up between McTavish and the man occasionally known as the King of Confusion. Or was it the Prince of Puzzlement? He was no longer quite sure. Indeed, at this particular juncture of the narrative, he was no longer quite sure of anything worth the time of day. Or night.

'So here's what we'll do.' HostageKaty popped a liquoricestick in her mouth and knotted her fingers as if kneading a blob of playdough. 'We're going halves and I'm calling the shots. Got it?'

After a moment to dissemble his discombobulation and another to unfuddle his muddle, The Professor muttered, 'I do not believe that this is happening,' and pinched a leg. 'You, my little canary bird . . .' he jabbed a finger at HostageKaty's cherubic face, 'have just made the biggest mistake of your premature life.' As a deathly silence sucked the sound out of the room, he fixed her in the eye with a maniacal glare and twisted his lips into a snarl. 'Let me introduce you to . . . the Jockal.' He swung around and aimed a spindly finger at McTavish. 'A ruthless killer whose depravity knows no bounds.'

'Whoa, steady on, Chief.' McTavish raised his hands in a gesture of defiant non-compliance. 'That was when I done ma course in pest control. Woodlice mainly. Teck it frae me, its murder trying tae get-rid of the wee pests from a tenement karzy.'

The Professor gave McTavish a despairing look, shook

his head, cleared his throat and turned to HostageKaty. 'Unless you do exactly as I say,' he said with a certitude that brooked no contradiction. 'The Jockel will snuff you out like a candle flame.' He went to jab a finger in her face then pulled back quick as a slick when she bared her teeth at him.

'Think you're Reggie Kray, do you, you big girl's blouse?' HostageKaty scoffed. 'You're thick as a plank, you are. Use that excuse for a luffa you call a brain. Do for me and you'll piss ten million quid up the wall. Fred's not stupid. Well, he is, but mam's not.' She cocked a snook at McTavish and said, 'if you think HairyFace is scary, wait till you meet my mam. I seen blokes twice his size piss their pants when she gives them one of her looks.' She crossed her arms and rocked back in her chair swinging her legs like a triptease artist on the high strapeze. 'So, we got usselves a deal or do I grass you up to the filth for banging me up in this smeggy excuse for a hovel and messing with me?'

'Enough.' The Blackened Man of Gloom hammered a fist on the table. 'How dare you have the brazen impudence to call Mission Control smeggy?'

'Tae be fair, Chief, it is a wee bit whiffy in here,' McTavish whispered in the Professor's good ear. 'Thought of tecking yaer frockcoat tae the cleaners to be fumigated?' He edged away when the man known as the Puppetmeister of Parsimony by those who knew no better pinned him to the metaphorical wall with a metaphorical flash of the eyes.

'Right then, we done?' HostageKaty said. 'I'm off for a Big Mac, and I don't mean you.' She tweaked her nose at McTavish and stuck out her tongue. 'I'll be back tomorrow in time for you to smack me about for the video. We do this shakedown proper or not at all.' She buttoned up her blazer, slung her satchel over a shoulder, skipped through the door, and melted into the night like a hot Malteser.

'Think the wee lassie will be alreet oot on her own this time of night, Chief?' McTavish asked as he stood at the window watching HostageKaty swagger down the road swinging her schoolbag like a satchel in the rye.

'I pity the misguided soul who tries to tangle with that spawn of Beelzebub,' the Professor muttered unquixotically. 'I will eat my spats if we see hide or hair of her again.'

ix

Heather Prendergast gave her head the mother of all scratches. Tricky, she thought. Very tricky. Unless she was very much mistaken, her father had just received a random ransom demand from a total stranger for an unknown hostage.

Although she didn't say as much, she was - to say the least - miffed. Masking her bamboozlement behind an expression of confident aplomb, she clapped her hands and said, 'righty-ho, daddy. Leave it to me. I'll handle things from here.' But despite her show of spunky esprit, if truth be told she had no idea where to start. After all, how does one negotiate with Micky Mouse for the release of person or persons unknown? She could only think that she must have missed that class at college – unlikely, as she had always been a willing if not an entirely able student. To add injury to ignorance, the chapter on cartoon kidnappers and unrelated relatives was missing from her hostagemurder textbook. Furthermore, the lack of any known precedent compounded her confoundment. You see, as far as she was aware - and she had spent years obsessively researching the pathology of true-life crime - not even Hercule Poirot had ever been called upon to exercise his little grey cells on such a mystifying case. Even the possessor of that most labyrinthine of deductive minds, the late, great Lieutenant Columbo, would have had trouble unshambling this cockeyed conundrum.

'Looks like I've brought you here on a fool's errand.' Sir Freddie polished his opera glasses with his top-pocket handkerchief and announced, 'now, I have work to do. Plug in the video projector on your way out and close the door behind you.'

To say that Heather was incensed by her father's callous malice would be an understatement. 'But you can't just ignore it, daddy,' she said. 'A helpless child is in deadly danger, and we are her only hope of rescue.'

'That, young lady, is none of my concern. In any event, I wager that you wouldn't have the wit to rescue her.'

Her father's snooty comment stiffened Heather's heckles to the hilt. 'Oh, is that so?' she said, barely able to stem her contempt. 'Well, let's see you put your money where your mouth is.'

'Preposterous,' Sir Freddie snorted. 'What do you take me for?'

'A chicken.'

Sir Freddie's face flushed a ruddy shade of puce and he thundered, 'watch your foul language, young lady.'

And that was when Heather's temper boiled beyond the brim. Her father's haughty dismissal of her professional credentials was the straw that cricked the camel's neck. Determined to prove her mettle, she threw pecuniary prudence to the wind and ventured a reckless, 'right. I bet you fifty pounds that I can crack the case.'

'Fifty pounds, you say?' Sir Freddie raised a scheming eyebrow. 'What say you we call it a hundred?'

Heather bit her lip, concerned lest she risk her entire Metropolitan Police pension pot. Why not, she thought? After all, as Aunt Elizabeth would say, in for a little, in for the lot. More to the point, an innocent little poppet's life lay in mortal danger. And so she held her breath and plucked up the gauntlet. 'Done,' she said. 'One hundred pounds it is.'

'Let's say guineas,' Sir Freddie countered with a mercenary glint in his monocle.

After a quick mental miscalculation, Heather went for broke and ventured a hesitant nod.

'By Jove, you're on.' Sir Freddie reached out to shake Heather's hand, then paused. 'But on one condition,' he said. 'I do not want darling Katy getting under her mother's feet during the summer recess. You must agree to let her assist with the investigation.'

Heather was shocked, nay she was horrified, nay she was mortified, nay she was all but lost for gratuitous words. 'Bratty?' she gasped. 'But that's like asking Sherlock Holmes to let Bart Simpson tag along.'

'I suggest that you keep your misplaced witticisms to yourself, young lady. Unless I am very much mistaken, this is her now,' Sir Freddie said as he heard the front door slam. He blustered to his feet and gestured for Heather to follow him to the Live-In Room.

Heather's jaw almost dropped through the floor - allegorically speaking - as she crossed the threshold of the Live-In Room. She hardly recognised the place. Another victim of Fifi's preposterous pomposity, the civilised if somewhat stuffy living room had been transformed into what she could only describe as an exhibitiontramp's garbagery. Papered from skirting boards to picture rails with embossed cupids, the sideboard, window ledges, mantlepiece and occasional occasional tables heaved with ticky-tacky knick-knacks – a gaggle of quackless plastic ducks, an embarrassment of scantily clad Russian dolls of differing shapes and malice, a stringless ukulele-banjolin, a drippage of ceiling wax artefacts, an uncountitude of busty busts of Fifi LaPorte, a flotilla of miniature squadronaires, two paperknives, three paperspoons and a paperfork, a smattering of *unspeakably* stained Christmas cards from geriatric Fou-Fou fans . . . and that was the least but by no means the last of it. The trivia of a trivial life was overwhelming in its imperspicacity.

To Heather's eyes, most nauseating of all were a plethora of silver-framed pornographs of Mademoiselle Fou-Fou LaPorte in her *chaton sexuel* days. Reminders of a short lived and critically mocked movie career, the yellowing snapshots included but were by no means limited to Fou-Fou LaPorte as Madame Pompadour in a Rococo mini-robe à la francaise, Fou-Fou LaPorte as Jeanne d'Arc in an immodest tunic and tightfitting bum-busting britches, Fou-Fou LaPorte as George Sand in a see-through crinoline and cape, Fou-Fou LaPorte as Sarah Bernhardt in an ankle length off-both-shoulders backless - and frontless - peasant dress, Fou-Fou LaPorte as Edith Piaf in a curvaceous haute couture pad-shouldered peekaboo skirt-suit, Fou-Fou LaPorte as Jessica Lapin in a revealing figure hugging split-to-the-crotch gown and Fou-Fou LaPorte as Picasso's golden muse, Marie-Thérèse, in a fig leaf. Not entirely flattering, it left *ne rien* to the imagination except why she should be wearing Wellington boots, smoking a pipe and fondling a ferret. All the poses had one thing in common, or rather two things in common. Enough said.

Furnituring the room were two clumpy reproduction Regency sofas, three matching love-chairs and a pebbledash coffee table. A brace of floor to ceiling French windows overlooked the lawn. Between these stood a mahogany bookcase stuffed to the beadings with Sir Freddie's prized collection of Victorian first-edition novels. Captured in the literary rye were Lady Pokingham, They All Do It, Sub-Umbra, Sport Among the She-Noodles, The Romance of Lust, Cruising Under False Colours, A Tale of Love and Lust, The Whippingham Papers – a spanking yarn, Sir Freddie maintained - Venus in Furs, The Autobiography of a Flea, The Lustful Turk and his favourite, Gynecocracy.

When, a month or two later Heather had a little time on her hands, she looked up the work in the Oxford Guide to British Romantic Filth. If that learned tome was to be believed – which she sincerely hoped it was not – the novella tells the story of a young man forced to wear a corset, hooped petticoats and silk stockings. The plot – if the smutty diatribe can be so described – revolves around the hero or would-be heroine serving dominant females' whims while dressed as a French maid. A series of miss-adventures include explicit encounters with predators of all sexes, carnal inclinations, humiliations and predations, bondage, discipline and what might be described as imaginative corporal punishment.

From what Heather could determine, it was pornographic titillation of the highest, or perhaps the lowest, order. In that they were contemporaries, how, she wondered - or more to the point *why* - had Sherlock not confronted the author, Viscount Ladywood, and given him a jolly-good talking to? The exigencies of time, she supposed. He was always frightfully busy cracking cases. And of course Doctor Watson was too timid to say boobs to a goose.

But that was then and this was now – another place, another page, another wart in time. And so, as yet blissfully unaware of her father's disgraceful taste in salacious reading matter, Heather sat down on a sofa nervously awaiting the moment of truth. Although it had been eleven years since she last saw her stepsister, to say that there had been no love lost between them would be a squanderous waste of virtual ink. Irrespective of the passage of time, her resentment had festered like a feculent skunk. To make no bones about it, she loathed Bratty – as she called her spoiled brat of a stepsister – with a vengeance bordering on the pathological. Nevertheless, as Aunt Elizabeth would say, crises call for compromises, so hard though she found it, she determined to be on her best behaviour.

Moments later Katerina Clark slouched through the door. At a glance, Heather took her to be a little under six feet tall in her sockless bovver-boots. She was wearing a pair of shabby-chic jeans, a snobby-chic jacket and a baseball cap emblazoned with the word *Available*. Much like a convent convict, her beach blonde hair was razored at the sides and floppy at the fringe. Her upturned nose was pierced with what Heather took to be a piggyring and her ears dripped with bling. Were Heather to be asked to describe her in one word, that word would be slut.

Sir Freddie's eyes lit up when he saw his stepdaughter. 'Hello Katy, my dear,' he said. 'How utterly charming you look.'

'Yeah, yeah, yeah. Speak to the hand, the face don't care.' Katerina spat out her chewing gum, slumped down on a sofa and fiddled with her nose piercing. 'Had to bunk off school to get my hair sorted. Cost a packet, but it's not like I had much choice,' she said. 'Hair extensions are *so* last month.' She lit a cigarette, crossed her legs and sat back blowing smoke. 'Anastasia says pixie cuts are cute and she should know. Both her fiancées are currency traders.' She examined her false nails, frowned, and muttered something about her manicurist being blind. 'Oh,' she said with a scowl. 'Baskerville's puked in the hall again.

Don't know why you don't have him put down. Might as well get Smothers done while you're at it.'

'Where have you been?' Sir Freddie asked as he coughed the smoke out of his eyes. 'Your mother has been beside herself.'

'Wouldn't have thought there was enough room. Slag.' Katerina muttered at the top of her voice.

'You will never believe what just happened . . .'

Katerina stifled a yawn. 'Yeah, yeah, yeah. Some other time, eh? I'm expecting Seb any minute. We're going clubbing.' As she slouched to her feet, she spotted Heather trying to slink out of the room. She narrowed her tweezered eyebrows in a show of stepfilial disgust. 'What's Spriggy doing here?' she said. 'Thought she wasn't allowed.'

'That is what I was about to tell you, my dear. I asked your stepsister here out of a sense of civic duty to help me rescue a damsel in distress,' Sir Freddie explained with a disingenuous expression of genuity. 'She agreed, but only on condition that I let you assist. Won't take no for an answer.'

Katerina rolled her eyes. 'Whatever,' she said. 'But it'll cost.'

'Of course, my dear. I would not expect you to invest any of your valuable time gratis,' Sir Freddie said as if his stepdaughter's gratuitous demand for a gratuity was reasonableness it's very self. 'What say you I raise your allowance by a hundred guineas a week?'

'I'd say wake up and smell the coffee, cheapskate.' Katerina chewed her bottom lip, deep in calculation. 'It'll set you back a Maserati Granturismo. Silver, so it doesn't clash with my hair.'

Surprisingly Sir Freddie did not appear unduly surprised. 'I have told you before,' he told her again with a longsuffering sigh. 'You are too young to have a Formula One runabout.'

'Too young?' Katerina snorted. 'Jeez, I'm nearly twenty-three.'

'Come, come, my dear,' Sir Freddie said. 'Let us not gild the lily. This isn't Tinder. You know full well that you are only seventeen.'

'You are *so* wrong. I am eighteen at the end of the week.' The floorboards rattled as Katerina stamped a petulant boot. 'You are always making out like I'm a little kid or something. Alright, I'll do it, as long as you let me have a dagger tattooed on my arm. Rachael says swastikas are *so* last year.'

'I will have a word with your mother when she is next in a good mood and let you know in a month or two,' Sir Freddie said with an accommodating smile. 'Just as long as you promise to behave.'

'Do this, do that . . . you're always bossing me about,'

Katerina stropped. 'Might as well be a nun.'

Having watched her stepsister's display of petty petulance in relative silence, Heather forced a smile. 'Katerina?' she said. 'Well I never. Haven't you grown? I hardly recognised you.'

Katerina's fringe flopped over her eyes as she tossed her head. 'Course not. You're a detective. At least, that's what my dizzy step-aunt tells me. Where's mum? Must show her my school report. She promised to take me shopping in Monte Carlo if I passed my exams.' She blew on her purple fingernails and polished them on a bra-strap. 'Got straight A's for all my homework. Slaved round the clock. Well, Seb did. I was too busy with my social media. Now if that's it, I'm off to change.'

'Don't be long, my dear,' Sir Freddie told her. 'Dinner is served at nine.'

'Yeah, yeah, yeah. Whatever,' Katerina mumbled and slouched off to her room.

Forewarned by Smothers that Sir Freddie required guests to be formally attired for dinner, Heather withdrew to her bedroom to change into something less comfortable. In any event, she had some serious thinking to do. The more she considered *The Curious Case of the Katenapped Girl*, the less sense it made. For instance, how did the sinister Mickey Mouse-alike know Sir Freddie's name? And he had referred to his hostage throughout as Katy, which was how Katerina was commonly known. What's more, the ransom note was correctly addressed, although . . . hmmm, now she came to think, the envelope hadn't borne a stamp. Which meant that either the hostageer couldn't afford one or he didn't have sufficient lickspittle to glue it to the envelope. The plot thickened.

She sat down on the shallow side of her bed, turned over a new leaf of her jotpad, licked the tip of her pencil and, with events still fresh in mind, wrote . . .

Unaware that daddy is being advised by the very foremost probationary crimefighter in the Met, the hostage takers have broadcast their demands. To my surprise and no little consternation, it would seem that they have kidnapped an innocent little poppet in error. Nevertheless, spurred on by a sense of public duty, daddy is adamant that I take the helm and secure her release. Oh, I may have found my Doctor Watson. My stepsister has begged me to let her assist with the investigation. For the sake of peace on earth, I may consent.

Delighted with Chapter Two of what she had no doubt posterity would regard as a literary masterpiece, Heather changed into her tweed twinset and kitten heels. She bunned her long hair, twizzled a snick of *ghastly* peach-pink sticktwist on her lips and, suitably stuffily attired, joined her father and stepmother in the Diner Room.

She was - to say the least - relieved to find the former Dining Room much as she remembered. At a stretch, the Georgian dropleaf table could accommodate a dozen or so diners or - at a squeeze, a grunt and a push - Fifi and eight guests. A matching hardwood sideboard homed a sundry of tablelay requisitories; damask tablecloths, lace serviettes and silver cutlery crested with the Trevelyan coat of arms - two lions rampant running away from a mouse. The only other item of furniture of notable note - chairs notwithstanding - was a scruffy vinyl covered bow-fronted drinks cabinet. This was replenished daily by Smothers, as Sir Freddie's idea of an after dinner tipple was to drain as many bottles as he could lay hands on before he passed out.

On the wall above this folly of indulgence hung an oily painting of Sir Freddie in mortarboard and ermine gown being awarded an honorary degree in Rubbers by the Royal College of Prophylactic Engineers. On the wall opposite was a portrait of Fifi. Sitting down with her legs crossed – she didn't do standing up, she told the portraitist – she was wearing a low-cut shocking pink chemise and a comely smile. As instructed, the artist had softened her curves – sliced them to the bone, it might be said – and turned back the clock by blotting out a grotesquitude of crow's feet, wrinkles, boils, molehairs, pimples, warts and all. The result was a perfect picture of perfidious perdition.

Sir Freddie was sitting at the head of the table sporting a dinner jacket, starched wing-collared shirt and red bow tie. Fifi occupied much of the opposite extreme. She was modelling a sequinned gold lamé evening gown with a diamond tiara perched on her silver bouffant. A peacock feather was tucked into her cleavage like a breastquill, should such an outlandish thing exist. Between them sat a curvy girl in a figure-hugging latex minidress, waist length shocking pink hair, studded leather choker, feathery eyelashes, black lipstick and mile-high platform boots.

Heather sat down beside her, said, 'I don't believe we've met. I'm Heather, Sir Freddie's daughter by his proper marriage,' then looked at her father, perplexed by his tipsy chuckle.

'Doesn't Katy look sophisticated in that wig?' he said. 'Unlike some I care to mention.' He ran a scornful eye over Heather's twinset and pearls.

Heather was about to ask if she should slam the door on her way out when Smothers shuffled in carrying a tray. 'Care for an hors d'oeuvre, Miss Heather?' He offered her a rice cake smeared with a splodge of *unspeakable*. 'Or would you prefer to start with the starter?' He deposited a silver platter on the table, lifted the lid and flourished a hand at what looked to be a fish head drowning in rice curd.

Heather patted her grumbling tummy and forced a smile. 'Looks scrumptious but I'm afraid I don't have much of an appetite.'

'That's because it stinks like Baskerville puke,' Katerina said and pretended to gag.

'I will have my usual. I am on the diet.' Fifi's reinforced chair wobbled as she patted her stomach. 'Steak cru, pommes de terres frites et crème de garlic, s'il vouz plait, Smotherers.'

'Excuse me . . .' Heather jumped up from the table, sprinted to the Coral Room – the downstairs restibule – knelt over the toilet and purged the contents of her stomach into the watery depths. On the way back to the Diner Room, she came across a scruffy youth being shown into the broom closet by Smothers.

When he saw her, the boy stuck out his tongue, said, 'yuck. Is that pukey peopleware for real? Hashtag Get-a-life,' and pointed to her twinset.

'Pleased to meet you, too.' Heather introduced herself with a limp handshake and a charmless smile. 'I'm Katerina's stepsister, Heather. I take it you must be Seb.'

'Yeah. Right. Cool. The namespace is Sebastian Marrowboan,' he said with inane grin on his inane face. 'Mad name or what?'

Heather's first impression of young Master Marrowboan was that he was almost as short as Katerina might be said to be tall. Her second impression was that he was a spotty little geek with a moppy shock of brown hair, thick bottlerimmed glasses, a spindly disposition and a sunken chin. Were she to be asked - which she hoped that she never would be - she would in all likelihood have said that he looked like a snotty little swot with measles. And that would have been doing him a kindness.

When he saw Katerina hipsway out of the Diner Room like a blowup fetish doll, Sebastian's eyes bulged halfway out of their sockets. 'Wowie-zowie, honeypie,' he said.

He swaggered up to her, stood on tiptoe, closed his eyes, puckered his lips and reached out for a kiss.

'Oh, just grow up, Seb, why don't you?' Katerina swatted him away like a scruff of fluff. 'Told you, look but don't touch. Don't even think about it. Smudge my lip gloss and you're yesterday's news. There's bound to be loads of dishy hunks at Viscount Perry's party, so drop me off and collect me when I text you.' She clicked her fingers to demand that he open the front door, swished her hair over her shoulders and sashayed out.

'Talk about a chip off the old block,' Heather mused as she watched Katerina fend off Sebastian's slavering advances as if he were a besotted puppy. 'Looks like this caper is going to be a thrill a minute,' she muttered sarcastically as she headed for the kitchen to give Smothers a professional hand with the washing up. Oh, how she regretted not having had the foresight to pack her rubber gloves and hairnet.

x

'Do ye want a deep fried Mars Bar and ketchup with yaer spats, Chief?' Groaty McTavish quipped as HostageKaty skipped through the swing doors of The Happy Thistle sucking a liquorice cheroot, pigtails all adangle. Tickled several shades of pink by the Professor's murderous glower, he followed her to the recreationary ready to get down to business.

HostageKaty hopped onto a bothy stool, tossed her satchel on the table, said, 'put it there, Groatface,' and tapped her chin with a grubby fingernail. When McTavish gave her a puzzled look, she grabbed him by the scruff of the neck and hauled him across the table until their noses were rubbing. 'Here, you listening, cloth ears? I said it's time you roughed me up.'

Cursing all humankind's sainted aunts, the man whose Dastardly Identity Would Never Be Unknowingly Unmasked shuffled through the door. He took off his frockcoat, rolled up his sleeves and clacked his bony knuckles with a sadistic, 'so you have a fondness for pain, do you my precocious little parakeet?'

'I can take it or leave it,' HostageKaty said with a shrug of her slight shoulders. 'If you ask me, it's all in the mind. But a girl's gotta do what a girl's gotta do.'

'You are about to suffer unimaginable agony

beyond your darkest imaginings,' said The Professor, not altogether charitably. Fists clenched, he turned to McTavish with a malicious snarl upon his lips. 'Spare the child no mercy, my tartan torturer. Do your very worst.'

McTavish arched his back and crossed his arms. 'I'm nai laying a finger on the wee lassie,' he said. 'I'll gas woodlice if I must, but I dinnae torture bairns. Do it yessen.'

'You will obey my command,' the Doom-meister roared.

'I will do nae such thing.' McTavish shook his head. 'Gratuitous sadism is nae in ma contract of employment.'

'Pah,' the Professor snorted. 'I take it that you have read the small print I added after you signed. You will do my bidding . . . or else.'

'Or else what?'

'Trust me, I will think of something inappropriate.'

HostageKaty rolled her eyes and groaned, 'like mam says, if you want something doing, do it yesself.' She took a deep breath, gritted her teeth and thwacked her head on the table. The room shook to the bothy beams as she grievous bodily harmed herself again and again until, dizzy with repeated headbangings, she slumped back on the stool, arms and legs akimbo. She drew a succession of jerky breaths, felt her bruises, winced, examined her reflection in a cooking glass, nodded, said, 'that'll do,' and broke into a pensive frown. 'Now I need blood,' she said. 'Lashings of fresh blood.' She grabbed McTavish by the throat and hauled him onto the table, buried her teeth in his arm and bit and bit and bit until blood gushed from the gnash. 'Oh, shut up, you girly wuss. Worser things happen at sea,' she scolded as he thrashed about in agony. Grinning, she spat blood into her cupped hands and splashed it all over her face. 'Scary, in't I?' she tittered as the Man Who Suddenly Felt Sick vomited into his top hat. 'So anyway, what is it you do round here when you're not being numpties?' she asked. 'I mean, who in their right mind would open a fast food joint under a flyover next to a motorway fenced off from the local housing estate by barbed wire? You bonkers, or what?'

Groaty McTavish looked round from the sink where he was splashing his gashes. 'Yon Professor reckoned he'd spotted a gap in the market,' he told her as he tourniquetted a tartan tea towel around his forearm.

'A gap? Blimey, you'd need a ladder and wire snips to get to this dump. That's if you're not flattened by a truck when you're crossing the road. I don't know . . .' HostageKaty shook her head and sighed.

'Ye ken, the wee lassie's got a point, Chief,' McTavish ventured timorously. 'Maybe that's why we only gan the one customer, Homeless John. Apart from The Happy Thistle, there's just undertakers and hardware shops this side of the road. All the takeaways, bistros, pizza joints and trattorias are across yon dual carriageway.'

'How long we got?' HostageKaty asked as she yanked out a hank of hair and stowed it in her satchel with her crib sheets, penny liquorice twists and photoshopped photosnaps of Robbie Williams humping Eastminster Academy's headmistress, Miss Ryder. Old Humpy as she was known to the fourth form gigglyswots, was sporting a humungous Shirley Temple bow in her straggly grey hair, a spiked leather collar, a peekaboo babydoll negligee and a pair of woollen booties. She had what could only be described a look of stark terror on her wrinkly face. Underneath was written, 'Take That.'

The Man Who Wished That He Was Somewhere Else took a gold watch from his waistcoat pocket, flipped it open, said, 'five minutes,' and tucked the ticker back into his tockpocket.

'Best get our fingers out, then.' HostageKaty skipped next door to the grainstore, sat down on a Miller's chair, tugged her gymskirt halfway down to her knees, halfmasted her blazer over a shoulder ripped open her blouse and said, 'you'll find a pair of handcuffs in me satchel with me knuckledusters. Give them us here.' She pressed her wrists together like Venus waiting to be chained and said, 'reckon I look suitably unfit for purpose? Or should I break me front teeth?'

'You look as cute as a Transylvanian trainwreck, my accursed little skylark,' the Professor muttered glumly.

'Proper,' Katy said and winked. 'Learned your lines? You better have,' she said, then told McTavish, 'chocks away, Biggles,' and giggled.

As the hands of the Professor's pocket-watch nudged midday, the sluice gates opened and HostageKaty burst into floods of hysterical tears. 'Do what they say, Fred,' she sobbed to camera. 'They in't messing.' She struggled with her handcuffs and screamed, 'there's six of them, big as brick shithouses. They're even eviler than mam's mate, Micky Agers.'

The camera panned from Katy's blood smeared face to a tall, lean, spindly man in a mothy frockcoat and - variety being the spice of life - a Donald Duck mask. Bald to the tip of his beak with wisps of lank hair limping over his frayed collar, he rubbed his hands and broke into sadistic cackle. 'Welcome to the latest episode of my little thriller, Sir Freddie,' he snarled. 'Are you sitting comfortably? Then I will commence.' The Professor - for unbeknownst to the viewers, it was in fact he - continued, 'as you can see, we are taking good care of Katy.' He stood aside to grant the camera a lens-eye view of the diminutive schoolgirl. Tears were streaming down her cheeks, her forehead was cauliflowered with bruises and her school uniform was dishevelled as if by the devil's own hand - an apt if somewhat melodramatic simile. As she chaffed at her hand-locked cuffs, a chilling Voice of Doom announced, 'you will receive a prepaid cellular telephone in tomorrow morning's post. Keep it with you at all times. A member of my organisation will contact you with instructions how to proceed if you want to see your precious little fledging again. Meanwhile, do not contact the police, do not leave the house, do not etcetera, etcetera, etcetera. You know the drill. And do not forget – we are watching you every minute of the day.' And with a pop of a flashbulb and a flicker of a camera shutter, he was gone.

The man McTavish sometimes called the Sultan of Stinge ripped off his mask and turned to Katy with a spine-curdling cackle. 'I believe that you have overlooked one tiny but terminal detail, my precocious little chough. Now that your hands are securely tethered, you are at my mercy to do with as I will.'

'You reckon?' HostageKaty slipped her wrists out of the handcuffs like a Whodunit Houdini, flew off the chair like a brat out of Hell, grabbed The Frockcoated One by the throat, wrestled him to the ground and pinned his arms to the flagstones with her knees. 'Listen, mush,' she growled into his nearest ear. 'Rat on me and you're fish bait. This is my gang now, and don't you forget it.'

Loath though he was to admit it, The Prostrate Professor feared that his best-laid plans had once more gan awry. It seemed that the Teutonic plates of power were shifting inch by pigtailed inch.

Heather Prendergast awoke with a jolt. 'Rats,' she expleted when she saw that she had overslept. But it was hardly her fault. Not everything was, despite what Chef Dibley maintained. You see, Smothers had neglected to tell her that the bedside clock had a windup mechanism and would cease to tick unless it was tended with tockwork clockularity.

Banishing default dreams of deductive fame and glory, she ran a drowsy eye around the bedroom with its puffin-patterned wallpaper and ornamental pony-prancing, flop-eared bunny and owlish pussycat figurines. For a moment she imagined that she was ten years old again. She rubbed her eyes, yawned out of bed, drew back the curtains and gazed down at the garden, sadly aware that she wasn't. Half-awake, she rooted though the ensuite wardrobe trying to decide what to wear. After agonising for an age - this maybe, or maybe that - she settled on a pair of jeans, a polycotton shirt and a lambswool jumper. The fact was that she was hardly spoilt for choice. Apart from her *ghastly* tweed twinset, they were the only clothes that she had packed.

Drawn like a moth to a blowtorch by the sizzle of sausages and bacon wafting up the stairs, she licked her lips, patted her stomach and hurried downstairs. Not watching where she was going, she almost tripped over a draggled figure squatting on the bottom stairstep glazing miserably at his cellphone. 'Sebastian,' she said. 'You look as if you've been up all night.'

'Katerina is going to ping me a text when she wants uploading,' Sebastian mumbled then looked round as he heard stilettoclacks behind him. His sunken jaw dropped halfway to his knees when he saw Katerina tripping down the stairs in high-heeled slippers, satin pyjamas and designer sunglasses.

'There was this bitch at the party wearing the same dress as me,' Katerina whinged. 'I slapped her face and got thrown out so cabbed it home and was in bed by midnight.' She tossed her fringe out of her eyes and stamped a petulant foot, showering Sebastian with pee-green stair-splinters. 'I was livid. I mean, jeez - who does Meghan Markle think she is? She needs to get a life. Slut.'

Sebastian's face plummeted like a slipshod steeplejack. 'I've been idling in standby mode all night waiting for you to ping me,' he mumbled as he pocketed his phone.

'Couldn't be bothered,' Katerina said with a toss of the head. 'Life's too short.'

'Well, if it isn't little Spriggy . . .' A frumpy woman in a floury dress ambushed Heather from behind and tweaked her cheek with a thumb and finger pinch. Missus 'Eggy' Beaten – for it was she – hugged Heather to her ample bosom and said, 'well just look at you. Not my little Spriggy anymore, are you? Dare say you're at big school now.'

'Actually,' Heather said as she struggled to unpinion herself from the housekeeper's pinny strings. 'I'm a Metropolitan Police officer.'

'Of course you are,' Missus Beaten chuckled. 'And I'm the Queen of Sheba. Now come along, dearie. I've made you a nice deep fried breakfast and a jug of your favourite chocomilk, chocabloc with sugar just the way you like it.' She brandished a jug of *unspeakable* goo in Heather's face. 'Sir Freddie is sleeping off a hangover in the Diner Room so I've done you a table on the veranda.' She cupped her hands to her mouth and bawled, 'Mister Smothers, where are you?'

'That is what I have been asking myself for the last forty years, Missus Beaten,' Smothers mumbled as he wheezed up the stairs from the Cook Room burdened with a breakfast tray the size of a silver surfboard.

'Just the same little madam she ever was, isn't she, Mister Smothers? Bless.'

'Begging your pardon, Missus Beaten, but who is Bess?'

'No, Miss Heather.'

'What about Miss Heather?'

'Still got a sweet tooth, bless her little cotton socks.'

'I should hope so, Missus Beaten.'

'You should hope so, what, Mister Smothers?'

'Still got her own teeth. And her own socks, I wouldn't wonder. Shame about Bess.' Smothers shook his head and sighed.

'I don't know - your hearing gets worse every day, Mister Smothers.'

'Nothing wrong with my ears. You can hear me all right, can't you, Missus Beaten?'

'Oh, Mister Smothers, really. You are as batty as a catheter,' Missus Beaten chuckled. 'Now come along, Miss Heather. Don't let your breakfast go cold. Eat up, then you can skip off and play with the fairies.'

'You have no idea how much I have been looking forward to seeing you again,' Heather said. And she meant every word . . . except the bit about looking forward to seeing Missus Beaten again.

Watching the demented domestics engage in a cross purposes confusation brought back memories; it seemed that some things had not changed. Or had they? Heather took a closer look and saw that age had indeed withered and custom staled their infinite varieties. Whereas Smothers appeared to have a shrunken head with the patina of a pickled walnut, Missus Beaten's jolly face now had a rashy bloom. A bosomy woman with ruddy cheeks, straggly white hair and mistley eyes, she was a good deal broader in the rump than in her pomp. But she still wore a permanent smile, the flipside of Smothers' maudlin moribundity; it seemed that nothing – not one thing –

could blunt her chirpy indomitude. Whereas Smothers maintained that every silver lining had a dark cloud, she saw sunny uplands in the deepest ditch.

Heather had a soft spot in her soppy heart for the doolally housekeeper. She respected the fact that after her mother died, Missus Beaten had agreed to stay on. Ostensibly this was to tend to Sir Freddie's needs, but in reality it was because she could not bear the thought of abandoning Baskerville to Smothers.

With nowhere else to go, Smothers had applied to join the Royal Navy. Turned down on the grounds that he was having a laugh, he was left with no alternative but to remain in service, though he made no attempt to hide his contempt for Fifi and Katerina, nor they for him.

Leaving Smothers and Missus Beaten to their own deranged devices, Heather wandered out to the veranda. At least, that is how Missus Beaten still referred to it. Fifi had rechristened it the Ballustradium when she replaced the Italianate marble tiles with slipeasy rubber decking, festooned a platoon of Graeco-Romanesque statues of her toga-clad younger self in the asphalt arboretums and replaced the azaleas and cyclamens with plastic palm trees.

Heather pulled a wrought iron barstool up to the corrugated tin table, took out her off-duty pocketbook and told Katerina, 'now let's get this straight. I am in charge of this investigation, so what I say goes. You are just my assistant, like Doctor Watson was with Holmes. I will expect you to make a detailed record of the case.'

'Expect away, sis. See where it gets you.' Katerina birdied her middle finger to indicate that she got the message. 'Must say, Sherlock Holmes was *so* dope.' She clasped her hands and fluttered her lashes. 'For a junky.'

Heather gritted her teeth and bit her tongue; hearing the great man's name on her stepsister's emulsioned lips was akin to blasphemy. But mindful that time was of the essence, she reached for a knife and fork. 'I'll brief you after breakfast,' she said with a lick of the lips. 'I'm starving. Haven't eaten for days.' She patted her pockets one by one and then patted them again for the avoidance of doubt. 'Rats,' she cussed. 'I've left my spycorder in my room. Won't be two ticks.' After telling Katerina and Sebastian to start without her, she ran upstairs and reappeared two ticks later with her miniature iSpy recorder. Tummy-flummoxed when she saw Baskerville standing on his hind legs with his front paws on the table cleanlicking her plate, she turned to Katerina and groaned, 'he's eaten my breakfast. Why didn't you stop him?'

Katerina stuck her nose-piercing in the air. 'So I'm supposed to do everything round here, am I?' she said. 'Typical. You're as bad as my stepdad.'

'Wowie-zowie,' Sebastian exclaimed when he saw Heather's high-tech playback recorder. 'Is that a Wangchung iSpy Patent Applied For?'

'Metropolitan Police issue. Cost an absolute fortune.'

Heather said proudly. 'Strictly speaking, I'm not supposed to have it, but I'm sure CID won't miss it for a day or two.'

Sebastian picked up the spy device, turned it through nineteen degrees, raised an eyebrow, said, 'so is this where you, like, insert a peripheral modifier key to overclock the secondary memory?' and jabbed a fork into a small aperture.

'Don't - that's the on-off switch,' Heather screamed as the digiblah recorder burst into flames.

Sebastian dropped the iSpy like a hot brick on a cold tin roof and dunked his hand into the pitcher of chocomilk to douse his fingers. As Heather clapped her hands to her cheeks, all but mortified to death, Baskerville picked up the smouldering device in his jowly jaw, high-tailed it to the rose garden, buried it in the compost heap, cocked a leg and watered it.

Hardly able to blink let alone think, Heather stared at the steamy mess. 'Golly,' she said. 'How am I going to record the kidnapper's demands now?'

'Seb can do it.' Katarina flicked a bangled wrist at Sebastian. 'He's geekileptic. Used to work in Silicon Alley till he got uninstalled for having his head in the Cloud. That's his laboratory.' She pointed to a tinny shed at the bottom of the garden.

'No probs.' Sebastian took a large metal box bristling with wires and sockets out of his hoodie pouch and posited it on the table. 'My latest invention, the Marrowboan

Spookcorder. Mad name or what? Right, then - crew and talent ready to squirt the bird?'

Heather gave him a quizzical look. 'And in English?' she asked.

'Come on, sleuth-babes. Let's log onto the World Wide Wait in my adminsphere.' Sebastian nodded at the tumbledown shed. 'I've got the widest broadband on the planet, enough parts to make every electronic device known to man and an electric kettle. Takes forever to boil.' He frowned and scratched his head. 'Might need to upscale it.'

With nothing much left to lose, Heather followed Sebastian and Katerina to Sebastian's outside laboratory. She made herself as comfortable as she uncomfortably could on an upturned beancrate and took in her surroundings while Sebastian rummaged through a junkitude of army-navy surplus detritus in search of a pair of pliers to boot up his computer.

More of a workslop than a workshop and small, but not too small, yet not large - at least not overly so - Heather's initial impression of Sebastian's shed was that it was . . . well, shed-like she supposed. Indeed, she fancied that it might be said to be cosy by those accustomed to life in a damp earwig-infested pothole; as a sufferer from acute earwigitis, she shuddered at the thought. Cluttered to the missing gutters with bygone mechanicals, shoeboxfuls of resistors, transistors, thyristors, semiconductors, demiconductors, valves, tubes, lubes and all sorts of assorted electronic allsorts, to her mind the workshop's biggest drawback – and sadly, she felt this to be insurmountable – was Sebastian Marrowboan in all his manifest malaffectations.

She sat forward - hands on knees - and screwed up her eyes as the monitor fuzzed to life with the familiar Ransom.com logo. 'It's very blurry, Sebastian,' she said. 'Seems to be some kind of bug in the system.'

'It's not a bug, it's a feature,' he said. 'You can have on or off but not both at the same time. I'm planning to quantumise it when I upgrade the software.' He fiddled with a tangle of wires behind the computer and hey presto – the picture focused into sharp relief.

Impressed, Heather said, 'that's much better. What did you do - install new software?'

'Uninstalled the kettle. Shhhh . . .' Sebastian pressed a finger to his lips as the logo faded to be replaced by a sinister Donald Duck.

Unable to believe her eyes, Heather held her breath as the camera zoomed in on a diminutive figure handcuffed to a chair. Her face was covered in blood, her pigtails hung in clumps over her shoulders and her school uniform was tattered and torn. A pathos of blubs, sobs and tears, she begged for merciful salvation as her ruthless captor laid down terms.

As the picture faded, Heather turned to Katerina. 'Watty,' she said. 'I mean Bratty. We are up against a criminal duck of unimaginable evil. But why? Sir Freddie swears that he has never set eyes upon that poor little mite before.' She checked her blank notepad and scratched her head. 'It doesn't make sense.'

Katerina sat back, stretched her long legs, kicked off her slingbacks and examined her fingernails. 'I'd have thought it's obvious. They think they've kidnapped me. Bozos.'

'Golly,' Heather gasped as she realised that for perhaps the first time in her life, Katerina might have a point. Quick as a flash, her mind moved to red alert as she figured that this was no textbook kidnapping. She had been taught that a police negotiator would know who the victim was and might even surmise the identity of the snatcher. But - negligently in her humble opinion - she had never been instructed how to proceed in the event of an unknown hostage being held for an unknown ransom in an unknown location by an unknown kidnapper. In the absence of a manual, she would just have to rely upon her soon to be legendary gut instinct. She was tempted to suggest that they track down the kidnappers, explain that they had made a ghastly mistake and swap the miss-taken girl for Katerina. On second thoughts, she thought it a ridiculous idea; tempting but ridiculous. As this was now her case, she determined to be decisive, commanding and authoritative. 'Right,' she said with a purposeful clap of the hands. 'Listening? Good. I've decided to wait for the cellphone to be delivered, then play it by ear. Until then, we do nothing. Got that?'

Katerina crossed her arms and narrowed her bat-lashed eyes. 'So you spent three years at college learning how to do nothing. Bet you graduated top of the class.' She turned to Sebastian. 'Play it again, Seb.'

They watched a digital catch-up in silence. When it finished Heather shook her head. 'No clues,' she said. 'They're obviously professionals.'

'What about her school uniform?' Sebastian asked timidly, not wishing to sound more stupid than he actually was. 'Could that provide a lead?'

'Brilliant.' Heather leant forward and gave Seb a patronising pat on the knee. 'There are thousands of schools in London,' she said with a snoot. 'Finding the right one would be like searching for a needle in a haystack.'

Katerina lit a cigarette, slumped back on the futon and blew three perfect rings of smoke. 'Blue gymslip and aquamaroon blazer . . . ring any bells, sis?'

'Of course,' Heather clicked her fingers as a mint of pennies dropped. 'Eastminster Academy for Young Gentleladies.'

Katerina mocked a round of applause. 'Got it in one, sis. I go there, your mum went there, my step-aunt went there . . .' She flicked cigarette ash into Sebastian's baseball cap and asked, 'can you freeze the frame?' When Sebastian dutifully did as instructed, she sat up - wide-eyed - and gasped, 'oh my God, I don't believe it. It's

Kickarse Katy, the school bully.' Her face went a whiter shade of pale beneath her spray-tan foundation. 'She's two classes below me, or she was until she got expelled for betting on a netball match and bribing the referee, barbecuing the school cat and selling the playground to a property developer. Three different developers, if I remember right.' She clasped her hands, held them to her chest and shuddered as if describing a teeny incarnation of an adolescent devil incarnate. 'Her mother had a word with the headmistress and she got reinstated, awarded straight A's for all the exams she'd missed and given a scholarship for initiative. Must say, Miss Ryder's new BMW convertible is the business.'

'Poor little poppet,' Heather said with all the empathy she could muster. 'We have no time to lose.' She jumped to her feet, tucked her blouse into her jeans and straightened her jumper ready to spring into action. 'Right,' she said. 'We'll make door to door enquiries. You take North London, Bratty. I'll do Chelsea and Seb – you handle the home counties. If we draw a blank, tomorrow we'll . . .'

Katerina cut her short with, 'or we could just check the CCTV outside the school tuck shop.' She smothered a yawn and said, 'elementary, or what?'

In a sleazy backwater of East London at roughly the same time - give or take - a curiosity of neighbours peeked through netted curtains as a newpin-shiny Rolls Royce pulled up at the kerb. A feather duster could be heard to drop as three burly hoods got out, stretched their arms to exercise their shoulders, buttoned up their mohair jackets, buttoned down their collars and straightened their kipper ties. All along the street a breathy hush descended . . . the Clark Gang's unannounced arrival on their arch-rivals' turf could only mean one thing. Trouble was brewing. Big, big trouble.

While the driver stayed behind to freshenup her makeup, the arrivalistas stood their ground and looked around. The smallest of the three, a leanish, meanish man in a snazzy suit, jazzy tie and snappy crocodile-skin shoes, ran shivers down the spines of those who cared to look upon his face. Like the Ozymandias of crime, his frown and wrinkled lip and sneer of cold command announced to all who dared to look upon his works, despair. A brutally disfigured figure, his worry lines ran deep. Some years ago his facial features had been callously refashioned by a gangland rival during an over-physical metaphysical debate about something trivial and, in hindsight, relatively inconsequential. As a result of his grossly disrespectful behaviour, the Butcher of Basildon - as cleaverman was known in underworld circles - is now swimming with the fishies in concrete flippers and a bespoke rope choker.

Fred 'Scareface' Clark – for it was he – turned to his right hand man. 'Brawns,' said he. 'See that geezer?' He nodded at an infant kicking a football against a wall. 'Sort him.'

Brawns clicked his fingers at his sidekick, a swarthy man with a criminal moustache. 'Mussels . . .' He pointed to the child. 'See that geezer? Sort him.'

'Oy, you. Hop it.' Mussels slipped the scamp a twenty pound note and shooed him away. 'That'll teach him,' he sneered as he watched the lad sprint off to the tobacconists with his football tucked under an arm.

Scareface cast his good eye about the street until it settled on a rundown pawnbroker's shop. Ordering Mussels and Brawns to watch his back, he walked in, flipped the open sign to closed and latched the latch. 'Nice place, you got here, Solly,' he said to a shifty-eyed man behind the counter.

Solly 'The Popweasel' Proust took off his beret and mopped his receding brow. 'Do me a favour, Fred,' he said. 'Come back in an hour. I'm closed for lunch.'

'Says who?' Scareface curled his top lip into a sneer and picked up a large jug-handled vase from the crockery display.

'Careful with that, Fred,' Solly said. 'It's genuine

Chinese. Minge Dynasty.'

'Really?' Scareface raised a cleavered eyebrow. 'Well it's ancient history now.' He let it go and laughed as it shattered on the parquet floor. When Solly pointed to a sign . . . *All Breakages Must Be Paid For. Easy Terms Available* . . . he said, 'put it on my slate, along with this.' He purloined the mother of all pearl necklaces from the jewellery display and stuffed it in a pocket.

'That's forty grand you owe me, Fred, plus interest at fifty percent a week.' Solly made a note in his ledger with a fountain-tipped pen.

'Awe, come on. The Prousts are worth millions,' Scareface said. 'Still, suppose I might as well go for broke.' He grabbed ahold of a carriage clock from the clock shelf, raised it pendulously above his head and flung it on the floor. As Solly shrank back quaking like a duck, he set his jaw and asked, 'the loan sharking business good these days, is it, Popweasel? You should know. You're the Proust Mob's bookkeeper. Thing is . . .' He made a play of inspecting his fingernails. 'Word on the street is, you're thinking about branching out into narcotics, protection, gambling . . . kidnapping.'

'Please, Fred,' Solly croaked. 'Told you, I'm closed for lunch.'

Barely had Solly finished grovelling than the door burst open and a small lipsticked moll with a bottle blonde permquake and bombshell breasts stormed in. 'Lunch is cancelled and so are you if you don't do exactly as I say,' she said in an ice cold voice redolent of an arctic breeze.

The blood drained from Solly's cheeks. A shamble of nerves, he opened the till, said, 'here, Dolores. It's all I got,' and tried to force the contents into her hand.

'That's not why I'm here.' Dolores pushed away his cash-handed advances. 'Tell him, Fred.'

'Thing is, my baby has gone missing,' Scareface snarled. 'And the Proust Mob is top of Dolly's list of suspects.'

'Your baby? Do me an effing favour,' Dolores groaned and rolled her eyes.

'Thing is, my girl has gone missing and I got a hunch your mob is responsible. No one else I know has got a big enough motive. Or a big enough death wish,' Scareface growled. 'She's only thirteen and . . .'

'Fourteen and a half,' Dolores corrected him.

'Thing is, she's only fourteen and a half, and never stays out all night. Ever.' Scareface said.

'Not much, she don't,' Dolores muttered.

'Thing is, from what I been told, she don't often stay out overnight. Not as a rule, anyway,' Fred snarled. 'If you hear a whisper, I want to know. There's a reward in it.'

Solly mopped his brow with his beret and gulped. 'What's the reward?'

'You get to carry on breathing,' Dolores said without blinking. 'With my effing-compliments.'

'A word of advice,' Scareface said with an ominous threat of menace in his voice. 'If you don't want the taxman knocking on your door at nine in the morning wanting to check your quarterly VAT return, you'll . . .'

Dolores barged Scareface aside with a bony elbow. 'I'll say this once and once only, Popweasel,' she said. 'The Proust Mob are dead men and women walking if they think they can get away with kidnapping my girl. I want her back and I want her back yesterday.'

Solly wrung his hands so hard that beads of sweat glooped on the counter, coagulating on the chipboard veneer. 'I got no idea what you're on about, Dolly. My mob are loan sharks. Might peddle a few drugs on the side, but we wouldn't know a kidnap from a catnap.'

Dolores Clark rocked onto her boot-tips and grabbed Solly by the scruff of the throat. She woman-handled him over the counter and glared him in the eye. 'I knew this fella once,' she said in a deadpan voice. 'A comedian, like you. He's a ventriloquist's dummy now.' She pushed Solly away and brushed her hands as he stumbled back gasping for breath. 'Now, you listen to me, Popweasel, and listen to me good,' she said. 'Unless my brat is released by the end of the week, I'm taking the Proust Mob down, and I in't talking a trip to Australia. Watch my lips . . . I own this effing manor. Got it?' She clicked her fingers. 'Mussels . . . Brawns - trash the joint and meet me back at the scrapyard.'

Having sworn her piece, Dolores 'Dolly' Clark helped herself to a handful of boiled fruitysucks from the sweetie bowl on the counter, told Solly to put them on her husband's slate and without so much as a parting suck, marched out and slammed the door behind her.

xiii

'For goodness' sake, Bratty, you've done nothing but whinge since we got here.'

'That's right, sis, have a go at me, why don't you? Any idea what it will do to my street cred if the Kensington Massive see us?'

'Oh, come on. Nobody will give a second thought to two schoolgirls hanging around outside Eastminster Academy for Young Gentleladies. It's the perfect cover.'

'You think? Don't suppose you looked in the mirror before we left home.'

'Must admit, my old gymslip is a little on the small side, but I doubt anyone will notice.'

'Not much they won't, sis. You look like a porn star.'

'Hark who's talking. At least I don't look like a teen escort. For goodness sake, Bratty, take that ridiculous padding out of your bra.'

'What padding?'

'And do you make a habit of wearing false eyelashes, bright red lipstick, fishnet stockings and suspenders to school?'

'Got a problem with that, sis? You sound just like

Humpy Ryder, my headmistress. Don't wear this, don't do that, put out that joint, leave those boys alone. I might as well be a nun. As if . . .' Katerina poked a finger down her throat and pretended to vomit.

Heather had the lightbulb moment when she was snatching a quick powernap. If, as they maintained, the hostageers were watching Trevelyan House twenty-four-seven three-six-five – three-six-six if it was a leap year, which it wasn't . . . probably – she would need a convincing disguise to slip the knot of scrutiny. So she thumbed through her wardrobe until she chanced upon her old school uniform. Perfect, she thought as her brain ticked into gear; let's face it, the kidnappers would hardly give a passing thought to two giggly schoolgirls popping out to play.

Needless to say, Katerina was not convinced, or she wasn't until Heather pointed out that the alternative would be to swap her for the hostage. And so a plot was hatched . . . in the guise of chummy school pals, she and Katerina would hotfoot it to Eastminster Academy and requisition the CCTV footage from the school tuckshop. It was a masterful - or to be more gender specific, a mistressful - ploy lifted straight from the pages of the Sherlock Holmes playbook.

It had taken Heather an excruciating twenty or so minutes to squeeze into her old school uniform and another ten to plait her pigtails. Indeed, she nearly abandoned the plan mid-grunt; the gymslip pinched like a girdle, the sandals bunioned her feet, the straw boater was half a head too small and the aquamaroon blazer itched like a worsted corset. On the other hand, her stepsister looked the epitome of school-chic in her designer gymslip, Jimmy Choos and faultless makeup.

Before venturing into the tuckshop, Prendergast of Saint Trinians - as Katerina had mischievously miss-nomered her - gave her boxed pleats a wishful tug in a fruitless attempt to grant her thighs an inch more modesty and a cinch less pinch. Needless to say, she felt a little . . . fleshy. But as Aunt Elizabeth would say, needs be as needs must in the line of duty, goosepimples notwithstanding. And so, adopting the gait of a jolly-hockeysticks schoolgal, she pushed through the sweetie shop door and demanded the attention of an acned youth picking his nose behind the counter. 'Excuse me, young man . . .' she said, then caught her tongue. Would a fifth-former address a shop assistant in such a manner? Probably not she thought, so she cleared her throat and tried again. '`Scuse me, mister,' she said in her chirpiest schoolgirl voice. 'Does that thing work?' She cocked a thumb at the surveillance camera outside the shop.

The boy's jaw dropped. 'Your mum lets you out like that?' He pointed to Heather's knees. 'She ought to be ashamed of herself.'

'Kindly watch your lip, young . . . mister,' Heather said, affronted to the nth degree; her knees were her Achilles heel. 'I must advise you that I am here on official business,' she said, reverting to type.

'Local massage parlour need a hand, does it?'

'I would ask you not to be so flippant, sir. Now, I wish to inspect your CCTV footage, if I may.'

Shop boy glanced at Katerina and mouthed, 'is she for real?' Then he turned to Heather and said, 'look, love, no-one is allowed to look at that footage without the boss's permission, not even a copper dressed like a porn star.' He shot her a wink. 'See that?' He pointed to the door. 'Close it on your way out. This is a respectable sweet shop.'

Wondering how on earth the *unspeakable* oik could have seen through her disguise, Heather arched her back to her full five feet and six inches, tucked her straw boater under an arm and said, 'what makes you think that I am a police officer?'

'Oh come on,' he sniggered. 'I wasn't born yesterday.'

Unminded to bandy words with the *pleb*, Heather derummaged her warrant card from her satchel, said, 'right you are. CID. Metropolitan Police Food Squad,' and flashed it in his face.

Shop boy put up his hands and backed away. 'It's a fair cop,' he said and winked at Katerina. 'I ran out of sherbet so used icing sugar in the lucky dips.'

Heather licked the tip of her pencil and jotted a note in her exercise book. 'Illicit sherbet substitution is no laughing matter,' she advised him. 'Now hand over the footage or I will arrest you for confecting an alibi.'

'Got a search warrant?' he asked.

Thrown off her stride by the unwarranted request, Heather said, 'rats - I left it in my cheerleader uniform. But take my word,' she fibbed. 'I assure you that the paperwork will be fully in order should the need arise.'

'Jeez, at this rate we'll be here all day.' Katerina groaned. 'I'll show him my credentials.' She barged Heather aside, scrambled over the counter, grabbed shop boy by the tie and dragged him into the stockroom. She reappeared a few grunts, groans and squeals later followed by shop boy with an asinine grin on his face.

'Golly, how did you manage to persuade him to hand over the footage?' Heather asked as she stowed the videotape in her satchel.

'Dunno.' Katerina shrugged. 'Suppose he must have taken a shine to me.' She refastened her bra straps, rebuttoned her blouse and fumbled in her makeup holdall for a compact to desmudge her lipstick.

Heather turned to shop boy, said, 'now mind how you go, sir,' tipped her straw boater and followed Katerina out to the street.

Sebastian was waiting in his Skodamobile, a four-wheel carwreck largely held together with duct-tape and blind faith. More rust than not, it was a prime candidate for a scrap museum and had been ever since it stalled on the malufacturer's assembly line. The very definition of a sloppy jalopy, it was his pride and joy - his ticket to ride, he called it in his more lucid moments.

As Heather squeezed into the passenger seat, Sebastian reached across to stow his graphic novel in the glove compartment. He sneaked a surreptitious peek at her thighs, loosened his collar, said, 'yeah. Well. Right,' and swallowed.

Katerina lent forward from her backseat perch, walloped him with her makeup holdall and meowed, 'keep your eyes on the road or you're Baskerville meat.'

Stirred but not deterred, Sebastian looked over a shoulder, put the car into the wrong gear, back-ended the vehicle behind, fiddled with the gearstick, bumper-crunched the car in front and stalled. He strayed another eye at Heather's thighs and whetted his lips before reignitioning the engine and lurching out into the road.

'So when did you pass your driving test?' Heather asked as Sebastian accelerated the wrong way down a one way street.

'They do driving tests?' he said as he veered into a pedestrian precinct to avoid an oncoming crash. 'Cool.'

Somehow, they made it home before dark. After a half a bottle of chilled Chardonnay to settle her nerves, Heather joined Katerina and Sebastian in Sebastian's adminbubble, as Seb referred to his shed. She found them arguing like Kats and dogs. Katerina was yowling at Sebastian and he was hanging his head with a hangdog expression on his pimply face.

Katerina screamed, 'couldn't take your beady eyes off her, could you?'

'But it's you I love, Katy. You,' Sebastian moped. 'You're my BFF.'

'Oh, just BFF-off and die, why don't you?' Katerina hissed, then zipped on a glassious smile as Heather walked through the door. 'Oh hi, sis. Me and Seb were just discussing global warming,' she said. 'It's a hot topic on TikTok.' She shuffled sideways to make more bumspace on the army-navy surplus futon, told Heather to sit down and remote controlled the video recorder with a handy broom handle.

Deep in concentration, Heather watched the footage of snotty Eastminster Academy girlyswots skipping through the school gates like pigtailed lambs exiting Daughterhouse Five. All of a sudden, she felt a clammy hand on her thigh. 'Behave,' she whispered and strayed Sebastian's hand back where it belonged. 'Cripes, that's her,' she gasped and pointed to the screen.

Kickarse Katy could be seen swinging her satchel at the tail end of a crocodile of jabbering schoolclones. As, one by one and two by two, her classmates drifted off, a man with a long white beard and a walking stick stepped out of the shadows, offered her a lollipop and whispered in her ear. Whatever he said seemed to set her at ease as she took his hand and they disappeared from view.

'Rewind,' Heather told Sebastian. 'Stop there. See that?' She pointed to a distinctive red birthmark on wierdy-beardy's neck. 'Golly, I don't believe it,' she gasped. 'It's Groaty McTavish.'

As one, Katerina and Sebastian turned to her and said, 'Who-ty McWho?'

Heather reached for a bottle of mineral water, took a sip and clutched it in her hands like a polyurethane comforter. Visited by the spirit of the late, great cicerone of crime, Sherlock Holmes, she stared into the near beyond with an expression of stony faced determination. 'Groaty McTavish is a nom-de-plume, a mere identification mark,' she said with a grimace, a shudder and a wince. 'But behind it lies a shifty and evasive personality. He is important, not for himself, but for the criminal mastermind with whom he is in touch.' She sat back, tidied her pleats over her thighs, crossed her legs and tapped her chin, deep in thought. 'Picture to yourself the pilot fish with the shark, the jackal with the lion - anything that is insignificant in companionship with what is formidable: not only formidable, Watty, but sinister - in the highest degree sinister.' She closed her eyes and took a deep - a very deep - breath to mollify her nerves.

'Pilot fish? Jackal? Lion?' Katerina turned to Sebastian and whispered, 'what did you spike her chocomilk with - acid?'

'I see you are developing a certain unexpected vein of pawky humour, Watty,' Heather chuckled, 'against which I must learn to guard myself. Now pay attention and take notes.'

Katerina wrote *pissed out of her skull* on her squibble-pad, underlined it several times and said, 'oh for pity's sake, sis, stop calling me Watty,'

'Don't be ridiculous,' Heather scoffed. 'Why would I do a thing like that?'

'Because you've got a Sherlock Holmes complex,' Katerina suggested. 'Either that or you're off your trolley.'

Heather ignored her. "You have heard speak of Professor Murray Harty, Watty?' she asked - rhetorically in her opinion; Harty's name was synonymous with villainy the length and breadth of New Scotland Yard. 'He is a famous scientific criminal,' she explained for the avoidance of doubt, should any such doubt exist. 'He is the scourge of law enforcement officers the world over. Said by some to be a deranged lunatic but regarded by others as an evil genius, he is the controlling brain of the criminal underworld, capable of making or marring the destiny of nations.' She wrapped her arms around her shoulders and shuddered as if chilled by a blast of wind. 'While he was incarcerated in Broadmoor Institute for the Criminally Insane, he wrote The Asteroidal Dynamics of Dynamic Asteroidal Queridium, a book which ascends to such rarefied heights of pure mathematics it is said that there is no man in the scientific press capable of making head or tail of it. Indeed, some maintain that it is beyond the wit of the most gifted astrophysicists. Mind you, others dismiss it as gobbledegook.' She broke into a wry smile and tapped her temple. 'You see, that is the genius of the man,' she said with an assuredness that brooked not one scintilla of doubt. 'Nobody is sure whether he stands on the shoulders of giants or cowers under the beds of midgets.'

After another sip of water to lubricate a frog in her throat, Heather, dabbed her lips with her tie and resumed her potted history of Harty's chequerboarded career. 'Nothing has been heard of him since he escaped from the maximum security wing of Broadmoor Hospital, leaving a trail of death and destruction in his wake. If, as I suspect, he is responsible for the poor little mite's kidnapping,' she said, 'rest assured, he will have an altogether more sinister agenda than a mere desire to enrich his bitcoin account. Take it from me, he is not a man to be trifled with.'

Katerina clicked her fingers, said, 'oh yeah, that Murray Harty,' gave Heather a strabismic look and squibbled *mad as a box of frogs* on her pad.

'Sorry, didn't mean to drift off like that.' Heather cleared her throat. 'It's just that I have always dreamed of pitting my wits against Professor Murray Harty. He is Prendergast of The Yard's arch nemesis. And we must not delay. If my hunch is right, the future of all mankind lies in our hands.' She cast a long, a lean, a lingering look at Katerina. 'And quite possibly, the future of all womankind.'

xiv

Professor Murray Harty sat at the recreationary table counting his remaining coppers. How, he asked himself, could the world's greatest criminal meglamind lose all his money playing snap with a pigtailed brat who hardly looked old enough to buckle her own sandals, let alone roll a liquorice cheroot on her milky thighs.

Heartened by the Professor's sulken expression, Groaty McTavish took the opportunity to rub a cellars-worth of salt into his wounds. 'Got tae hand it tae the wee lassie, Chief,' he said with a nod of respect. 'She can sure hold her drink.'

'Pah,' Professor Harty scoffed in an attempt to reassert his threadworn credentials. 'It is only barley water.'

'So how long we got?' HostageKaty asked as she counted her winnings. Again.

The Professor wrested his pocket watch from Katy's clutches and flipped it open. 'By now Sir Freddie will have received the prepaid cellular telephone,' he said as, reluctantly it must be held, he gave her back his watch - or rather her watch as it now was following one too many ill-considered wagers. 'I will contact him forthwith with instructions how, where and when to hand over the ransom.' He narrowed his eyes and jabbed a spindly finger at HostageKaty's cherubic face. 'And then I will pay back Solly Proust, retrieve my domestic Hadronette Collider and ColdFusion Centrifuges and you, my flighty little sparrow, can return to your nest.'

HostageKaty shuffled the cards in one hand, flipped them into a fan, closed her eyes, asked McTavish to pick a card - any card - told him what it was, relieved him of his last ten pence and banked it in her pencil case with Harty's pocket watch and treasured Parker quill. 'So then, muppets,' she said. 'What's the plan?' When, studiously avoiding her eyes, the Professor's looked away, she rolled her eyes and groaned, 'don't tell me you're just going to wing it like you did when you opened this sorry excuse for a pig trough.'

'Pah,' Professor Harty scoffed at the suggestion that he might not have considered every conceivable eventuality to the infinitesimalist degree. 'I will instruct your doting father to deposit the cash in a disused drain on Eastminster Common,' he told HostageKaty with the clinical precision for which he was famed. 'McTavish will be hiding in a nearby tree and when he is quite sure that nobody is looking, will collect the ransom and return hotfoot, making sure that he is not followed. Once I am satisfied that all the money is sufficiently present and correct, I shall release you relatively intact.'

'Gawd give me strength.' HostageKaty rolled her eyes. 'I seen cleverer plans than that in a Christmas cracker. And what if my scummy dad stitches you up, eh? You tell me that?'

Professor Harty rubbed his hands together as if maliciously milling corn. He cackled, 'you die a terrible and agonising death, my little turtle dove.'

'And?' HostageKaty asked.

Professor Harty stared at her. And he stared at her. 'What in Lucifer's name are you implying, you misbegotten spawn of Diabolis?'

'Rubbish at this, in't you?' HostageKaty popped a liquorice twist in her mouth and spoke between chomps. 'So let's say you do the dirty . . . fat chance,' she said. 'But suppose you get me before I get you, then what?'

The Professor gave her a puzzled look as if to say, does that not go without saying, my child? 'Weeell,' he said guardedly, fearing that he might be the unwitting victim of a maladroitism. 'The Jockal will chop you into tiny pieces. Then he will bury your remains in the footings of a flyover or throw them into the canal or . . .'

'Whoa . . .' McTavish lumbered to his feet, raised his hands and backed away. 'Count me oot, Chief. I telled ye before, I dinnae do egregious bodily harm, except tae woodlice and the like.'

'Very well, you lily-livered turnkilt. It is my intention to end the world but if needs must, I will start by ending hers.' Professor Harty turned to HostageKaty and snarled, 'it will give me the greatest pleasure to rip out your innards with my bare hands and dispose of your mangled remains in the central heating furnace.'

'It disnae work,' McTavish reminded him. 'The gas gan cut off because we didnae pay the bill.'

Professor Harty slammed a fist on the table. 'Does it matter? You will be as dead as a cadaver, my little nightingale. Why should you care whether you are buried, cremated or devoured by an unkindness of ravenous ravens?'

HostageKaty sat back with her feet up on the table chewing liquorice and swigging barley water from the bottle. 'You're missing the point, numpty,' she tut-tutted. 'So, let's say Fred tucks you up with a brick in a box and you snuff me out – as if. What then? You'll still be broke, but you'll have my mam on your case. And believe me, you don't want to know what she'll do when she gets her hands on you. And I do mean when.'

'Ye ken, the wee bairn's gan a point, Chief.' McTavish tugged his kilt over his knees and screwed up much of his face.

HostageKaty rocked back on her stool and said, 'so here's what we'll do. Listening? Right . . .' she ticked her fingers one by one. 'First off, this is going to take time. Knowing Fred, he'll drag out negotiations long as he can while mam tries to find me and rips your bollocks off one at a time before cutting off your ears and burying you alive in an anthill. Fred didn't get filthy rich by paying full price for anything, and mam's hobby is inflicting pain.'

Professor Harty glanced at McTavish as if to say,

'hmmm . . . '

'Then there's the handover,' HostageKaty ticked her middle finger. 'Fred will have snoops all over the drop-point. Better believe, there'll be heavies everywhere dressed as letter boxes, dogs, bushes . . . you name it.'

Professor Harty threw back his head and cackled out loud. 'Think I have not considered that, my little cocksparrow?'

'So what you going to do about it?'

'Never you mind,' the Professor growled.

'Nae, gae on,' McTavish said. 'After all, it's me up that tree waiting tae collect the ransom.'

'Pedant,' Professor Harty hmphed, despite inwardly acknowledging that McTavish might have a point. 'Well, what do you suggest?'

'Drones,' HostageKaty said.

'Enough of your damned impertinence, I say,' Professor Harty roared.

'Ooh, touchy in't we?' HostageKaty giggled. 'We'll tell Fred where to stash the cash and that, then collect it with a remote controlled drone. Once we've counted the quids and made sure he hasn't stitched us up, I'll take my cut, bunk off somewhere with a sunny beach, a liquorice parlour and loads of fit talent and you can subjugate the universe or whatever. As if I care.'

'Sounds like a plan, Chief.' McTavish nodded approvingly and gave HostageKaty a pat on the head.

'Easy-peasy,' HostageKaty said. 'But it'll take time to sort. And it'll cost.' Her lips moved as she totted up the ante on a paper hanky. 'Five grand, I reckon, give or take a monkey. How much you got?'

The Professor turned his frockcoat pockets inside out and stared glumly at a fistful of fluff. 'What do we have in the bank, keeper of the corporate reserves?' he asked McTavish.

'Tae the nearest muckle?' McTavish asked and tapped an app on his Mc-ayePhone. 'Nae a mickle, gie or teck.'

HostageKaty shook her Pollyanna pigtails and groaned. 'Ever thought of getting a proper job, muppets?' she asked. 'Suppose I'm just going to have to bankroll this shakedown messell.' She thought a moment, stuck up a finger, asked, 'got a chew-proof box big enough for a starving rat?' and broke into a gap-toothed grin. 'Time to pay the pasta joint over the road a visit and make them an offer they'd be numpties to refuse.' She hopped off the stool and skipped to the door. Struck by a thought, she turned and asked, 'fancy a takeway pizza while I'm at it?'

Freshly showered, jeansed and jumpered, Heather Prendergast flopped down on her bed and nibbled the blunt end of her pencil. This writing lark is tricky, she thought as she pondered the latest chapter of her epic casebook. Then, inspired by the Holmsian bible on the bedside table, her trusty pencil seemed to take on a life of its own, much like a Harry Potter wand. In no time at all to relatively speak of, words gushed forth, unbridled and unabridged.

Chapter Three. Day two of The Curious Case of the Katenapped Girl. After interviewing suitably qualified candidates I have assembled a crack team to assist with the investigation. By painstakingly analysing the available data in forensic detail, I have come to the conclusion that the kidnapper is none other than Professor Murray Harty in cahoots with his very ruthless henchman, Groaty McTavish. As taught by my professors at Merton Police College, I will proceed with the utmost care and leave no stone unturned, aware as I am that Professor Harty has evaded justice for absolutely ages.

I am expecting a package from the kidnappers at any moment containing a mobile cellular phone. Given a direct line of communication, I have every reason to believe that I will have the villains bang to rights in very short order. In the likely event that daddy's chum, The Commissioner of Police, sees fit to promote me, I will accept the honour with my trademark humility and request a minimum of publicity.

After reading the chapter back several times, Heather scored a line through *and request a minimum of publicity.* That's better, she thought. After all, why hide her achievements under a bushel? A tingle of excitement jitterbugged up her spine as it struck her that this could be one of the most celebrated cases that she might ever be called upon to crack, so why not shout her worth from the rooftops? And then, all of a moment, she was riven with doubt. Was she yet ready to pit her young wits against Professor Murray Harty? It was, after all, a giant slop from squeegeeing kitchen floors to tackling the Controlling Brain of the Criminal Underworld. Although failure was not an option, it was a distinct possibility.

As her misgivings multiplied like fruit flies on a rotting quince, Heather's every instinct told her that this was a case for the redoubtable Inspector Obafemi rather than a trainee kitchenary assistant. But then her gaze fell upon her trusty Sherlock Holmes Omnibus. What would her mentor do, she asked herself? Turn the case over to Inspector Lastrade or solve it himself? Needless to say, the answer went without saying.

Heather's idling thoughts were interrupted by a knock on the bedroom door. She pricked up her ears, zipped up her jeans, called, 'come in, Smothers,' and added a smug, 'I recognised the shuffle of your slippers on the landing. And if I'm not mistaken, that pungent aroma is the distinctive brand of hand-rubbed pipe tobacco you smoke in bed. Of course, the clincher was your hesitant knock, unmistakably that of an elderly gentleman suffering from lumbago. Elementary, if I may say.'

'Yeah, Right. Cool.' Sebastian Marrowboan slouched into the room with an inane grin on his face.

Heather sat up and cleared an embarrassed frog from her throat. 'Has the post arrived?' she asked. When Sebastian nodded, she crossed her fingers and took a deep breath. 'Was a cellphone delivered?'

Sebastian shook his head. 'Negatory. Only this.' He handed her a small parcel glitter-wrapped in silver paper. 'It's bookmarked for you.'

'But nobody knows I'm here.' Profoundly puzzled, Heather tapped her chin with the unnibbled end of her pencil. Thinking aloud, she said, 'I bet the kidnappers have been tipped off by a grass.' She clicked her fingers. 'You know, I wouldn't be surprised if the gardener isn't a plant.' Determining to make further enquiries when she next had a window in her busy schedule, she examined the parcel. 'So this must be the cellphone we were told to expect. Stand back, Sebastian,' she cautioned as she ran a varnished thumbnail down the Sealotape. 'Golly.' She threw up her hands in delicious delight. 'It's a box of yummy chocolates.' She gave Sebastian a puzzled look. 'Any idea who delivered this?'

Sebastian's cheeks flushed a blushy shade of cherry and he squirmed like a worm. 'Yeah, well, right . . . beats me. It's beyond my bandwidth. Don't you like them?' he asked anxiously. 'Wouldn't be surprised if chocolates like that don't cost near enough a whole week's pocket money.' When Heather gave him the blankest of looks, he shrugged and changed the subject. 'Oh, Katerina needs a facetime conflab. Says she wants you to open-source her in the meetspace.'

'I beg your pardon?'

'Our carbon community needs to be on the same page, Spriggsy. You don't mind if I call you Spriggsy, do you?'

'I'd rather you didn't.'

Sebastian's shoulders slumped. 'Yeah. Right. Cool,' he mumbled. 'See you in the adminsphere at zero hour.' He stuffed his hands in his pockets and slouched off down the stairs.

Not having eaten a bean worth eating since sneaking a surreptitious finger of fudge in the sweetie-shop the previous afternoon - needless to say, she left ample remuneration on the counter - Heather sampled a few mystery choconuts, licked her lips and sampled all the rest. Chocked up to the gills, she tucked her trusty Sherlock Holmes Omnibus under an arm and hurried downstairs, where she found Missus Beaten scrubbing Baskerville sick off the doormat.

Missus Beaten sat back on her haunches, mopped her brow with the scrubbing brush and smiled her perpetual smile. 'My, my, Miss Heather, don't you look grown up in those jeans and that jumper? Tell you what, why don't I take your twinset and blouse to the cleaners? This weather is as stuffy as a Christmas goose, so dare say you won't be needing them for a day or two.' She took a five-penny piece from her apron pocket, cocked an eyebrow in mock surprise, said, 'well I never, what have we here?' pressed it into Heather's hand and winked. 'Don't spend it all at once, dearie. Now off you pop and play with Baskerville in the sandpit. I'll have Mister Smothers dig you up when lunch is ready.'

Katerina and Sebastian were waiting in Sebastian's shed when Heather arrived. She sat down on vacant trolley and called the meeting to order. 'The hunt is on,' she said with note of purposeful determination in her cultured voice. 'Thanks to my keen powers of observation, we now know who the hostage is. And I have a hunch that the kidnapper is none other than Professor Murray Harty, the organizer of half that is evil and nearly all that is undetected in this great city of ours. He may have lost touch with reality, but he is nevertheless a genius - a philosopher and an abstract thinker of the first order.'

'A high-dome,' Sebastian said.

Heather nodded. 'That is putting it mildly,' she said. 'He is a man of good birth and excellent education, endowed by nature with a phenomenal mathematical faculty. But insanity runs in his blood, which has been rendered infinitely more dangerous by his extraordinary mental powers. If I am right,' she said with a certitude that brooked no doubt, 'this is a ghastly mistaken case of identity. Professor Harty believes that he is holding Katerina and will torture the poor little poppet to death unless daddy pays the ransom.'

'As if . . .' Katerina flopped the fringe out of her eyes with a toss of her head. 'Tight isn't the word. Know what he gave me for my twelfth birthday? A pony,' she said, barely able to stem her contempt. 'What was I supposed to do with that - wear it?'

'Daddy bought you a pony?' Heather swallowed a lump in her throat. 'All he ever gave me was a mangy puppy that snarled whenever I went near it. That was fifteen years ago and Smothers is still trying to housetrain him.'

'Get on with it, sis,' Katerina said as she inspected her acrylic fingernails. 'Seb's taking me clubbing later so I need to put on a cute face and change into something easily rip-offable.'

'As you will,' Heather said with a culpatory scowl. 'So, we were supposed to get a prepaid cellphone in the post . . .'

'A burner,' Katerina interjected.

'No, a prepaid cellphone. Pay attention, Bratty,' Heather scolded. 'It hasn't arrived, so I suspect that Harty is playing games to keep us on our toes. He will probably make contact in some other way to catch us unawares. We must try to get into his diabolical mind and stay one step ahead. Meanwhile, Sebastian, in case he does phone, can you put a trace on the call? And you, Bratty - keep an eye out for any strange men.'

'You bet.' Katerina licked her plummy lips. 'And what will you do while I keep them occupied?'

'One of these days, young lady, we will have words. You can count on it,' Heather said with a humdinger of a scowl as she got to her feet. 'Come on, we have no time to lose.' She checked her watch and tucked her notepad under an arm. 'By now, the poor little mite must be frightened out of her wits. Bless.'

xvi

'What you mean, you sent that burner second-class post?' HostageKaty landed a brain-juddering blow to the thick side of McTavish's skull with the business end of a broth ladle. 'Told you, they're expecting it today. I don't know. . .' She pointed to a tendrilous plant on a plant shelf by the serving hatch. 'Next to you, that Venus Flytrap is dead brainy.'

McTavish cowered his head in his hands and whimpered, 'I was strapped frae cash, lassie. Many a mickle mecks a muckle.'

'Mickle, muckle, wiffle, waffle, piffle, puddle, piddle,' HostageKaty scoffed. 'We're talking ten million squibs here - ten mill - and you think it's clever to save fifty pence on a first-class stamp? Do me a favour.' She clambered onto a bothystool, propped her elbows on the table and fiddled with her pigtails. 'From now on, you do what you're told, Haggisface, or you're sacked.'

Professor Harty fixed HostageKaty in the eye with a spine-curdling stare. 'Unless it has escaped your notice, my little song thrush,' he snarled, 'a hostage does not sack her kidnappers. It is strictly against the rules of nefarious engagement.'

'Alright clever-clogs, so how you going to pull this off without me, you tell me that?' HostageKaty turned to McTavish, demanded, 'milkshake, Groatface, now, or you're quarantined,' and pointed to the McIcecream whisk. 'While you two muppets were sat here plotting the end of time or whatever, I been grafting me fingers to the bone to fund this sorry excuse for a shambles. If you reckon the world is going to end of its own accord, you got another thing coming.' She slammed a wad of cash on the table, said, 'plenty more where that come from,' and rooted through her satchel for her Bootleg Barbie Diary. 'Here . . .' she flung it at McTavish and said, 'you keep tabs on the clientele, and you, the Carpenter of Noon or whatever you call yesself . . .'

'The Harbinger of Doom,' Professor Harty gnarled through his remaining teeth.

'Please yesself. I'm putting you in charge of housekeeping. Ta.' She licked her lips as McTavish handed her a Malty McOatshake and sat back slurping through a bendy straw. 'I already signed up the pizza joint over the road. Six hundred nicker a week they're good for. The Indian takeaway should be worth loads more. What you reckon – a grand?'

'I dinnae understand,' said McTavish with the verbose equivalent of a frown. 'Why are all the local restaurants donating money tae finance our operation?'

'Didn't they learn you nothing at school, Groatface?'

'School?'

'You know, that place you went when you were a kid.'

'You mean borstal.'

'Your parents sent you to borstal?'

'Parents?'

HostageKaty narrowed her eyes at McTavish. 'I'm that close to calling it a day.' She pressed two fingers together and held them up for him to count. 'That close.'

'You will go when I say and not before,' Professor Harty roared.

'You reckon?' HostageKaty scoffed. 'And how you going to stop me?'

Harty shuffled to his feet, drew his cloak of visibility about his shoulders and thundered, 'I will strike you down with a bolt of electricity so powerful that it will reduce you to a crisp.'

'Best be quick, Chief,' McTavish whispered, 'the `lecky's ganna get cut off any time the noo.'

'Once you have paid the electricity bill, my little chuff, I will strike you down with . . .'

'Shut your face, knobhead. Right, take this down.' HostageKaty tossed McTavish a red crayon and pointed to a blank page in her Bootleg Barbie Diary between All Dressed Up and All Bets Off. 'Wednesdays - Papa Papagone's. Rats. Six hundred. Got it? Good. Thursdays - Taj Mahal. Mice. A grand. Fridays - Maison Blanche. Cockroaches. Twelve hundred.' She rummaged through her satchel and frowned. 'Bollocks, I'm clean out of cockroaches. Never mind, we got loads in the kitchen.'

All of a dither, McTavish scratched his head with the crayon. 'So all the local restaurants got vermin?' After an inordinate pause for thought, he raised a finger. 'Why dinnae I offer tae get rid? I got a certificate in pest control, ye ken,' he said proudly.

'Don't get it, do you? Stand back . . .' HostageKaty took a deep breath, pointed to the skirting board and let rip with an hysterical scream. 'A rat . . .'

'Where?' McTavish leapt onto a chair and looked desperately around.

'Shut your gob,' HostageKaty said. 'I in't finished.' She screwed her face into a walnut of verminary disgust and howled, 'this place is infested with rats. I'm going to tell on you to the Public Health unless you compensate me for my trauma with three takeaway pizza margaritas - extra capers and olives - that tiramisu on the pudding trolley and six hundred quid in used readies to buy me silence. Ta very much. Most generous. I'll be back next week to do me civic duty and check the rats have gone. Same time, same table, same deal.' She had to check her tongue from adding, 'same rat.'

'You fiend,' Professor Harty snarled, all but lost for gratuitous words. 'You are the kind of unscrupulous hostage that gives blackmail a bad name.'

HostageKaty hoisted her button nose in the air. 'In't

blackmail,' she said snootily. 'It's protection services. Entirely voluntary. The client gets to choose. Pay me and stay in business or don't and don't. Totally up to them. It's a legitimate enterprise. Little Breeders Limited. I registered it at Companies House. I've a good mind to put in for half a dozen government bounce-back loans to invest in a scummier class of vermin.'

While HostageKaty slurped the dregs of her McOatshake, Professor Harty took McTavish to one side. 'I fear that this is not going entirely as intended, my hairy Highlander.'

'Aye, Chief. The best laid plans of mice and men . . .'

'Less of the mice, dolt.' The Professor cast a surreptitious glance at HostageKaty, who was wiping whipped cream off her nose after polishing off a hostage-sized carton of takeaway tiramisu. 'We must regain the initiative. When the meddling brat's back is turned, throw a barley sack over her head, bundle her into the grainstore and make sure to padlock the door securely.'

'Do that and we'll be brassy afore the week is oot,' McTavish whispered back. 'Yon wee lassie is bankrolling the operation.'

'Hmmm . . .' Professor Harty stroked his chiselled chin and creased his bulbous brow. 'I suppose that for once you may have a point, my hirsute Highlander. Very well. We will let her have her way until the ransom is paid and then . . .' He rubbed his hands and clacked his bony knuckles. 'She dies.'

Taking care not to let the Professor hear what he was thinking, McTavish muttered, 'unless the wee bairn gets us first.'

And so the first small fissure of dissent appeared in the Katenappers' ranks. It was not by any manner of means to be the last.

A raggletaggle gypsy princess.

xvii

Bleary eyed and not so bushy-tailed, Heather Prendergast lay on her bed watching the newday dawn seep through the bedroom curtains like shards of luminous flux, butterkissed and morny. Day follows night as surely as night follows day, does it not? she mused philosophically. Profound. She glanced at the bedside clock, rubbed her eyes and stretched her arms in a fulminant yawn. If she felt as though she had hardly slept, it was probably because she hardly had. Despite the passages of time, her father's house held memories that she would rather blanket from her mind.

As a dewy-eyed pre-teen, she had been a raggletaggle gypsy princess here. She had played with faeries at the bottom of the garden here. She had sought refuge from the puppy dog from Hades here. More to the point, this is where she watched her mother fade away to join the heavenly host, never understanding why. When her father banished her to live with Aunt Elizabeth in deepest Kent, she vowed that she would never return. Yet here she was, on a nomadery mission to rescue a helpless miss-taken stranger from the clutches of the deranged Caretaker of the Criminal Underworld - Professor Murray Harty.

Consigning girlhood memories to the cabbage-doll patch of her mind, she rolled off the bed and prepared to face another day. After sluggishly acquitting her morning ablutions, she ventured downstairs to await the postman's knock. Shortly before nine, a menacing growl announced the arrival of Baskerville. When she knelt down to pat him on the muzzle, he snarled and bared his fang. Well that brought back memories, she thought, so she retreated a safe distance and sat down on a stairstep varnishing her toenails until a posthand poked a few letters and a small plasticated parcel through the letterbox.

Growling like a hound dispossessed, Baskerville pounced on the package and masticated the plastic with his gums. After fending him off him with a chair and a broom-handled mop, Heather wrestled the package from his growly maw and, leaving him to rip up the remaining letters to his caniniverous content, beat a fleeting retreat to the first floor bathroom – the Flipper Room as it was now called. She closed the door behind her, turned on the light and clamped a hand to her mouth to smother the mother of all groans.

Spotlit on all sides, the see-through Perspex bathtub was mounted on a plexiglass plinth affording the bather an unobstructed view of the world beyond the plate glass window . . . and a passer-by's eye in. Heather could well imagine Fifi wallowing *au naturel* in full view of the neighbours in a splashback to her tit-ilatory moviestar career. It would seem that her despicable apology for a stepmother knew no shame – no shame whatsoever. It was hardly surprising that Katerina had grown up to regard clothes as designer wrappings to be shed at the drop of a predatory zip. Following in her mother's mule steps, she was doubtless destined for a life of insanitary vanity, drooling canoodlers and remorseless divorces fuelled by oodles of alimony.

What a life, Heather thought. How desperately sad.

The Flipper Room's ceiling and three of the walls were tiled with mirrored glass. A gargantuan pea-green toilet, sink and bidet were plumbed into the other. The linoleum floor tiles and frilly nylon curtains were clashing shades of maroon and orange, malpatterned with buttercup-yellow daffadoodles. The overall effect was . . . the word nestled on the tip of Heather's tongue. As it wriggled free, she clicked her fingers. That's it . . . excremental.

Swallowing her colour clash disgust, Heather thumbnailed open the parcel and yes – it was indeed, a burner phone as Katerina had streetnomered it. How typical of Professor Murray Harty's cunning to send it by second class post, she thought with a wry smile. He was obviously planning to catch Sir Freddie unawares, dissanimate him in suspense, pile on the pressure, leave him guessing and stay one trip ahead. Whelmed with admiration at Harty's demonic cunning, she balanced the cellphone on a bath stool, sat on the side of the tub and rummaged through her shoulder-bag for her travelling forensics kit to check for fingerprints. She unpacked her workaday essentials – handkerchief, canteen keys, sneeze-tissues, bedsit keys, Harry Styles photograph, lip balm, emergency chocolate orange, spare false eyelashes, Harry Styles Diary, good luck pebble, hairbrush, social distancing mask, makeup compact, official off-duty pocketbook, police whistle, Harry Styles Fan Club membership card and a roll of Sealotape, ever more frantic until - panicking like a manic-stricken gannet - she shook out the remaining grunge. And that was when she remembered that Naff had borrowed her forensics kit to go phishing.

What to do, she fretted. 'Come on, Heather,' she told herself. 'You're a fully badged-up Girl Guide. Improvise.' After all, when push comes to shove, what is the difference between Metropolitan Police Issue fingerprint powder and Rimmel Stay Matte Pressed-Mineral Powdered Foundation Veil? She was reaching for her compact, blusher brush and Sealotape at the ready, when she was almost jumped out of her skin by a loud knock at the door. As she flustered to her feet, she stumbled into the bath stool sending the phone spiralling into the toilet. She clapped her hands to her cheeks and stared into the murky water. Oh how she wished that she had had the foresight to flush twice. She was about to burst into tears when a shuffly figure in a scruffy fleece slouched into the bathroom clutching a humungous bunch of red roses.

Sebastian Marrowboan - for it was he - stared at his sandals, squirmed and chewed his bottom lip. 'Yeah, well, pharmed these from the garden, Spriggsy. I bookmarked them for you.' He surreptitiously removed the Interflowera purchase receipt and held them out for her to sniff. As she backed away, he caught sight of the cellphone festering in the fetid loo water. 'Uncool,' he said. 'User error.' He rolled up his sleeves and reached into the urinary goo. 'Needs downloading in some rice,' he mumbled as he retrieved the waterclogged device. 'See, rice soaks up moisture and reformats memory leaks.' He gave the phone a vigorous shake, stowed it in his combat trousers, glanced at Heather, blushed and slouched out.

Rather lost for words, Heather sighed and shook her head. She felt tired; weary; neuralgic. She decided that there was only one thing for it – medicinal chocolate. She tossed the roses out of the window and retreated to her attic bedroom. Taking care to lock the door, she raided her emergency sweetmeat reserves, wolfed down her last chocolate orange, smacked her lips and licked her fingers – sheer indulgence. Then, candyfilled and tummyguzzled, she slumped down on the bed for a quick powernap. Some time later, she was roused by the raggle-naggle ringtone of her cellphone. When she saw the caller ID, she broke into a smushy smile, pressed the phone to her lips and cooed, 'missing you, darling. Where are you?'

'At your gaff in Crouch End. Popped back to grab some gear. And you?'

'You're not going to believe this, Naff, but I'm on a top secret undercover mission.'

'Well, stone me, babe. Me too.'

'Where?'

'Timbuktu.'

'Golly, how terribly thrilling.'

'Just pulling your leg, honey. So what you up to?''

'Can't tell you. Someone might be listening.'

'Like who, babe? The Someone Squad?'

'Why do you never take me seriously, darling? I bet you change your tune when I crack this kidnapping case.'

'You on a kidnapping case?'

'Who told you? Have you been talking to daddy's gardener? Look, I should go. He's waiting for me downstairs.'

'The gardener?'

'No, daddy. I'm late for lunch.'

'You staying with your old man?'

'You have been talking to daddy's gardener, haven't you?'

'No way, honey. Just a hunch.'

'Love me?'

'Like crazy, babe. I should be done in a week. Then we can grab that break in Huddersford we got planned.'

'Promise?' Heather cooed smoochily.

The line went dead.

Luncheon was served in the Chandelerium. Aptly named, a score of stalactiform chandeliers of various shapes, sizes and luminosity dangled from the ceiling like bunches of crystalline grapes. They were sneaksakes pillaged from *Le Château des Parures,* the mansion where Fifi was bedridden by her first husband, Baron Enfantépicier, after their elopement. Wed when she was sweet sixteen and he was sour sixty-six, tragically the tryst unravelled faster than a crotched woolly in a tumble dryer. For barely had Fifi been consummated than the Baron was exposed in *Le Monde* for indecent exposure and paedophilia. It seemed that his carnal desires knew no bounds. Or age limits. After a whirlwind divorce, she pillaged the chandeliers, a selection of doorhandles and a stuffed ptarmigan from the family home before the huissiers stripped the place of saleables.

To remind her of the first great lust of her life, Fifi had converted the former Breakfast Room into a shrine for her dearly incarcerated ex-husband. The doorhandles were incongruously screwed about the room like porcelain wall-warts and the ptarmigan – now infested with fleas – occupied pride of place on the Formica table. The walls were festooned with posters of the teenage Fou-Fou LaPorte in various states of undress, including one of her modelling an itsy-bitsy teensy-weensy one-piece polka-dot bikini and a bashful smile. She was pictured smoking a pipe and fondling a ferret but not wearing Wellington boots; in her formative years it would seem that she wanted for wantonness.

'You are late,' Sir Freddie thundered as Heather walked in. He ran a disparaging eye over her designer jeans, cashmere sweater and *fiendishly* expensive and *groovilly* fashionable trainers. 'Are you in the habit of wandering the streets dressed as a man, young lady?' he snapped.

Heather ignored him and sat down beside Katerina. 'Going to a party?' she asked. 'Must say, that's a very short dress.' She thought to add, 'is it a negligee?' but checked her tongue in the nick of time. In any event, her stepsister's diaphanous excuse for a frock was a good deal less jawdroppingly eyepoppingly nauseatingly revealing than the tent-sized babydoll teddy that her stepmother was flaunting.

'I got a session booked with my personal trainer,' Katerina told her. 'We're going snogging in his Beamer.'

Sir Freddie looked up from his carpe pâté avec œuf glacé and frowned. 'Try not be home too late, my dear. You know how your mother worries.'

'Do this, do that. I'll be back when I'm back. Seb's going to pick me up when I get bored.'

'Are you sure that is wise? You know what a hopeless driver he is,' Sir Freddie said.

'You are *so* annoying,' Katerina stropped. 'Any chance you'll drop dead and leave me loads of money?'

'Do not be disrespectful to your father, mon petit chou,' Fifi scolded between drools of glutinous gorgonzola fondue.

Katerina narrowed her swallow eyes and pursed her

lips. 'That disgusting man is *not* my father,' she stropped. 'My real dad is dead.'

'You know perfectly well that papa n'est pas mort, ma cherie,' Fifi said with an insufferably longsuffering smile. 'He is en vacances in Alcatraz.'

'He is dead,' Katerina howled and stamped a needle sharp stiletto on the waxed linoleum. 'Anyway, nobody made all those old wrinklies invest in his zeppelin factory, did they? He was doing them a favour. I mean, where else can you get a thousand per cent interest on a poxy million dollar loan?'

'There was no zeppelin factory,' Sir Freddie muttered through his moustache.

'So? There would have been if dad hadn't run out of hot air. Wasn't his fault. Costs a fortune to live in Las Vegas. Where's Eggy?'

On cue, Missus Beaten flustered into the Chandelerium carrying a silver tray. 'Carp kedgeree. My old mum's recipe,' she announced proudly. 'Don't go telling Delia Smith, but the secret is a cupful of salt and a dozen cloves of garlic,' she confided as she dished out ladles of sludge for Heather, Sir Freddie and Katerina before emptying the ballast into Fifi's gobble bowl.

Heather prodded the festering mess with a fork and was plucking up the courage to sample a soupçon when it buzzed. Puzzled, she dug into the slush and pulled out a half-baked cellphone. She held it to an ear, said, 'hello?'

gave it a shake, shook it again, gave her head a shake and tossed it on the table. 'Sebastian Marrowboan,' she yelled. 'In here. Now. We need a word.'

Sebastian shuffled into the room with his hands in his pockets, took one look at the burnt burner-phone and raised an eyebrow. 'Cool,' he said. 'Thought I'd recyclebinned it in error.'

'You put it in Eggy's rice sack to dry, didn't you?' Heather said, stating the blaringly obvious.

'So, is that a thing?' Sebastian expressed surprise at Heather's turn of voice. 'Anyway, what did the kidnappers say?'

'No idea. That phone has been soaked, boiled, baked, salted, carped, egged, curried and peppered. Dare say the warranty is void. It tastes foul.' Heather screwed up her nose in a show of cellularphonic disgust.

Sebastian picked up the sorry contraption, sniffed it, said, 'want me to give it some percussive maintenance?' and shrugged when Heather glared at him. He stuffed his hands back in his pockets and turned to go but paused. 'Oh, I triangulated the call like you said,' he said. 'I programmed the coordinates into my Marrowboan Tracknav. Mad name, or what?'

Heather leapt to her feet and clapped her hands. 'Come on Bratty,' she said, 'Drink up and follow me.' She was reaching for her glass when Sebastian stumbled into the table sending the stuffed ptarmigan flying. As she tried to catch it, a glassful of full bodied claret splashed all over her shoes, jeans, blouse, jumper, face, hair – everywhere. Drenched from moptop to toetip, all but rendered speechless - not - she screamed, 'you oaf. My twinset and blouse are at the cleaners. These are the only clothes I've got.'

Hearing Heather's anguished howls, Missus Beaten blustered through the door in a fluster of starched pinafore. When she saw Heather flailing her arms about her head and stamping her feet in a frenzied fit of pique, she said, 'goodness me, Miss Heather, just look at you. Still the same messy little madam you always were. Now come along, dearie. I'll do you a nice hot tub in front of the fire in the servant's quarters, just like old times.' She broke into surrogate smile and gave Heather's cheek a thumb and finger tweak. 'Now, let's throw those soggy clothes in the twintub and find you something nice and comfy to wear, you little scamp.' She cocked her head, tapped her chin, thought a mo, then winked and said, 'I believe I may have just the thing.'

The finger stays on. I'm attached to it.

xviii

The recreationary was shrouded in gloom, reflecting the Professor's cadaverous mood of mind. A combination of bricked up windows and blackened walls contributed to the air of a furibund funeral parlour. Homely, Groaty McTavish called it. Cosy. He said it reminded him of his formative years growing up at Her Majesty's Displeasure in Barlinnie.

Professor Harty stalked the echoic void with his shoulders hunched and his hands clasped behind his back. The clutter of liquorice packets, hairpins, empty FizzyBru cans and dead cockroaches strewn about the floor offended his sensibilities. All he craved was a little peace and quiet to ponder life's vicissitudes. That and world domination. Not too much to ask, surely?

'Listen to this, Chief.' McTavish looked up from a copy of the Pest Control Times he was perusing by candlelight to pass the time of day. 'Ye'll nae guess what a group of rats is called,' he said with a gruff chuckle. 'A mischief. That's what it says here anyway, so must be true.' He turned the page and raised a ginger eyebrow. 'Well I'll be a Sheltie's uncle . . . seems a group of crows is called a murder. A murder, would ye believe? And it's a parliament of owls. Well, who would have thinked it?'

Professor Harty drew to an abrupt halt, turned and

glared at him. 'Dolt,' he growled. 'Even a retarded chimpanzee with half a brain knows that.'

A sullen scowl eclipsed McTavish's pockmarked face. 'All reet, Chief, if yaer sae clever, tell me this . . . what's a group of Scotsmen called?'

'A brawl, of course. Fool.'

McTavish flung the newspaper on the floor, huffed to his feet, clenched his fists and narrowed his eyes. 'I've had it up tae here with yaer Sassenach insults, pal. Ye can call the dole office and get yesself a new trainee thug for all I care.'

The Professor raised his hands and boldly backed away. 'Calm down, my petulant apprentice. I was not insulting your noble brethren, I was merely describing them.'

'That's alreet, then.' McTavish took a calming breath, unclenched his fists and sat back down. 'So anyways, what did Sir Freddie have tae say when ye telled him how much he was ganna have tae pay tae get wee Katy back?'

'You may well ask, my sporraned accomplice. I fear that I may have underestimated the little gull's doting stepfather.' Professor Harty knotted his fingers and clacked his bony knuckles. 'Let me put it this way,' he said. 'When I asked if he was sitting comfortably and had a quill and parchment to hand, the line went dead. Clearly a delaying tactic. The oldest trick in the almanac.' He broke into a pinchlipped smile. 'But if Sir Freddie thinks that he is fooling me, he is only fooling himself.'

'Are ye sure ye dialled the reet number?' McTavish asked. 'I telled ye tae write it doon on yaer hand like I done. But, oh no. Ye said ye'd remember it, just like ye remembered tae tell me what this job was all aboot when ye took me on.' He made a pretence of scratching his head. 'Now I come tae think, ye didnae tell me the half of it, did ye? In fact, ye didnae tell me the any of it at all.'

'Pah, it was but a trivial oversight. No harm done,' the Professor scoffed, as if accusing him of a breach of trust was a slur upon his indignity. 'Still, I am minded to agree, but then we would both be wrong. Let me try Sir Freddie again.' He grabbed McTavish's hand, twisted it through one hundred and eight degrees, read his palm and, ignoring McTavish' pathetic moans and groans, redialled the number. 'The line is dead,' he muttered as he listened to a crackle of static. 'So Sir Freddie thinks that this is a game of telephonic tag, does he? Unsheathe your dirk and halberd, my Highland terrier. It is time to call our adversary's bluff. Prepare to slit young Katy's throat and bury her mutilated body in the footings of the flyover.'

Unmoved, McTavish sat firm and crossed his arms. 'Nae on yaer life, Chief,' he said with a defiant shake of the head. 'She'll scratch ma eyes oot if I gan tae lay a finger on her. Anyway, ever thought Sir Freddie might want us tae bury the wee lassie under a flyover? I know I would if she was ma bairn.'

'Impossible,' the Professor snorted as if the suggestion

was hardly worth the sniff of day. 'It is a well-known fact that Sir Freddie Prendergast's world revolves around her. She is his everything. And more.'

'Has the eejit been at the barley wine?'

'That may well be, but do not forget that beauty lies in the apple of the eye of the beholder.' Professor Harty stroked his chiselled chin, vague in thought as his mind cranked into a higher gear. 'But there may be more to Sir Freddie's silence than meets the eye,' he said as he weighed an infinite possibility of probabilities and whittled them down to one. 'How often have I told you that when you have eliminated the impossible, whatever remains, however improbable, must be the truth?' he asked with a rhetoricallity that brooked all illogicality. 'I fear that we may be engaged in a fiendish game of devil's bluff,' he said. Having reached an accommodation with the vagaries of uncertainty, he donned his frockcoat and top hat, balanced his pince-nez on his hawk nose and prepared to venture out for his daily recreational - feeding poisoned insects to lizards at the zoo. Struck by the eerie silence, he asked, 'so where is our precious little hummingbird, anyway?'

'Roond at the mini-mart stocking up on fizzies, lollipops, barley water, liquorice and rat-treats,' McTavish explained.

Enraged, Professor Harty slammed a fist on the table. 'You mean to say that she is squandering our precious resources on frivolities?'

'Gimme a break, Chief. Ye ken as well as me, she gets tae help hesself and in return, yon supermarket is allowed tae stay in business. She told me it's called free trade `cause nae money changes hands.' McTavish's gruff voice brimmed with respect. 'Seems a pestilence of blood-sucking bats isnae good fer trade in these parts. But like she says, fair trade is nae robbery.'

A clatter of laptop keys announced HostageKaty's return. She kicked open the door and staggered in weighed down with the mini-mart's cutprice hardware bin. Environmentally conscious to a fault, she was frugal with her strong-armed demands. 'Here, Groatface, grab this.' She thrust a bargain bucket of tar into McTavish's hands. 'See them double-yellows?' She pointed to the road outside. 'Get rid while I sort the bollards and no-parking signs.' Sweating like a polyurethane lettuce, she slumped down on a chair, propped her sandals on the table and dewidgeted a can of loganberry fizz. 'So what's occurring, muppets?' she asked. 'When am I getting out of pokey?' She looked from McTavish to Professor Harty, rolled her eyes and groaned, 'don't tell me it's all gone Pete Tong.'

Professor Harty cleared a nervous tickle from his throat. 'It would appear that a minor hitch has arisen, my little finch,' he mumbled, hoping that HostageKaty would not detect a nuanced note of panic in his voice.

'Fred blanked you, didn't he?' Dismayed by yet another sorry spurn of events, HostageKaty slumped back in her chair and stared miserably at a biocular arachnid scuttling along the picture rail towards a panic stricken fly. 'Told you he'd play you for a sucker, but did you listen? Oh, no. Not you. Brain as big as a planet? Doggy-doo between your ears, more like. Oh well, not to worry,' she said with a sophical sigh. 'I got me hands full just at the minute. See, me and Uncle Groaty got plans. This time next week The Happy Thistle is going to be the busiest takeaway this side of Disneyland.' She broke into a mischievous smile. 'If I was you, the Possessor of Gloop or whatever you call yesself, I'd do a runner before my mam finds you and sends you swimming with the fishies.'

Professor Harty threw back his head and - despite his better nature - laughed out loud. 'If you think that I intend to let your ill begotten mother play mind games with me, you have another thing coming.'

'Oh, so you reckon I'm dicking you about, do you?' HostageKaty said. 'Well, take it from me, the last person who tried to play mind games with my mam ended up in the lobotomy farm. I seen grown men cry when she gives them one of her looks. And what's with all this Sir Freddie bollocks, anyway? You know something I don't?' She shrugged when the Professor scratched his cranium and frowned. 'All right, so don't tell me. See if I care.'

In the face of HostageKaty's acrimonious animosity, Professor Harty and Groaty McTavish retreated into a conspiratorial huddle, leaving her to prime her cockroach army in readiness for another hard night's scuttle in the neighbourhood kitchens.

'World domination or nae world domination, I've a mind tae gan back tae ma old job gassing woodlice in the Gorbals,' McTavish whispered. 'Next tae yon wee lassie, exterminating pests is a barrel-load of laughs.'

'Hmmm, for once you may have a point, my cerebrally challenged friend,' the Professor conceded in a rare gesture of concurrent. 'It is time to take off the kidskin gloves and show Sir Freddie that we are not hostage takers to be trifled with.'

'How we ganna do that, Chief?' McTavish asked.

Professor Harty stared into the middle distance and broke into the sinisterest of smiles. 'Another missive, only this time I will include a little present. Fetch a pair of scissors, a newspaper and a pot of glue.' He adopted his trademark Voice of Doom stance – arms outstretched, head thrown back – as was his wont when dictating threats.

To Whom It May Concern,

Henceforth I will only communicate by means of cryptic messages in the classified advertisement columns of the Pest Control Times. As a token of my dishonourable intent I hereby include a free gift with this letter. Ignore it at your peril.

Kindest Regards,

The Pachydermatous Purveyor of All Evil.

McTavish snipped and glued and glued and snipped with a dexterity belying his hamfistedness until he came to the last line. 'How ye spelling that, Chief?' he asked, scissors and gluepot at the ready.

'E-v-i-l. How else, you sporraned cacographer?' the Professor snarled.

'Gie me a break, Chief,' McTavish said. 'I mean, how ye spelling patchydermatitis?'

'On second thoughts, sign it the Perfumed Purveyor of All Evil.' Professor Harty rubbed his hands and cackled. 'I fancy that will throw Sir Freddie off the scent.'

McTavish looked about and scratched his head. 'So where's this present yaer on aboot?'

'There.' Professor Harty swung around and pointed a finger at HostageKaty. 'Sever her pinky and enclose it with the letter.'

No sooner had the Perfumed Purveyor of All Evil spoken than HostageKaty flew at him. She clamped her teeth around his outstretched finger and hissed, 'I got a better idea. Let's send them one of yours instead.' Giggling as Professor Harty's eyes watered, she ventured a muffled, 'give in?' and when he nodded, unchomped her fangs and licked the blood off her lips. Eyes like pissyslits, she rammed a fist in his face and said, 'if you're nice to me, I'll let you have a lock of my hair, but the finger stays on. I'm attached to it. Got that?' She closed her eyes, took a deep breath, yanked out a hank of hair and tossed it on the table.

As the Professor stared at her, lost for unrepeatable words, she planted one hand on a pleated hip and held out the other, palm up. 'What you waiting for?' she said. 'Bleed in there, you big girl's blouse. We got to soak the hair in blood so Fred knows we in't messing. Mam will never take us serious unless she reckons you maimed me. Like I said, we do this shakedown proper or we call it a day.' She stuck her button nose in the air and tossed her head. 'I in't risking me retirement fund on some half-baked plan cooked up on the fly by a bunch of daffy chancers who couldn't organise a piss-up in a pissoir to save their lives. So do what you're told or you'll be looking for another hostage.'

Heather Prendergast wolfed down a Finger of Fudge and licked her lips . . . yummy, yummy, piggy tummy. Elevenses over, she reviewed the latest chapter of The Curious Case of The Katenapped Girl.

I have requisitioned vehicular transport and enlisted the services of one of the very foremost computer technicians in all of South Kensington to assist with my enquiries. With the eyes of the world upon me, I have decided that it would be appropriate to wear a uniform commensurate with the authority vested in me by King and Country. Anyway, Aunt Elizabeth would never let me hear the end of it if I wasn't looking my best when I address the nation with news of the dramatic rescue. I shall, of course, behave with my usual modesty and make quite clear that it was a team effort, albeit masterminded and largely conducted by my good self.

Heather nibbled the unrubbered end of her pencil, thrilled to bits with her authorly voice; although sophisticated, it had a down to earth sense and sensibility. She used verbs in most sentences, colourful adjectives where required - though not too many - and full stops in all the right places. Commas were an issue, but she was sure that her publisher would have a girly swot to deal with the *ghastly* little blighters. All in all, she was smugly satisfied that her cultured prose would put established chroniclers to shame . . . eat your heart out, Agatha.

Wrist aching from writing, editing, revising and redrafting, Heather filed the notepad in her shoulder-bag and took a last look in the mirror. Although the skirt was somewhat on the immodest side, she supposed that it would have to do. The fact was that she was hardly spoilt for choice; it was either this, her cutesy teen sailor suit, her stepsister's cast-off jodhpurs and hacking jacket or a revolting Addam's Family brocade bridesmaid's dress that Katerina once wore to a Halloween party. Ghoulish was not the word. On second thoughts, maybe it was. Still, as Aunt Elizabeth would say . . . blather, blather, blather.

Reminded that beggars cannot generally be choosers, she joined Katerina and Sebastian in the Bumbershoot Gallery, as Fifi had christened the Coat Hall when she painted it a urinary shade of seasick yellow and decked the hall with plastic ivy. After a quick head count, she marshalled her forces for what she was confident would be the final chapter of the hostage-rescue mission.

Following complaints from the neighbours and a High Court injunction, Sebastian Marrowboan now parked his Skodamobile half a mile or two from Trevelyan House. And never had Heather Prendergast endured such a shaming trudge through the highways and byways of humiliation. Indignity was piled upon ignominy when the expeditionary sleuth party bumped into the local postman plying his morning trade.

'Katy Clark, isn't it?' Postie nodded an amiable good day to Katerina. 'And who have we here?' He cocked a wink at Heather.

Katerina took Heather's hand and said, 'she's my kid sister.'

'Didn't know you had a sister, Katy,' Postie said. 'Bonnie little thing, isn't she?'

Heather arched her back and tucked her beret under an arm. 'How dare you?' she gasped, offended to the enth degree.

'Temper, temper,' Postie said. He slung his postbag over a shoulder, said, 'give my best to Brown Owl,' and with a parting, 'diddums,' married on his way.

When Katerina wagged a tickoff finger and warned Heather that if she didn't behave, she would be packed off to beddy-byes without any din-dins and no night-night story, Heather exploded with, 'very funny, I don't think.' Quaking from beret to sandals, she said, 'let me be clear . . . if I had anything else to wear, there is no way on this good earth that I would be seen dead at my own funeral dressed like this. I have never been so embarrassed in all my life. For heaven's sake, I haven't worn this Brownie uniform since I was ten.'

Although Katerina tried to keep a straight face, she didn't try particularly hard. 'Lucky you were tall for your age,' she said as she looked Heather up and down as if she was an animated beany doll. 'Must say, the dress is a bit tight around the tits and the tush. Just as well you haven't got any.'

Ignoring Katerina's giggles, Heather asked, 'and why, may I ask, does Missus Beaten keep all my old clothes?'

'Oh come on, sis,' Katerina said. 'You know as well as me, her golden rule is waste not, want not. She never throws anything out. That's why Smothers and Baskerville are still cluttering up the place.'

Fed up to the back teeth with her stepsister's gawky mawkishness, Heather breathed a profound sigh of relief when they arrived at Sebastian's carwreck. After mulling it over for half a nanosecond, she plumped to sit in the back beside Katerina, partly for propriety's sake but largely because Sebastian's Tracknav was bolted to the passenger seat.

'OK, let's juice her up.' Sebastian ratcheted the driver's seat into position, grinned over a shoulder and stuck up a thumb. 'This is your captain speaking,' he intoned in a robotic voice. 'I'll pilot the mission while you two sleuth babes navigate.'

Heather pointed to the Tracknav and joked, 'looks like an ancient black and white television set hooked up to a car battery.'

'Thanks,' Sebastian said, impressed by Heather's perspicacity. 'Now belt yourselves in - we're going hypersonic.' He rolled up his sleeves, set his sunken jaw, ignitioned the engine, slammed the jalopy into gear, put his foot down on the brake and stalled. 'Forgot to boot her up,' he said sheepishly. 'Ready to rap? Right, watch the fuzzy white blip on the screen. If it moves right, say . . .'

'Take a right?' Heather hazarded.

'Spot on,' Sebastian said. 'And if it moves left . . .'

'Get on with it, Seb. I'm late for my date.' Katerina walloped him with a rollupped copy of Teen Vogue. 'If we don't get a move on, Danny will start without me. Probably finish without me, too,' she muttered under her breath.

A hazy, lazy, alliterative kind of lackadaisical dog-daisy day was setting in by the time the undercover sleuthers hit the road. After stopping to buy cigarettes for Katerina and replenish Heather's depleted chocolate reserves, Sebastian rammed the Sebmobile into cruise control. 'Hold tight,' he shouted over the crank of the engine. But rather than take off like a pocket rocket, the Skoda sputtered to a stall and freewheeled to a stop.

'Bum-mer,' Sebastian mumbled. 'Must have forgotten to hyperventilate the warp drive and top up the radiator.'

'Is it far,' Heather asked as she scrambled out of the backseat, brushed the grime off her pleats and readjusted her toggle.

Sebastian squinted at the Tracknav and pointed. 'According to the coordinates,' he said, 'it's over there, then right, right again and down an alley. I'll show you.'

Leaving the Skodamobile to let off steam, the intrepid adventuresses and their geeky guide continued on foot.

Should they pass a passing passer-by, Heather shrank into the shadows and feigned invisibility. She had never felt so conspicuous in all her born days. However, spurred on by Aunt Elizabeth's adage - needs be as needs must in a righteous cause - she swallowed her blushes and put her best sandal forward. And so, stoically reminding herself that Prendergast of The Yard knows no shame when duty calls - neckerchiefs and toggles notwithstanding - she soldiered bravely on. In no small part, she was spurred on by the knowledge that she was about to pit her wits against the most formidable foe that she might ever cross words with. One of them would emerge victorious, she knew. And the other? Probably not.

Sebastian led the way, Heather followed and Katerina trailed behind, pausing every now and then to exchange phone numbers with eligible strangers. As per Sebastian's directions, they turned right, turned right again and ventured warily down a straight-and-narrow alley. The tension mounted like a rickety stile until they reached an impossible impasse.

'Looks like we've hit a null node.' Sebastian pointed to an imposing ivy-clad wall barring their progress. 'Ground Zero must be on the far parameter.' He nodded at the loomy impediment. 'Guess we'll just have to navigate back to home page.' Although he didn't say as much, he was relieved; he worried that his Skodamobile might be towed away and dumped at the neighbourhood car crusher - as coincidence would have it the same place he found it.

As a nearly qualified probationary police officer, Heather assumed command. 'I'm going in,' she said with a determination than brooked no confutation. 'You two stay here and keep a look out. If any problems crop up, deal with them. If I'm not back in an hour, wait a bit longer. Right . . .' She took a deep breath and grabbed a fistful of ivy. 'Give me a leg up,' she ordered, then squealed and slapped Sebastian's hand when he did just that with more alacrity than decorum.

'Really, sis, you don't have to,' Katerina pleaded as Heather tackled the perilous north face of the ivy with the lithesome ease of an arthritic sloth.

'Please, Bratty. I was trained to climb inanimate objects at college,' Heather said as she wiped a zest of sweat out of her eyes. With a determined grit of the teeth, she eased herself up, pinch by pinch and notch by notch. Overgrowth prickled her arms, vines snagged her neckerchief, twigs snaggled her toggle. As she searched out footholds in the flaking brickwork, a sandal spiralled down to earth leaving her footloose and dangle free. Puffing like a puffin, battered as a codfish, skirt frayed to within an inch of her clinch, she hauled herself up and up and up, hand over fist. Undeterred, she climbed on . . . on . . . on, until, like Sir Edmund Hillary before her, she summited the peak and fisted the air in triumph. Exhausted by her Hillarian efforts, she flopped down on the coping stones gasping for breath, questioning her inanity and doubting her sanity. Although she went to inordinate pains not to burst into tears, inwardly she cursed her accursed dumbwittery.

Why, oh, why she asked the Gods of Obduracy, had she had the temerity to embark upon such a foolhardy feat of daring-do without due thought and consideration? If truth be told, she told herself, there was much to be said for keeping her feet on terra firma in New Scotland Yard's staff canteen.

She was summoning the wherewithal to clamber down when she heard a shout . . . 'Jump, sis. We'll catch you.' Puzzled, she brushed the hair out of her eyes and looked down, astonished to see Katerina and Sebastian standing on the far side with their arms upstretched.

'Tried to tell you, sis,' Katerina shouted. 'They always leave the gate open.' She pointed to a wrought iron gateway a little way away.

Bruised, battered and bewildered, Heather scrambled down and picked a *ghastly* appurtenance of fungal matter out of her hair. Although her Brownie uniform was marmaladed to shreds, she was mightily relieved to still be in one piece . . . or she was until she saw her hands. She stuck out her tongue and ucked – her nail varnish was *unutterably* scuffed. But not to be panicured, she consigned her vanity to the annals of expedience and asked, 'how did you know about the gate?'

'Because it's the servant's entrance of Trevelyan House.' Katerina glared eyedaggers at Sebastian. 'Seb triangulated the wrong phone and programmed his own coordinates into his dumb-arsed Tracknav.'

In a rare show of contrition, Sebastian hung his head and skulked. 'Yeah, right. Total pwnage.' He stared at his feet and shuffled – more of a squirm than a shuffle if truth be told. 'Looks like I had a headcrash and blew my buffer,' he whimpered. His cheeks flushed cherry-berry and he swallowed. 'Don't go postal on me, Spriggsy,' he begged. 'Could happen to anyone. I mean, NASA didn't put a man on the moon at the first attempt.'

'Actually, they did,' Heather reminded him as she dabbed a balm of lickspittle on her bruises and put her chipped nails out of sight, if not out of mind. But looking on the bright side - as was her wont - she was relieved that the journey home wouldn't take long. And so, resigned to another day of frustration, obfuscation and Sebastian, she followed Katerina down the steps to the servant's quarters. She was about to knock on the door when Katerina tugged her arm, said, 'oh my God,' and pointed through the window.

Heather pressed her nose to the glass, clapped a hand to her brow and gasped, 'crickey, I do not believe it.'

Yes miss, no miss, three bags full.

xx

At more or less the same time, big, big trouble was brewing in the East End of London. Humungous.

To cut a tedious backstory short, when a turf war broke out between two notorious gangland rivals, the Clark Gang and the Proust Mob, collateral damage led to the closure of a number of pavement florists rumoured to be fronts for the drugs trade. Things came to a head on Valentine's Day when the Home Secretary was unable to find any daffodils for his wife or orchids for his mistress. Incandescent at this blatant breach of his human rights, he demanded that the security services make the matter their number one priority.

Accordingly, under the watchful eye of The Right Dishonourable Minister, the Flying Squad pulled out all the stops and within six months, Detective Simon 'Naff' Robinson had been seconded from the North Huddshire Organised Crime Unit to augment the Special Branch unit keeping the Clark Gang under surveillance. Not known to London's criminal fraternity, he was ideally placed to infiltrate the murky substrata of East End gangland. Needless to say it was a hazardous assignment ideally suited to a detective who thrived on danger and had a reputation in law enforcement circles as something of a loose howitzer.

Sworn to silence, Naff researched his mission with all due diligence, aware that his life might depend upon it. From what he could glean from a variety of snarks, narks, snouts and grasses, the Proust Mob worked out of a nightclub in downtown Hackney Wick – The Sundown Strip – and the Clark Gang was based in a scrapyard in a broken down neck of East London colloquially known locally as Forgottenham.

Clark's Scrappery - as the unsightly blight of unrecyclable crappage was known in the rough trade - was *rumoured* to be a hothouse of every kind of organised crime worthy of the name, *rumoured* being the italicised word. Naff was to learn that everything in those parts was *rumour* rather than fact. For example, Fred 'Scareface' Clark was *rumoured* to be a kingpin of the drugs trade, *rumoured* to run a protection racket and *rumoured* to be creative with his tax returns. Scurrilous rumour all of it, as Scareface's distinguished barrister maintained at his client's numerous court appearances and equally numerous acquittals, jurisprudence dictating that any judge worthy of his gilt edged pension preferred to live to enjoy it rather than go swimming with the fishies under Blackfriars's Bridge, a victim of a midnight hit, stun, splash and run.

If the streets of Forgottenham were paved with gold, it was not apparent to the naked eye. On the contrary, Naff's intelligence sources suggested that the vicinity was rife with rickety pickpockets, riddled with dodgy fiddlers and squirming with two-legged vermin. Clark's scrapyard was *rumoured* to be the main employer in the area, not that it was a thriving hive of activity. Upward of a baker's dozen overalled scrappers - as the hired hands were known - filed through the gates each and every morning. They banged a few cylinder heads together, recycled the odd bicycle and stripped a pusillanimous panoply of paraphernalia to harvest spare parts. However, most of their time was *rumoured* to be spent drinking tea, playing two-hand brag and keeping an eye out for prying eyes.

Although in a number of respects Forgottenham reminded Naff of his home town of Huddersford, by and large he thought it a festering mess of environmental distress in sore need of redress. Scavenged metal carcasses and mechanical hulks formed rusting heaps of tottering neglect and overloaded garbage skips brimmed to the rim with discarded cardboard and mouldy old household detritus. However, according to Special Branch, the scrapyard was merely a mercenary diversion. The nerve centre of the nefarious operation was *rumoured* to be a shabby Portacabin in a corner of the yard. This was Dolores Clark's office, or rather it was *rumoured* to be Dolores Clark's office. As not all those who went in came out, Naff was unable to determine what was *rumour* and what was, in fact, fact.

Although it was an age since Naff last had a routine job - a mundane nine-to-five in common parlance - he took advantage of a lapsed friendship from his army days to infiltrate the scrappery as a stand-in scrapper. On the face of it he was a likely rogue, but behind the rear he was an experienced under-the-covers operative briefed to soap up any suds of information that might lead to the apprehension of the puppetmeister and puppetmeistress of what was *rumoured* to be a hotbed of organised crime.

On day one of his covert assignment, he was de-ballbearinging a rust-encrusted sprocket when he was accosted by a burly man in an ill-fitting suit and dark glasses.

'Oy, you,' the man shouted across the yard.

Me?' Naff pointed to his chest.

'Yeah, you with the long hair and the tattoos. What's your name?'

'Naff.'

'What kind of name is that?'

'Dunno. Ask me folks.'

'New round here, ain't you?'

'I'm filling in for Grizzly while he's inside.'

'Know how to operate a car crusher?'

'Sure. Trained on Aljons but spent a bit of time on Hammbreakers when I were in the army.'

'That'll do. Follow me. The boss wants a word.'

'Can't it wait? I'm due a tea break.'

Brawns - for it was none other - turned to a lumbering brute of a man at his shoulder. 'Mussels, tell the new boy how things work round here.'

'All right, punk, you asked for it,' Mussels snarled. 'We start at eight. Lunch is from one to two and we clock off at five. You get two tea breaks, statutory holidays, optional membership of the staff pension scheme and . . .'

'What my henchman means,' Brawns said, 'is that when Dolores whistles, you come running.'

'Dolores?'

'The guv'nor's missus. She's the brains behind the outfit.'

'Is that the small bird with the imitation leopard skin coat who parks her Jag in front of the Portacabin?' Naff asked. 'Face like it was chiselled out of granite. Bottle-blonde perm. Well built. Crazy high heels. Always wears short skirts. Big boobs. Got a wandering eye. A real piece of work.'

'Might be. If you know what's good for you, you'll keep your mind on the job and your lip zipped. Here she comes now.' Brawns nodded at a petite vixen-dressed-as-cub in a faux-fur coat, a microcosmic skirt and high-heeled boots striding across the scrapyard smoking a cigar. 'If she asks you anything, just say, yes miss, no miss, three bags full.'

Naff frowned and scratched his head. 'Thought you said she was the guv'nor's missus. So why call her miss?

'Know what, Brawns? The lad's got a point,' Mussels said with a shrug of the shoulders.

Before Brawns had time to engage in a deeply meaningful debate about semantics - a rose by any other name and all that blather - Dolores Clark strode up to Naff and gave him a wandering eye. 'Fancy yourself, don'tchya, fella?' she said and blew smoke in his face.

'Yes miss, no miss, three bags full,' Naff said with a deferential cough.

'Lippy, in't ya?' Dolores gave him a lipsticked wink. 'Grizzly reckons he knew you in the army.'

'We were in the same outfit,' Naff told her.

'Know how to handle yesself?' Dolores asked.

Naff shrugged. 'I guess.'

Dolores turned to Brawns. 'He'll do. Brief him while I see how Fred's getting on.' She checked her watch. 'Unless the Prousts release my brat by the end of the week, I'm taking them out, starting with Priscilla . . . and I int talking tickets to Strictly Come Effing Dancing. If they think they can mess with me, they got another thing coming.'

'You sure the Proust Mob's got her?' Brawns asked.

Dolores grabbed Brawns' kipper tie and yanked until his face went purple. 'Who else would pull a stunt like this?' she growled. 'Course it's the Prousts. Well, take it from me, they just signed their own effing death warrants.

Anyone except me lays a finger on my brat is fish bait.' She pushed Brawns away and narrowed her eyes. 'Understand?'

'Yes miss, no miss, three bags full,' Brawns stuttered as he staggered back gulping for breath.

Behind a casual expression of indifference, Naff pricked up his ears. As luck would have it, it seemed that he might have just hit paydirt. Although he had heard rumbles in the concrete jungle that something was afoot, news that a rival mob had kidnapped the Clark's only daughter was precisely the breakthrough he was hoping for. Because the upshot was that not only had the infamous Dolores 'Dolly' Clark emerged from the murks of shadowland to assume the reins of gangsterdom, her husband, Fred 'Scareface' Clark had called in favours from the brylcreemed scum of East London.

As various representatives of the sump of the earth parked their Mercs and Beamers outside Dolores's Portacabin, Naff made a mental note of their faces. Some, such as Phil 'the Pill' Plumber, Marc 'the Nark' Davis and Micky 'the Artful Codger' Agers he knew from their mugshots, but others were not on file. Within half an hour, more or less a dozen freelance hoods and hoodesses were waiting to be briefed. As one they stood to attention when Dolores strode through the Portacabin door followed by her husband. She tossed her moleskin coat on a chair, propped her backside on the desk and inspected her oxblood nails while the assembled gangsters took their seats.

'Thanks for coming,' Scareface said. 'Cup of tea, anyone? Biscuit?' He clicked his fingers at Brawns and snapped, 'ginger nuts.'

Micky 'the Artful Codger' Agers gave Naff a thoughtful look, took a step back, closed one eye, raised a thumb, rotated it through ninety degrees and sized him up like an exhibit in a wax museum. 'Very pre-Raphaelite. Definitely something of the Dante Gabriel Rossetti's about him,' he said with a pensive stroke of his goatee beard. 'I believe I may have a display cabinet his size at the gallery. Give me a shout if you want to sell him.'

'Hands off. That's Naff. He's new.' Dolores glared at the Artful Codger and said, 'listen up, Micky. I will tell you once and once only. Friday night, I'm sending you to the Proust's nightclub. Take Naff with you. He's new on the manor so Priscilla Proust in't gonna clock him. After the cabaret, create a diversion while Naff snoops around backstage to see if they got Katy banged up there. Nothing but trouble since the day she was effing born, that one.' Dolores's wirewool eyebrows met as she narrowed her pit bull eyes. 'The rest of you get tooled up,' she said. 'If I don't get my girl back pronto, all hell is gonna break loose. Synchronise watches and get ready to rumble.' Briefing over, she got to her feet and reached for her coat.

As the motley crew shuffled out to their getaway wheels, Dolores placed a hand on Naff's shoulder. 'If you know what's good for you, New Boy,' she said with a note of ominous intent in her gravelly voice, 'you'll keep your hands off Priscilla Proust. The last member of my gang who tried it on with that bitch is adjusting to life as a tailor's dummy. You wouldn't want me to give your handsome face an acid bath, would you?' She broke into a twisted smile as Naff's jaw dropped. 'Glad we understand each other,' she said, then added, 'a word of warning. Watch out for Blojob, Priscilla Proust's minder. That mutant is effing trouble . . . with a capital eff.'

This little piggy went to market.

xxi

Heather Prendergast smeared a peek hole in the window with her neckerchief and squinted in. From what she could see, the butler's parlour was much as she remembered. She could not help but smile as she recalled how, as a little slip of a thing, she used to sit on Smothers' knee picking moths out of his stubble. Sometimes Missus Beaten would join them and hum a nursery tune while crocheting a tea-caddy or knitting a pair of muffles by the fire.

'Clippety, cloppity, clop,

The horse fell in the dock.

The clock ran down,

And horsey drowned,

Clippety, cloppity, plop.'

was little Heather's favourite, although she also had a fondness for the toe-rhyme . . .

'This little Spriggy went to market,

This little Spriggy stayed home,

This little Spriggy had her throat cut,

This little Spriggy got boned,

And this little Spriggy went wee, wee, wee,

And piddled all the way home.'

'When I was a little girl, about your age, Miss Heather,' Missus Beaten would reminisce like a groove stuck in a gramophone needle, 'my old mum taught me all she knew.' She rocked gently to and fro in her bentwood chair with a fondness-of-ages smile. 'Oh, but she was batty as a brush, was my old mum. You'd not want to eat her cooking. My little Nannie Doss, our dad used to call her. Mind, she kept her kitchen as nature intended. Good, honest old-fashioned Burkshire clutter. None of this trendy new-fangled recyclable rubbish. Bless.' She chuckled like a country drain as her thoughts meandered back to a more innocent age. 'There were fourteen of us little-uns. Two girls, a boy and eleven cats,' she said. 'Our dad was an unemployed slacker. Had been ever since he got kicked out of school.' She put aside her knitting, knotted her fingers, folded her hands in her pinafored lap and gazed into the past. 'I started out as a parlour maid for Lord Jinx when I was a lass, and in no time at all got demoted to kitchen skivvy.' She lapsed into a smile as the memory took hold and refused to let her go. 'That's when cook took me under her wing and taught me how to boil rice. Must say, I never looked back. When cook died after that terrible muddle with the ricin, Lord Trevelyan advertised the position in The Lady. If you want the honest truth, Miss Heather, I never posted the letter. Couldn't for the life of me work out how to do it.' She nodded at a yellowing envelope on the mantleplace with a skulky look on her florid face. 'When nobody applied, your grandfather give me the job. I wet-nursed your mother, Lady Rose, and dry-nursed her younger sister, Lady Elizabeth. Must admit, I was in two minds about staying on after Sir Freddie married that revolting French tart, but I couldn't leave Baskerville, could I? So I decided to stay on until Smothers died.' She scowled at Smothers from the corner of an eye. 'Wish he'd get on with it.'

Ah, memories, Heather thought. Grim, grim memories. The stuff of sleepless nights. But that was then. This was now. Or was it? To all intents and purposes, the butler's parlour looked much as it had back then; fading paintwork; clumpy settee; broad sideboard; messy dresser; chestless drawers; standing lamp with missing shade; wrought-iron tigerlilies creeping up the chip-tiled fireplace; floor standing planters potted with wilty begonias and a veritable plantitude of dizzilizies on the windowsill. However, despite the familiar trappings, the habitants were, to say the least, different.

Katerina sneaked a peek and elbowed Heather in the gusset. 'Why is Eggy dressed like a French maid?' She pointed to a portly woman beside the sideboard busying herself with a feather duster. Although her back was turned, there could be no mistaking the maidly regalia – skimpy black satin dress, white half-apron, ruffled headpiece, silk stockings, gartered suspenders and high heels. A glossy tress of jet-black hair tumbled over her puff-sleeved shoulders and coagulated just above the small of her back.

Heather grabbed Sebastian's arm as she heard footsteps in the hall. 'Duck,' she said.

Sebastian looked up, shielded his eyes with a hand, mumbled, 'is it a bird, is it a plane, is it a duck?' as a *something* waddled through the door - a grotesquerie of flabby flesh squeezed into a seem-busting leather corset, fishnet stockings, thigh-high stiletto boots and a featureless rubber mask.

The *something* turned on the light and wobbled across the room madslapping a bullwhip against a thigh. 'Tu es une vilaine petite fille coquine,' it scolded as it whipcracked away. 'I will give you the punishment until you beg my mercy.'

'Oh my God, it's mum,' Katerina gasped and covered her eyes with a hand. She tried not to peek through her fingers but curiosity got the better of her. It always did.

'Come on, Bratty, we don't have a moment to lose.' Heather straightened her beret and reknotted her neckerchief, ready to spring into action like the heroine of her yet to be written blockbuster novels, Bruyère 'Kitten' Galore. She was about to force an entry as taught in Drugsbust class when Katerina tugged her arm and pointed.

Heather caught her breath as the French maid turned around and revealed himself in all his draggy glory. Sir Freddie – for astonishingly, she was in fact he - bent over, pulled down his panties, closed his eyes and chortled in orgasmic ecstasy as the leather-clad dominatrix scolded him for being 'la vilaine petite fille coquine,' and horsewhipped him to within an inch of his frills.

Lost for anything meaningful to say, The Infamous Threesome gaped through the window, mouths wide open, as Smothers shuffled into the butler's parlour carrying a small pill bottle on a silver tray.

'Not now, Smothers,' Sir Freddie said with an intemperate grunt. 'Can you not see that I'm busy?'

'Begging your pardon, Me Lud. Me eyesight is not what it should be. Time for your recreational medication.'

Sir Freddie pulled up his panties and readjusted his wig. 'Very well,' he said tetchily. 'What have we got?'

'I am afraid that I could only get poppers, Me Lud. Me usual provisioner is indisposed with an acute attack of the kneecappings,' Smothers said by way of a lame apology. 'I gather that discord has broken out in the East End of London. It would seem that a hoodlum has misappropriated the daughter of a rival.'

'Bother. Oh well, suppose poppers will just have to do,' Sir Freddie grunted. He sat down on Missus Beaten's bentwood chair, straightened his stockings, crossed his legs and gestured at the sideboard. 'Leave the tray there, Smothers. Now off with you. My good lady wife and I have pressing matters to attend to.'

Shocked by the spectacle of depravity unfolding before

their shrinking eyes, Katerina turned to Heather and whispered, 'Jeez, sis, did you hear that? A turf war has broken out in East London.'

'Unbelievable,' Heather stared into the fjords of abstraction and fingered her toggle. 'Do you think this could have anything to do with our Katenapping case?'

xxii

Professor Harty returned his quill to the inkpot and read aloud. 'Little Breeder for sale. One previous owner. Good working order. Ten million pounds cash or part exchange for four Zippe Gas ColdFusion Centrifuges and Hadronette Collider with quantum control or what have you.'

Satisfied that the advertisement struck just the right note - vague yet to the point - he folded the parchment, tucked it in an envelope with a forged postal order, secured the flap with sealing-wax and handed it to McTavish. 'Make haste, my slovenly Groat,' he said with an urgency that brooked no delay. 'Unless you deliver this to the Pest Control Times by midday today, I will forfeit my prompt payment discount.'

'How is Sir Freddie ganna ken it's wee Katy?' McTavish asked in a rare moment of filamental enlightenment as he stowed the letter in his sporran with his sgian-dubh.

'Dolt,' the Professor snorted with all the contempt he could bluster. 'Who else could it be?'

'Just saying, that's all, Chief,' McTavish said. 'Wouldnae it be easier just tae pop roond and have a quiet word in Sir Freddie's ear? Say yaer doing a favour fer a mate so he disnae get suspicious.'

'Brilliant. Alternatively, I could incarcerate myself in the grainstore for fifty years, exist on a diet of oat slops and fetid water and save the long arm of the law the inconvenience of staging the trial of the millennium,' Professor Harty suggested, tongue pressed firmly in his sunken cheek. 'Where is she, anyway?'

'Gan tae get the permit rubberstamped fer that new toll road she's planning.'

'Toll road, you say?' the Professor raised a receding eyebrow. 'What toll road, pray tell?'

McTavish unfurled a map on the recreationary table and pointed to a bendy squiggle. 'See yon stretch of double-carriageway marked in blue crayon? Well, she's ganna put a toll booth here . . .' He tapped a pencilled cross outside The Happy Thistle. 'The deal is, she's ganna charge motorists twenty poond a pop tae drive through, but they gets a Malty McOatshake throwed in for free. That way she gans tae write off the cost against tax as a legitimate business expense. She calls it free-market enterprise. See, the punters gan tae choose. Cough up or queue fer the next ten year.'

'Pah,' The Miserly Minister of Misery scoffed. 'The regulatory authorities will never allow it.'

'That is what I telled her, Chief, but she gie the Lord Mayor an offer he couldnae refuse.' McTavish said, respect growing by the breath. 'See, he waked up this morning with a sheep's head in his bed. His missus wasnae best pleased, I can tell ye. Made a reet mess of the bedlinen.' He screwed up his stubbly face and grimaced. 'So anyways, when the pompous eejit belled wee Katy back tae gie her a mouthful, she telled him she had a giraffe and two wildebeests stashed in her karzy. So he backed off and gie her the green light tae do what she wants.' His eyes lit up like smog lamps on a summery Glasgow day. 'The wee bairn disnae mess aboot,' he said. 'Not like some I care tae mention.' He gave the Professor the kind of look that spoke for itself.

Faced with signs of mutiny in the ranks, Professor Harty simmered. And he brooded. And he simmered. And he brooded. Up until that juncture in the time-space continuum, he had never had cause, good, bad or ugly, to call McTavish's loyalty into question. After all, who else would pay a moronic fool a muckle a month plus sleeping bag and floorboard to do . . . what? Bastardise the English language and serve an occasional McBreakfast to Homeless John. And the sorry truth of the matter was that the Jockal showed markedly less ruth than he claimed when applying for the post. To put it in a nutkernel, he had massaged his CV. Nowhere in the coldblooded murder section had he made mention of woodlice. He simply stated that he was licensed to kill by the local authority. Professor Harty cursed his naivety for jumping to the conclusion that the victims in question were of the two-legged rather than the insectivorous variety.

But looking on the bright side - as the Professor went to great pains to rarely do - for the first time in months, the organisation's bitcoin account was in the black, notwithstanding HostageKaty's lavish expenditure on liquorice, whoopee-cushions and itching-powder. She had recently signed up a Japanese sushi bar – snakes - a Thai takeaway - spiders - and the Fish and Chippery round the corner - silverfish. Granted, it had taken the best part of two days, but she had taught McTavish how to secrete a variety of vermin about his person - he was a natural, she claimed - and instructed him to collect pestilence insurance with good-natured malice from a burgeoning portfolio of clients. Meanwhile, she amused herself by vandalising swings and roundabouts in nearby parks, strongarming liquorice from small children and blagging her way into Soho strip joints on the pretext of looking for her guardian.

For the first time since a lizard masquerading as a psychiatrist committed him to an asylum for the criminally insane, Professor Harty felt forebodened by a sense of unappreciation. While HostageKaty and Groaty McTavish were out terrorising the neighbourhood or hunting for vermin in sewers, he was abandoned to his own devices. At a loose end, he passed the time of day calculating the meaningless of life with his slide rule or counting his thumbs . . . 1 + 1 = 2. It was undemanding work and, to be frank, within a micronanosecond, boredom set in leaving him with little else to do but fret.

To add to his frustration, without prior consultation, discussion or authorisation, HostageKaty had taken to referring to Mission Control as Little Breeder's Head

Office. It was, the Professor thought, presumptuous to say the least. At times he had an uneasy feeling that his authority was being usurped by a foulmouthed pigtailed schoolbrat with gap teeth, a grime stained gymslip and an irreverent disposition towards her elders and infinitely betters. Indeed, he was beginning to suspect that she might be in league with the alien lizards. Although she didn't tick all the boxes, she did tick some; she had an uncanny ability to accumulate money and a formidable knack of disrupting other people's lives. He decided to check if giant lizards had a fondness for liquorice. He made a note in his almanac to surf the World Wide Web; it was awash with sites hosted by fellow believers who, like him, had been messaged by The Voice.

As a loss what to do, a disheartened Professor Harty ticked off the dwindling arcs of time on his fingers. He was desperate to cash in his hostage chips. He lived and breathed for that happy, happy day when he could install the ColdFusion centrifuges in his laboratory, bombard Queridium with Higgs-Boson particles, ionise it into pure energy and resume his life's purpose - world domination.

His musings were interrupted by hoots of laughter as HostageKaty and Groaty McTavish swaggered through the door chatting and giggling like bosom buddies.

When she saw Professor Harty glaring at her, HostageKaty let go of McTavish's hand, pointed to a damp patch in a corner and said, 'hoy, the Protractor of Gloop or whatever you call yesself - thought I told you to clean the place up. So why's there still blood on that wall?' Ignoring his ferocious glower, she hopped onto a bothy stool, upended her satchel on the table and said, 'they had scorpions on offer at the pet shop so I grabbed me one.' She dangled a writhing stinger in the Professor's face, announced, 'the bistro is being bolshie so I'm upping the ante,' kissed the pincersaurus on the mandibles and tucked it in a blazer pocket. 'I been thinking,' she said. 'Not sure I want to go home. It's dead cushty here. A laugh a minute. I know . . .' She stuck up a grubby finger. 'Why not tell Fred I snuffed it? Say you can't for the life of you remember where you put me, so I starved to death by mistake.'

'Pah. I do not make mistakes, my little skylark,' Professor Harty snarled, then bit his tongue as the biggest mistake of his life shrugged her small shoulders. 'In any event, it is too late. I have already posted my ransom demand. By this time next week, I will be rich beyond my wildest imaginings and you will be free to wreak havoc upon your pitiable parents.' He broke into a fiendish cackle and rubbed his hands as if cleansing his soul with the devil's own sanitiser.

'What aboot me?' McTavish asked. He had half a mind that the Professor might be planning something untoward. But as his probation officer used to say, half a mind is better than usual.

'Good question, my Highland henchman.' Professor Harty looked at McTavish askance and stroked his chin.

'What about you?' The fact was that McTavish's casual remark had punctured a raw nerve. For although not written into McTavish's contract of employment - at least not in so many visible words - Professor Harty intended to dispense with his kilted minion's services the moment they were no longer required.

Over the course of the last few days, Harty had devised a malicious plan in keeping with his standing as a malevolent employer. He would set McTavish a simple puzzle – something along the lines of . . . if $ax^2 + bx + c = 0$, where $a = 1, b = -7, c = 12$, and $ib^2 - 4ac = (-7)^2 - 4(1)(12) = 49 - 48 = 1$, allowing for the fact that $x = -b \pm \sqrt{(b^2 - 4ac)}/2a$ and $[7 \pm \sqrt{1}] / 2(1)$ unless $x = [7 \pm \sqrt{1}] / 2$, then what is the length of a piece of string? While the heathen Highlander was solving the petty poser, he would shuffle up behind him, bludgeon him to a pulp with a cromach, rip out his heart and eat it for lunch. Then he would dismember the body with a body saw, feed the pieces through the haggis mincer, add a touch of pepper, a pinch of salt and a sprig of parsley and serve the sumptuous delicacy to Homeless John in a toasted Bannockbun. To add insult to mortal injury, he would donate McTavish's kilt, sporran and tam o'shanter to the English Bigots Protection League.

But for now this must remain his secret. He feared that it might demotivate McTavish should he get wind of his murderous intent. And so he bluffed . . . 'you know, my faithful postilion, I am minded to promote you to Guardian of The Cosmos on double your current salary.'

'Gie me a break, Chief. Ye nae paid me a muckle. Ye been docking ma wages in lieu of board and lodgings ever since ye tecked me on. Anyways . . .' McTavish rocked back on his stool, tidied his kilt over his knees and folded his arms. 'I been gie a better offer.' Tickled pink when he saw Professor Harty's face turn a chalky shade of white, he broke into a semi-toothless grin. 'Yon wee lassie is ganna start a pest control division of Little Breeders and wants me tae run the show. Let's face it, I'd be a glaikit not tae bite her hand off.' He leant forward and jabbed a finger in the Professor's face. 'So unless ye gets yaer act together, pal,' he said with a contempt that brooked no favour. 'I've a mind tae teck her offer and leave ye be.'

And so the first small rupture of discontent became a fissure of malaise. Little did the Professor Harty know, but before long it would become a chasm of revolt.

xxiii

All but at her wits' end, Heather Prendergast pummelled a pillow with her fists. She had lost count of the number of times she had asked Katerina to take notes and the number of times that Katerina had stuck up a finger and told her to get a life. What was the point of her, Heather asked herself rhetorically? And as for Sebastian Marrowboan's brainstorms . . . stormdrains, more like.

Although she resented having to carry her own notepad – as if she did not have enough on her hands – it did at least mean that the lucky publisher who snapped up the rights to The Curious Case of The Katenapped Girl could rest easy that it would be an unimpeachable, forensically detailed, historiologically accurate account, unlike the piffle that clogged the Kindlesphere these days. A school for wizards? Oh, really - who believes that twaddle?

Reminding herself that Prendergast of The Yard is *not* a snivelling girly wuss, she dabbed her eyes, blew her nose and reached for her pencil. Brow furrowed in concentration, she nibbled her bottom lip and, in the neat copperplate script that she learnt at finishing school – the only thing she had learnt at finishing school - wrote . . .

Chapter Four.

Following a tip off from one of my snouts that Professor Harty was bunkered down in a very remote backwoods of South

Kensington, I led an expeditionary party on a terribly daring recce. In the line of duty I had to climb a very big wall and suffered severe abrasions to my person; viz, my fingernails. Unfortunately due to factors beyond my control, the bird had flown the nest before I could spring my trap.

I am now faced with a desperate quandary as my uniform is in a frightful mess and my twinset and blouse are at the dry cleaners. When I telephoned the oiks with instructions to jump to it and tend to my needs as a matter of urgency, they were very rude. Until Eggy finds my jeans and jumper I am therefore left with no alternative but to requisition appropriate garmentry from my stepsister. After all, as Aunt Elizabeth would say, it is better to face the world with humility than naked. To be on the safe side, I have ordered supplemental casual wear online and paid a very hefty premium for express delivery.

On a more positive note, my ploy of refusing to respond to Professor Harty's demands has clearly got him very rattled. In desperation, he sent a message to say that from now on he will only communicate by means of classified advertisements in an obscure journal. Little does he know that this plays right into my hands.

However, the truth was more prosaic as the truth so often is.

With her twinset backclogged in a queue of puked suits and messy dresses at the local dry-cleaners, catastrophe struck when her jeans and jumper went walkabout. 'But you promised to wash them,' she wailed when Missus Beaten broke the news. 'Now I don't have a thing to wear.'

'My word, you and your tantrums, Miss Heather. Just the same little madam you always were.' Missus Beaten ticked her off with a finger. 'It's Baskerville you need to have a word with, not me. He went all growly and had them away when I left them to dry by the fire. Bless,' she said, as if Baskerville was a mischievous pup not a malicious mutt. 'Not to worry. I found you something nice and comfy to wear,' she said with a breezy smile as she bundled a jumble of clothes into Heather's reluctant arms.

'Why are you wearing my smeggy old jodhpurs and hacking jacket?' Katerina asked when Heather appeared for breakfast on the Ballustradium.

'I fancied a change,' Heather said with a pony smile, all the while straining her every facial sinew to hold her embarrassment in check. The truth was that were she not in dire need of sustenance, she would have stayed in bed all day rather than parade in public like a Gymkhana Chameleon. If it was not enough that the jodhpurs and hacking jacket were several sizes too large, the riding boots almost came up to her thighs. Gross was hardly the word. But mindful of Aunt Elizabeth's maxim - it is not the clothes that maketh the woman but the labels within - she tightened the waistband of the Harrods jodhpurs to the nethermost notch, slackened her tie and pulled a barstool up to the table. Ignoring Katerina's hoots of laughter, she put her riding helmet and crop on the floor, licked her lips and tucked into a plateful of lukecold eggyrice on fried toast. She was so hungry she could eat her horse, in large part because she had excused herself from joining Sir Freddie and Fifi for dinner the previous evening on the grounds that she was suffering from a perforated appetite. The fact was, she found it impossible to look her father in the face . . . or anywhere else for that matter. Especially anywhere else.

While they breakfasted, Heather and Katerina engaged in a jentacular confabulation about the spectacle of domestic depravity they had witnessed the previous afternoon. 'You're a police officer, sis,' Katerina said with a barely disguised note of contempt in her whiny voice. 'Is it allowed to blackmail your stepfather?'

'Cripes, Bratty, it most certainly is not.' Heather choked as a gulp of chocomilk went down the wrong way. 'It's strictly against the law.'

'Well, what if I dress up like a French maid, wave a feather duster in his face and say if he doesn't buy me a Maserati, I'll tell his golf club chums he's got a bent putter?' she asked as she tossed her cigarette end in Sebastian's grapefruit juice.

'Hmmm . . . suppose that would probably be alright,' Heather said with a thoughtful nod. 'I'm pretty sure that soliciting parental gifts is allowable as long as it's not accompanied with menaces. I'll check with the Commissioner when I get back to The Yard.' She jotted a reminder in her My Little Pony pocketbook. 'I say, did you hear Smothers mention that gang warfare has broken out in the East End?' she asked. 'Now I come to think, I seem to remember hearing rumblings at The Yard.' She chose not to say that this was because she had emptied a bucket of dried prunes and a bumper pack of max-strength Senocot tablets into a vat of lamb curry in the mistaken belief that it would take the edge off a superfluity of chilli powder she had mistakenly used instead of curry powder. The upshot was that New Scotland Yard's plumbing had gone into meltdown. The repercussions were still being flushed.

Sebastian derummaged a copy of the Pest Control Times from his backpack and unleafed it on the table. He pointed to a classified advertisement on an inside page. 'Hey guys, take a look at this.'

Heather read aloud . . . 'Little Breeder for sale. One previous owner. Good working order. Ten million pounds cash or part exchange for four Zippe Gas ColdFusion Centrifuges and Hadronette collider with quantum control or what have you.'

'No, not that. Down a bit.' Sebastian tapped the bottom of the page. 'See? Atari ST1040 computer with cracked copy of Cubase and mouse. One careful owner.' His face fell. 'Oh, and six careless owners. Bum-mer.'

It went without saying that Heather ignored him. With Hostagemurder class in mind, she said, 'of course the kidnappers will expect us to negotiate.'

'Are you kidding? They'll make mincemeat of Kickarse Katy if we mess them about. How about this . . .' Katerina scribbled a note on a napkin and read it back. 'We are in the market for a fully functioning Little Breeder for a new adventure playground and would be happy to agree your terms. Please advise how, where and when to conduct the transaction.' She sat back with a smirk on her face. 'That should do the trick. Only one problem,' she said. 'We're ten million quid short, give or take.'

And that was when Sebastian Marrowboan came up with an unusually pertinent interposition. 'Don't shop me to the cybercops,' he whispered, 'but I just invented a killer device to quomodocunquize currency - the Marrowboan Notocopier. Mad name, or what?' He looked from Katerina to Heather expecting a round of applause then shrugged when they stared at him as if he had just announced that he was engaged to a shrub. 'Come on, guys. Don't look at me as if I've just got engaged to a shrub,' he said. 'This is for real. I can print off ten million, easy.' He gulped down the dregs of his grapefruit juice - pith, pips, soggy fagend and all - and led the way to his laboratorium. After showing the girls in, he looked over a shoulder, glanced over the other, locked the door, peeked through the keyhole and - satisfied that Baskerville was nowhere to be seen - whipped a dusty dustsheet off a bulky mechanical contraption.

Unimpressed to say the least, Heather turned up her nose. 'Looks like an ancient photocopier hooked up to a primitive computer.'

'Yeah, right. A Sinclair ZX80. Months ahead of its time,' Sebastian said with a puff of pride. He smoothed out a five pound note, fed it into the paperfeed and after a bump, a shunt and a grind, a replica note spewed out of a covert orifice.

Heather held both notes up to the light and examined them forensically from a variety of angles. 'Sebastian, this copy is identical to the original,' she said. 'The only problem is, it's possible your Notocopier might break the law.'

'Wouldn't worry if I were you, sis.' Katerina picked up the note and turned it over. 'Says five pounds on one side and fifty on the other.'

Sebastian frowned and scratched his head. 'Programming error. Problem in chair, not keyboard.'

While Katerina was otherwise engaged painstakingly messying her hair in Sebastian's prototype Reflectometer, Sebastian sidled up to Heather, cleared his throat, lowered his eyes, mumbled, 'bought you this,' and presented her with a small onion shaped bottle.

Heather read the label and raised an eyebrow. 'Oh I say, Essence of Garlic. How sweet. What girl doesn't like North Korean perfume? Tell you what, I'll give it to my stepmother as a go-away present.'

Sebastian's cheeks flushed a pimply shade of pink. Avoiding Heather's eyes, he fiddled with his hanky as if it was a snotty comfort rag. 'Can I ask you something, Spriggsy?' he asked.

'Anything, Sebastian. Don't be shy.'

'Can we go riding? I was thinking, like, tonight when Katerina goes out clubbing. Ping me a text,' he called over a shoulder as Katerina collared him by the scruff of an ear and frogmarched him out of the door.

Moments later the hissy fit to end all hissy fits rent the garden air asunder.

xxiv

Professor Murray Harty lay on his fourposter bed jabbering to himself. For the want of anything more productive to occupy his lithiumed cells, he stared at the ceiling counting blinks. *Two thousand and one, two thousand and two, two thousand and three . . .*

The slime encrusted grime brought to mind his padded cell at Broadmoor Institute for the Unjustly Victimised. He cast his mind back to his escape and cackled out loud. If his memory served him well - sadly, not always the case these days - he had wriggled out of his straight jacket, ripped out the lizard head-doctor's epiglottis with his canines, skinned him alive with his fingernails and left the stinking carcass on the bed under a blanket to fool the nurse-lizards. He then crawled through a maze of sewers under the secure wing before emerging into an excrement processing plant. After bludgeoning the night-watchlizard to death with a rock hard turd, he tossed the carcass onto a dung heap and hailed a cab to a nearby burger joint for a celebratory snack. Appalled by the extortionate prices and shoddy service, he strangled the waitress with her pinny strings, stabbed the chef repeatedly with a skillet-knife and made off into the night with the contents of the till – seed corn capital for a string of daring heists and gratuitous murders that were to elevate him to the top of New Scotland Yard's Celebrity Most Wanted list.

Life was so carefree then - a leisurely stalk in the park. Happy, happy days, so different from the gruelling bouillabaisse of ennui that stewpified his current malaise. The fact of the matter was that he felt ignored. He felt neglected. He felt taken for granted. What he wouldn't give to unburden his soul to his dearly dismembered mother - Diabolis rest her soul.

That evening was typical of the Professor's fallen state of grace. His Highland henchman and the pigtailed brat had left him holding the fort. Holding the fort for good grief's sake? In his prime he had held more forts than the gap-toothed spawn of Beelzebub had held hot dinners. In a Pavlovian response he patted his tummy and licked his lips. Loath though he was to admit it, there was an upside to his accursed hostage's extra curricula activities - a bountiful fount of gastronomic gratuities strongarmed from her reluctant clientele. As he waited for this evening's gourmet takeaway - Chinese, he hoped, or maybe Thai - his thoughts turned to the early days of his quest for the holy grail of physics . . . dark matter.

In his formative years, young Master Harty had been a prodigious musical prodigy. His pushy parents – a would-be Doctor of Linguistic Morphology and an Honorific Blue-Stockinged Dragon – instilled a belief in their only child that he would one day be the greatest composer that the world had ever heard. It was his destiny they insisted. His birthright.

'Pah,' Doctor Harty told the nursery nurse when she

questioned why his ambitions for his son were so far adrift from reality. 'Ludwig van Beethoven?' he scoffed. 'His music was a symphonic cacophony. Hardly surprising that the dolt went deaf. So would you if you had to compose that racket all day long.'

By the time that he was five or possibly six, young Harty had composed three symphonies and an atonal operetta - The Flying Duckman. Despite being works of brilliant originality, he discarded them on the grounds that they did not measure up to his demanding standards. There was a nebulous fundamental missing, he boohooed to nanny as he slumped over his Casio keyboard in floods of tears. And so began a search for the mislaid chord, a quest that was to lead to an obsession with harnessing dark matter.

Frustrated that mankind dismissed his infantile genius as signs of nascent maladjustment, master Harty applied his analytic mind to nuances of time, tempo and timbre. Why, he puzzled, must conventional wisdom dictate that each note follow the last rather than precede it? Was this a fundamental law of nature or merely a handy convenience to suit the anatomical needs of the performer? What if a sequence of notes could be re-ordered so that the first came last, the last came first and those in between either appeared at the beginning or the end - a process he called vice-verses? This would open up a universe of extrapolations and render structure an infinity of possibilities rather than a symmetry of limitations.

The breakthrough came one enchanted evening when he accidentally hit upon a random black key during a recital of one or other of his burgeoning catalogue of unfinished symphonies. Amazed that it made a sound – he had always assumed the little thin ones were purely decorative – it unlocked a harmonious mystery . . . dark musical matter. And so an obsession was born. Convinced that he could utilise the black keys to pre-empt the white ones - effectively to anticipate subsequent notes and thereby disrupt the sequential order - his research led to a preoccupation with gravitational distortionism, time-shift determinism and – inevitably – world domination.

Of course, as every retarded chimpanzee with half a brain knows, sound is a longitudinal wave carried by air molecules. It struck young master Harty that there should be a simple equation for the timbre produced by a single note . . . perhaps $sin2\pi ft$ if the corresponding tone has frequency f. But as he delved beneath the lid of his Casio keyboard, he realised that this was only the case for tones that were produced electronically. He had long since realised that natural sounds carried overtones and had a Fourier series, $\sum(a_n sin2\pi nft + b_n cos2\pi nft)$, where the coefficients a_n, b_n determined the timbre. He suspected that this was why different instruments - say a xylophone and a kazoo - sounded different when playing the same note and probably had to do with the physics of vibration. So adding two and two and two together and subtracting the number he first thought of, he deduced that any tone he heard at frequency f almost certainly also had components at frequency $2f, 3f, 4f,$.

Elementary, one might say. ABC in the lexicon of tonal XYZ. All very well, but Harty was still a very baffled six year-old. He was playing chess with his best friend, Aristotle Rubberduck - the inspiration for his operetta - in the bath one evening when, struck by a sudden splash of inspiration, he realised that intervals were a function of convenience. They *had* to be - there was no other logical explanation. Inspired, a cog dropped as master Harty realised that since time immemorial human beings required musical frequencies to be nice ratios of small integers. Pah, he scoffed. That might be good enough for Mozart, but not for him. And so he stayed up way past bedtime until, with a lisped, 'eureka,' he saw that he was faced with a massively convenient mathematical coincidence. He slapped his bulbous brow and cursed his stupidity. He had overlooked the obvious fact that several of the powers of $2-\sqrt{12}$ were merely good approximations to ratios of small integers. And this excited him; it excited him a great deal. Indeed, it might be said to have aroused him.

Brain spinning like a turvy top, Harty rubbed his sleepy eyes and scribbled down a formula in his colouring book. He started with C and went up a fifth to get G, then D, then A, then E, then B. So far, so good, but what next? Bingo . . . in a radical departure from full tone determinism, he went down a fifth to get F. He got the black keys from there using the rest of what he defined as the circle of fifths. Gadzooks – he was cooking on gas.

He rolled up his pyjama sleeves, rubbed his hands and set about redefining the parameters of tonal architecture. After he had gone up a 'perfect' perfect fifth twelve times, he found that he had a frequency ratio of $3^{12}:2^{12} \approx 129.7:1$. To put it in words that even Aristotle Rubberduck could understand, $\log_2 3 \approx \frac{19}{12}$ happened to be a good rational approximation and that, my fearless featherless rubber friend he announced triumphantly, was the basis of equal temperament.

Splish, splash, splosh. Slam dunk.

As if an arithmetic deity had flicked a switch, he had a sudden lightbulb moment. Of course . . . it was blindingly obvious that he could use other types of temperament, such as well-temperament. If so, maybe - just maybe - some intervals would sound better. Of course, some would sound worse, but that was no reason to throw his toys out of the cage. But he fretted that if he did not use equal temperament, different keys might sound different. Why, he asked himself? The answer struck him like a bolt from the blue . . . light diffracts from black keys at an infinitesimally lower marginal velocity than from white.

And that was when and why and how and where little Murray Harty's mind turned to dark matter, or rather to the distorting gravitational effect of semitones on a well-tempered scale. An hour or two spent brushing up on Newton and Einstein before he tootled off to bed convinced him that although the canon of physics might profess to accommodate known unknowns, it failed to take into account unknown unknowns. From there it was but a short shoe shuffle to a determination to join the pantheon of scientific greatnesses by unravelling the mysteries of dark matter. If this required a minor detour into world domination, so be it. As nanny would have said before her murderous demise, 'such is life. Now off to bed with you little sleepy-head, before the alien lizards slither down the chimney and gobble you up.'

Professor Harty was jarred back to the present by the cackle of his cellphone. He glanced at the caller ID and groaned. What the devil did Popweasel Proust want at this time of night? More with a grimace than a scowl, he took the call. He listened, frowned and snapped, 'told you, Proust, I will have the cash next week. Until then, those reconditioned centrifuges go nowhere.' His jaw dropped halfway to his breeches as, outraged, he thundered, 'how dare you, you blasphemous spawn of a mutant gecko. Do you have any idea who you are talking to? Oh, you do.' He cleared his throat. 'Very well. One week it is. But I am telling you . . . damnation.' He cursed the unreliability of primitive technology as the line went dead.

If it wasn't enough that HostageKaty had usurped his dastardly domain, Solly 'Popweasel' Proust was now threatening to sell his precious centrifuges and Hadronette Collider to a malevolent Mullah in Iran if he did not stump up five million pounds in used readies within seven days.

The pressure was well and truly on.

xxv

Heather Prendergast rolled onto her back, propped a pillow behind her head and stared up at the ceiling. Her nightie was drenched in sweat, her skin itched like a celibate priest and her sheets were stickier than the lickside of a postage stamp.

It had been a catch clickety-clack sort of a night; open the skylight and let the gnats swarm in or stuffocate in the lung busting heat. Unable to sleep, she had been in and out of bed all night like a peripatetic glasshopper opening and closing windows in alternating bouts of swatting and sweating, tossing and turning, napping and tucking. To make matters worse, her mind just would not stop churning. Why, oh, why, she asked herself, had she become embroiled in a hostage-kidnap case that had nothing whatsoever to do with her? Stubborn pride, she supposed, and an innate pig-headedness that threatened to become her Achilles trotter. Not for the first time she cursed her foolish mulishness. For goodness' sake, had she had the sense to walk away, by now Kickarse Katy would be happily dead and buried and she would putting the finishing touches to her first blockbusting novel at Aunt Elizabeth's humble Tudor mansion in St. Mary Nook.

Stoically gritting her teeth, Heather told herself, enough of such vicissitudes. Consigning her brain fatigue to the fliptop-bin of never-say-die-isms, she yawned out of bed ready to brave another brave new day. After rope-a-doping her grunge in an invigorating power-shower, she knuckled down to work. Nothing if not assiduous, she unpolythene-bagged the evidence on her duvet in polychronological order - the collaged demands from the hostageers, some blood soaked strands of hair and a floppy-copy of the tuckshop CCTV footage. After carefully mulling over the pros and cons, the ins and outs and the thisses and thats of the case, she strode purposefully to the window and stared out at the garden, flummoxed. Oh, how she wished that Naff was here. He would know what to do. But he wasn't. So he didn't. And neither did she.

For the want of anything more constructive, she settled down to write the next chapter of her casebook. For the better part of two whole minutes, she stared blankly at a blank page nibbling the thick end of her pencil wondering what Doctor Watson would do if he had writer's block. Not to be defeated, she dredged the sump of her literary reservoirs and wrote . . .

Chapter Five. It is very hot today.

She read it back and shook her head. Somehow, it didn't feel right. She couldn't put a finger on quite what, but something was missing – a nebulous je ne sais quoi. Of course . . . her fingers snapped. It lacked tension. Drama. A gripping sense of foreboding. She recalled Aunt Elizabeth's telling her that the opening line of a chapter must catch the reader's attention, and as a best-selling romantic novelist, Aunt Elizabeth - or rather Melissa Moncrief to use her nom de plume - should know. So she turned over a new leaf in her notepad and had another go.

Day four of the investigation was very hot and stuffy.

Delighted to have unblocked a mental drain, Heather captured a fleeting thought and, keen not to let it slip through her fingers, wrote,

The sun shone down very brightly.

No, no, no, she said to herself. That lacked gravitas. How about,

 The sun shone like a gaslight in the sky.

Pretty darned good, she thought. But could be better. So she tried again.

The sweltering sun gaslighted the very blue sky.

Wait - hadn't she used the very verb or adverb or pronoun or whatever it was already? Grammaticalisation had never been her strongest suite, but not to worry - her editor's intern was bound to have post-doctorate degree in creative writing so could correct any punctuation or; spelling mistooks. With the literary bit now firmly between her teeth, she revised the sentence.

The blazing sun gaslighted the clear blue sky like a chariot on fire.

'Awesome,' she squealed and clapped her hands. Mann-Booker Prize winning stuff. Purring with pride, she read the finished chapter out loud . . .

Day four of the investigation was very hot and stuffy. The blazing sun gaslighted the clear blue sky like a chariot on fire.

Brilliant. It conjured up images of hot sunny days and blazing chariots. She suspected that it might need a little fleshing out before she put it to bed, but that could wait until bedtime. For now she had more pressing matters to attend to.

She cast a weary eye at her stepsister's jodhpurs and hacking jacket. There was no way that she was prepared to suffer her stepsister's adolescent castoffs for one more minute, let alone another day. The spurs snagged her elasticated leggings, the jodhpurs sagged half way down to her knees, the waistband flopped about her belly like a trouserflap, the hacking jacket flapped around her chest like a duffleflag. And boy, oh, boy, was it stuffy . . . sweatiferous was not the word. But dress relief was nigh. At any moment she was expecting a delivery from PartyGirl Online. It was all that she could do not to salivate out loud at thoughts of the summerlusciously cute frock she had ordered the previous morning before dashing down to breakfast.

Just as she was beginning to think that PartyGirl had let her down like a pair of pound shop tights, Katerina sashayed into the room carrying a package. 'This what you're waiting for, sis?' she asked. 'It arrived two hours ago but I couldn't be bothered to tell you.'

Choosing to keep her feelings to herself for the sake of peace on earth, Heather ripped open the box, rustled through the packaging, removed a dress and held it up. 'This isn't a size six,' she gasped as she inspected it from every angle in the hope that her eyes were playing tricks.

'No, it's age six.' With a deliciously malicious smirk, Katerina said, 'that's what you ordered, bozo,' and tossed an invoice on the bed.

Trying with all her might not to burst into tears, Heather stared at the kiddie frock, lost for utterable words. Not for the first time it would seem that her online impetuosity had trumped her digital perspicacity. And much as it was in her nature to blame technology, now she came to think – really think – it was possible that in her haste she had ticked the age six box mistaking it for size six. Rats . . .

'Not even you can squeeze into that,' Katerina said. 'Suppose you'll just have to wear those again.' She pointed to the jodhpurs and hacking jacket. 'Sooner you than me, sis. It's hotter than Lady Gaga's muff out there.'

Heather buried her head in her hands and wailed, 'I can't wear those disgusting clothes again. I'd rather die.'

Katerina clicked her tongue, cocked her head, tapped her chin and said, 'now there's a thought.'

Pointedly ignoring Katerina's snide aside, Heather gritted her teeth. 'Desperate times call for desperate measures,' she muttered and - reminding herself that Prendergast of The Yard was a pending mistress of disguise - thumbed through her wardrobe in search of sartorial salvation.

While Katerina retired to her bedroom to change into something disgustingly lusty, Heather swallowed her blushes and – with the greatest reluctance, it must be held – squeezed into the most appropriate item of frockwear she could find. Assuring herself that it was merely a stopgap measure until she could buy something more fitting at the nearest TopCop Boutique, she ventured downstairs to bid a less than fond farewell to her father. In the cold light of day she concluded that she was out of her depth and should stick to scouring nonstick saucepans. To put it in words of one feather, despite a catalogue of clues, she had not a clue where to go from here.

She found Sir Freddie perusing the tipster supplement of Forbes Magazine in the Poo Bar, as the Billiards Room was now known. In a tribute to her Adult Video Smut-Hussy of The Year Award for her role as Clonnie Dyke in Le Sale Chercheur D'or, Fifi had installed a reproduction saloon bar, carpeted the floor with plastic sawdust and replaced the candelabras with fluorescent candles. A blowup image of Fou-Fou LaPorte in a Cat Ballou hat was etched on a silvered mirror by the poker table. Naked from tummy to tit, she was sipping a glassful of a viscous green liquid. Emblazoned across her breasts in bold print was . . . *La déesse du sexe Fou-Fou LaPorte boit Shampagne de Dupont en exclusivité.*

Nattily attired in a black velvet smoking jacket, silk

cravat, flat cap, plus-fours, tartan socks and patent-leather slip-ons, Sir Freddie looked up when he heard Heather venture timidly through the door. He stubbed out his cigar, adjusted his monocle and broke into what might be loosely described as a smile. 'Well, well, well,' he said as he ran his monocle over her white pleated gabardine skirt, floppy-collared middy blouse, navy blue scarf and neck-bow, knee-socks and Mary Jane sandals. 'I see Katerina has smartened you up. Must say, I have always had a soft spot for a swabbie, but who in their right mind doesn't like a Jenny Wren?' he said with a lascivious twinkle in his monocle.

Trying her utmost not to blush, Heather brushed the creases out of her sailor suit and toyed with the lanyard. She said, 'thought I'd say goodbye. Maybe see you at your funeral. Here - your winnings.' She thrust an elasticated band's worth of five pound notes into Sir Freddie's hand and turned to go.

'A quitter, eh?' Sir Freddie rubbed thumb and forefinger together in an age-old gesture. 'You are just like your mother. A born loser.'

And that was when Heather's temper snapped like an overwrought bedspring. 'You are beneath contempt,' she screamed at the top of her voice. 'You have never done a day's work in your life and you have the nerve to insult my mother. Without the Trevelyan family fortune, you would still be slumming it in a caravan in Pinner.'

Sir Freddie's face turned a humourless shade of purple

and the veins in his neck pumped fit to burst. 'I have never been so insulted in all my life,' he thundered.

'Then you can't have been listening,' Heather yelled.

'Think you're so high and ruddy mighty, do you, Lady Muck?' Sir Freddie railed. 'Well let me tell you, your mother's father, Lord Jinx, came from a long line of robber barons. His forebears were slave traders, rogues and pirates ennobled for pillaging the Empire.' He slammed a fist into the palm of his hand and roared, 'I would remind you that my grandfather was a self-made man. The Prendergasts have been in prophylactics for generations. And as for Lady Rose, your mother didn't even have the gumption to bear me a son.' He looked down his nose at Heather and sneered, 'even a common alley cat can do that. My word, Helen, you take after her.'

Heather stamped a sandal and screamed, 'Heather, Heather, Heather.'

'Have it your own way. You are nothing but a dreamer. Always have been, always will. A lily-livered quitter.'

'I'll show you who the quitter is round here.' Heather snatched the notes out of Sir Freddie's hand. 'It's time to play hardball. I'm upping the stakes.' She closed her eyes and swallowed. 'I bet you a year's salary that I can crack the case,' she said. 'And if I don't, I'll go on a bread and water diet.'

'And if you do?' Sir Freddie asked with a mercenary glint in his monocle.

'Fifi goes on a bread and water diet.' Heather said. 'What's good for the goose is good for the gander.'

Sir Freddie threw back his head, slapped a knee and roared with laughter. 'I see you are spunkier than I gave you credit for, young lady,' he said as he dabbed the motes of hilarity from his eyes. 'All right, Midshipwoman Easy - you are on. Starve and be damned.'

xxvi

Dolores Clark kicked open the pawnshop door and marched in with her husband close at heel. Dressed to murder in a bellicose figure-hogging shammy-leather miniskirt and pad-shouldered donkey jacket, she tossed her cigar butt on the floor and ground it into the lino with a stilettoed boot. At her click-fingered command, Brawns, Mussels and Naff took up position behind her with their arms crossed and their lips snarled.

Scareface strode up to the counter, uncased a violin and demanded, 'what'll you give me for this, Popweasel - it's a genuine Strativarius.' He pointed to a label inside the eff hole. 'Real wood. Took it in payment for a gambling debt. The geezer said it was worth a bundle.'

Solly polished his bottlerimmed glasses with his beret, balanced them on the hook of his nose, examined the violin with an expert eye and shook his head. He said, 'you've been fiddled, Fred,' and tucked his glasses into a pocket. 'It's a cheap Chinese copy. Maybe worth a tenner. A score with the wind behind you. Put it with the others.' He waved a hand at the Musical Instruments and Bagpipes section. 'Now if that's it, I'm late for lunch. Close the door on your way out.'

'You will have lunch when I say and not before.' Dolores pawn-handled her husband out of the way and hammered a fist on the counter. 'Where is she, Popweasel?'

Solly raised his hands and backed away. 'Don't know what you're on about, Dolly,' he croaked. 'Honest to God.'

'God? You wouldn't know her from Adam. That's it, time for talking is over.' She turned to Brawns and clicked her fingers. 'Bring him in.'

Brawns turned to Mussels and snapped his fingers. 'Keep schtum and bring him in.'

Mussels gave Brawns a blank look. 'Bring who in?'

Brawns sidled up to Naff and whispered, 'bring who in?'

Rather than squander precious breath that he might later need for any manner of means, Naff cut straight to the chase and ushered in a suave sophisticate in a camelhair coat, bespoke handmade suit, silk scarf and felt-tipped hat.

When Micky Agers – for if you hadn't guessed, it was he – strolled through the door with a silver handled cane in one hand and a rusty chainsaw in the other, a pregnant hush fell over the pawnshop like a duckless quack. He looked slowly around the assembled hoods, broke into a guileless smile and asked, 'pleased to see me, kiddiewinks?'

Of an instant, the blood drained from Solly Proust's cheeks; the mere mention of Agers' metaphysical deconstructivism sent shivers abseiling down the spine of every culture-vulture worthy of the name. Trembling like a gimbal in the wind, he raised his hands and begged, 'no, please - not the Artful Codger.'

Caught between two minds - or better said, split between two personalities - Agers ran a bulging eye around the cluttered shelves. Intrigued, he fiddled with his pencil moustache and said, 'interesting place you have here, Proust,' labouring the word *interesting* as if said in jest.

'Seen anything you fancy for your gallery?' Dolores asked with a note of disdain in her sandpaper voice. Crappy old antiques were not to her taste. She preferred to ramraid the latest gadgets from High Street stores or scam high-tech portals with hacked debit cards.

'Possibly,' Agers said. 'But then again, possibly not.' He strolled through the pawnshop swinging his chainsaw, poking into drawers and fingering bric-a-brac until his interest was taken by a display of gold watches. He turned to Solly, asked, 'these for sale?' and when Solly nodded, took out a jeweller's loupe and examined the hallmarks. Satisfied, he broke into a crooked smile, said, 'not any more, they're not,' and pocketed the lot. For all the world as if out for a jolly in the National Gallery, he sauntered around the showroom until a *something* caught his eye. Curious, he kicked aside a hapless firedog, cleared an aisle through the clutterbish and drew to a halt in front of a painting half-hidden by a carousel of hot electrics. 'You know,' he said as he stood back stroking his goatee beard,

'I would have bought that Matisse if it wasn't signed Picasso.'

'Two for price of one,' Solly said with a pecuniary rub of the hands. 'As it's you, I'll do it you cheap.'

'How much?' Agers asked, sorely tempted to raise an eyebrow.

'How much you got?' Solly's gold tooth glinted as he broke into a pawnographic smile.

Agers took out his wallet, counted out a wad of counterfeit notes then paused when he saw Solly drool. 'I'll think about it,' he said teasingly and repocketed the cash. 'Aha, just the thing.' He swung around and aimed a finger at Solly. He said, 'I will take that loan shark, if I may,' and turned to Brawns. 'Measure him up for a tank, my good man. I will saw him in half, suspend him in formaldehyde and sell him to the Saatchis at my next rigged auction.' He slapped his cane against the palm of a hand and looked Solly over like a *thing*. 'Or maybe I'll slice off his face, bracket it and display it at my gallery.'

Solly's eyes opened wider than seemed anatomically possible. 'What?' he gasped, scared witless or scared shotless or an anagrammatism of the two. 'You're going to frame me for the Clark girl's kidnapping? You're insane.'

'Wash your mouth out with turpentine, Proust,' Dolores snapped. 'Micky in't just insane, he's certifiable. I seen the paperwork.' She summoned Brawns with a snappy thumb and finger. 'You . . . see if they got my brat

214

banged up out back.'

A rummage or two later, Brawns returned brushing dust mites off his mohair suit and unspiderwebbing his shaven head. 'There's a bunch of aluminium jibby-jobbies in the stockroom, about so big.' He stretched his arms in all dimensions. 'Looks like the Proust Mob are distilling moonshine back there. Want me to rip them apart and see if they got Katy stashed in one?'

'No . . .' Solly gasped, wide-eyed and panicky. 'Them are ColdFusion nuclear centrifuges. They're reserved for an important customer. Anyone lays a finger on them and I'm history.'

'Don't give me that, Popweasel,' Scareface snarled. 'You honestly expect me to believe there's a nutter wants a shed full of nucular centrifuges? Pull the other leg. It's got bells on.'

'Nucular?' Dolores gave her husband an inphonate look.

Trembling from the points of his winkle-picker shoes to the bobble of his beret, Solly went a deathly shade of pale. 'Please, Dolly . . . help yourself to what you want, but don't touch them centrifuges,' he begged. 'You know well as me, the Professor ain't a man to be trifled with. I'd sooner spend the rest of my days in formaldehyde than have that homicidal maniac on my case.'

Naff pricked up his ears. He suspected that his superiors would be most interested in this snippet of information. Most interested indeed. To make quite sure that he hadn't crossed the wrong wires, he asked, 'so who is this Professor bloke Popweasel's on about, Boss?'

'If you think I'm dumb enough to tell you that, New Boy, you got another thing coming,' Scareface said. 'Murray Harty's name is the best kept secret on the planet.'

Difficult though he found it, Naff somehow managed to keep a cool face. He knew that it might blow his cover skywide were he to acknowledge a name that ran seismic shivers down the spines of every law enforcement officer this side of beyond.

Patience running thin, Dolores grabbed Solly by the tonsils and slammed him up against a stuffed bear. 'Don't mess with me, Popweasel. Don't even think about it. The last man who tried is still adjusting to life as a woman.' She jabbed a finger in Proust's face and narrowed her eyes at the bear. 'The Professor don't dirty his hands on scum like you. He's class. Thinks big.' She took a deep breath and spoke deliberately, one word at a time. 'Now listen up `cause I in't gonna tell you again,' she said. 'I want my brat back and I want her back yesterday. Mess with me and Micky will formaldehyde you. Think I'm bluffing?' She cast one eye at the Artful Codger and the other at his rusty chainsaw.

Solly Proust mopped his brow with his beret and pleaded, 'see reason, Dolly. Why would we kidnap Katy? She's one of our best customers. We sold her the franchise to peddle drugs at Eastminster Academy for Young

Gentleladies. Brings us in a bundle.' He scratched his stubble with a thumbnail and stared towards the margins of credulity. 'Come to think,' he said, 'I ain't seen her for a while. I reckoned she must have gone rogue, like Marlon Brando done in that film, Poxylips Now.'

Enraged beyond all fury, Dolores slammed Solly's head against the bear's muzzle and slapped his chin with her knuckles. 'It's Apocalypse Now, nonce, and don't you forget it,' she growled. 'Now listen up, and listen good, Popweasel. I will say this once and I will say this once only,' she said. 'You are living on pawned time. If you've not got my brat, find out who has or I'm taking the Proust Mob out, and I in't talking a trip to Alton Towers.'

Having sworn her piece, Dolores Clark hitched up her miniskirt, toggled up her jacket and snapped her fingers at all and sundry. 'Scareface, Micky, Mussels, Brawns, follow me. And you, New Boy,' she jabbed an oxblood talon at Naff. 'Give Solly the third degree and find out if he knows where the Professor is holed up. This town in't big enough for the both of us.'

Scareface's face lit up like a spandex ballet. 'Sparks. This Town Ain't Big Enough for The Both of Us,' he said as he opened the door to see Dolores out. 'Got to number two in the charts in Nineteen Seventy-Three. Daylight robbery. Had number one all over it.'

Dolores poked a finger in her husband's disfigured face and snarled, 'it was Nineteen Seventy-Four, moron. Everyone knows that.' And with those words of songular wisdom, she stormed out and slammed the door behind her.

So duh ya' wants' to jump mah' sista' o' duzn't ya?

xxvii

Even the most upstanding police officer may on occasion be called upon to compromise her standards when working undercover. For example, she may be required to don a disguise not entirely of her own choosing to infiltrate a viper's nest. Under strict instructions not to blow her cover she may even have to turn a blind eye to very illicit activities that she would otherwise feel duty bound to report to the Commissioner. And so it was that I . . .

'Rats,' Heather cussed as she was interrupted by a loud knock at the door. She stowed her notepad on the bedside table with her Sherlock Holmes Omnibus; she would finish Chapter Six later when she had something more to report. 'Come,' she shouted.

Katerina swished through the door with her Gucci makeup holdall slung over a shoulder. 'Hot to trot?' she asked and mopped her brow with an exaggerated expression of perspiration.

'For heaven's sake, Bratty,' Heather said. 'If that skirt was any shorter, I would have to run you in for indecent exposure.'

'Talk about the pot calling the kettle black, sis. That sailor suit hardly leaves anything to the imagination.'

'Think I don't know it? I have never been so embarrassed

in all my life. Well, not since yesterday anyway. If anyone from The Yard sees me, I'll never live it down.'

'Say cheese and I'll email them some snapshots.'

'Do that, and I will never speak to you again.'

'Cross your heart and hope to die?'

'I would advise you to watch your tongue, young lady. Kindly show some respect for your elders and betters.'

'Introduce me to some and I'll give it a go. Jeez, sis, you are *so* dumb.'

'Right, that's it. Miss Katerina Clark, I am cautioning you on suspicion of committing Gross Affrontery Without Due Respect. Anything you say will be taken down and thrown back in your face when you least expect it.'

'Yeah, well, sorry, sis. When I said you were dumb, I didn't mean to insult your intelligence. I didn't know you had any.'

'Apology accepted. But are you sure it's wise to go to Drugsville dressed like hookers?'

'It's totally dope. Compared to the local talent, we'll look like midwifes.'

'I'm really not sure. I may be off duty, but I'm still a police officer.'

'Yeah, well, if you stopped acting like one maybe no one would notice. You are *so* not cool, sis. Just leave the talking to me. We don't want to spook the locals by telling them to kindly watch their lip or you'll have to ask them to accompany you to the station every time they open their mouths. They might rumble us.'

'Please, Bratty, I am perfectly capable of rapping with the riff-raff, thank you very much. I will have you know that I almost passed my Metropolitan Police street-cred exam, and at only the second time of asking.'

'All right, so tell me - what's a Ho?'

'A gardening implement.'

'And the Hood?'

'Milliner's slang for a hat. No use trying to catch me out, Bratty. I'm down with the kids – hot diggity-dawg, no mashing, pony-sitter.'

'I can see we're in for a really dope time - not. Come on, sis. Seb's waiting.'

It was the only plan that Heather had been able to hobble together in the circumstances; track down Smothers' illicit provisioner and somehow persuade him to dosh the dirt. With luck, by this means she hoped to undig some information about the gang warfare rampaging in East London. After all, it would be stretching coincidence to both margins if the misappropriated girl Smothers mentioned was not one and the same one that she was looking for.

In the event, tracking down Smothers' nefarious

medicationer proved more easily done than said. As the fickle demands of the plot would have it, Katerina had arranged to visit Drugsville to score some blow, as she referred to her illicit victuals. Being the eve of her eighteenth birthday, she planned to celebrate in style with double hubble-bubble, toke and trouble. Fortuitously it turned out that she and Smothers used the same provisioner. Indeed, she had introduced the doddery old butler to her main man, a snarky narcotics dealer known in the hood by the Milliner's Massive as Muggy. Accordingly, she volunteered Sebastian to drive them to Drugsville as soon as her suntan was dry.

Sebastian's eyes lit up when he saw Heather. 'Why is Spriggsy dressed like a Japanese schoolgirl?' he asked. 'Wouldn't mind giving her attributes some content curation. Mushy-mushy.'

Katerina walloped him with her makeup holdall so hard that his brain rattled. As he slumped down in the Sebmobile's driver's seat shielding his head with his hands, she hissed,' if you want to live to see puberty, keep your eyes on the road and your hands to yourself.'

Doing her best to avoid being seen by ambulating perambulators or articulating truck drivers, Heather huddled beside Katerina on the backseat of the Skodamobile while Sebastian lost his bearings behind the wheel. No matter how scanty her attire, she felt positively matronly compared to Katerina. Exhibitionist tramp was not the word. Or words. After all, when all is said and done, what is the difference between a skimpy halter neck and a brassiere, she asked herself as she ran an eye over her stepsister's relative state of undress. Nomenclature, she decided. Simply that. As if that was not enough, to her mind Katerina's microskirt redefined the Wikidefinition of micro. And skirt. To be brutally blunt, she fancied that her stepsister looked like a Barbielicious slut with her long legs, exaggerated curves, fake suntan and lashings of gaudy bling - a comparison she suspected would puff Katerina's pride beyond vainglory.

It came as no surprise that although Sebastian claimed to know the way to Drugsville like the back of his hand, it transpired that he didn't know the back of his hand particularly well. For this, that and innumerable other malfunctioning SebNav reasons - mad name or what? - it took him the best part of three hours to circumnegotiate the North Circular Road, not helped by a queue of traffic backed up at a pop-up toll gate in Willesden.

'Twenty pounds?' he whinged as he emptied his backpack on the passenger seat in search of his cardboard wallet.

'Aye, but ye gets Malty McOatshake throwed in fer free,' the burly tollmiester told him with a semi-toothless grin. 'And ye gets fifty percent off takeaways with yon voucher.' He handed Sebastian a paper beaker brimming with viscous slime and a flyer promoting a variety of bargain-basement tempts.

Sebastian tossed the discount voucher on the

Skodamobile's floor with a miscellany of empty crisp packets, jack-spanners, fire exterminators and other keepsaves he was hoarding for a rainy day. Tummy guzzled to the fill, he double-dechoked the engine, crunched the gears and rejoined the snake of slime-slurping motorists on the road to next to nowhere. Sometime later, he dropped the sleuth sisters off in a murky backwater of Drugsville. As they bailed out of the sloppy jalopy gulping for air, he told them, 'I'll back up the Sebdrive and wait here. Ping me a text when you need uploading.' All set, he checked his missing wing mirrors, ground the gears, flooded the engine and stalled.

Leaving Sebastian to naval-gaze, Katrina led Heather into a dim-lit alley where a wiry man with an Afro haircut, shades, a woolly Rasta hat and crutches was waiting. She breezed up to him and slapped his hand in a ho-bro street-greet. '`Sup, Dude dere, Muggy,' she said and pointed to his splints. 'Trouble wid yo' kneecaps?'

'I fell waaay down de stairs,' he said unconvincingly. 'My, you's looking good, hoocher-coocher. Want kibbles and bits?'

'No way. Just de usual herb. Do me good measure, mah man, coz it's mah buthday tommora'.'

Muggy cast a furtive glance about, took a polythened bag out of his pocket, said, 'here y'are, hunny,' and exchanged it for a fistful of bills. He moistened his lips when he caught sight of Heather lurking in the shadows pretending not to be there. 'Hey, whose yo' homey?' he asked. 'Looks like some skeeger. All da badasses dig a ho-pipe in da scuppers wid a sailor. Whuts de goin' rate?'

'Take a chill-pill, Muggy. The ho is out uh yo' league.' Katerina lowered her voice. 'Got some minute?' she asked, 'I wants info'mashun. I's lookin' fo' some goat.'

'But you's already gots some.' Muggy cast a lustful glance at Heather who was hiding behind an undercover dustbin sweating like an off-duty pig. 'Gotta say, da ho's threads dun't leave much to the 'magination.'

'Back off, homey. She's mah' kid sista`.'

Muggy stroked his scruff of a beard. 'So whut gotss'ta it cost fo' ha' t'be mah' sister too?'

'Give me da info'mashun I's afta' and she's yo's all night.'

'We got us some deal, hunny.' Muggy slapped Katerina's hand downside-up and gave her a high five. 'So whut duh ya' wants' t'know?'

'De goat I lookin' fo' bin lifted fro' the street by some badass. Whut's da word fro' da herd?'

'Know ha' name?'

'Katy. She's little-ass. Goes t'mah farm. Gone missin' last week.'

'If ya' know whut's baaaad fo' ya', ya'll fo'get about ha'.' Muggy took a nervy glance over a shoulder. 'Look, ya've gotss'ta dig, if ah' jimmey mah' mouth, I'll be in big-ass trouble. Dere's some whole load uh heavy dudes lookin' fo' dat goat.'

'Like who, fo' instance?'

'If ah' tell ya' dat, ah' be out uh business.'

Katerina flicked her head in Heather's direction and made a crude gesture with a fist. 'So duh ya' wants' to jump mah' sista' o' duzn't ya?'

Muggy's crutches wobbled like whammybars as he battled the serpent of temptation. 'OK. Wo'd on de street be dat da Proust Mob bin askin' quesshun,' he said in a hushed voice. 'And dey're not da only ones.'

'Who else?'

'I kin't say.'

'Look at da sista'.' Katerina cocked her head in Heather's direction and clicked her tongue. 'Pretty little wahtahmellun, ain't she? Are ya' sho' ya' kint tell me?'

Muggy cast his shady eyes to the heavens and chewed his bottom lip. 'Scareface bin askin'.'

'Scareface?' Katerina gave Muggy a suspicious look. 'Dat's not `nough, Muggy. Ah' need his dojigger if ya wants ta' dance da hornpipe wid ma' kid sista'.'

'Dat's all yo' gettin'.' Muggy zipped his lips with a finger. 'Now move yo' ass, mamma. Ah' gots some hot date wid yo' sista'.'

'In yo' dreams, homeboy.'

'Hey, cut me some slack, hunny.' Muggy raised his voice. 'We got us some deal.'

'So sue me.' Katerina grabbed Heather's arm and high-heeled it down the alley.

Needless to say, Sebastian was nowhere to be seen when they got back to Skodamobile. 'He's Baskerville meat when I get my hands on him,' Katerina growled as she sat on the Skoda's bonnet sampling Muggy's wares. 'Come on, sis.' She pointed to a nearby arcade. 'Let's go shop.'

'So what were you and Muggy talking about?' Heather asked as they walked.

'Cupcakes,' Katerina said. 'We were swapping recipes. Can you believe, he doesn't use cochineal in his icing? Not as a rule, anyway.'

'How very odd. But did he know anything about the case?'

Katerina tossed the roach into a passing gutter and took out her compact to freshenup her makeup. 'Not a lot,' she said. 'He clammed up when I pressed him.'

'Did you offer him an inducement?'

'Of course.'

'What?'

'Oh look,' Katerina pointed to a tree. 'A tree.' She stowed her lip gloss in her makeup holdall, replaced her everyday lashes with fluttery eveningwear, shaded her eyelids with mellow-yellow and gave Heather a curious look. 'Heard of the Proust Mob?'

'The notorious crime syndicate? Golly,' Heather gasped. 'They operate out of a nightclub called The Sundown Strip in Hackney.'

'My fave rave.' Katrina pouted her lip and kissed the air. 'What about Scareface?'

Heather stopped in her tracks and clapped her hands to her cheeks. 'Cripes, Muggy mentioned Scareface?' When Katerina nodded, she took a deep - a very deep - breath. 'You know what this means, don't you, Bratty?'

'What?'

Deep in thought, Heather stared unseeing into a distance of distraction and fingered her lanyard. 'I don't know,' she said in a barely audible whisper. 'I only wish I did.'

xxviii

Oh, how Professor Murray Harty sulked. Oh, how he brooded. Oh how he cursed his accursed stars.

As he sat on the edge of his fourposter bed darning his frockcoat, he puzzled how - or more to the point, why - his best laid plans had gone so spectacularly awry. After all, had he not considered every conceivable hitch, glitch, snag and snafu to an infinitesimal degree? As if that was not enough - and to his mind, nothing ever was - to be on the safe side, he had put contingency plans in place to cover every foreseeable eventuality, no matter how far-fetched; viz, that McTavish might bungle the kidnapping; viz, that his unwitting hostage might suffocate in the trunk of the getaway wreck; viz, that she might have the brazen gall to escape; viz, that her wealthy steplizard might refuse to pay the ransom. He had even allowed for the possibility that the sky might evaporate at an inopportune moment. The list was as long as his yarn.

Bereft of logarithmic rhyme or quadratic reason, he shook his head and sighed then shook his head and sighed again. As far as he could tell, he had accounted for every possible scenario - except one. But it was hardly his fault. Nothing ever was. For Lucifer's sake, how could any diabolical criminal mastermind worth his Largactil have the wit to predict that his hostage would refuse to be released? But the fact of the matter was that this was, in fact, the fact of the matter.

As if it was not enough that his teeny tormentor failed to afford him the respect rightly due to an upstanding denizen of his standing, she was carrying on as if Mission Control was an adventure playground. Within the space of one short week, she had built a business empire to rival Legoland. What was more, during the midmorning McMilkshake break, Harty was sure he overheard her say that she intended to annex Willesden and have Pope Groaty the First anoint her Empress of Verminland. He had little doubt that she would succeed. It seemed that everything the despisable little urchin prodded, scratched, snatched or spat at turned to gold.

'Talk of the devil's spawn,' he muttered under his halitosis as, without so much as a kick at the door, HostageKaty barged into his private quarters chewing a liquorice cheroot.

She checked her Princess Elsa watch, planted her hands on her pleats and said, 'not done yet? We got a shipment of barley due any minute. I left Homeless John manning the toll gate and roped in that bag lady he hangs out with to run the takeaway. Uncle Groaty's doing his pestilence rounds, so that means you got to unload the barley truck on your tod. Get your act together or I'm putting you in social isolation.' Having laid down the law, she stuck out her tongue and swaggered out without even having the temerity to slam the door behind her.

'Be gone with you, accursed wretch,' Professor Harty

snarled the moment she was out of earshot. Brooding like the mother of all hens, he put aside his needle and thread, turned his frockcoat the right way in and examined his handiwork with a critical eye. Not bad . . . not bad at all. Although not one to blow his own bugle, he fancied that he had done a first rate job; that correspondence course on Quantum Invisible Mending had been a dud cheque well bounced. His mood now merely sombre rather than hypercholic, he toggled up his frockcoat, straightened his spats, tipped his top hat and admired his reflection in a glisten of wall slime. Very dapper, he thought as he plucked a loose thread from his sleeve. 'Darn it,' he cursed as the stiches unravelled before his eyes, much like his plans for world domination. All but at his wits end, he reached for his remedial needle and, as he sewed, wrestled a quandary of mind-beguiling proportions.

The bad news was that Solly Proust had issued an ultimatum so he only had a scant seven days to find a bountitude of cash, failing which his precious ColdFusion Centrifuges and Hadronette Collider would be heading for Tehran fallaciously way-billed as Home Gymnasiums. The good news was that according to a classified advertisement in that morning's Pest Control Times, Sir Freddie Prendergast had agreed his terms. It seemed that the money was in the bag, so to speak. The Professor cackled at his ruthless play on words. The problem was that Little Miss Not Very Big - as HostageKaty was known to her burgeoning posse of fawning acolytes - had made her feelings abundantly clear. She was having a whoopee time and was no way - *no way* - going nowhere without five million cashpoundnotes stashed in her satchel.

So where did it all go wrong, Professor Harty asked himself as he gazed despairingly around his bedroom? Whereas once upon a time the cobwebbed rafters, candle-waxed furnishings, homegrown mould and cultivated slime had been comforting in their gloom, he was now beginning to dread his own company.

For longer than he cared to remember, The Professor of Perpetual Procrastination - as he was given to understand that he was known in the Court of the Lizard King - had found solace in his solitude. He had been content to share his personal space with Aristotle Rubberduck, the only toy duck who had ever truly madly deeply understood him. So what if man and womankind dismissed his one-tonal music as cacophonic? One day his genius would be recognised as having been aeons if not more before its time.

But was that not the story of his life? Harty cast his mind into the chasmic fractures of his past. He recalled that by the ripe old age of twelve, he could and should and would have been acknowledged as one of the greatest natural scientists of his age had he not been ridiculed by those who knew no better. Professor Brian so-called Cox, he scoffed. What did that simpleton know about anything? The lizard had his head in the stars. And so like every philosopher of note before him and doubtless many to come, he had forged a lonely path, driven by the certainty that he was unique - a breed apart. Following a string of harmless corporate hacks, petty bank heists and sapless murders, he had been on the cusp of achieving the celebrity status he so craved when a lengthy period of incarceration intervened. But at least confinement in a padded cell afforded him time without distraction to dwell upon the mundanities of life, the universe, anything and everything, including but not limited to dark matter, the Big Bang and alien lizards masquerading as politicians, bankers and shrinks.

But now, as he teetered on the limbs of immortality, the Professor feared that his destiny was being undermined by a pigtailed brat with gap teeth and the sensibilities of a guttersnipe. If HostageKaty refused to be liberated, there was nothing for it but to engage in a fiendish game of devil's bluff. Although it was not in his nature to go back on his solemn word – heaven forfend – he was left with no alternative but to persuade Sir Freddie Prendergast to hand over the ransom prior to his step-daughter's release on the pretext that she had overslept or somesuch. Then he would tell the little witch that Sir Freddie had reneged on the deal, repay Solly Proust while her back was turned and install the centrifuges and Hadronette collider in his laboratory. If he rose at the crack of dawn and skipped breakfast, he calculated that he should be able to ionise sufficient Queridium to power his Time Projection Chamber before Sir Freddie, HostageKaty and Groaty McTavish wised up to the fact that they had been triple-crossed. Of course, being a man of honour, in due course he would apologise . . . once he had enslaved them, along with the rest of humanity.

Professor Murray Harty rubbed his hands in a show of portentous glee. 'Prepare to eat thy just desserts, my little snow goose,' he cackled. 'We will soon see who wears the breeches round here.'

Dolce vita. Mona Lisa, Pizza Quattro Formaggi.

'Bratty, I've been thinking.'

'Steady on, sis. You'll ruin that new dress you just bought at the Drugsville branch of Monica's Ladieswear, Hippydashery, Bongs and Chillums.'

'Oh, do you like it?'

'What's not to like? The Mary Poppins look is *so* dope.'

'Thanks ever-so, Bratty. Must admit, I wasn't sure when I tried it on in the shop. You see, I have an awful lot on my mind. The thing is we can't afford the ransom. Let's face it, ten million pounds is rather a lot to find at short notice.'

'Don't say? So what do you suggest?'

'We'll just have to bluff it. I don't see we have a choice. Do you think Professor Harty would let the poor little mite go if I say daddy will pay in ten instalments, starting next month? That would buy us enough time to think of something. Crowd funding maybe, or a raffle. I know it's a long shot, but as Aunt Elizabeth says, take care of the millions and the pounds will take care of themselves.'

'Hello, anyone home?' Katerina rapped Heather's head with a knuckle. 'Jeez, sis, you are *so* dumb. Everyone knows my stepdad has never kept his word in his life. If you don't believe me, ask Smothers. Sir Freddie promised he could retire twenty years ago. Every time Smothers reminds him, dad claims his watch is at the menders. I know . . .' She clicked a finger. 'Why don't we forget all about this dumbassed hostage rescue lark? It's all right for you in that potato sack and shawl, but I'm freezing my nipples off in this drag.' She wrapped her arms around her shoulders, fluttered her lashes and sighed, 'the sacrifices a girl must make to look drop-dead gorgeous . . .' Alerted by a tuneless whistle, she looked round, broke into a scowl and said, 'about time. Thought you'd forgotten about us - I should be so lucky.'

Sebastian Marrowboan sidled up to Heather and Katerina, said, 'hi there, eye-candies,' then took a step back and scratched his head. 'Why is Spriggsy dressed like Whistler's mother? She looks like my gran.' He nudged her in the girdle and winked. 'Right, give me a minute to adjust the bounce-rate on my tyre,' he said. 'My guess is there's a spike embedded in the firmware.' He knelt down and took a closer look. 'Cool, the tyre's not flat - just irregular. Still, to be on the safe side, I better autocorrect the combustion and optimise the drive engine. Stand back . . .' He ratcheted open the Sebmobile's bonnet, scrolled up his sleeves and emptied a tube of lube over the carburettor. All set, he clambered into the driving seat and cross-wired the ignition.

Without stopping to think, Heather climbed in beside him. Having realised the error of her ways, she was about to bail out when Katerina leant forward, clipped Sebastian round the ear and demanded, 'take us to The Sundown Strip.'

Sebastian's face lit up. 'We off clubbing?'

'Less of the we, loser,' Katerina said. 'Me and sis need to see a man about a dog.'

'They'll never let her in looking like a retired schoolteacher,' Sebastian mumbled as he slammed the Skodamobile into the first gear he could find and lurched into the evening traffic. 'Spriggsy,' he said as he pulled up at a green light and leant over to adjust her seat belt. 'Mind if I ask you something?'

'As long as it isn't personal.'

'Hardly.'

'All right, then.'

'Are you a virgin?'

'How dare you.' Heather slapped Sebastian's straying hand. 'And will you please look where you're going?'

'I did,' Sebastian said with a snigger. 'Yeah. Right. Cool.'

Downtown Hackney was but a crow's throw from Drugsville Central, give or take a pigeon's smidgeon. Sebastian drew the Skoda to a juddering halt in a narrow alley behind the infamous den of iniquity that styled itself The Sundown Strip. 'I'll come with you,' he volunteered as he helped Katerina out of the back.

'I'd rather eat glass,' Katerina said and shooed him away with a fist. 'Wait here. We might be a while,' she told him. 'And whatever you do, don't breathe.' She tiptoed to the fire exit, looked furtively around and, satisfied that nobody of any consequence was looking, swiped the latch with her stepfather's charge card. 'Come on, sis,' she whispered and crept in.

Appalled, Heather shrank back and gasped, 'you can't do that.'

'Watch me. If anyone asks, tell them we're the cabaret act. Say I'm Cinderella and you're my ugly stepsister. Might as well be straight with them.' After making sure the coast was clear, Katerina yanked Heather through the fire exit and eased the door to behind her.

From what Heather could see – and to her relief she could almost see quite clearly – backstage at The Sundown Strip was far from sunsety and strippy. Dank and dingy, the corridors were quieter than a softshoe shuffle. The all-encompassing silence was broken only by the distant chatter of clubbers filing into the glitzy nightclub on the far side of the curtained stage.

Katerina paused at the first door she came to and took a peek inside. Satisfied that the coast was clear, she crept in and turned on the light. 'Come on, sis . . .' She dragged Heather into an artiste's dressing room - lightbulb-mirrored dressing table, costume wardrobe and casting couch. She broke into a wicked grin and clapped her hands. 'Let's make whoopee.'

'I cannot believe you said that,' Heather gasped. 'If it hasn't escaped your notice, Miss Clark, we are trespassing on private property. If anybody catches us, I might as well kiss my career goodbye.'

'Jeez, you are *so* uptight, sis. Let your hair down for once,' Katerina said as she rummaged through an oddjobbery of baubled, bangled and beaded costumes in the wardrobe. Dress by dress, leotard by leotard, tutu by threetu and bunny infested top hat by floral magic wand, she tossed a miscellany of stage wear over her shoulder until a *something* caught her eye. 'Hey, sis, look at this dope Sally Bowles drag.' She unwardrobed a coat-hangered costume, held it to her chest, examined the fit in the mirror and nodded. 'Anastasia says I look just like Lisa Minelli, only loads younger and miles cuter,' she said with a vanity that brooked no sanity.

'Was she having a total eclipse of the brain?' Heather asked as her stepsister disappeared behind a screen to change into another gear.

In two shakes of a quail's tail, Katerina reappeared fully Bowlsed-up in a black halter-topped waistcoat, short shorts, suspendered-stockings and a bowler hat. She was cavorting with a chair in front of a mirror singing 'moneeey makes the world go round, the world go round, the world go round,' when two girls walked in.

When she saw Katerina, the taller of the two clenched her fists and hissed, 'che cazzo . . .'

'Che whatso, hunny?' Katerina tipped her bowler hat and twizzled her cane.

Girl number two broke into the most saccharine of smiles. 'Ciao bella. My name is Gina, but call me Salome,' she said in a thick Italian accent. 'Mio amici, Calypso, say, vaffanculo da qui?'

'Dolce vita. Mona Lisa. Pizza quattro formaggi.' Having exhausted her lingua Italiana, Katerina gave Calypso a tiddly wink, tipped her bowler hat and doffed her fringe.

Calypso glared at her, straightened her back and snaked her eyes. 'Che diavolo ci fai qui, stronza?' she demanded, which for the benefit of any uniglots still reading, lewdly translates as, 'what the ^*¬;**fk;$$?'

'Calypso, she want to know who you are,' Salome said.

Heather cast a hopeful glance at Katerina. 'Sally Bowles?'

Calypso shot her a death-wish glare and tossed her head. 'Sembri un uomo con le tette,' she said, implying something transcendentally different.

'Calypso, she pleased to meet you, Signorina Bowles,' Salome said with a murkish smirk. 'You are . . .?'

'Shirley Holmes.' Heather held out a hand. 'The pleasure is all mine.'

Calypso brushed Heather's hand aside, stuck her nose in the air and snorted, 'dì a queste fottute troie di uscire da questo camerino,' or to put it another way, 'go ^*¬;** yourself, b!$$tch.'

Salome miss-translated for Heather's benefit. 'Mi amici, Calypso, she want to know if you need help.' When Calypso added a brusque, 'per l'amor del cielo, Salome, le cacci fuori o devo chiamare Blojob?' or in common parlance, '^*¬kssmy$$*rse,' Salome chuckled. 'She is . . . how you say? Si, she is curious to know why you are here.'

Katerina kicked over the chair, twirled her walking stick in the air like a drumstick majorette, caught it behind her back and raised her bowler hat. 'We're the dope new cabaret act.'

Calypso stuck up her middle finger in what was to Heather's way of mind, a rude, not to say crude, not to say perfunctory breach of accordo cordiale. With a parting, 'femmine imbarazzate,' she span on her Cuban heels and stormed out.

'My friend, she think Priscilla double booked the cabaret. She wish you buona fortuna.' Salome handed Heather a small vanity case and said, 'prego, please to use our costumes. Break the leg.' She kissy-kissed Katrina on both cheeks, blew Heather a parting kiss and with a shout of, 'voglio una parola con te, Calypso,' ran after her friend, heels clacking like duckquacks in the empty corridor.

'Cute, or what?' Katerina nudged Heather in the ribs. 'Watch the door while I get changed. If Seb turns up, scream.' She slipped behind the screen and reappeared a few minutes later in her civvies. After touching up her makeup, she tiptoed out of the dressing room, looked everywhichway including up and pointed to a light seeping under a door at the far end of the corridor. Hauling a reluctant Heather behind her, she sneaker-pimped along the passageway, picklocked the door and crept into the manager's office. In the middle of the room stood a reproduction utility desk on which was a silver-framed photograph of a glamorous platinum blond in a bikini with the words, 'I Love Me,' scrawled in one corner. Other snapshots of the same woman draped on the arms of a rollcall of soap stars, musclebound studs and celebrity hoods hung on all four walls.

Katerina's attention was taken by a white mink coat languishing on the sofa like a poleaxed polar bear. She tried it on, turned up her nose, muttered, 'trailer trash,' tossed it on the floor and told Heather, 'I'll do this room while you check the loo,' and nodded at a glass-frosted door.

As instructed, Heather set to task. Hardly had she lifted the toilet seat than Katerina rushed in, pressed a finger to her lips and turned off the light. Moments later voices could be heard in the office.

'Packing a piece, Blojob?' A woman drawled in a nasal mockney accent.

'Sure thing, Priscilla,' a basso-gruffundo voice grunted.

'Solly reckons a deranged lunatic has kidnapped Katy Clark. Dolores thinks we done it and says if we don't hand her over pronto, she ain't gonna be best pleased.'

'Could get messy, Boss. Bad for business.'

'You can say that again.'

'Could get messy, Boss. Bad for business.'

Patience running thin, Priscilla said, 'listen up. Phil the Pill reckons the Clark Gang are gonna send a snoop to case the joint. I gave her a monkey for snitching them up. She wanted an ape but I told her to take a hike. Keep your good eye out for strangers and tip me the wink if you see anyone acting suspicious.'

'What do I do if I see anyone sniffing about?' Blojob asked.

'Waste them and dump their bodies outside Clark's Scrappery as a warning to Dolores to keep off our patch. Shoot first and ask questions after.'

'How can I ask questions if they're dead?'

'Easy,' Priscilla said. 'Just don't expect any answers.' She followed Blojob out and turned off the light.

'Cripes,' Heather said as she ventured warily into the darkened office. 'Sounds like Murray Harty has kidnapped the daughter of the most notorious gangland moll in London by mistake. Dolores Clark's rap sheet is as long as my arm. Drug trafficking, possession of firearms, grievous bodily harm, double parking . . . you name it.'

'Tell you what,' Katerina suggested, 'why don't just we knock this rubbish idea on the head and go clubbing to celebrate my birthday?' She peeked her head through the door, looked about and chivvied Heather into the corridor. They were within sniffing distance of the fire exit when a brute of a man stepped out of the shadows. Taller than Naff by an eye-patched head, he wore an ill-fitting suit on an outsized body. His metallic teeth glinted as he snarled, 'hello girls, and who may you be?'

Thinking fleetly on her feet, Katerina blurted out, 'ciao, bruv. We're the dope new cabaret act, Salome and Calypso, aren't we, sis? Jeez, is that the time?' she said as she glanced at her watchless wrist. 'Arrivederci. Must fly. Hasta la vista, amigo. See you in a bit.'

Blojob – for it could have been no other – scratched his pumice-stone jaw and gave the girls a dubitable look. 'Get a move on, scrubbers,' he said. 'Showtime is in ten minutes and you better deliver, `cause if you ain't who you say you are, Priscilla will want a word in her office.' He broke into the sinister smile to trump all sinister smiles. 'And take it from me, slappers, you don't want to go there,' he said with an ominous glint in his unpatched eye. '`Cause if you do, you're coming out in a box.'

xxx

Naff straightened his bow tie, plucked a stray hair off his tuxedo and adjusted his reflection in a convenient window. Satisfied that he looked the part, he asked himself, 'who is that smooth operator?' and broke into a wry-martini smile.

If he felt pleased with himself, it was for good reason. As was invariably the case when it came to the fairer sex and their mothers, flirtery had got him everywhere and Dolores Clark had fallen head over boots for his rugged good looks and roguish charms. Hopelessly smitten, she dismissed her husband's words of caution as petty jealousy and inducted Naff into her inner circle. She even monikered him with a mobster handle – New Boy.

Smugly confident that his cover was now rockfast, Naff cast his mind back to the briefing in the Godmother of Crime's Portacabin shortly before he and Micky Agers set out for their clandestine mission.

Dolores rocked back in her chair with her feet up on the desk, kicked off her stiletto boots and wiggled her toes suggestively. 'Scrub up well, don'tchya, New Boy?' She twitched her bent nose and fluttered her horsey lashes. 'Time to see what you're made of.'

'Sugar and spice and all things nice, Dolly,' Naff told her with the smarmiest of smiles. 'I'll give you a taster later if you promise not to behave.'

Bored to the numb with the adolescent flirtage, Micky Agers examined his fingernails with an expression of casual indifference. 'Get on with it, kiddies,' he said, 'I got punters to fleece and auctions to rig. I'm only doing this `cause I got Monet problems.'

Delores sat forward, planted her elbows on the desk, bridged her hands and scowled at all and sundry. 'Listen up. I will say this once and I will say this once only,' she said. 'I'm sending you to The Sundown Strip tonight to see if the Proust Mob got my brat banged up backstage. Now eff-off, Micky, while me and New Boy have a quiet flirt in private.' Having given the Artful Codger his mooching orders, she turned to Naff and batted her bristly lashes. 'When you're done,' she schmoozed, 'why not drop by the bungalow for a candlelit debriefing? I got a few bottles of vintage stout put by for a special occasion. Don't worry about my no good husband,' she said when Naff raised an eyebrow. 'Friday night is Gangster's Anonymous. He won't be back till late.'

So it was that two hours later, Naff and Micky Agers could be found kicking their heels in a queue of inebriated gangsters and their incelibate floozies outside The Sundown Strip in Hackney Wick. As they filed past a miscellany of blousy streetwalkers, predatory pimps, dopey drug peddlers and musclebound bouncers, they were greeted by a glamorous platinum blonde in a shimmery evening gown.

'Well, hello, Micky,' Priscilla Proust drawled in a husky voice that sent shivers scuttling down Naff's spine. 'Not seen you since the Conceptual Existentialist Art exhibition at the Tate Modern. What is Tracey Emin on these days – glue?' she laughed – a common heehaw sort of a laugh markedly at odds with her sophisticated frockings. She looked Naff up and down, pouted her bee-sting lips, shot Micky a wink and asked, 'so, who's the beefcake?'

'Banksy,' Micky said, as direct and to the point as his trusty chainsaw.

'Really?' Priscilla arched a pencilled eyebrow.

Micky shrugged. 'Might be. Your guess is as good as mine.'

'Looks like it's your lucky night,' Priscilla said. 'I was keeping a table for the Archbishop, but Danny the Deacon just phoned to say the old dog is auditioning choirboys in the catacombs so won't be able to make it.' Insisting that Micky put away his stolen charge card - tonight would be on the house - she escorted them to a stage-side table and asked, 'can I get you boys a drink?'

'I'll have a Scotch on the rocks,' Micky said as he sat down, exercised his shoulders, stretched his legs and made himself comfortable. 'Make it a double.'

'And you, Banksy?'

'Same, but with ice instead of rocks,' Naff said. Eyes glued on Priscilla's pert derriere as she minced to the bar, he shuddered and gave his wrist a metaphorical slap. Reminding himself that he was here to work not window shop, he took in his surroundings.

He had heard tell of The Sundown Strip – of course he had. It was a legendary underworld hangout for legendary underworld hang-outers. But this was the first time that he had seen the notorious fleshpot in the flesh, so to speak. It was much as he expected - trashy, brashy and flashy. Classy, it was not. His kind of place, in other words. Muscle in dinner jackets and cheesecake in eveningwear canoodled, smooched and snogged at candlelit tables. Scantily clad waitresses in puff sleeved satin dresses squeezed through the crowd taking orders, delivering drinks, fending off customers' advances, pickpocketing tips and peddling illicit substances. Seemingly intent on drinking themselves under the table, the clientele paid little heed to the cacophonic disco, although every once in a while, a couple took to the dance floor and shuffled to a medley of old-romantic blasts from the past.

Hardly had Naff finished his scotch on the ice than the music faded and Priscilla Proust hipswayed onto the stage. She clapped her hands to demand the audience's attention and, as the clatter of chatter died down to a smatter of patter, announced, 'and now, ladies and gents, The Sundown Strip is proud to present an exciting new cabaret act. All the way from the Sheik of Araby's harem in Mesopotamia, give it up for Salome and Calypso performing The Dance of the Seven Veils.'

With a shimmer and a swish, a velvet curtain parted to reveal a stage-set of potted palms and mini-minarets. To a scratchy soundtrack of tambourines, ouds and mizmars, Salome bounded on stage blowing kisses to the crowd. A tall, well-built blonde draped from head to thigh in chiffon scarves, like Alibaba's bride, her face was hidden by a beaded veil. Dangling from her ears were pendulous earrings that tinkled like windchimes when she moved. Egged on by whistles, whoops and thighslaps from the audience, she clomped around the stage headbanging like a moshpit terrier in idiosyncratic synchronicity to the music.

As Salome took a bow to catch her breath, Calypso stumbled on from the wings. A blushing redhead, she was a good deal shorter than Salome and a full belly skinnier. Like her partner, her features were masked by a flimsy veil except for two panic-stricken eyes. At Salome's nudged prompt, she held her arms aloft, leapt into the air like a skittish frog, twizzled a clumsy pirouette, landed with a curtsy and pas-de-deuxed around the stage in an awkward combination of short pointe steps, petite batteries and balletic attitudes.

Struggling to be heard above the wolf whistles, Micky Agers cupped a hand to Naff's ear and shouted, 'very avant-garde. Post-impressionist, one might say, with a hint of Dada and a nod to Charlie Chaplin.'

'Not backwards coming forwards, is she? The blonde with the body,' Naff said with a nudge and a wink as the tall girl ripped off a veil and tossed it into the crowd. 'Not like her skinny mate. I pity the geezer who pulls the short straw. She looks like a bolshie reject from the Bolshoi.'

Veil by teasing veil, Salome revealed more of her fake suntan to a raucous chorus of wolf-whistles, cat-calls, bear-grunts and man-hoots. To a countdown of *seven, six, five, four, three, two, one*, she stripped down to the bare essentials with Calypso cowering behind her trying to look invisible. As the audience held its collective breath, Salome could be heard to say, 'awe, come on, sis - anyone would think you've never stripped off in front of two hundred randy drunks before.' As she ripped off her final veil and exited stage left blowing kisses to the crowd, her earrings snagged in Calypso's costume and all seven veils fluttered off like moths in a Serengeti breeze.

With nowhere to hide and - more to the point - no one to hide behind, Calypso stared at the audience with her knees pressed together, her mouth and eyes wide open like a rabbit frozen in onrushing headlights. As Micky Agers was later to remark, with her tumbling red hair and bemused expression, she looked for all the world like Botticelli's Venus rising from the shell – she most definitely looked shellshocked, that was for sure. As the audience erupted like adolescents at a ribald panto, undecided whether to clamp her hands over her ears or keep them clamped elsewhere, she burst into tears and ran off stage.

Dumbfounded, not to say flabbergasted, not to say

discombobulated, Naff's jaw dropped halfway to his knees. 'I do not friggin` believe it,' he gasped, unable or unwilling to trust his eyes. And that was when Micky Agers leapt to his feet, upended the table and yelled, 'call that art? I want my money back,' at the top of his voice.

Well, needless to say pandemonium broke loose. A waitress screamed, the barman pulled down his shutters and scores of punters whipped scores of coshes and knuckle-dusters out of scores of dinner jackets, fur coats, handbags and manbags.

When he saw Blojob elbowing his way through the melee like a bull in a chinastrop - fists clenched and teeth glinting in the glitterballs - Micky pulled a spray can out of his pocket, raised it menacingly and snarled, 'back off Bloey, or you'll be a red man walking.'

Leaving Micky to wreak havoc as only he knew how, Naff hurried backstage in search of Katy Clark . . . and more to the point, to find his girlfriend. He wanted a word in her ear. Two, maybe. Chapter and friggin` verse, in fact. He was casing the joint when he sniffed a whiff of pungent Wild Swan perfume wafting down the corridor. He swung around to see a platinum blonde in a skintight frocktail dress brandishing a pearl-handled revolver.

'Drop `em, big boy,' Priscilla Proust - for it was she - ordered.

'Take it easy, babe. I ain't armed.' Naff raised his hands and edged back to the dressing room door.

'Your pants. Drop `em,' Priscilla said. 'Let's see what you're packing.' She turned up her nose when Naff undid his cummerbund and his trousers slithered to his ankles. 'Poser.' She nodded at the fire exit. 'Fuck off.'

As Naff fumbled to hitch up his trousers, a husky voice behind him whispered, 'not yet, you don't,' and a sinewy arm reached out, dragged him into the dressing room and slid across the bolt.

xxxi

There is no Chapter Seven of *The Curious Case of The Katenapped Girl*. Actually, that is not quite true. Topping a blank page are the words, *Chapter Seven has been redacted on the grounds of national security.* It was all that Heather could think to write in the circumstances. Anyway, when push comes to shove, what is the point of a detective mystery where nothing is left to the imagination? Hardly a mystery, is it? But the hardboiled truth of the matter was that she regarded some things as private; personal; difficult. Better left unread.

It is fair to say that Heather 'Bam-Bam Shazam' Prendergast - as she was known to her legion of newfound fans - was not feeling her best after her miss-adventure the previous night. Never had she felt so demeaned. Ever. Of all the places to flaunt her stark bare-nakedness, The Sundown Strip ranked only marginally lower on the rungs of shamefaced humiliation than the House of Lourdes. In her lurid imaginings, every sleazebag on the planet had been ogling her puny body, clapping, whistling and knee-slapping in hoots of riotous laughter.

Hardly surprising, then, that she ignored the knock on her bedroom door. Wishing that she could hide forever and a day, she tugged the duvet over her head and played dead. She was firmly intentioned to stay in bed until Hell froze over . . . or lunchtime. She had not yet made up her mind. As the doorknocking continued - each knock louder than the last and quieter than the next - she poked her head above the covers and asked herself, is that dead spider dangling from the lampshade symbolic of my punctured pride or merely past its web-by date?

Rat-a-tat-tat . . . there it was again. Insistent. Persistent. 'Go away,' she shouted. 'I'm not here.'

'Please, Spriggsy. You're stressing my biometrics.'

Sebastian's whiny voice took Heather back to the night before the morning after when she discovered that there was a more sensitive side to young master Marrowboan's lack of personality than met the eye.

Following her de facto fiasco, not knowing where to turn or where to look or what to do, Heather threw on her dress and ran out into the cold night air flushed to the gills with humiliation. She was banging her head against a brick wall when she felt a hand upon her shoulder.

'Need some help with that wall, Spriggsy?' Sebastian asked, uncertain what to make of her display of nihilistic masochism.

'Leave me alone,' she wailed. 'I want to die.'

'Uncool,' Sebastian said. 'Come on, let's get you home.' With a maturity beyond his immature years, he helped her into the back of the Sebmobile and propped his backpack under her head as she curled up in floods of tears. 'Don't worry,' he said as he pulled out over the kerb, 'I've had a headlight fitted.' And with those reassuring words, he chauffeured her back to Trevelyan House. After making sure that she was safely in safety mode, he jerked off into the night with his headlight flickering like a candle of mercy.

With Sebastian's gallantry in mind, Heather dabbed her eyes and relented. 'Come in,' she called. 'The door is open.'

Sebastian poked his head into the room and asked, 'you decent? I got you some chocolate. You like chocolate, don't you?'

Heather blew her nose, sat up and fussed her nightdress over her knees. 'How sweet,' she said as he gifted her a large tub of chocolate spread. 'Did you bring a spoon?'

'You don't eat it, you wear it. Here . . .' Sebastian took a trowel from his hoodie pouch and hopped up on the bed. 'I'll smear it on and we can take turns licking it off.' A glint lit up his spectacles. 'It's adult edutainment.' When Heather clipped him round the ear and pointed to the door, he stuffed his hands in his pockets, cocked her a wink, said, 'configure you later,' and shuffled out smirking like a demented Smurf.

Soggy-eyed and saggy-tailed, Heather trudged to the Flipper Room to freshen up. She was soaping her bits and boobs in the shower when she spotted a *something* bolted to the ceiling. Fuming like a gate, she stood on a stool, ripped the Sebcam down, flung it in the toilet and grunted,

'I will have the oik's guts for garters - after lunch.'

After towel drying her flyaway hair, she dabbed a smidge of shadow on her eyelids and a twist of lipstick on her lips, donned her unfashionably comfortable new dress and ventured downstairs to the Chandelerium. Salivating at thoughts of hot buttered crumpets and chocolate spread, half way down, she bumped into Smothers wheezing up the other way.

'Oh, there you are, Miss Heather.' Smothers paused to mop his brow. 'Might I ask if you have seen Miss Katerina? Her bed has not been slept in and the current Missus Prendergast is faking one of her panic attacks.'

'Golly,' Heather said. 'I left her at The Sundown Strip.' Not a little concerned, she abandoned Smothers to his bends and continued on her way. She found Missus Beaten in the hall clearing up after Baskerville. 'Oh, Eggy, could you fix me a light lunch, please?' She gave her tummy a pat and smacked her lips. 'I've hardly eaten for days.'

Missuses Beaten got up off her knees, dunked her scrubbing brush in the sick bucket and peeled off her rubber gloves. 'Of course, dearie. Scrambled eggs on bread all right?'

'I'd rather not. Scrambles give me terrible indigestion. Think you could manage something a little more substantial? Preferably with no rice or fish.'

'Really now, you little monkey, what a question. Tell me what you fancy and I'll boil it up in a jiff.'

'I could kill for a ham omelette and baked beans,' Heather said with a glutinous drool.

'Not sure I've got the recipe for ham. And beans take an age to bake. Tell you what, there's some carp kedgeree left over from breakfast. I'll boil it up with a bit of cabbage and . . .'

'Isn't that made with rice?'

'Only a pinch.'

'If you don't mind, I'll give it a miss. How about bangers and mash?'

'Mashed rice?'

'Mashed potatoes.'

'I'll see if I've got any left. It's Miss Katerina, you see. She's such little greedy-guts. Demands chips with everything. Bless. I know, why don't I boil you up some left-over risotto?'

'Rice risotto'

'No, carp.'

'But made with rice.'

'Just a little.'

'Tell you what - you used to make the best steak and kidney pudding in South Kensington. Makes my mouth water just to think about it. Any chance of some yummy steak and kiddley pud with lashings of your special lumpy gravy?'

'What a memory you've got, Miss Heather. I only wish I still knew how to make it. It's been an age. I know, do you like Paella?'

'Made with rice?'

'Now there's a thought. Or how about something continental like a nice Goldfish Biryani or a Carp Bhatt.'

'By continental, I presume you mean the Indian subcontinent? If you don't mind, Eggy, I'd rather have something more traditional.'

'Jambalaya? Gumbo? Sushi?'

'You know, now I come to think, scrambled eggs on bread sounds yummy,' Heather told her and, masking her famishment behind a glassy smile, proceeded to the Chandelerium.

Sir Freddie looked up from the Gambler's Gazette as Heather walked through the door. He rested his cigar in an overflowing ashtray, straightened his dickey bow, took off his monocle and scowled. 'Get your clothes from a charity shop, young lady? I don't know . . .' he shook his head as if to suggest that no matter what his daughter did, she would never measure up to his malign standards. 'You should follow Katerina's example,' he told her, 'and dress with more panache.'

At mention of Katerina, a simmering volcano of blubber on the love-settee erupted in tears. 'Mon pauvre, pauvre bébé,' Fifi wailed. 'She has had the accident, I know it.' She made a theatrical show of dabbing her eyes with a frill of her passion pink negligee.

'See what you've done?' Sir Freddie shot Heather the frostiest of glares. 'You have upset your stepmother.'

'Me?' Heather gasped, all but speechless for words.

'I leave you in charge of your stepsister for a day and you ruddy-well mislay her. She is just an innocent child, Helen. Easily misled.'

'Innocent?' Not for the want of trying, Heather could hardly believe her ears. 'And for the last time, you old fool, my name is Heather.'

'How dare you bandy words with me, young lady.' Beside himself with apoplexy, Sir Freddie fumed, 'I will have you know that I knew your name before you were even born.'

'She is l'enfant de sa mère horrible,' Fifi sobbed. 'She has led ma chère petite astray. Sacré blue, what is to become of me?' She clapped a hand to her brow and feigned the bargain-basement of all swoons.

'Want me to ask Smothers to bring you some recreational medication?' Heather asked with an expression of disingenuous concern. 'Or maybe daddy can make you better by tickling you with a feather duster if you pull down his panties and slap his botty hard enough.'

A prickly silence fell. Fifi cast a nervous glance at Sir

Freddie, who avoided Heather's eyes with the guilty skulk of a child caught rummaging through his mother's naughty knicker drawer. 'Now, now, Heather,' he said. 'Let us not be hasty.'

'Helen,' Heather screamed. 'Helen, Hel . . . oh.' She bit her lip. 'Golly, you remembered.'

Sir Freddie shunted the stuffed ptarmigan aside to make room on the Formica table for a decanter of his favourite Old Grouch whisky. He filled his tumbler the brim, downed it in one gutshivering gulp and topped it up again 'What say you we forget about matters that are none of your concern, eh, my dear?' he said. 'As I recall, we have a wager. How is the investigation progressing?'

Heather's reply was pre-empted by the creak of the door as Missus Beaten bustled in carrying a plate of mangled eggs on bread. 'Here you are, dearie.' She moved the ptarmigan back to its rightful place in a hopfest of disgruntled fleas, posited the scramblage in front of Heather, said, 'bless,' gave Heather's cheek a stinging fingerpinch and bustled out.

Despite a churning stomach, a combination of malnourishment and hunger pangs got the better of her and Heather was about to tuck in when a flabby hand whipped her plate away.

'Ne rien perdre.' Fifi licked her lips, scooped the *uneatable* mess into her slavering maw, sat back, belched and lapsed into a snore.

'Hope she enjoyed my lunch,' Heather said with a malicious smirk. 'She'll be living on bread and water soon. You see, I know who the kidnapped poppet is and who is holding her hostage. As soon as I find out where she is, it will be game over.'

Sir Freddie took off his monocle and stared out of the window. He was about to renege on the deal when the door flew open and Katerina blew in. She tossed her baseball cap on a chair, hitched up her tights, slumped down on a sofa, kicked off her Jimmy Choos and announced, 'so the deal is, I got us a six month residency.' Hardly able to contain her thrall, she gushed, 'dope, or what?'

Heather raised both eyebrows and shook her head. 'I don't think so,' said she.

'Awe, come on, sis. This could be our big break. I can see it now.' Katerina sketched a billboard in the air. 'Sexy Salome and Cute Calypso, the hot chick and the naked dick. We'll pack `em in.' She pulled a contract out of her cleavage and waved it in Heather's face. 'We get five hundred a show, double bubble at weekends and commission on all the Albanian champagne we can unload on dozy punters.' She licked her lips and twinkled an eye. 'After the show, we get to help ourselves to any costumes we fancy to play the field. I dolled up as Ivanka Trump last night, charged ten bucks a snog and raked in almost five grand. Woke up with a splitting headache . . . and a dreamy eighteenth birthday present.' She clapped her hands and squealed. 'I can leave school and you can quit your crappy job. Las Vegas, here we come.'

'That's my girl.' Sir Freddie raised his glass. 'Following in your mother's footsteps, what?' He downed his snifter in one go and dabbed his lips with his top pocket handkerchief. 'Oh,' he said by way of an afterthought, 'while you are in Las Vegas, could you check if your mother's divorce has been finalised yet? It is taking an age.'

As one, Heather and Katerina stared at Sir Freddie. As one, their jaws dropped. As one, they looked at one another. As one, they mouthed, 'yet?'

xxxii

'Who blabbed?' HostageKaty waved a copy of the Pest Control Times in Groaty McTavish's face. 'Look – says here, someone's blown the whistle to the Health and Safety. Bet it was that Italian fella from the pizza joint.' She narrowed her eyes to venomous slits. 'Luigi's been angling for a discount since day one. Know what he done to my head rat when I told him to take a running jump? Ratatouille, that's what. With Dolcelatte. Dolcelatte, would you believe? What kind of cheese is that? Poor little mite. Frightened the life out of him, it did.' She fought back a tear, unrummaged a grubby hanky from her satchel, dabbed her eyes, blew her nose and put on a brave face. 'Now I'll have to train up a new one, unless you want the job, mug face - the Nitty Numpty of Bleedin` Nora or whatever you call yesself.'

'The Dark Knight of The Necronomicon, you little turd,' the man known for no good reason as the Dark Knight of The Necronomicon growled as he retrieved the newspaper from the waste-newspaper bin and turned to the classified advertisements section. To be honest - which was not much in his nature - he was fed up to the back cavities with HostageKaty's extracurricular activities. Although no slavedriver – perish the thought – to his way of thinking, being held hostage should be a full time occupation. For that reason and for that reason alone, he determined that when the time came he would rule the world with a rod of iron, no longer a spineless rule taker but a ruthless dictator. Which is not to say that he would not be beneficent to supplicants who grovelled at his feet, kissed his pinky, praised his devilish good looks, sent him pure sweet love on the wings of a snow white dove - that kind of thing. Nevertheless, he vowed that his first proclamation upon assuming omnipotence would be that a certain teeny pigtailed terror be thrown to the Presidential crocodiles. On second thoughts, maybe not. Even a crocodile deserves a fighting chance.

'Interesting. Very interesting,' Professor Harty said to himself as he ran an eye over the classified advertisements. 'Pah, I see that Sir Freddie has taken the bait.' He read out loud . . . 'I will leave payment in a place of your choosing. pp Sir Freddie.' He turned to McTavish with a crooked sneer. 'There you are, my aiding abettor. My adversary is putty in my hands.'

'What does subject tae contract mean?' McTavish pointed to the small print. 'Says there he'll pay ten percent four weeks after we release the bairn and the balance in monthly instalments - subject tae contract.' He shook his ginger head. 'Ye ken, yon wee lassie will nae leave unless she gets her cut first. Says she'd rather poke yaer eyes oot with a sharp stick.' He nodded at HostageKaty who was idly crayoning a doodle of a matchstick-boy in a wizard's hat with blood gushing from his shorts.

'Hold your tongue, you Highland blasphemer,'

Professor Harty thundered. 'The misbegotten spawn of Satan will do as I say . . . or else.'

'Or else what?' McTavish asked, genuinely interested.

'I will rip off my pinafore and go on strike.' The Professor arched his back and crossed his arms with a defiant snarl upon his lips. 'Let us see how our fiendish little mistle-thrush copes without clean spoons. She will soon do my bidding.'

'Ye'll have tae do better than that, Chief. The wee lassie gan spoons coming oot of her ears.'

Professor Harty flung out his arms, threw back his head and let loose a spine-curdling cackle. 'Alright then, forks. Knives. Broth ladles. What difference does it make? The Happy Thistle will be subsumed in filthy cutlery in no time.'

'Here, you listening, dickhead?' HostageKaty yelled across the room. 'I said, I've a good mind to torch that crappy pasta joint and snaffle the pizza chef for our takeaway. Make him an offer he'd be a numpty to refuse. That'll teach Luigi to keep his big mouth shut.'

Unable to cope with HostageKaty's mindless banter a moment longer, Professor Harty withdrew to his quarters and slumped down on a Gothic beanbag. He had reached an impossible impasse. On the one hand, Sir Freddie Prendergast had agreed to pay a handsome ransom for his accursed stepdaughter, mad fool that he was. But on the other, it seemed that he was not prepared to part with a bagged bean until the accursed wretch was released alive and no doubt kicking. Worse still, he was offering to pay in instalments. Instalments, for Diabolis' sake. What use was that? Professor Harty needed his ColdFusion centrifuges up and running within a week, not at monthly intervals. Even he, the greatest genius who may ever have lived, could not ionise atoms one at a time, cold fusion or no cold fusion.

What made the Professor's icy blood run hot was the implication that Sir Freddie impugned his integrity. Was the simpleton not aware that the name Harty was synonymous with probity in all the best circles? Or was it synonymous with depravity? Either word would suffice he supposed; in his book they were one and the same. But the fact was, he was caught in a devil's fork. He would not receive a brass farthing until HostageKaty was released but he could not release her until he had been paid in full; she had made it a condition of her incarceration that she was no way - *no way* - prepared to set a sandalled foot beyond her new fiefdom until her share of the ransom was safely lodged in her offshore piggy bank.

And that was when a devious brainworm burrowed its way into Professor Harty's bulbous cranium. There were three players in this game of chance, were there not? For in addition to him and the foulmouthed stepdaughter of a fabulously wealthy lizard, it struck him that he should also factor Solly Proust into the pic n` mix.

It only took an elementary leap of genius for the

Obelory Obganiator of Oblectation to reason that if Solly Proust could be persuaded to trade HostageKaty for the centrifuges, the shady loan shark could then sell her to Sir Freddie by means of a multimillion pound payday loan. And of course, Proust could charge an extortionate rate of interest. He was, after all, in business to make obscene profits on his nefarious activities. And the Proust Mob had the means to enforce the bargain. Should Sir Freddie renege on the deal, Blojob would bury his metal canines into Sir Freddie's throat and rip out his oesophagus.

Inspired by his inspired stroke of quadrilateral thinking, Professor Harty reached for his cellular phone and dialled the magic number. Making sure to muffle his voice, he whispered a throaty, 'Popweasel, it is I.'

'Who?'

'Who do you think, dolt?'

'Kylie Minogue? I should be so lucky.'

'Do not bandy pop songs with me, Proust. I am The Man Who Shall Not Speak His Name.'

'Hello, Murray. Got my cash?'

'That is why I am breaking my sworn silence to communicate with you.'

'Yes or no.'

'It is not as straightforward as you think.'

'Sure it is, Harty. Yes or no.'

'Pay attention. I have a proposition for you and your siblings. A means whereby you can multiply the return on a modest investment manyfold and . . .'

'So it's a no. Bell me back when you're flush.'

'Hear me out, fool. I have a valuable property on my hands and am prepared to trade her for my ColdFusion centrifuges and Hadronette Collider. Moreover, I can introduce you to a willing buyer prepared to pay a handsome price for her release.'

'Her?'

'I said it, not her, cloth-ears.'

'No you didn't. You said her.'

'A slip of the tongue.'

'So, if you got such a stonking deal lined up, why do you need me?'

'The fabulously wealthy individual in question wishes to pay in instalments and I am not licensed by the Financial Regulatory Authority to offer credit terms.'

'I'll have a word with Priscilla and get back to you. What's your number?'

'Pah. Do you think that I was born yesterday, you imbecile? No one on the face of this or any other planet is privy to my confidential cellular phone number. Not even the devil himself.'

'No probs, it's come up on the screen. Leave it with me and I'll get back to you. Give my best to the lizards and keep taking the med,' Solly said and rang off.

Cackling to himself, Professor Harty powered down his cellphone supremely confident that Popweasel would call back in short order. After all, was Solly Proust's middle name not Greed? All that remained was the trivial matter of forcibly persuading HostageKaty that it was in her best interests to cooperate.

What could possibly go wrong?

xxxiii

Heather Prendergast was taking the afternoon air when she came across Katerina tending the psilocybin in her herb garden. Deeming this to be as opportune a moment as any, she took her to one side and had a quiet word in her ear. 'Bratty,' she said quietly, 'did you know that your mother was still married to your father?'

'I'd hardly called them married, sis,' said Katerina as she packed her fork and trowel into her Louis Vuitton gardening bag. 'Let's face it, dad's in Alcatraz.'

'That's not the point.'

'It is too. I mean, how can he bonk mum if he's banged up?'

'There is more to wedlock than exercising one's conjugal rights, you know,' Heather pointed out.

'Really? That is *so* gross.' Katerina could hardly abject her revulsion. 'Something ought to be done about it.'

'The point is, if your parents aren't officially divorced, legally speaking they must still be married.'

'Yeah, well. Suppose so. Sort of. But only a bit.'

'Bratty, it doesn't work like that. You're married or you're not. There's no in between. It's like pregnancy. It is biologically impossible to get a bit pregnant.'

'Jeez, you are *so* dumb, sis,' Katerina folded her arms and stuck her nose chain in the air. 'Course you can,' she said. 'Happens all the time.'

Heather shook her head and tut-tut-tutted. 'Hate to tell you, Bratty, but you could not be more wrong. It's strictly one or the other.'

'For real?' Katerina's eyes opened wide and her face turned a pasty shade of pale. She grabbed her carrybag, gave Heather a panicky look and said, 'look, I got to log onto Tinder and ping a few texts. I may be all day.' Clutching her stomach, she ran to her room to burn some cellular rubber.

'Must be something in the rice,' Heather muttered as she wandered back to the house to freshen up. If truth be told, she was feeling a good deal better, in no small part because if Katerina's face was anything to go by, her *unspeakable* stepsister was feeling a good deal worse.

She was about to flop down on the bed for a quick powernap when a *something* caught her eye. Most odd, she thought. Most odd indeed. She was absolutely, utterly, positively, possibly sure that she had closed the wardrobe door before going out. But unless her eyes deceived her – unlikely, although not beyond the bounds of astigmatism - it was now mostly ajar. Summoning all her reserves of nerve, she took a wary peek inside and to her puzzlement and no little surprise saw that her old school gymslip was nowhere to be seen. At first she assumed that Eggy must have taken it to wash but a niggling doubt took hold when she found a stray hair on her nightdress. Determined to get to the nub of *The Curious Case of the Fibrous Follicle*, she unshoulderbagged her most magnifying glass and donned an everyday pair of rubber-glovewear. After forensically examining the foreign fibre with an expert trainee eye, she deduced that it was brown, lank and *unspeakably* greasy. And that meant it could not possibly belong to Missus Beaten. What was left of Eggy's hair was as white as driven rice. Upon closer inspection, she realised that it was . . . ughhh – pubic . . . and screwed up her face as far as it would go.

As Heather was polythene-bagging the evidence, she noticed indentations on the duvet as if a *someone* had been trampolining on her bed. Upon microscopical examination, she surmised that in all probability the dents had been made by a man or perhaps a woman of average weight and height, assuming the average woman to be of the same probable weight and height as the average man she had in mind. And what was that faint smell on the pillow, she wondered? Eau de Cologne? Aftershave? Skunk? Suspicious that a *someone* or some *someones* had been in her bedroom, the clincher came when she spotted that her underwear and makeup were strewn all over the floor. Well, it went without saying that she was furious beyond all bounds. Determined to give the intruder an unedifying piece of her mind, she stormed downstairs to the servant's quarters where she found Missus Beaten scrubbing Baskerville vomit off the boot-scrape. 'Eggy,' she demanded. 'Have you seen any strange people in the house lately?'

'What a question, dearie. Of course.' Missus Beaten mopped her brow with the vomit-scourer, licked her fingers and ticked them one by one. 'Well, apart from Mister Smothers, there's Sir Freddie and that foreign lady he plays dress-up with. Bless,' she said with a sloppy smile. 'My, my, people don't come any stranger than her. Oh, not forgetting Miss Katerina, of course. What a little scamp.'

'But no strange men?'

'Well, there's young Master Marrowboan, but I would hardly call him a man. Talking of which, are these your undies?' Missus Beaten took a pair of sorrowful panties from her pinafore pouch and dangled them in front of Heather's boggling eyes. 'Young Master Marrowboan left them in the bathroom, bless his little cotton socks.'

'I swear to God that I have never seen those flannelette knickers before in my life,' Heather fibbed, meaning that she never wanted to see the *unwearable* things again in this or any other life. Regretting that her college course hadn't included a module on how to throttle a geek, she set off in search of Sebastian. She whithered upstairs, downstairs and in her metaphorical lady's chamber determined to take him by the left leg and throw him down the stairs. As not taught in Elementary Deduction class, she left the most obvious place to last and stomped across the lawn to his outside laboratory. She barged in, yelled, 'Sebastian Marrowboan, we need a word. Now,' and grabbed him by the ankles as he tried to crawl under the futon.

As she loomed over him clenching and unclenching her fists, Sebastian whimpered, 'I had a memory leak and suffered an influencer fragmentation so used my modifier key to hack into your home domain. Hope you don't mind, but I went phishing in your drawers and did some character encoding. You won't tell Katerina, will you? If she finds out, she'll terminate my recursive functions.'

'Take off my gymslip and burn it this minute, you revolting specimen.' Heather demanded. 'If you don't, I will throw it on a bonfire with you in it. I'll say it was an accident.' She ground the words through gritted teeth. 'And before you say anything, I'm allowed to bend the truth. I'm a police officer.'

As Heather was about to strangle Sebastian one breath at a time, the door burst open and Katerina swished in. 'False alarm,' she said with a look of infinite relief. 'Constipation.' She took off her designer sunglasses and gave Sebastian a risible look. 'Why are you wearing sis's smeggy old gymslip? You look ridiculous. If you said you were a deviant, I'd have lent you mine.'

'Have I died and gone to Hell?' Heather asked herself out loud. 'Sebastian has turned into Ru Paul, Bratty is acting like a rabbit on pheromones, I'm risking my career trying to solve an unsolvable kidnapping case and now I'm told that my stepmother is a bigamist.'

'Only slightly.' Katerina said. 'So does this mean we're

not proper stepsisters anymore?'

'You know, I hadn't thought of that.' Heather clapped her hands and twizzled a twirl. 'Isn't it a wonderful day?'

Leaving the girls to revise their filial relationship, Sebastian slouched off to change into his least grubby combat trousers and hoodie. He rejoined them with a determined look on his pimply face. 'Let's just bookmark this page and not overclock our multiprocesses, eh?' he said as he booted up his computer with a mallet. 'Chocks away, sleuth babes. Retrieve data, reformat and scroll on.'

'He means, let's work out where we go from here, sis,' Katerina interpolated for Heather's prehensile apperception.

Heckles on the rise, Heather raised a don't-go-there finger. 'Please Bratty, you are no longer entitled to call me sis,' she cautioned. 'And I feel it only fair to warn you that as soon as I get back to The Yard, I intend to report your mother's bigamous behaviour to the Commissioner.'

'Yeah, you do that.' Katerina lolled back on the futon, flicked a flop of fringe out of her eyes and fiddled with her nose-piercing. 'If you try to stitch him up, my stepdad will have a few words in a few ears and you'll like as not be looking for a new job before you put the phone down. Anyway, for your information, he's already lodged a bribe with the relevant authorities to have the paperwork backdated. It cost him an arm and a leg, but if anyone bothers to check, the official records will show that my real dad divorced my mum two days before he married her.' Having stated her case, she turned the screw with, 'anyway. if I was in your revolting shoes, I'd be more concerned with trying to win my bet with Sir Freddie . . . sis.'

Trying not to show how hurt she was by Katerina's unwarranted slur on her fab new patent-leather lump-heeled pumps, Heather swallowed her pride and recapped for everybody's benefit, but largely her own. 'So we now know that the hostage is the daughter of two notorious gangland mobsters, Scarface and Dolores Clark. If my hunch is right, she is being held against her will by Professor Murray Harty, the unhinged Controlling Brain of the Criminal Underworld.' It was all that she could do not to shudder as Professor Harty's name soiled her lips. 'The problem is, we don't know where she's being held.' In search of inspiration, she tapped her chin with a relevant fingernail. 'If only we had something with her scent on it, like a handkerchief or a lock of hair.' She clicked her fingers as a lightbulb dithered to life somewhere in her cranial extremes. 'Bratty, you don't happen to remember what was in the envelope with Harty's last ransom note, do you?'

'Wouldn't have been a lock of KickarseKaty's hair by any chance?' Katerina suggested with an expression of bored numbdom.

'Gadzooks . . .' Heather jumped to her feet ready to spring into action. 'All we need is a sniffer dog and we'll have as good as found her.' She scratched her head and stared into the infinite beyond. 'Any idea where we can get hold of a bloodhound?'

xxxiv

Dolores Clark kicked open the swing doors and stormed into The Happy Thistle. Singularly unimpressed with the Highlandish décor and bagpiped muzak, she expleted, 'what the effing-eff is this - a theme sewer?' Scowling like fussle, she took off her rat-fur jacket and ordered Naff to hang it on the ornamental antlers by the marinated saltweed bar. 'Watch the door,' she told him. 'If any customers want in, tell them to eff-off. We're not to be disturbed.' After ordering Brawns and Mussels to watch her back, she demanded McTavish's attention with a piercing two-fingered whistle. 'Table for three, Jock,' she said. 'I'm expecting company.'

With the deferentialest of smiles, McTavish showed her to his best table. He brushed the grime off the tartan tablecloth with his tam o' shanter, flicked the moss off a reproduction crofter's stool and stood back eagerly awaiting his first order of the day . . . of the week maybe. Actually, truth to tell, there was no maybe about it.

Dolores sat down, unfastened the top buckle of her blouse, itched an armpit, crossed her legs and picked up the handwritten menu. 'What the effing-eff is a Bannockbun when it's at home? Sounds foreign.' She tossed the menu aside and ordered a coffee. 'The proper powdered stuff, not that fancy imported muck. No sugar.'

'Sweet enough already, are ye, missy?' McTavish quipped as he reached into his sporran for his order pad and pen.

Mortally offended, Dolores turned to Brawns and said, 'wipe the smile off the joker's face.'

Brawns turned to Mussels and clicked his fingers. 'Wipe the smile off the juggler's face.'

Mussels found a dish cloth behind the bar, squirted it with washup liquid, held McTavish's head under the coldwater tap and scrubbed his mouth until his teeth chattered. 'The lady don't like sweetener, Jock,' he snarled, 'and don't you forget it.' Job done, he rinsed out the cloth, draped it over the side of the sink and sanitised his hands with dishinfectant.

Dolores sat back, crossed her lamp-tanned legs, muttered, 'what's keeping the slut?' and gave her counterfeit Rolex an impatient tap. Roughly translated, her body language read that she wanted to get the pow-wow of war done and dusted before the tartan décor made her lose the will to swear. 'The geezer who owns this dump must have effing bollocks for a brain,' she muttered as she looked around. 'Whose idea was it to meet here, anyway?'

'You said to find somewhere quiet and out of the way, boss.' Trapped like a rabbi in Dolores's lasered glare, Brawns fidgeted uneasily. 'Take it from me, joints don't come no quieter than this.'

Dolores narrowed her buckshot eyes. 'You're having a

laugh. It's next to the effing North Circular Road, for effing-eff's sake.' Ready to rumble, she brushed the cigar ash off her blouse, zippered up her mini skirt and straightened her fishnet stockings as a shocking pink stretch-limousine smoothed to the kerb outside and a shapely blond in a white fur coat minced out of the backseat cocktail bar.

When Priscilla's minder - a man-mountain of a growl in a loose-fitting suit and tight-fitting eyepatch - lumbered through the door, Mussels stuck up a thumb, said, 'hiya, Bloey, how's it hanging?' and cocked him a wink. 'How's the missus - still editing the Daily Mail, is she, or has she knocked it on the head and gone back to pole dancing?' Too busy to stand around chewing the flab, Blojob gnarled a cursory grunt before checking under the tables and poking his broken nose into every nook and corner before shouting, 'clear,' to indicate that the restaurant passed mustard.

Priscilla Proust breezed through the doors in a waft of rose petals with a hint of distilled juniper, closely followed by a stubbly man in a shabby double-breasted suit, pinstriped shirt, patent leather winklepicker shoes and a blueberry beret. She handed Naff her fur coat, said, 'don't I know you, big boy?' and looked him over like a leg of mutton. 'Oh yeah, you're that fella from the other night. All ding and no dong,' she said and zipped him a wink. When she saw Dolores glaring at her, she broke into a honeychew smile, blew her a raspberry kiss, hitched up her skirts and tottered over to join her. 'Don't get up, Dolly,' she said. 'I know it ain't easy at your age.'

'It's been a long time, Cilla,' Dolores growled.

'Not long enough,' Priscilla said as she sat down. She patted an impermanent wave back into her lacquered hair, took a gold cigarette case from her handbag, lent across the table and offered Dolores a Sobranie cigarette.

'Keep it, scrubber. I'll have a real smoke.' Dolores lit a panatela and the two molls murdered time by trading insults for old times' sake while they waited to be served.

Unused to multitasking, a flustered McTavish put his thoughts on hold, rooted through the kitchenware for his faithful mortar and pestle and set about powdering The Happy Thistle's last few coffee beans. Although elated to have customers, he was deeply troubled that they were blatantly disregarding the Nae Smoking signs. At a loss what to do, he intercommed HostageKaty. In the flicker of an och-aye, she slouched into the kitchen and stretched her arms in a humungous yawn. 'What's occurring, Groatface?' she asked. 'I was catching up on me beauty sleep.'

'We got customers,' McTavish said with a puff of Highland pride. 'But they're smoking in a public place. I dinnae ken what tae do.'

'Leave it to me, you big girl's blouse.' HostageKaty spat on her fingernails and buffed them on her slumberjacket. 'I'll shove the dogends up their arse.' She stood on tiptoe, peeked through the service hatch and gasped, 'strike a light, its mam.' The blood drained from her dimpled cheeks. 'That's Brawns and Mussels with her. Don't recognise the tall numpty with the girly earring and tattoos. He must be new.' She cast a murderous scowl at the tradesperson's entrance. 'I bet the Blabbermouth of Toytown or whatever he calls hisself has grassed me up. Where is he, anyway?'

'Gan for a wander. Said he had some existential thinking tae do. Something aboot lizards messaging him,' McTavish told her. 'So who's the braw lassie with the big yin?'

HostageKaty clambered onto a crofter's stool and sneaked another peek. 'Blimey, don't believe it. It's only Priscilla Proust, that's all. Mam's sworn enemy. The weedy one is her brother, Solly, the Proust Mob's bookkeeper, and the ugly one is Blojob, their minder.'

'Why's he called Blojob?' McTavish asked.

'Search me. Why you called Groaty?'

'Long story, lassie,' McTavish said with a faraway look in his eyes.

'Please yesself,' HostageKaty said with a hapless shrug. She shuttered the hatch, pressed a finger to her lips and lowered her voice. 'Something big is occurring, Groatface. Must be. Look, if they ask about me, just act normal and play dumb. If Farty Harty shows his ugly mug, tell him to make hisself scarce. Say if he don't keep his big mouth shut, I'll shut it for him.' She bared her fangs and whetted her lips with a snarl of the tongue.

With a contrived show of waiterly nonchalance, McTavish strapped a tartan apron over his kilt and delivered a piping hot beaker of McCoffee to Dolores's table. 'Yaer starter, missy.' He tipped his tam o'shanter and doffed his ginger forelock. 'And what'll it be for yoos?' he asked Priscilla. 'Care tae see the menu?'

'Don't bother. I'll just have a salad and a mineral water,' Priscilla said.

'A what, missy?' McTavish gave her a blank look. 'And a mineral what?'

'Forget it.' Priscilla shood McTavish away with a flip of the wrist. 'Looks like I'm on a diet.' Ignoring Dolores's barbed mutterances about spare tyres and girdles, she turned to Solly. 'Tell grandma why we wanted to meet on neutral territory.'

Solly Proust propped his beret on the back of his head, lent forward and lowered his voice. Unaware that McTavish was standing behind him straining both ears, he whispered, 'a little bird just told me he's got your daughter.'

Dolores stared at Solly. Hard. 'Got a death wish, has it, this little birdy?' she said. 'It better start squawking and start squawking fast if it don't want to spend the rest of its life as a feather duster.'

Caught in Dolores Clark's unblinking glare like a minnow snared in a mixed-metaphorical web, Solly cleared a rasp from his throat. 'Says he's willing to trade her for certain valuables I got in my possession,' he said with a simpering smile.

Dolores studied her chipped nails, frowned, took a nail file out of her patent-leatherette handbag, reached across the table and buried it in Solly's hand. 'Look, schmuck,' she growled over his howls. 'Just do the deal and charge my card. You can hack it online. So, that it – we done?'

As Dolores got up to leave, Priscilla grabbed her arm and tugged her back. 'Your plastic good for twenty mill, is it, gran? Don't think so,' she said with a toss of her platinum locks. 'See, that's our asking price.'

Dolores flabbered a gasp and turned to Brawns, 'that's well out of order. What do you think, Brawns?'

'Yeah, it's well outta order.' Brawns looked over a shoulder at his henchman. 'What you think, Mussels?'

Mussels scratched his head and mumbled, 'think?'

Dolores expleted a mouthful of deletives and rolled her eyes. 'Might as well talk to my effing hand,' she groaned. 'Best see what Scareface has to say.' Ignoring McTavish as if he was a piece of furniture - as coincidence would have it, his childhood ambition - she turned her back, autodialled a number and pressed her cellphone to a cauliflower ear. She nodded, nodded a few times more, put the call on hold, turned to Solly and asked, 'is the price negotiable?' When he shrugged, she returned to back-turned cellphone mode. 'You sure we can find that much cash at short notice, Fred?' she asked and raised a bristly

eyebrow. 'Yeah, yeah, I'll write it down so I don't forget.'
She pinned the phone to an ear with a bony shoulder and
clicked her fingers. 'Brawns – pen.'

Brawns snapped his fingers. 'Mussels - pen.'

Mussels caught McTavish's eye. 'Here, you in the
tartan skirt,' he snarled. 'Lend the lady your pen, please.
And jump to it.'

Dolores jotted a figure on a McNapkin and slid it
across the table. 'Our final offer,' she said. 'Take it or leave
it. And tell your feathered friend he's nuggets if he even
thinks about pecking a hair on my brat's leg.'

Priscilla read the napkin, laughed out loud, screwed
it into a ball and tossed it into the Happy McYucky Bin.
She said, 'I'll get back to you, Dolly, but don't hold your
breath. You ain't got much left.' Having instructed Blojob
to make sure that the street was clear of passerbyes with
prying eyes, she draped her mink coat over her shoulders
and sashayed out to the waiting limo.

Dolores Clark tossed a cigar butt on the table, told
McTavish, 'there's a tip, Jock,' put on her rat-fur jacket,
clicked her fingers at her entourage and swaggered out to
her waiting jag.

As soon as he was alone, McTavish retrieved the
McNapkin and delivered it to HostageKaty in the
kitchenary area. She took one look and burst into tears.
'Five hundred quid?' she blubbed. 'Is that all I'm worth?'

'There, there, lassie.' McTavish wrapped an arm around her quaking shoulders. He had never seen HostageKaty cry before. Indeed, the very concept defied credulity. All of a moment, she seemed a vulnerable wee bairn rather than a maniacal mistress of misanthropic monetary mayhem. 'It's nae but a wee bluff, lassie,' he said. 'Ye ken as well as me, Sir Freddie is ganna break the bank tae gan ye back.'

HostageKaty dabbed her eyes with the back of a hand and wiped her nose with the back of the other. 'Please, Uncle Groaty,' she said with a sniff and a snuffle. 'What's with all this Sir Freddie bollocks? My dad's called Fred. Just Fred, got it? Fred Clark.'

Cast into a dithering dichotomy of dialectical indeterminism, McTavish clapped a hand to his brow and staggered back into the turf burning stove. 'Hoots mon,' he gasped. 'Ye mean, yaer nae Sir Freddie Prendergast's stepbairn - Katy Clark?'

'Do us a favour. She's that snotty sixth form twat. Thinks she's Taylor Swift,' HostageKaty said with a derisory twitch of her button nose. And then, as a terrible truth dawned, she stared at McTavish, eyes opening ever wider to a soundtrack of clunking pennies. 'Uncle Groaty,' she said with a note of guarded dread in her voice. 'Mind if I ask you something?' As McTavish slumped down on a stool and buried his head in his sporran, she said, 'you in't gone and kidnapped the wrong Katy Clark by mistake, have you? Not even the Protester of Muppetville or whatever he calls hisself could be that much of a dickhead.' When McTavish avoided her eyes and broke into a gibbering sweat, she fiddled with a pigtail and stared unblinking at the bricked-up window. 'Love a duck, you have, in't you?' she groaned as the magnitude of the cockup sank in, settled and congealed like a curdle of rancid gloop.

Caught midway betwixt panic and blind panic, McTavish pinched himself and then pinched himself again. Bereft of sense or sensibility, he could only think that he had unwittingly stumbled into a parallax universe where everything was tiptopturvy or, as his favourite warder used to say, sporran aboot kilt. As he struggled to unmuddle his fuddle, his nightmare became worse by a factor of degrees when he heard the spit of spats shuffling down the corridor from the tradesperson's entrance.

A jitter of nerves, McTavish took a deep breath and whispered, 'let's just meck this our little secret, lassie, on a strictly need tae know basis.' He glanced at the door, gulped and mopped his brow. 'And teck it frae me - yon mad Professor strictly disnae need tae know.'

xxxv

'I was pulling your leg, Bratty. Couldn't you tell?'

'Yeah, right, sis. You had me in stiches.'

'But seriously, do you think Baskerville is up to it?'

'He's a bloodhound, isn't he? That's what he's designed for. Let's face it, he's rubbish at anything else.'

'Ah, but it's not as simple as that. You see, a dog reflects the family life. Think about it . . . whoever saw a frisky dog in a gloomy family or a sad dog in a happy one?'

'And your point is?'

'Well, you could say that Smothers and Missus Beaten are Baskerville's family. He might be confused.'

'Hmmm . . . see what you mean.'

'We'll just have to risk it. We have no time to lose There are heroisms all around us waiting to be done. I'll grab a quick shower while you get changed.'

'Don't you like my new shorts? They're Dolce and Grabita. Cost an arm and a leg.'

'For heaven's sake, Bratty, you can hardly go out in public wearing a designer thong. Can't you find something less conspicuous - a clown's outfit perhaps or a Teletubby costume?'

'Hark who's talking. You look like Emily Pankhurst in that dress. I'll never live it down if any of the bruvs in the Kensington Massive see us. They'll think I'm taking my gran for a night out at the Bingo. Time you learnt to dress to thrill, not chill.' Katerina looked at Heather from the corner of an eye, screwed up her nose piercing and shuddered. 'I know,' she said. 'Why don't I send Seb to Camden to score you some dope new drag with my stepdad's charge card?'

'If you must,' Heather agreed with a biddable sigh. The fact was that she thought her new dress stylish and a la mode, if not exactly a la this year's mode. If truth be told, she supposed that it was a little staid. Arcane some might say, though preferably not to her face. Too much embroidery on the bodice and the cuffs, possibly. And around the ankles. The hardboiled fact of the matter was that although perfect for lounging about, the skirt was so tight that it was all she could do to hobble to the loo, let alone sprint after a rampant bloodhound hotfoot on a scent. 'Very well,' she said reluctantly, minded that her twinset was at the cleaners, her jeans and jumper had gone walkabout and her Brownie uniform was marmaladed to shreds. For a moment she regretted having gifted her cutesy sailor suit to the sales assistant at Monica's Hippydashery to wear to a Gay Pride Eurovision song contest orgy. But only for a moment; the reality was that if she never saw the yucky thing again, it would be too soon. Her sailor suit, that is, not the Eurovision Song Contest. She wouldn't miss that for the world. La, la, la, la, la, la, la, dum-de-dum-de-dum, ding-a-ling-a-ling, muppet on a string. She licked her lips . . . fantabulosa. Back on point, she said, 'tell Seb to make sure he buys me something fashionable. Now, synchronise watches. We'll meet in the Bumbershoot Gallery at three.'

After a trip to the Flipper Room for an invigorating powersplash, Heather returned to her bedroom squeaky clean and towel-wrapped. Taking care to hold her nose at arms' length, she picked up Katerina's jodhpurs betwixt finger and thumb and tossed them out of the window . . . out of sight and out of mind. Having sprayed the chair with seat-freshener, she sat down with her notepad on a knee and reached for her trusty pencil.

The Curious Case of The Katenapped Girl. Chapter Eight.

I have enlisted a crack sniffer dog team to assist me in a very daring rescue mission. I am afraid that I cannot elaborate as I am under strict instructions to keep operational matters strictly under wraps. Should word leak out that Professor Murray Harty is up to his old tricks again, there might be panic in the streets. The government might even fall. Suffice it to say that the case is progressing apace. I have little doubt that the end is very nigh.

Exhausted after baring her soul, Heather flopped down on the bed to grab a quick powernap. As her eyelids drooped, she felt a tingle spinnaker up her spine at the prospect of an abundance of *groovissima* new casualwear. What would Sebastian choose, she wondered – a chic pantsuit, a demure floral print dress, a floaty lowcut off-the-shoulder frock or a pair of hip designer jeans and a jazzy silk blouse? Maybe all of the above, she hoped with a sartorial smack of the lips.

Hardly able to precipitate her anticipation, Heather drifted into cottonwool dreams of raindrops on roses and whiskers on kittens, bright copper kettles and warm woollen mittens, girls in white dresses with blue satin sashes, lashings of mascara on her brows and eyelashes, brown paper packages tied up with string and all sorts of bodaciously eyepopping lipsmacking kneetrembling headturning manbaiting things. She was roused from her slumbers by a loud knock on the door. 'Come,' she called and jumped out of bed, hardly able to sublimate her thrall.

Sebastian Marrowboan slouched into the room weighed down with carrier bags. 'The e-mall server told me these are the latest software revisions,' he told her. 'Seems everyone is uploading them.' He tossed the bags on the bed, stuffed his hands in his pockets and shuffled out.

Tingling from tip to toe, Heather unwrapped a spuriosity of needless tissue-paper, polythene species exterminants, polystyrene planetary contaminants and plasticated landfill clutterants until she reached the kernel of the package. Shocked, she threw up her hands in what she was later to describe as 'horror.' After a moment to come to her senses and another to gnash her teeth, she strode to the door and yelled, 'Sebastian Marrowboan. Come here. Now. We need a word,' at the top of her voice.

Sebastian trudged up the stairs with an expression of bemusement on his pimply face. 'What's wrong, Spriggsy?' he asked. 'Don't they fit?'

Incandescent beyond rage, Heather snaked her eyes and said, 'if you think I would be seen dead in a satin bustier, a leather choker, suspenders, fishnet stockings and those ghastly high heels, you must be out of your mind.' Taking care not to burst a blood vessel, she wrapped her hands around Sebastian's neck, dug her thumbs into his Adam's apple and squeezed and squeezed and squeezed until his face turned a breathless shade of purple. Ignoring his inane grin, she hissed, 'if you want to leave here with all your bodily parts intact, tell Missus Beaten to find me something respectable to wear. And no gymslips, Girl Guide uniforms or jodhpurs. Remember, you are drinking at the last chance saloon.' Having laid down the law, she stuffed the *unspeakable* fetish wear into a carrier bag, thrust it in Sebastian's arms, marched him to the door by the scruff of the neck and helped him down the stairs with a well-aimed boot to the butt.

Wondering why things that she used to take for granted such as popping out for a casual manhunt should have assumed the convolutions of a four-dimensional Rubik's cube, Heather joined Katerina and Sebastian in the Bumbershoot Gallery shortly after the appointed hour; Aunt Elizabeth had taught her that it is a girl's prerogative - nay, her solemn duty - to always be late for a date. Indeed, one of her *stupefyingly* wealthy, *stunningly* attractive and *dippily* dizzy aunt's oft-repeated adages was that time may wait for no man, but all men will wait for a woman . . . if they know what's good for them.

It must be said that Heather had mixed feelings about Missus Beaten's idea of respectable. On the one hand, she would be the first to accept that Katerina's Addam's Family fancy dress bridesmaid's frock was demure after an adolescent fashion. But on the other hand, she thought it a mite incongruous with her stab vest. But stoic as ever, she reminded herself that when nudge comes to shove, borrowers can't be choosers. The fact was that Missus Beaten was adamant that it was the only dress that she could find in Heather's size that would marry up to the little madam's demanding standards. Bless.

And so, not for the first time, Heather swallowed her misgivings. Admittedly, she looked like a refugee from a vampire wedding, but what firmed her resolve was the knowledge that Prendergast of The Yard was, or would one day be, a mistress of disguise - although quite where a black calf-length satin bridesmaid dress with Goth embellishments ranked in the canon of subterfugery was a moot point. Still, as Aunt Elizabeth would say, needs be as needs must in the line of duty, net petticoats and diamanté tiaras notwithstanding.

Having coaxed Baskerville off Smothers' bed with a juicy doggy-tempt, Heather took her courage in both hands and attached a sturdy chain to his collar. She handed the leash to Katerina, hitched up her petticoats, squatted down and waved the lock of Kickarse Katy's hair under his muzzle. When he reacted with nary a flicker of a twitch, she shrugged and - taking care not to dislodge her tiara - shook her head. 'He's half asleep,' she told Katerina, stating the oblivious. 'It's all he can do to keep his eyes open.'

'Nothing a few party drugs can't sort.' Katerina rooted through her makeup holdall for her groove-all-night pills. When Baskerville next yawned, she popped a handful of energy accelerants into his mouth and stood back waiting for the show to kick off.

The effect was instantaneous. Swishing his tail and yelping like a puppy, Baskerville sat on his haunches, pricked up his floppy ears and thrust his muzzle between Heather's legs. When Katerina tried to drag him away, he howled, turned tail and galumphed out of the front door hauling her behind him like a kitemark in a force-nine gale.

'Grab this before I ladder my stockings.' Katerina thrust Baskerville's leash into Heather's hand. She stumbled to a halt, caught her breath, uncrinkled her coatigan, straightened her skirtigan and propped her designer sunglasses on her pixie-cut, bimbo stylee. 'Knew I shouldn't have worn these six-inch heels,' she muttered. Drastic times calling for drastic measures, she swallowed her pride, ordered Sebastian to take off his sandals, swapped them for her ankle boots and toddled off to join the hunt.

'He's picked up a scent,' Heather shouted as she

struggled to hang onto Baskerville's leash. 'Cripes,' she screamed as the bloodhound leapt over a fence, dragging her behind him. He yapped, barked, howled, disappeared into a hedge and reappeared a few moments later with a dead rat the size of a beaver in his droopy jaw. Panting like a puffadder, he dropped it at Heather's feet and looked up at her expecting a pat on the head.

Heather raised a finger and waved the lock of Kickarse Katy's hair under his muzzle. 'Kidnapped girl,' she said. 'Go find. No fetch rat.'

'Why are you talking to Baskerville like that, sis?' Katerina asked.

'Please, Bratty, kindly don't interfere. I work with sniffer dogs at The Yard all the time,' Heather told her, choosing not to say that her canine duties amounted to slopping canteen leftovers into designated doggy feed bins.

Hardly had Heather finished massaging her credentials than the bloodhound hared off again. He scrabbled through a hedge into a neighbouring garden, quarried a pit in the bowling-green lawn, buried the rat, dug up the vegetable patch, cocked a hind leg and watered the marrows then cocked the other and hosed the asparagus. After ripping the sun lounger into a tangle of aluminium and canvass, he sniffed around, pricked up his ears and shot through the gate into the main road howling like his legendary namesake.

Puffing and panting to keep up insofar as her petticoats allowed, Heather sprinted after him with Katerina hot on her heels. 'Look out,' she screamed as an articulated truck came speeding down the road towards them. As they stood stock-still rooted to the spot like helpless carrots, Baskerville galumphed into the road, sat down in the truck's path, bared his fang and let loose a bloodcurdling howl. Frightened out of his wits, the driver slammed on the brakes, swerved and jack-knifed into a supermarket.

'No,' Heather yelled as Baskerville bounded through the shattered shutters and made a bee-line for the butchery counter. Unable to hold on any longer, she let go of the leash as he leapt into the meat display snarling, growling, ripping, shredding, munching, crunching, pawing and gnawing like a hound possessed.

'Oh-oh, he's off again. Come on, sis.' Katerina grabbed Heather's hand and dragged her after the rampant hound, now bloated by a side of beef, a bellyful of pork-bellies and several legs of lamb. 'Oh my God, that is, like, totally gross.' Katerina hid her eyes as Baskerville sniffed the fruit and veg display outside a greengrocer's shop and vomited all over the strawberries.

When the irate shopkeeper raced out of the shop brandishing a broom like a pikestaff, Baskerville sank to his haunches, growled, and flew at the man. Having seen shopman off with a nip and a yap, he watered the apples, fertilised the pears and bounded down the road in the direction of Trevelyan House. Glad to be home, he unbolted the back gate with his tooth and hightailed it into the garden.

Heather and Katerina followed at a distance. When they reached the gate, Heather rested a hand on her stepsister's arm and pointed to a mound of earth on the far side of the lawn, barely a bone's throw from Sebastian's shed. 'Look, Baskerville has dug something up. Golly, I don't believe it. It's a decomposed body,' she gasped, unable or unwilling to believe her eyes. 'Wait here, Bratty. Leave this to a professional.' She was about to move into panic mode when Baskerville came bounding across the lawn clutching a *something* in his mouth.

Heather recoiled as she realised that the hound from Hades had unearthed a leg and, yes . . . an arm. The blood drained from her freckled cheeks as she saw that the hands and feet were missing. 'Look away, Bratty,' she urged. 'Harty wasn't bluffing. He's murdered the poor little mite, dismembered her body and buried her remains in daddy's garden. He's not just evil, he is a sadistic monster.' She clutched her hands to her stab vest, closed her eyes and broke into a fit of uncontrollable shivers.

'Sis . . .' Katerina shook Heather's arm. 'You better take a look.'

'I can't.' Heather covered her eyes with the tiara. 'It's too awful.'

'Yeah, it's, like, totally gross,' Katerina said. 'I mean, who shops at Dorothy Perkins these days? Doesn't bear

thinking about. Their fashions are years behind the times.'
She wrestled a pair of waterclogged jeans and a sodden
jumper from Baskerville's growly maw. 'The stupid mutt
just dug up your missing clothes.'

Nae McTavish worth his sporran would let a wee bairn be took alive.

xxxvi

The Unprincipled Possessor of Imperspicacity, as Professor Harty was given to understand that he was known to his scaly tormentors, squatted on the throne of the ensuite poo-chamber abutting his fourposter bedroom. To pass the time of day while passing stools, he jotted an idle thought on a sheet of toilet paper with a poostick; $52-x+x-5x+2+3x+8x2-40 \setminus frac\{5\}\{2x\}+ \setminus frac\{x+2\}+ \setminus frac\{3x+8\} \{x^2=02-x5+x+2x-5+ x2-43x+8=0$. All well and good, he thought, but would it not be more elegant to say $2x2 + 5x + 3 = 0$ and so $x = -3/2$?

'Pah, enough of such child's play,' he grunted. Having put the toilet paper to more pertinent use, he flushed the throne, laced up his undergarments, buttoned up his breeches and knotted his belt. With half an eye on the mirror and the other half elsewhere, he ran his hands under the hot tap and whistled *Rule Satania* as his gruesomely departed nanny instructed him so to do before her premature demise . . . another fit of temper, another life, or so it seemed. Ablutioned to his eminent satisfaction, he wandered back to the outer sanctum - as he wittily referred to his bedchamber – to simmer and to brood. He was fed up to his missing molars with vacillations, aberrations, obstructions, adjournments, postponements and similar spurious tautologies.

Harty had grown ever more frustrated, infuriated and irritated as the days ground by, one to the next, the next to another, each a mirror image of the last. Warthog days, he called them. Why, he asked himself, did Groaty McTavish and the pigtailed brat retreat into a conspiratorial huddle whenever and wherever and however he fell upon them, be it by accident or design? It was almost as if they owned the franchise to an exclusive secret and did not wish him to partake. He worried that unless he nipped their unsociable behaviour in the bud, it might trigger another attack of what Nurse used to call his persecution complex.

Professor Harty had long suspected that at the root of his paranoia lay a fear that that he never quite knew who was plotting against him or quite why. As he felt the foundations of his certitude crumble like a sandcastle in an incoming tide, he wondered whether Solly Proust might be in league with HostageKaty. That would explain why Solly had not yet responded to his bargain basement blackmail-hostage offer. Come to think, was Proust perhaps an alien lizard masquerading as a human weasel? After all, he had often seen a reptilian glint in the accursed loan shark's eyes when he was counting cash.

And so Professor Harty determined to bring matters to a head. For the clock was ticking ever down and would so do, he knew, until he could fabricate enough microscopic black holes to distort the space-time continuum and exterminate the alien lizards. If wiping humankind from the face of the earth was an unintended consequence, so be it. After all, you cannot break eggs without making an omelette . . . assuming that his theoretical calculations held water. But why in Diabolis' name would they not? He had done the math to the n-teenth place and despite the occasional glitch – most notably when he could not for the life of him work out how to connect a printer to his laptop - the world and its oyster knew that he was infallible.

But now the Professor faced a conundrum of chicken-and-eggial proportions. He could not manipulate time until he had sufficient fuel to power his Time Projection Chamber but could not ionise Queridium to produce that fuel without more time. He was in an oxymoronic quandary. Which came first, he puzzled, the Higgs or the Boson? Enlightenment came there none.

To his simmering frustration, the one and only gap-toothed means to his one and only end grinned him in the face, morning, noon and night. Enough, he decided. Determined to spin the chapter to a timely end, he stormed into the recreationary to have it out with his accursed tormentor once and for all. As a hushly silence fell, he drew his batwinged cloak about his shoulders and demanded, 'you will tell me what is afoot, you pigtailed spawn of Diabolis, or I will smite you from the face of Willesden.'

'You do that, mugface. See if I care.' HostageKaty stared into her Malty McOatshake, eyes focused on the last few slurps.

'Gie the wee lassie a break, Chief,' McTavish said. 'Can

ye nae see she's depressed?'

'Depressed?' Professor Harty thundered. 'Pah, that will be the least of her moods when I have done with her.'

McTavish hitched up his kilt, gritted his teeth and clenched his fists. 'I telled ye, Chief, leave the wee lassie be,' he demanded - with menaces. 'Yaer asking fer a Glasgae handshake if ye dinnae back off, pal.'

Harty boldly edged away and stuttered, 'can you not take a joke, my jocular Jock?' He dabbed his brow with a cuff of his cloak and forced a feeble smile. 'Maybe I can help contextualise the little skylark's issues? After all, a problem shared is a problem halved, is it not? Or to put it at its simplest, $1/0.5 = 0.5$.'

'Ye reckon? Well gan a load of this . . .' McTavish fixed Professor Harty with a Highland glare. 'A well-wisher's gan and offered Homeless John a job tending a wee wishing-well in his fairy grotto. Baglady's packed her carrier bags and gan to stay with the vicar. And look . . . the Mayor has ratted on his deal.' He pointed through the window at a fleet of bulldozers chugging down the North Circular Road towards the tollgate. 'And tae cap it all, the Public Health just told her they're ganna send a team of well-intentioned bastards tae rid the area of harmless vermin. The poor wee bairn stands tae lose a fortnight's worth of beetles, all her spiders, a mischief of rats, a nest's worth of wasps, a cluster of mice and a shoal of silverfish. All that hard work down the pan.'

'What a calamitous catastrophe.' Professor Harty masked a joyous smirk behind a solicitous sigh. 'Never mind. At least she still has a dungeon over her head.' He reached out to tickle HostageKaty under the chin then, quick as a flick, drew back when she bared her teeth and snarled at him. 'Cheer up,' he told her – as if he gave a caber's toss. 'As soon as your doting stepfather, Sir Freddie Prendergast, hands over the ransom and a little extortionate interest, you will be free to go on your merry way.' He feigned a smile. 'I would not be in the least surprised if he does not gift you a bounty of venomous spiders to welcome you home.'

'You going to tell him or do I?' HostageKaty asked McTavish. 'No, let me. Might cheer me up.'

Professor Harty looked from HostageKaty to Groaty McTavish and back again at HostageKaty. 'Tell me what, pray tell?'

HostageKaty reached into her satchel for a liquorice twirl, slumped back in her chair and stared unblinking at a people's army of worker ants lollygagging up the wall towards the condiment shelf. 'You've only gone and kidnapped the wrong Katy Clark, that's all. Numpty.'

'I am not as a rule given to respond to flippant humour, but on this occasion I will make an exception,' Professor Harty said and faked a belly laugh.

'Please yesself,' HostageKaty said. 'Problem is, Dolores and Fred don't want me back. Even if they did, I in't going.

We got other plans, don't we Uncle Groaty?'

'I . . . I . . . I do not understand,' Professor Harty stuttered. 'Who in Diabolis' name are Dolores and Fred?'

'Me mam and dad. Jailers, more like.'

The whites of the Professor's eyes bulged like hardboiled eggs. 'But surely you are Katy Clark, the mote of Sir Freddie Prendergast's eye?'

'Gan a minute, Chief? A wee word . . .' McTavish took Professor Harty to one side and whispered an altogether different truth in his ear.

The Professor clapped a hand to his bulbous brow. Unsteady on his feet, he stumbled into the eat-as-much-as-ye-ken oatmeal bar and gasped, 'you mean to say that the pigtailed spawn of Beelzebub is an imposter?'

HostageKaty spat the masticated knockings of her liquorice into her hand and tucked it in a blazer pocket. 'Now just you listen here, the Necronomicon of Numpyville or whatever you call yesself.' She raised her voice to shrieking point. 'I didn't ask to be kidnapped. You lifted me off the street without a bye your bleedin` leave and banged me up in that smeggy grainstore like I was a sack of yeast. If you'd had the common decency to ask me who I was, none of this would have occurred. But oh no - not you. Brain the size of a planet? Shit between yer ears, more like.' She birdied a finger in Professor Harty's startled face. 'So don't lay this cockup on me. I'm the best hostage a snatcher could wish for. I been good as gold.

Pulled me weight, paid all yer bills and even put yer poxy restaurant on the map. So don't call me an imposter or I'll scratch yer eyes out.'

As Professor Harty cowered in a corner like a wee timorous beastie, she turned to McTavish with a maniacal grin on her dimpled face. 'Thing is,' she said and rubbed her hands, 'there's been a change of plan. Same scam, different hostage.' She burst out laughing as McTavish bundled a barley sack over Professor Harty's head and trussed him up like a haggis with a Highland reel of Scotch-twine. 'Bang him up, Uncle Groaty,' she ordered. 'See how he likes it.'

After strapping his former employer to his fourposter bed, McTavish returned to the recreationary shaking his head. 'I dinnae feel well aboot this, lassie. I dinnae feel well aboot this at all. Let's be honest, I never shafted a co-conspirator before. It's near as not criminal.'

'Don't be such a wuss,' HostageKaty scolded. 'All in a day's work. Right, let's see what he's good for.' She rifled through Professor Harty's wallet. 'Bollocks. Empty, except for this.' She ripped up the Professor's treasured British Tarmacademy membership card and tossed it in a flop-top bin. 'Must be someone willing to stump up a fair few quid for a criminal mastermind, even if he's off his trolley. Wonder if he's got any mates?' She frowned, thought for a nanosecond and shook her head. 'Ask a stupid question, get a stupid answer. Suppose the Old Bill would probably stump up a reward,' she said to herself. 'But that would be peanuts compared to what I'm after. I know . . .' She clicked her fingers. 'I'll bell the Artful Codger. Let's face it, must be shitloads of dozy punters willing to pay a tenner a pop to see a mad professor in the buff, rattling his cage and spouting bollocks. Wouldn't be surprised if I can't sell the film rights to Hannibal Lecture.'

McTavish knelt down and reached for HostageKaty's hand. 'Ferget aboot the Sassenach, lassie,' he said. 'Yon Professor's ganning nowhere withoot yaer say-so.' Struck by what passed for a thought, he said, 'if we can find oot where he's stashed the Queridium, we can mebe turn it over to the National Science Museum, pocket a tidy reward and do a runner somewhere no one's ganna find us.' He fingerclicked a thumb as an idea snuck up on him. 'Tell ye what, ye can breed pedigree vermin and I'll set up a wee pest control business tae get rid. It's called symbiosis.' He squeezed her hand and coaxed a smile to her lips. 'If I ever have a bairn,' he told her. 'I want her tae be just like yous, except ginger. Be good if she was polite once in a blue moon.'

HostageKaty rested her head on McTavish's shoulder 'Oh, Groatface,' she sighed. 'Under all that hair, you're just a soppy big girl's blouse.' She snuggled to his side and closed her eyes. 'Uncle Groaty,' she said with a shudder. 'I'm dead scared.'

McTavish gave her a reassuring cuddle. 'That's nae ma wee Katy,' he said. 'I never seen yous withoot a snarl on yaer bonnie face.'

'When mam finds me, and she will, I'll be fish fodder. I been happy here with you and the Dumpster of Doom, or whatever he calls hisself.'

Groaty McTavish drew his sgian dubh, plucked a hair from the back of a hand and sliced it in two with a deft flick of the wrist. 'Dinnae fear, lassie,' he said with a note of steely determination in his gruff voice. 'Nae McTavish worth his sporran would let a wee bairn be tecken alive.' He broke into a reassuring smile and patted HostageKaty on the head. 'Dead, mebe, but nae alive.'

xxxvii

Rising star of New Scotland Yard staff canteen, probationary Metropolitan Police officer Heather Prendergast, summoned her crack flying squad for a confab of war in Sebastian's adminbubble. They would not be disturbed here, she said; Baskerville was sleeping off his excursionary exertions in the butler's parlour; Smothers was scratching his head in the broom closet; Sir Freddie was nursing a hangover in the Chandelerium and Fifi was stuffing her face in the Poo Bar. 'Where's Sebastian?' she asked as she cleared the nuts and bolts off an army-navy surplus pouffe and sat down.

'Looking for the till receipt for that romper suit he bought you,' Katerina told her. 'I said if he didn't take it back for a refund, I wouldn't let him keep my ankle boots. He thinks the ticket might be on the Skodamobile's floor with the remains of the clutch.'

Heather checked her watch, frowned and shook her head. 'Rats,' she cussed then blushed, said, 'pardon me,' and bit her lip. 'Oh, well,' she sighed, 'Suppose we better start without him. The game is afoot.'

'How thrilling,' Katerina said, barely able to suppress a yawn.

Before getting down to business, Heather rummaged through her shoulder-bag for her trusty Sherlock Holmes

Omnibus. 'Righty-ho,' she said as she opened it on her lap on the off chance that she might need a prompt, hardly likely as she knew Sherlock's theorisms better than Doctor Watson ever had. 'So, what do we know so far?'

'Well for starters, we found out that Baskerville is a fraud,' Katerina said. 'Not sure what the point of him is. He's a waste of a dog, almost as useless as Sebastian. Talk of the devil . . .' she looked round as Sebastian slouched through the door carrying a large box-shaped cardboard box.

'Hi, sleuthbabes,' he said as he emptied a miscellany of funky junk on the barenaked floorboards. 'Fragmentations of microkernels and breadcrumbs I downloaded from the Sebmobile's mother board. If it's all right with you, I'll process the data while we commune in the chatroom.' He pointed to the Sherlock Holmes Omnibus on Heather's lap. 'What's that dead tree on your floppy drive, Spriggsy?'

'Every detective's bible. My first point of reference when I'm faced with a difficult case,' she told him with a wry smile. 'I know it by heart. Sometimes I quote dear old Sherlock word for word without realising it. A Freudian slip, I suppose.'

'Yeah, right. Cool. Like a pre-Gatesian Google,' Sebastian said as he scrunched up an empty crisp packet and tossed it on his workbench for safekeeping.

Needless to say, Heather ignored him. 'So we now know that Professor Murray Harty and Groaty McTavish have mistakenly kidnapped Katy Clark, the daughter of two notorious East End mobsters, believing her to be you.' She glanced at Katerina and scowled. 'Please, Bratty, could you please paint your toenails some other time?'

Katerina crossed her arms and flopped back on the futon with an exaggerated expression of wtf on her face. 'What I don't understand,' she said, 'is why we're wasting valuable shopping time on this.'

Heather drummed her fingertips on her trusty sleuth-bible. 'Because, my dear Bratty,' she said, 'it is every man's business to see justice done.'

'So go find a man,' Katerina said. 'Tell you what, find a few and I'll take care of any leftovers.'

'Bratty, will you kindly stop breathing and pay attention?' Heather said, unamused by her stepsister's filial flippancy.

'Please, sis, let's call it a day and leave it to the cops. Someone might get hurt.' Katerina gave Heather a pertinent look to suggest whom that someone might be.

'We don't have time. Do you have any idea how bureaucratic The Yard is? You would not believe how much paperwork is required just to get a carton of cream crackers for the staff cafeteria. Takes forever. And as for replacement crockery . . . forget it. You might as well ask for the moon.' When Katerina raised an eyebrow, Heather looked quickly away and swallowed. Hurriedly covering her skid marks, she said, 'of course, I'm speaking hypothetically. I have my people deal with that kind of thing. But take it from me, the red tape involved in a complex kidnapping case like this would take time we simply do not have.' She tapped her Holmsian bible with a fingernail. 'No, like my mentor, I will follow my own methods and tell as much or as little as I choose. That is the advantage of being unofficial.'

'Whatever you say.' Katerina stretched her long legs and kicked off her shoes. 'Mind if I clip my toenails while you sober up?'

'Do put away that canister of spray-tan, Bratty. This is important.' Heather sat to attention, brow creased in concentration. 'There are eight million stories in the naked city,' she said, 'and this is one.'

'Oh, give me a break, sis.' Katerina rolled her eyes and - not one to squander energy– touched up her mascara.

'Shhhh, I'm thinking.' Ignoring Katerina's *unmutterably* rude aside, Heather said, 'there is nothing more stimulating than a case where everything goes against you.' She tapped her chin and stared out of the window at the compost heap - Mister Smothers' flower garden, as Missus Beaten referred to it. Bless. 'Wonder what Sherlock would do if he was faced with the kind of problems I'm up against?' she wondered aloud. 'I suppose he would accidentally stumble across a clue that would reveal the whereabouts of his evil nemesis.'

'How?' Sebastian asked as he scooped the last few

pieces of wastepaper into what he referred to as 'a pile.'

Heather shrugged. 'Well, he would probably bend down.' She bent down. 'Pick up a scrap of paper.' She picked up The Happy Thistle discount voucher from Sebastion's clutterbish. 'Give it a quick look.' She glanced at the flyer. 'And the answer would be staring him in the face.' She frowned and scratched her head. 'Bratty,' she said with a note of guarded caution in her voice. 'Don't suppose you remember the ransom demand Professor Harty posted in the Pest Control Times?'

'Sure. He wanted ten million but said he might part exchange her for something or other. A kaleidoscope, I think.'

'My, what a prodigious memory you have for a vain narcissist, Bratty. But can you recall what he claimed to be selling?'

'A little bleeder. No . . .' In lieu of a lightbulb, Katerina raised a finger. 'A Little Breeder. Must have been a typo.'

'I think not. Listen to this . . .' Struggling to stem a rising tide of excitement in her voice, Heather read out the small print at the foot of the flyer . . . *Season tickets available from Little Breeders Limited, The Happy Thistle restaurant, North Circular Road, Willesden.* 'Sherlock was right,' she whooped and waved the flyer in the air. 'The world is full of obvious things which nobody by any chance ever observes.'

'And Seb is the Walrus.' Katerina tapped her temple,

turned to Sebastian and whispered, 'straitjacket. Now.'

'Don't you see, Bratty?' Heather gushed. 'We now know where the poor little poppet is being held. The case is as good as solved.'

'So you reckon Kickarse Katy is in that smeggy Highland restaurant by the pop-up toll road?' Katerina clasped her hands to her chest and shuddered. 'Oh my God, a fate worse than death. Did you get a load of their Bannockbuns? They stink worse than Baskerville.'

'Ah, but their Malty McOatshakes are happy-face emoji,' Sebastian said and licked his lips.

Erring on the safe side of caution, Heather consulted her trusty Almanac of Deduction. Her lips moved as she read, 'you can't see the lettuce and the dressing without suspecting a salad, so I would say it is more than possible, it's probable.' She slammed the book shut and jumped to her feet. 'You see, Bratty? Great minds think alike. We have the missing piece of our jigsaw. Game, set and match to me, I think. Can't wait to see daddy's face when I break the news.'

'Whoa, slow down, sis.' Katerina raised a red flag finger. 'Aren't you jumping the gun? I mean, you haven't rescued her yet.' Although loath to put a dampener on her stepsister's spirits, she applied the disc brakes to her impetuosity. 'So what you going to do? Knock on Professor Harty's door, tell the psychopathic maniac the game is up so could he please let his hostage go or you'll give him a jolly-good talking to?'

'Don't be ridiculous,' Heather said, stung to the quick by her stepsister's snarkasm. 'I'll bang him to rights and free the hostage.'

'Jeez,' Katerina sighed, 'next to you, Sebastian is James Bond.'

'Yeah, right. Cool.' Sebastian admired his reflection in his prototype Reflectometer, slicked back a hair, set his sunken jaw and muttered, 'shaken not stirred.'

'Well, what do you suggest?' Heather asked, making no attempt to bridle her contempt or harness her disdain.

Katerina traded her mascara for eyeliner and applied a vanity spot to her upper lip. She admired the results in her compact, muttered, 'cutie pie – you are delicious,' and blew herself a kiss. Back to reality, she packed her panstick and paint pots in her makeup holdall and turned her mind to the matter in hand. 'Well, if you're dumb enough to try and rescue Kickarse Katy, sis, you're going to need backup.' Struck by a sudden bolt of common sense, she said, 'I know - what about your boyfriend? Think they'll let him out of the asylum long enough to give you a hand?'

Heather thought for a moment, thought a moment more, then shook her head. 'I only wish I could get hold of him. Trouble is, he's on a top secret undercover mission in Timbuktu.'

'Then leave it to the Feds, sis. Please.'

'Really, Bratty, I am the Feds,' Heather said. Caught in the moment, she closed her eyes and drifted into a Technicolour daydream of her moment of glory. In her mind's eye, she was leaning on the duty-sergeant's desk casually examining her fingernails. 'Throw the book at him, Sarge.' She cocked a thumb at the infamous Professor Murray Harty, Controlling Brain of the Criminal Underworld. The nation's most-wanted was slumped on a bench, head bowed like a broken kitten, sobbing as he imbibed the last taste of freedom he would likely lick for the next one hundred years – two hundred, in all probability. To add humiliation to indignity, he was shackled to a ramshackled Groaty McTavish. 'It was an elementary collar, Sarge,' she said with her trademark modesty. 'I knocked on the door and when Harty saw who he was up against, he threw in the towel and said fair cop.'

All of a sudden her fantasy bubble burst in a putrid stench of ammonium sulphide. Her vainglorious imaginings were replaced by a lurid vision of a mangulated body lying in an earwig infested ditch. It was her worst, worst, *worst* insectmare. 'On second thoughts,' she said as she mopped her brow. 'Maybe I'll just pass the details of Katy's whereabouts to the appropriate authorities.'

'So you're going to hand this clusterfuck over to the top brass at The Yard?' Katerina breathed a sigh of relief.

'Don't be ridiculous, Bratty. They are far too busy locking up environmental protesters. I intend to have a word with Katy's parents.'

Katerina stared at her aghast. 'Jeez, sis, that is *so* dumb. You reckon you can just waltz into the lion's den looking like Dracula's bridesmaid and expect them to take you seriously?' She poked a finger down her throat and pretended to vomit. 'Yeah, right. Don't forget to send me an invite to your funeral.'

'You know, Bratty, for once you may have a point. I wonder . . .' As the tendrils of an idea took root in the fallow pastures of her mind, Heather Prendergast came up with what was, in the circumstances, an inspired plan. 'Time to call on the services of the British Empire's most fearless secret agent.' She pointed to a yellowing photograph on the Sebfrigerator. Taken several years ago on the Junior Superheroes Float at the annual Eastminster Carnival, Katerina was modelling a skintight leather costume and had a wicked grin on her whiskered face. One hand was groping a rip-chested Batmanalike and the other was fending off the Incredible Skulk - Sebastian Marrowboan by any other name.

With thoughts of the glamourous heroine of her yet to be written blockbuster novels in mind, Heather turned to Katerina and asked, 'you wouldn't happen to know if Missus Beaten still has your old Superheroine costume?'

Chapter Nine.

Posterity will record that that The Curious Case of The Katenapped Girl was ultimately cracked by one of the most audacious acts of subterfuge in the annals of all history. Although an acknowledged mistress of disguise, I nevertheless saw fit to enlist the services of one of the very foremost make-up artists in the whole of South Kensington to ensure that I would not be recognised, with unthinkable consequences for humankind. Having all but passed my undercover method acting course at Cadet College, to make very sure that I would not arouse suspicion, I adopted the guise of a typical resident of Forgottenham. And so it was that under the cover of darkness, I ventured bravely into the viper's nest confident that I would pass unseen by the very heavily armed guards manning the perimeter. It was my intention to alert the poor little poppet's distraught parents to their precious daughter's parlous predicament and by this means augment my forces prior to mounting a very dare-devil rescue mission. Dismissed by my curmudgeonly stepsister as a rubbish idea but lauded by my chief technical officer as a cool stroke of zoanthropic cunning, I dutifully set about my purpose with scant regard for my personal safety or bodily comfort.

PC Bruyère 'Kitten' Galore of New Scotland Yard Continental Catering Detail flattened her ears and flexed her claws. 'Zut alors,' she mewed under her breath; she could hardy credit how itchy her stepsister's old KittenGirl costume was. But stoic as ever, she stiffed her whiskers and reminded herself that the *infurriating* disguise was all in the line of duty. As Aunt Elizabeth never tired of saying, needs be as needs must. Or was it, needs must as needs be, she wondered, her insatiable curiosity roused. Never mind. Now was not the time to split hairs.

Satisfied that there were no gardeners packing loaded hosepipes lying in wait, she gripped the wire with her claws and scrabbled up the fence. 'Les rats,' she meowed under her breath as her hind quarters became entangled in the mesh. Undeterred, she mopped her muzzle with a paw, gritted her incisors, yanked her tail free and scurried on up.

Part one of her mission accomplished, Gendarme Galore crouched on the fence pretending to be out for a night on the tiles. Whiskers twitching, she sniffed the air, pricked up her ears, sprang to the ground and, crouching like a cougar, looked quickly left and right. Satisfied there were no dogs in sight, she padded across the car park and took cover behind a disused refuse skip to snatch a quick catnap.

She was about to break cover when two burly hoods strolled into view shining their torches into the shadows. Fur bristling, she arched her back and extended her claws ready to fly at them and scratch their eyes out should they attempt to flea-collar her. But when she realised that she was cornered like an alley-cat in a cul-de-sac, she bluffed a half-hearted meow.

'Relax,' Brawns told his henchman. 'It's only a cat.'

'Careful,' Mussels said. 'Could be feral.'

'Get away,' Brawns said with a chuckle. 'How many feral cats you know got a mobile phone?' He shone his flashlight at Kitty Galore of Quai des Orfèvres – for it was she – and saw her frantically fiddling with her cellphone, whispering, 'not now, Bratty. I'm busy.'

'Oy – you . . .' Brawns grabbed Heather by the scruff as she tried to scamper through a gap in the fence. 'What's your game?'

'Purr.'

'Don't give me that,' Brawns snarled.

'Didn't you hear the man? He told you not to give him that.' Mussels pushed her cellphone away.

Having decided that there might be more to this particular puss than met the eye, Brawns cathandled Heather through a scrappagery of cars, hillocks of dismembered electricals, carcasses of car-crushed carburettors and a pusillanimous miscellany of motley mechanicals to a shabby Portacabin to one corner of the yard. Outside, a dapper man in a camelhair coat, double-breasted suit, Banray sungoggles and a porkpie helmet was hard at work welding scrap metal into spindly sculptures with an oxyacetylene torch.

Micky 'the Artful Codger' Agers - for it was he - flipped up his visor, sat down on a rusty cylinder-barrow and took a pinch of chemical snuff. 'Go in.' He nodded at the door. 'Dolly's stocktaking.'

'Hey, Micky, like the sculptures,' Mussels said. 'Careful you don't flood the market with fake Giacomettis.' He stroked his bulldog chin as he examined Micky's counterfeit masterpieces with a dilettante eye and nodded. 'Tell you what," he said, 'why not knock up a bunch of Henry Moores and a few Barbara Hepworths to keep them morons at Sotheby's on their toes?'

'When I want your advice,' Agers snarled, 'I'll ask for it.'

'No problemo. Just give me a shout.' Mussels tipped his baseball cap and followed Brawns into the Portacabin.

Dolores Clark looked up from her desk as Brawns cathandled Heather through the door. She pushed aside the pile of cash she was stocktaking, scowled and said, 'what you got there, knucklehead? Looks like something the effing cat dragged in.' She rocked back in her chair, propped her stiletto boots on the desk and examined Heather like a hard boiled cat fancier inspecting a mutant stray. 'So what you want, moggie?' she demanded. 'This is private property. Didn't you see the sign? Trespassers Will Be Effing Wasted.'

Doing her utmost to resist an urge to scrabble onto Dolores's desk and sniff about for treats or a rubber band to play with, Heather said, 'I bring tidings of your missing daughter,' and held out a paw.

Dolores stared at her, rubbed her eyes and turned to Brawns. 'My hearing playing up, or did that cat just speak bollocks?' She brushed Heather's proffered pawshake aside. 'Sort her, Brawns. I don't have time to play cat and mouse with no one, let alone a nutter in an effing catsuit who spouts rubbish.'

Brawns nudged Mussels in the ribs. 'You heard the boss. Sort her.'

'I'm on it, Brawns.' Mussels towered over Heather, straightened her whiskers and growled, 'consider yourself sorted, puss.'

Dolores groaned, 'don't know why I bother,' and snapped her fingers. 'Get New Boy in here,' she told Brawns. 'I'll have him do the business.' She rolled her eyes when Brawns turned to Mussels and clicked his fingers. 'If you want something doing, do it yerself,' she muttered. Shaking her head, she strode to the door, stuffed two fingers in her mouth and whistled. When Naff wandered in eating a sandwich, she pointed to Heather and told him, 'chip an ear and spay her. You'll find chloroform, a boxcutter and a Covid mask in me gun-drawer. On second thoughts, forget the chloroform. I want to hear the scaredy-cat yowl. Nothing like a bit of gratuitous sadism to put a smile on me face.'

'Sure thing, Boss.' Naff handed his sandwich to Mussels, blew on his knuckles and ripped off Heather's mask. 'Stone me,' he gasped as she gaped at him, almost if not more shocked than he was. Struggling to keep face, he swallowed and turned to Dolores with a feeble, 'mind if I do it after me tea break?'

'What the effing-eff you think this is?' Dolores roared. 'The civil effing service?'

At this point, Mussels intervened. 'As his union rep, I got to tell you that under clause eight, subsection five, paragraph two of the Criminal Working Practices Protocol, the lad's well within his rights. You're welcome to lodge an appeal to . . .'

He was interrupted by Heather's sharp intake of breath. 'Naff,' she whimpered. 'Aren't you supposed to be in Timbuktu?'

'On my way, babe.' Naff doffed his forelock and edged towards the door. Before he could take flight into the night like a lily-livered sprite, Dolores collared him and yanked him forwards until their noses were almost rubbing.

'So how come this pussystunting kitty knows your name, New Boy?' she demanded with the unblinking glare of a great white shark eying up a snack-attack.

'Take your hands off him, you . . . you . . . painted harridan,' Heather caterwauled. She brushed Brawns' hand off her front leg, reached a paw into her kittensuit and pulled out her warrant card. 'I must caution you that I am a plainclothes police officer,' she said with all the authority at her command.

'Call that plain clothes?' Mussels pointed to Heather's

tail and whiskers and collapsed in a fit of sidesplitting bellyaching tummywobbling kneeknocking flatulating laughter.

Dolores, on the other hand, was highly not amused. 'Filth, eh?' She cast a wary eye at Naff. 'Got sand in yer ears, New Boy? I said, how come pussy knows you?'

Naff stammered, 'I . . . er . . . I'm wanted by the cops for you name it. That cat's a top dog in the Met,' he bluffed in an attempt to salvage what was left of Heather's curried favour before their relationship became permanently vindalooed. 'She's been on me case since forever.'

'Oh yes, I'm on your case all right,' Heather muttered darkly. 'Timbuktu my foot. Wait till I get you home.'

'What the effing-eff is going on here?' Dolores asked with a medley of rank bemusement and frank suspicion. 'I got a feeling we've caught two snitches, and that's two too many.' She clicked her usual fingers. 'Brawns, Mussels, sort them.'

Before Heather could turn tail and bolt through the nearest cat flap, Brawns clamped his arms around her soft underbelly, dragged her hissing and scratching to a radiator and cable-tied her front paws to a pipe. When Naff tried to rally to her assistance by way of Timbuktu, Mussels blocked his exit. 'Dog,' he snarled and delivered a brutal punch to Naff's withers, twisted a foreleg behind his back and coshed him on the snout with a muzzle duster.

Dolores sat back down at her desk, brushed a strand of brittle-blond hair out her eyes and took a Havana cigar out of the gun pocket of her donkey jacket. She rolled it between forefinger and thumb, gave it a sniff, sighed, 'a fella is a fella, but a cigar is a smoke,' and lit up. 'Mussels, dump New Boy in the car crusher and slice pretty kitty's face to shreds,' she said. 'Scar her for life like my no-good husband.' She flicked a wrist at the door, licked a thumb and put it to purpose re-thumbing her cash pile.

'Don't you dare,' Heather yowled in a combination of unadulterated rage and hyperadulterated fear. 'Touch one hair on my body and I'll report you to the RSPCA.'

'Skittish, in't yer, puss?' Dolores turned to Brawns. 'Cut out her tongue and declaw her. And for effing-eff's sake get on with it. That scaredy cat has got more rabbit than Watershed Down. She's worse than my foulmouthed daughter.'

Just as Brawns was about to remodel Heather's face with a cut-knife razor, Micky Agers strolled into the Portacabin smoking his trademark quarter-bent squat-bulldog pipe.

'This a private party or can I bring my chainsaw?' Micky asked. When he caught sight of Heather crouching on all fours shivering with fear, he grabbed Brawns' wrist mid slash and gave it an Indian twist. 'Friends, let us not be hasty,' he said with a pensive twiddle of the moustache. He stepped back and examined Heather from muzzle to tail as if eying up an al-fresco fresco. As she looked up at him whimpering in gratitude, he said, 'cute little exhibit, isn't she?' Intrigued, he cocked his head and examined her like an old master inspecting a new mistress. 'Mind if I put in a sealed bid?' he asked. 'I believe I may have a counterfeit sarcophagus exactly her size at the gallery. You know, if I amputate her whiskers, gold plate her face, and weld a beard to her snout, I'm sure I can pass her off as Tutankhamun and make a killing.' He broke into a maniacal chuckle and made an exaggerated play of rubbing his hands as if kneading a pliant wheel of wholemeal cheese.

Frightened as near as not out of her hide, Heather tucked her tail between her legs and struggled to free her paws as the Artful Codger took a horse syringe and a phial of permanent paralyser out of his portfolio. Ignoring her pitiful meows, he searched for a puncture point in her fur that wouldn't mark her glossy coat. 'Wait,' she wailed. 'I know where Katy is.'

A hushed silence fell over the portacabin like a dumb waiter. Dolores stubbed out her cigar, looked up from her money pile and narrowed her eyes at Heather. 'Brawns, Mussels – lock New Boy in the Portaloo and make yerselves scarce. Micky, get back to work. Them sculptures in't going to counterfeit thesselves. Me and Miss Kitty need a word . . . alone.' As the room emptied, she kithandled Heather to the floor and planted a needle sharp heel in her stifle. 'Start squealing, puss, or I'll neuter you. Mess with me and the only litter you'll ever have will be wastepaper.'

Helplessly pawcuffed to the pipe, Heather closed her eyes and gulped. 'I know where your daughter is,' she whimpered.

'Working for Priscilla Proust, are you, moggie?' Dolores forced her lethal heel further - harder - into Heather's groin.

'No. Please,' Heather yowled as her nine lives flashed before her eyes. 'I'm Sir Freddie Prendergast's daughter by his legal marriage,' she yowled. 'Professor Murray Harty kidnapped Katy by mistake, believing her to be my stepsister. He's demanding ten million pounds to free her.'

'What a load of effing-bollocks,' Dolores scoffed. 'I'll hand you over to Micky Agers if you can't do better than that.'

'No. Please. Anything but Tutankhamun, I beg you,' Heather wailed. 'Look, if you don't believe me, call daddy. His phone number is in there.' She twitched her whiskers at her wallet.

Dolores was, to say the least, dubious. She thought it the kind of cock-and-dick story that could have been lifted straight from the pages of a ludicrously far-fetched novel. 'So why don't I just tell your old man I'll release you if he forks out ten million?' she said. 'Then I can pay off Harty, get Katy back and read her the riot act.' Deaf to Heather's catophonic yowls, she reached for her cellphone and dialled Sir Freddie's number. 'Well, well, well,' she said as she rung off. 'Seems you're on the level, kitgirl.'

'So will daddy pay the ransom?' Heather asked, bristling with anticipation. On the one paw she had high hopes but on the other three, she feared the worst.

'In your dreams, kitty. The weird thing is, for some reason he kept calling you Helen. Still, he thanked me for the call, told me to euthanize you, toss your carcass to the crows and asked me not to bother him again. He bet me a tenner you'd wet yerself when I broke the news. We got on pretty well as it happens. He's my kinda guy.'

'Wait, please,' Heather pleaded as thoughts of crows pecking at her underbelly frightened her to within an inch of her ninth life. 'If I rescue Katy, will you forget all about this little misunderstanding?'

'You taking the piss, puss?' Dolores Clark stared at Heather if she was a whisker short of a full mouse. 'If I let you scamper out the door, I'll never see you again. Leastways, not if you got any sense, I won't. Not that you have. Seen yourself? You're a disgrace to your litter.'

'What if I give you my word?' Heather begged.

'A regular Boris Johnson, in't you? Think I'll just auction you to Micky and have done with it.'

With thoughts of the last gasp saloon uppermost in mind, Heather tossed her only remaining metaphorical card onto the allegorical table. 'Look, keep Naff as security and lend me something to wear that doesn't clash with my hair. If I don't rescue Katy, you can do what you want to him. The more terminal the better.' She flattened her ears, blinked several times and swallowed. 'He may cook pasta to die for, but it's only fair to warn you that his socks stink of gorgonzola.' She screwed up her muzzle and shuddered.

Dolores stared at her. And she stared at her. 'Wake me up, someone,' she said after a pun-ishing paws. 'I'm having a bad dream. Must be. Seems I'm negotiating with a copper dressed as a cat – an effing cat, for effing-effs sake – who just offered to rescue my brat in exchange for a police nark with smelly feet.' After a moment to reludicrous her bearings, she nodded. 'All right, I'll have a word with Scareface and if he agrees, we got a deal. Get my girl back and that scumbag copper mate of yours goes free.'

Dolores 'Dolly' Clark, godmother to the Clark Gang and pariah of Forgottenham, reached into a drawer for her snub-nose revolver and said, 'try anything clever, puss, and lover-boy is dead in a box.' She levelled the gun at Heather's snout, unlatched the safety catch and broke into a quantumphysical smile. 'And so, perhaps, are you, Policecat Officer Schrodinger.'

I am rescuing you in the name of the law.

xxxix

The tradesperson's entrance had been left ajar. Careless, Heather thought. Shoddy. An open invitation for any novelist worth his, or more probably her, gruel to avoid having to fabricate a more dramatic means of entry. Such as . . .

Our intrepid sleuth crouched outside the old bakery like a tigress on the prowl. As a full fat moon broke through the cottonwool clouds, she spotted a convenient half-open window at the building's uppermost height. Although all but beyond the reach of mortal hand or eye, her legendary gut instinct told her that it was the only means of gaining access without alerting those inside.

Left with no melodramatic alternative, our heroic heroine shimmied up a convenient drainpipe - she had been trained to climb inanimate objects at l'Université de Criminologie. As the pulsing background music ratcheted up the tension, she edged on up, hand over hand, foot by foot – fifty metres, one hundred, two hundred, five hundred until . . . Her heart missed a beat when a hand came adrift leaving her dangling perilously in mid-air. She looked down and shuddered, dizzy with the realisation that if she survived the breakneck plummet, she would in all likelihood be ripped to cutlets by one of the marauding packs of ravenous wolves roaming the streets of Willesden. Taking her courage in her free hand, she reached out for a nearby window ledge. In a scarce to believe feat of breath-denying derring-do, she hauled herself to safety by the skin of her nail varnish. However, her relief was short lived as, without warning, she was attacked by a flock of ravenous pigeons hell-bent on her annihilation. But spurred on by her mission of mercy, rather than fight back as her every sinew demanded, she punched a hole in the window with a jujitsu chop and slithered headfirst into the void.

Imagine our intrepid heroine's shockhorror when she found herself in a disused lift shaft. As she tumbled in a freefall spiral, she grabbed ahold of the first thing that came to hand – a convenient rope abandoned by a long forgotten maintenanceer in a moment of misbegotten forgetfulness. Gripping the dangle between her knees, she abseiled down the twisted twine. Several close-ups of her sweaty face when her hands slipped, her palpitating chest as debris rained down upon her head, her taut thighs as she gripped the rope between her knees and countless other arty edits, wipes, fades and cuts later, she found herself knee deep in *unspeakable* in a sewer in the subterranean depths.

Undeterred by the turds - determent was not in her nature - she held her nose and waded through the effluence towards a pinprick of light in the distance. At incalculable cost to her manicured nails, she fended off frenzied attacks from rabid rats and vampire bats until - sweating like a mop-bucket - she punched a hole in the sewer wall with a jujitsu kick and hauled her bruised body into a disused currant-bunnery.

As she looked about, her eagle-eye fell upon a goatskin rug. Inspired by the Gruffalos of her youth, she disguised herself as a little kid and strayed into receptionary bleating for nanny. When the hostageers went to pet her, she battered them into submission with a flurry of expertly executed jujitsu head-butts. Her daring ploy worked like a polyphyletic taxon and, realising that they had met their match, the kidnappers ran up the white flag; they knew the game was up. Mission accomplished, our bold adventuress goat-herded the traumatised poppet out to the safety of . . . *fill in the blank*.

But no – such and similar dramatic devices must wait for another yarn because the prosaic fact of the matter was that the tradesperson's door had been left ajar.

Sporting a natty rat-leather minidress, an ex-subwayarmy greatcoat and a porkchop hat borrowed from Dolores Clark, Heather tiptoed into the old bakery. Taking care not to rouse the dog - should there be one - or draw attention to her presence - should she have one - she crept along a lamplit corridor until she chanced upon a padlocked door. A clunk of keys hung on a nearby hook next to a sign that read *Return After Use or You're Fishbait.*

Aware that this might be Prendergast of The Yard's first and perhaps her only encounter with her evil nemesis, Heather took copious mental notes which she was later to regurgitate verbatim as the penultimate episode of her pending number one best-seller.

Chapter Ten

I must confess to rarely, if ever, having felt fear in the discharge of my detective duties. Aware that what was to transpire would go down as a red letter day in the annals of crime busting mythology, I unlocked the door, pocketed the keys and ventured boldly in.

I found myself in a singular bedroom carpeted with a green mould-like substance. As I crept in, a figure bound hand and foot to a fourposter bed opened his eyes and a tremendously virile and yet sinister face turned towards me. With the brow of a philosopher above and the jaw of a sensualist below, one could not look upon his cruel eyes, with their drooping, cynical lids, or upon the fierce, aggressive nose and the threatening, deep-lined brow, without reading Nature's plainest danger-signals. It was clear to the most dispassionate eye that Professor Murray Harty - for I took it to be no other - was not a man to be trifled with. Nor was he a man to let the grass grow under his feet for there was not a follicle of foliage in plain sight.

"Professor Harty, I presume," I ventured as he set eyes upon me.

"Who in Beelzebub's name do you think I am?" he retorted, "Miss Kylie Minogue?"

"Would that I were blessed with such good fortune," I replied with a wit that brooked no favour. "The game is up," I told him as I stood at the foot of his bed. "But first, if you will, some discourse. Let us see," I said, "if there is justice upon the earth, or if we are ruled by chance."

"Dolt," he thundered, quite plainly tongue in cheek. "That head of yours should be for use as well as ornament."

"Professor Harty," I said, "if I may make so bold as to call you that, you really are an automaton – a calculating machine. I confess that there is something positively inhuman in you at times."

"And I confess that I covet your skull," he roared as he thrashed about to free his arms from the ropes that bound him in captivity.

"Lest you think that I regard you as an eccentric, I would mindfully point out that in my vast experience the charlatan is always the pioneer and the quack of yesterday is the professor of tomorrow," I told him as I edged away.

To which he replied, "$x^2 + (x+1)^2 = 5^2$."

"Please, Professor, do not bandy Pythagoras' theorem with me," I scoffed, amused by his presumption. "It is my second nature. Indeed, it is said by some that but for Pythagoras, I might have conceived it."

"Pah," he snorted, "let me tell you that while the individual man is an insoluble puzzle, in the aggregate he becomes a mathematical certainty. You can, for example, never foretell what any one man will do, but you can say with precision what an average number will be up to. Individuals vary, but percentages remain constant. To put it at its simplest, $h(x)=-0.017x^2+1.09x+6.1$, where x represents the horizontal distance from the start and $h(x)$ is the height of the cerebellum. So says the statistician."

"So say we all," I quipped. "But misadventures come in pairs. One is a punishment and the other is a misfortune."

"Fool," he raged like a ruptured metatarsal as he thrashed about to free his limbs from the tethers of bondage. "You see, but you do not observe."

"Your course is run, Professor," I told him. "Because it is done by a girl who cannot afford to fail, one whose whole future career as Prendergast of The Yard depends upon the fact that all she does must succeed. I talk of the Science of Deduction. Admittedly, it is crushing the nut with the triphammer — an absurd extravagance of energy — but the nut is very effectually crushed all the same."

At this, Professor Harty sank into the mattress, his spirit broken. He sighed, "so help me, I give up," and closed his eyes.

Satisfied that I had defeated him with the objectivity of my logic, I left Professor Harty to his slumbers, tiptoed out of the room and gently eased the door to behind me. In the knowledge that the sands of time were fast diminishing, I prepared to seek the object of my quest and release her to the merciful embrace of her mother.

Leaving her lawyers to deal with spurious claims of unintended plagiarism, Heather crept along the corridor until her progress was impeded by a sturdy door. She knelt down and peeked through the keyhole. From what she could see, there were two occupants - a burly man in a kilt and a small girl in a shabby blue gymslip and a liquorice-stained blazer. They appeared to be searching for something as they were upending sofas, pulling out drawers and rummaging under the rugs. Intrigued, Heather pressed her nearmost ear to the door.

'Must be here somewhere, Unc, unless he's stuffed it up his frockcoat,' the girl was saying. 'What's it look like?'

'Suppose ye might say a rock. Aboot so big,' the kilted man told her.

'I know what a rock looks like, numpty. But I never seen a meteorite of Queridium.'

'Oh, see what ye mean, lassie. Well, it's silver, or mercury. Platinum maybe. Shaped like a cumquat. Size of yaer average haggis, gie or teck. Checked in there?'

'Course. It's the first place I looked.'

Having heard enough, Heather kicked open the door and limped in. 'Don't anybody move,' she ordered.

'What if I need to scratch me bum?' the pigtailed teen asked.

'Scratching is allowed. But no funny business.' Heather thrust a hand into a greatcoat pocket and pointed a finger to make believe that she was packing a gun.

'Uncle Groaty,' the girl said.

'Aye, lassie?'

'You go that way, I'll go the other and when I say boo, jump her.'

'Oh no you don't. One false move and I shoot.' Heather narrowed her eyes, set her jaw, edged slowly back and - as McTavish lunged - let him have it between the eyes . . . bang, bang.

HostageKaty - for it was of course she - planted her hands on her pleated hips and tossed her pigtails in a show of scorn. 'That the best you can do, Miss Muppet - bang, bang?' she said. 'You're rubbish at this, in't you?'

Heather slumped down on the sofa, stared miserably at her finger and mumbled, 'blanks.'

HostageKaty gave her a puzzled look. 'She with you, Uncle Groaty?' she said.

'Me?' McTavish pointed to his chest. 'Nae, bonnie lass. Assumed she was a customer.'

HostageKaty sat down beside Heather, took her hand in hers and said, 'thing is, ducky, you didn't ought to be here. See, me and Uncle Groaty's pressed for time and can't take no orders just at the minute.'

It goes without saying that Heather was shocked to be taken for a civilian; she naturally assumed that her air of calm, cool, collected officiousness would speak for itself. For the avoidance of doubt, she said, 'this may come as a surprise, but I'm not a customer. I am an undercover police officer.' She stood up, tucked her porkchop hat under an arm and arched her back. 'Miss Katy Clark,' she said with all the authority at her command. 'I am hereby rescuing you in the name of the law.'

336

HostageKaty stared at her for a full ten seconds then turned to McTavish and scratched her head. 'What you reckon, Uncle Groaty - is she for real or has she escaped from a farm?'

Heather took out her warrant card and flashed it in HostageKaty's face, but to her surprise and no little consternation, rather than showering her with kisses, HostageKaty bared her teeth and snarled, 'you got five seconds to make yesself scarce, copper, or you're on the menu.' She grabbed McTavish's sgian dubh from the table and jabbed it at Heather's chest. 'One, two, three . . .'

'Golly, they've brainwashed you,' Heather gasped, appalled at the spectre of non-surrender brandishing a dagger before her startled eyes.

'Chance would be a fine thing,' HostageKaty scoffed. 'I'm staying put with Uncle Groaty, so there. I got Copenhagen Syndrome.'

'I think you mean Stockholm Syndrome, poppet.'

'This a geography lesson?' HostageKaty screamed. 'You're as bad as my mam, you are.'

'Dolores is worried about you, sweetheart.'

'Tell her I'm swimming with the fishies. Say I suffered a really, really painful death. Say it took forever. That'll put a smile on her face.'

Heather was, to say the least, profoundly miffed. Despite the hours – quite literally – that she had spent studying hostagemurder at college, she could not for the life of her remember the correct procedure for a police negotiator to pit his – or in her case, her – wits against a hostage who refused to be rescued. Forced to improvise, she determined to tread with the utmost care; she was later to liken her approach to walking on eggshells in ballet shoes. In the hope that cool, calm, calculated reason would prevail where authority had failed - in technical parlance, gentlee gentlee catchee cheekee monkee - she donned her soothiest smile, adopted her nursiest voice, reached out the hand of sisterhood and said, 'now don't be silly, Miss Clark. Kindly buck up your ideas and come with me before I lose my temper.'

HostageKaty's jaw dropped and she glared eyedaggers at Heather's epiglottis. 'You're dead, you are, copper, if you don't shut your gob, in't she, Uncle Groaty?'

But rather than rally to HostageKaty's corner, Groaty McTavish slumped down on a bothystool, stared miserably at the floor and shook his shaggy mop of ginger hair. 'Best do as the filth lady says, lassie.' He dabbed a tear from the corner of an eye. 'Dinnae worry yesself aboot a sad old Jock like me. Yaer mammy needs ye home.'

'Oh, Uncle Groaty, I in't leaving you. Never.' HostageKaty took McTavish's hand and gave it a heartfelt squeeze. 'I never had no one care about me before. You give me all your liquorice, even though I know you been saving it for a rainy day, you kept me safe from the Muppet of Miseryville or whatever he calls hisself and

tucked me up snug as a bug in a rug when I went beddy-
byes.' She rested her head on his shoulder and broke into
a soppy smile. 'Mam's got Scareface to threaten. She don't
need me.'

'Ye belongs back at the family scrapyard,' McTavish
told her. 'Blood is stickier than water.' He stared into a
distance of forlorn regrets. 'See, I dinnae have a family
to care for me. I was left on a crofter's doorstep when I
was a wee bairn, brought up in a pigsty on a diet of raw
porridge and went straight from truant tae borstal. Apart
from ma certificate in pest-control and a doctorate in
social anthropology, I nae got a trade tae fall back on. Ha,'
he scoffed with a wry grimace, 'the closest I ever had tae a
friend afore I met ye was yon mad professor, and he hates
ma guts.' He clasped his hands between his kilted knees
and swallowed a Highland sob. 'Forget aboot me, lassie.
I'm nae worth the time of day.'

HostageKaty swung around and glared at Heather,
eyes ablaze. 'See what you done, piglet? Uncle Groaty's
gone all Charles Dickens on me.' She huddled up to
McTavish and gave him a cuddle. 'I in't leaving without
you, Unc,' she whispered, 'so Miss Marbles can go play
with hesself for all I care.'

And that was when Heather Prendergast came up with
one of the most brilliantest ideas of her career to date – of
her career to any date, most likely. When she looked back
upon that moment with the lucidity of time and place, she
could scarcely believe the audacity of her perspicacity.

'What if I were to arrange for Mister McTavish to be employed in the family firm?' she said. 'I have a hunch that your mother might have an opening for an experienced mobster.' She clicked her tongue and winked. 'The new boy she recently took on has . . . well, let's just say, he's blotted his copybook.' *And mine,* she muttered under her breath.

HostageKaty's face lit up. She jumped off McTavish's lap, skipped over to Heather and shook her hand so hard that she almost dislocated her wristwatch. 'You got yesself a deal, Miss Piggy.' Over the moon, she kissed her pet scorpion on the sting, nested him in a tobacco tin and stowed it in her satchel with her handcuffs, knuckle dusters and emergency liquorice. 'Pack your sporran and let's hit the road, Unc. I'm dying to introduce you to Brawns and Mussels. They're prize numpties - a laugh a minute.'

PC Heather Prendergast breathed a heady sigh of satisfaction as she watched McTavish pack his few belongings into a tartan bin-liner. It had, she thought, been the longest day of her career by a metropolitan mile. If there had been eight million stories in this naked city, there was now one more. And what a story. She couldn't wait to tell Aunt Elizabeth. She closed her eyes and tried to picture Sir Freddie's face when she broke the news that she had been promoted to Chief Inspector Prendergast of The Yard or possibly Commander Prendergast of The Yard. Or even . . . she bit her lip. Come on, she told herself, let's not get ahead of ourselves. But the fact was, she had all but wrapped up the case of the century and recognition was bound to follow as surely as recriminations follow a hen party.

Only one small niggle remained to be crossed and one naggle dotted before she could stride off into the dawn silhouetted by the rising sun, a latterday legend on a par with - dare she say - the late, great Sherlock Holmes. She reached for her cellphone to break the glad tidings to the Commissioner. It hardly took a hop, a skip and a leap of the imagination to picture the conversation . . .

'PC Prendergast here, sir. That's the one. Catering Induction Detail. No, I'm not ringing to apologise for putting prunes and Senocot in the lamb curry. It was an honest mistake. Anyone could have made it. Sitting down?' she asked. 'Would you believe, I've got Professor Murray Harty under lock and key? Indeed, that's him – the Controlling Brain of the Criminal Underworld, no less. Thing is, I'm on leave for another two weeks so do me a favour and send some of the lads to collect him. Believe you me, he's going nowhere except the secure wing at Broadmoor. I'll leave the key under the mat.' In a Pavlovian response, she reached into a pocket and pulled out a bunch of keys.

'What you got there?' HostageKaty asked, hoping upon hope that her ocular perception was playing up.

'Golly.' Heather's cheeks flushed a cringy shade of cherry-berry. 'Looks like I might have made a bit of a blooper.' She forced an embarrassed smile. 'It's possible I forgot to lock Professor Harty's bedroom door.'

In the flutter of an eyelash, HostageKaty raced to The Professor's four poster bedroom. She returned a minute or so later effing and blinding as taught at her mother's knee. 'The Doomster of Gloom or whatever he calls hisself has only gone and done a runner. Can't trust no one these days,' she said as she flopped down on the sofa, her face more miserable than sin. 'Wouldn't be surprised if he didn't pocket that cumquat of Queridium before he scarpered,' she said. 'Here – found this on the bed.' She thrust a scrap of parchment into Heather's hand. It bore the spinechilling equation $E = mc^2$ in Professor Harty's spidery scrawl.

Heather Prendergast - Probationary Catering Assistant Second Class of The Yard for the unforeseeable future - read the quadratic runes and shuddered. Deep on the wings of distraction, she stared into the ever expanding space-time continuum and, with a deep midwinter's distance in her voice, said, 'this can only mean one thing.' She took a slow - a deliberate - breath. 'Professor Harty must be plotting a sequel. The fiend.'

xl

Naff picked up Heather's notebook and read the cover. 'So, what's this, babe?' he asked. 'The Curious Caper of ...'

'Case,' Heather corrected him. 'The Curious Case of the Katenapped Girl.'

'Oh, yeah,' Naff said. 'Write it yesself?'

'All my own work,' Heather told him modestly.

'Mind if I take a look?'

'Mind? I'll be upset if you don't.'

An avid aficionado of Who-done-its, Naff turned straight to the last page and read aloud ...

Chapter Eleven.

Mission accomplished. As the hands of the clock of time nudged inexorably towards midnight, knowing that it was now or never, I mounted a very daredevil raid on the fortified garrison where the helpless moppet was being held. After a Mexican standoff lasting absolutely ages, I rescued the poor little mite and reunited her with her overjoyed parents. To my acute embarrassment, they invited me to be guest of honour in a tickertape parade through the streets of Forgottenham. Needless to say I declined. I have never nor ever shall be a glory hunter. My reward is simply to know that I am helping forge a better future for my brothers and sisters should I ever have any, which is about as likely as sprouting wings and flying to Jupiter or Mars bearing in mind my despicable father who I never want to see again. To my profound regret, when he realised that his course was run, Professor Harty jumped ship like a cowardy custard rather than face his just desserts. But never fear. I shall not rest until he is safely under lock and key and civilisation can breathe easy again.

Naff turned the page and then turned another. 'So where's the rest?' he asked.

'Volume two, you mean.'

'This ain't exactly what I'd call a volume, honey. More like a postcard.'

Heather and Naff were relaxing in Heather's bed-living room after a roller-coaster week of ups and downs, smiles and frowns, thrills and spills. But what a result . . . Katy Clark had been reunited with her parents, Groaty McTavish had a bludgeoning new career, Naff had been released relatively intact and, of greatest import, Heather would never have to speak to her *unspeakable* father again - God willing. All that remained was to mend a few loose ends and they could set off for a truncated vacation in Huddersford; it would be another twelve days before Heather had to grind her nose back to the griddlestone in the Metropolitan Police staff canteen. But first they had some air clearing to do.

'So, babe, let's get this straight,' Naff said as he stirred a handful of chopped garlic into a yumptuous pasta sauce. 'You're saying it weren't you at The Sundown Strip the other night?'

'Don't be ridiculous,' Heather said without looking up from the Police Gazette fashion supplement; she was sorely tempted to lash out on a natty spandex stab-vest, polka dot riot helmet and pink truncheon – the height of fashionable millennial riot wear. 'What do you take me for?'

'Don't ask,' Naff muttered under his breath. 'So where exactly was you Friday night?'

'If you must know, I spent the weekend with Aunt Elizabeth. We went to the St. Mary Nook Women's Institute sowing bee and had a whale of a time. It was such fun,' Heather said with a buttermelt smile.

Naff leant back against the sink with his arms crossed and gave her a cockeyed look. 'The old biddies wouldn't run a strip joint down Hackney way, would they?'

'As if . . .' Heather dismissed the idea with a toss of the head and a flick of the wrist.

'Don't come the innocent with me, babe,' Naff said. 'I seen you with me own two eyes. Hate to say it, but you're a rubbish dancer. You need to take a few tips from your mate – the headbanger with the body and the fake tan.'

'How dare you cast aspersions on my balletic prowess?' Mortally affronted, Heather tossed aside her reading matter. 'I will have you know that I was offered a six month contract.'

'Who by - Billy Smart's Circus?'

'Don't be so rude. Priscilla Proust. I gather Micky Agers told her that he thought my performance was very avant garde.'

'You can say that again. Never seen nothing like it in me life.'

'And what, may I ask, were you doing at a strip club, you unspeakable man?'

'If you must know,' Naff said with a defensive pretence of offence. 'I were there on business. What's your excuse? Oh, forget it,' he said with a shrug of the shoulders. 'I best sort dinner. I ain't eaten since them jellied-eels Delores done me for breakfast, and she ain't no Egon Ronay.' To the mood music of a rumbling tummy, he rooted through the fridge-cum-larder more in hope than expectation. 'Bollocks,' he said as he inspected the sad sorry fester of mouldy ice, fetid feta and past lay-by eggs. 'We're clean out of Parmesan. I best shoot out and score some.' He took off his pinafore and, much to Heather's disgust, tossed it on the sofabed. 'Don't forget to stir the sauce,' were his parting words as he donned his motorcycle jacket, supercool shades and bandana. Having morphed from Michelin-starred chef to Michelin-tyred dude, he left Heather to simmer the dinner on the bedsit heater-cum-stove.

Shortly after her boyfriend had gone in search of a gourmet lump of cheese to grate, a loud buzz roused Heather from her daydreams. 'Who is it?' she asked the doorcom, assuming it would be a bobbybuzzer, a battybrush salesman or a postman in seek of directions; her inner, outer and every other circle of friends had just popped out for cheese. Even her Facebook page was a blank - apart from Holmes and Watson. She had personally posted their witty have-an-elementary-birthday greetings on her socially bereft media. After all, what are fantasy friends for if not to rally to her side when celebrations are in order?

'Come on, sis, buzz me up,' a whiny voice demanded. 'There's this really creepy bloke bugging me. Won't leave me alone.' The volume faded as the mouth belonging to the voice could be heard to say, 'won't tell you again, Seb. Take your finger out of your nose and park the car.'

A few minutes later, Katerina staggered through the bedsit door puffing and wheezing after climbing six flights of stairs. She tossed her half-smoked cigarette down the stairwell, looked about and turned up her nose, now diamond studded in keeping with her *swishingly* sophisticated new image. 'When you said you lived in a penthouse apartment,' she said with a snoot, 'didn't think you meant a shoebox on the top floor of a multistorey slum.'

'Small is beautiful,' Heather said wishfully, bitterly regretting not having had the fleetness of mind to tell the doorcom she was out.

'Yeah, there is that.' Katerina cast a condescending look around. 'But there's small and there's itsy. I've seen bigger Wendy Houses. And is it me, or does the place stink of gorgonzola?' Taking care not to inhale, she flicked Naff's pinafore off the bed-settee, sat down and stretched her long legs halfway across the room. Holding her nose, she unrummaged a bottle of *horrendously* expensive sweatmask from her makeup holdall, dabbed a liberal splash behind her ears and an illiberal splash on her wrists.

'Like the drag?' she asked when she saw Heather admiring her pussy-bowed silk blouse, pencil skirt and kitten heels. 'Had to get poshed up for a job interview as a currency trader at my stepdad's bank. It's as good as in the bag,' she bragged. 'Told him I'd email a snapshot of him in his fetish gear to the Board if he didn't give me the job.' She tapped her chin with an ivory fingernail. 'Might tuck him up anyway,' she said, 'just for a giggle.'

'So what does the job involve?' Heather asked, not that she gave a tuppenny fig.

Katerina licked her plummy lips and said, 'I'll be doing exactly what it says on the tin. Trading my stepdad's currency for designer clothes, handbags, shoes, holidays in the Bahamas, that kind of thing. Of course, I'll be expected to look the part when I'm escorting clients to his Knightsbridge casino to piss their money up the wall. I get commission - half their winnings and half their losses - so it'll pay to keep them sweet. Not sure how though,' she said as she fussed her skirt over her thighs, undid the top few buttons of her blouse and lounged back on the sofabed with her legs apart. When Heather scowled, disgusted by her stepsister's hypermercenariness, she groaned, 'oh, come on, sis. You know well as me a girl's got to make a living. Talking of which, mind if I take a look?' She picked up Heather's payslip from the coffee table-cum-desk and gave it a quick look. 'So they pay you tips on top of your salary. Sick,' she said. 'That is *so* dope.'

Not so much embarrassed as mortified, Heather mumbled, 'that is my salary,' and stared into her lap as her stepsister's tweezered eyebrows all but went orbital.

'Really, sis - you need to have a word with someone.' Katerina tutted. 'My stingy stepdad gives me more pocket money than that.'

Feeling smaller than a smidgeon, Heather tossed her head in a show of impecunious piety. 'A detective's profession is its own reward', she said with a self-righteousness bordering on wrong- headedness.

'What I can't understand is why you don't just get a rich boyfriend and shop till you drop like any normal girl. I can lend you a few titled dimwits if you like,' Katerina said, then gasped when she gave the payslip another look. 'Oh my God - it's addressed to PC Heather Prendergast, Probationary Assistant, New Scotland Yard Catering Induction Detail.'

Humiliated from the gingertips of her split ends to

the pinkytips of her pedicured toes, Heather ripped her payslip out of Katerina's hand and filed it in the wastepaper basket - out of sight though sadly much in mind. 'So, to what do I owe the pleasure?' she asked with an irony that brooked no misinterpolation. 'Or did you just come here to make me want to give up the ghost?'

'Jeez, you are so uptight, sis. Live a little, why don't you?' Katerina broke into a brattish scowl. 'Anyway, can't stop. Just dropped by to say your twinset and blouse are back from the cleaners. Not sure where you'll put them, though.' She cast a catty eye around Heather's dimensionally challenged bedsitting flat. 'Seb's going to bring them up when he's parked the car, if he can manage the stairs without getting lost.'

Concerned that she might have forgotten something - to add a pinch of sea salt or somesuch - when she saw smoke billowing from the frying pan-cum-wok on the cooker-cum-radiator, Heather was sorely tempted to take remedial action. But on second thoughts, she decided that it was probably supposed to do that. Spag sauce flambé rang a bell. And it smelt utterly yummy, if a little brittle, so not to worry. In any event, she was entertaining, although entertaining was not a word she would choose had she more control over the narrative. Despite being unmooded to be sociable, Aunt Elizabeth had brought her up to put hospitality before hostility in the A to Z of etiquette, so she filled the multipurpose kettle and plugged it into a multipurpose socket. 'Have you time for a quick a cup of tea?' she asked, hoping that the answer would be a definitive no.

'Got anything less non-alcoholic?' Katerina asked as she took a gold-leafed tobacco pouch out of her makeup holdall and proceeded to roll a spliff.

'I would ask you not to smoke illegal substances in my apartment, if you don't mind,' Heather said huffily.

'Don't mind a bit. Ask away. See where it gets you,' Katerina said as she lit up.

Although loath to waste more breath than she could readily afford - and she feared that her daily quotient was already running at a deficit - Heather asked, 'how are things at home?'

'Home - is that what you call it? Prison more like. Might as well be a nun.' Katerina poked a finger down her throat and aped a vomit. 'My stepdad bosses me around like he owns the place. Don't do this, don't wear that, don't stay out partying all weekend, don't use my corporate charge card . . . Treats me like a child.' She flicked fag ash on the rug and sat back inspecting her nails.

Heather changed the subject while she still had the will to live. 'So how are Smothers and Missus Beaten?'

'Same as always. Smothers wants to retire but Sir Freddie says he can't. Something to do with the small print in his articles of indenture. You'll never believe, but Eggy has enrolled in a mail-order postal course. Better late than never. Haven't heard a peep out of Baskerville. I think he's dead . . . as if I care.'

Of course . . . Heather clicked her fingers as she remembered what she had forgotten. And that was when she discovered that better late than never doesn't necessarily apply to Spaghetti Bolognese. As she scraped the last burnt testaments into a floptop bin, she asked, 'has your mother gone on a diet?' not that she imagined for one moment that she would have; as far as Fifi Clark-Prendergast was concerned, binge-eating was not so much a predilection as an addiction. Nevertheless Heather harboured hopes. After all, as Sir Freddie would say, a deal is a deal . . . unless I change my mind.

'Oh yeah, that. Strictly bread and water from now on,' Katerina said. 'Mind, not sure Mum should eat so many condiments. Salt, pepper, mustard, garlic, fillet of roast hog, lobster thermidor, rice pudding and clotted custard . . .'

'Those aren't condiments,' Heather said, shocked beyond the benefit of doubt.

'Try telling mum that.' Katerina sniffed her tea, turned up her nose and pushed it away. Not having touched up her face since she arrived, she was rooting through her makeup holdall for a liptwist when a fifty pound note fluttered to the floor. Initially minded to ignore it, she had second thoughts. As she bent down to pick it up, Naff walked through the door carrying a slab of fresh Parmesan and a bottle of bargain bin screwtop wine.

When he saw Katerina stooping down, Naff whipped off his sunglasses and broke into a foxy smile. Making sure that Heather wasn't looking, he was about to give Katerina a helping grope when she looked round and winked.

'Well, hi there, handsome.' She batted her lashes. 'Bonking my stepsister too, are you? Good luck. You'll need it.'

All but speechless, Heather planted a hand on each of her hips and glared at Naff and Katerina - first one, then the other, then both at the same time. 'You two know each other?'

'Never seen her before in me life,' Naff lied through his lying teeth as he bravely backed away with his hands raised in a show of insouciant innocence. 'Thought she were my sister.'

'You don't have a sister,' Heather reminded him in unambiguously unequivocal terms.

'Well if I did, bet she'd be the splitting image of whoever that is.' Naff gave Katerina a shifty grin.

Katerina sidled up to Heather and whispered, 'found him backstage at The Sundown Strip. Now that's what I call a birthday present.' As Heather sputtered for words, she nudged her in the ribs. 'I know, why don't we call ourselves Thelma and Louise, like in that dope movie?'

Heather ground the words, 'or Dumb and Dumber,

like in Dumb and Dumber,' through clenched teeth.

'So, then, sis,' Katerina said. 'What's our next case?'

'How about The Curious Case of the Castrated Casanova and the Strangulated Slut? Could be a cracker.' Alerted by a shuffle behind her, she looked round to see Sebastian Marrowboan cowering in the doorway clutching her polythene bagged twinset.

'Too much information,' Sebastian whimpered. He slid to the floor, tugged his hoodie over his head and huddled on the doormat hugging his knees. After a few jerky breaths, he took off his glasses, looked up at Heather and begged, 'please buffer your aggro, Spriggsy. I'm having a headcrash.'

And that was when an irresistible urge flushed between Heather's ears. Unable to subjugate her primeval evil for a neurosecond longer, her imagination ran riot. In her mind's eye, she was wielding pair of pinking shears and glaring from Naff to Katerina to Sebastian with a who's-first hunger in her eyes. As the tension mounted like mountain goat ratcheting higher and higher in bleats and bounds, nary a twig could be heard to creak, nary a mouse could be heard to squeak, nary a mute could be heard to speak. Just as she was about to plunge the shears into whoever's whatever – she was spoilt for choice – her cellphone rang. She grabbed it and screamed, 'go away. I'm about to do something I will regret for the rest of my life.' Before she could fling her phone on the floor and stamp on it, she heard a familiar voice sobbing on the other end of the line.

Alarmed, Heather slumped onto a multipurpose stool. 'What's wrong, Aunt Elizabeth?' she asked. 'Golly. Uncle Monty has been arrested for doing what to a what with a what?' she gasped, unable to believe her ears. 'But he wouldn't hurt a fly.' She held the phone at arm's length and stared at it as her aunt gabbled incoherently into the ether. 'Stay where you are,' she demanded. 'I'll be there as soon as I can.'

In the hope that rallying to his girlfriend's side might unblotter his copybook, Naff asked, 'trouble?' - in the circumstances as dumb and dumber a question as they come. 'Pack an overnight case and get changed. It gets well chilly on the back of the Bonneville,' he said - as if Heather didn't know. Moving swiftly into action mood, he stuffed a change of underwear, a razor and a toothbrush into his camera case and checked his watch. 'If we get a move-on,' he said, 'we should be there by eight.'

Five minutes later, suitably besuited in her *grooviest* designer jeans, a woolly jumper and a *zootishly* cute leather jacket, PC Heather Prendergast of the crack CID Egg Squad tucked her trusty Sherlock Holmes Omnibus under an arm, picked up her overnight case and slung her shoulder-bag over a shoulder. All set, she told her *unsufferable* stepsister that she would be back to throttle her when she next had a minute and put her best foot forward and her least foot back. Decided and determined, if a little apprehensive, she stepped over Sebastian Marrowboan and strode out into the cool night air. Keeping her upper lip stoically stiffed, she took the long and winding staircase to the lobby en route for the crime-riddled depravities of the Home Counties, boldly missioned to ratchet her sleuth-credentials up to the next hilt.

As she mounted the pillion of her boyfriend's ripsnorting mechanical steed, she was visited by the spine-curdling realisation that she was heading for a great unknown. For it seemed that a deathly game was afoot in that den of depravity known to all who dared whisper its name as . . .

The Municipal Borough of Royal Tunbridge Wells.

I hope you enjoyed reading this book as much as I enjoyed writing it.

Find out more about our intrepid sleuthess by nosebagging Volume One of The Prendergast of The Yard Casebooks – Elliefant's Graveyard – The Curious Case of the Throatslit Man – available now on Kindle and paperback from the prime suspect. Sign up to my newsletter at em-thompson.com for details of volume three, Murder on the Ordinary Express – The Curious Case of The Butcher of St. Mary Nook, due shortly, and The Making of Prendergast of The Yard, destined to hit the Kindlesphere early in 2025.

And finally - honest – if this riproaring pageturner has put a smile on your face, I would humbly beseech you to put a smile on mine by leaving a review.

Thank you kindly, Heather Prendergast and em thompson.

What reviewers say about Elliefant's Graveyard;

"I found the writing to be like nothing I had ever read before, and there were quite a few laugh out loud moments along the way making this a delightful read!" **Imar. USA**

"This book is a breath of fresh air. It has all the elements of a crime mystery but has a quirky and funny edge to it. It's the first book I've actually had a laugh at for a while! The story is engaging and keeps you gripped and entertained the whole way through, with a great plot that comes together brilliantly!"

Taylor AC. UK

"This is one of those rare gems that hits you with its originality and charm. Thompson writes with a clever, whimsical style. He plays with words and language, telling the story of an aspiring detective, and probationary constable, Heather Prendergast, as she investigates what she believes are two cases of murder and one unfortunate death. As someone born and raised in Yorkshire, the characters, landscape, and attitudes are all too familiar and Elliefant's Graveyard made me smile, wince, and homesick. Wonderful." **David M Cameron - Australia**

"Em Thompson's Elliefant's Graveyard is like stumbling upon a hidden door in a London alley, one that leads to a parallel universe where tea is spiked with mischief and the fog has a mischievous grin. The prose dances (part waltz, part jig) through this delightful mystery. Expect puns, chuckles, and a dash of whimsy. If you're tired of mundane reality, step into Elliefant's Graveyard. Just be careful not to trip over the invisible gnomes!" **Steve Exeter. UK**

"Make a cup of tea and settle down for a fun read." **Book Lover. USA**

"A uniquely fascinating read. Its narrative style is more akin to Lewis Carroll's works than your average detective thriller. Ideal for wannabe detectives worldwide and lovers of whimsical mysteries." **Ronnie. USA**

"A uniquely entertaining read. Perfect for fans of whimsical

mysteries and aspiring detectives everywhere." **Andrea. Italy**

"Elliefant's graveyard was the first ever book that I found funny. It is not just a story; it's a celebration of the heartfelt connections we share with those who have passed and the impact they leave behind. Through its imaginative lens, Thompson encouraged me and all the other readers out there to cherish memories, honor the past, and find comfort in the beauty of life's series. I personally liked the character Heather Prendergast so much. This book is amazing." **Nahaa. India**

"Really shines with its engaging characters and a suspenseful plot. FULL of clever wordplay, making it a really enjoyable read. Hoping the next volume of this series will come soon." **E.L.Y USA**

"Keeps you glued to each page wanting to know more. Uncovering murders, investigative reporting, and also different twist and turns. Read this book with your favourite beverage on the side during the weekend." **Ekta Chandale. India**

"A fun and well written story with mystery and suspense that will have you turning pages from the very beginning. I truly enjoyed reading this book and I look forward to the next book of the series and reading about Heather's next adventure." **Reviewer. USA**

"If you love a fun, imaginative mystery, you'll love this book!" **Emir. USA**

"I couldn't put this book down! The quirky crime mystery had *me laughing and guessing until the very end. The author's clever plot twists, engaging characters, and witty dialogue made for a truly enjoyable reading experience. The vivid descriptions and creative use of language brought the story to life. I highly recommend this unique and entertaining whodunit to anyone looking for a fun read."* **Cliente Kindle. Brazil.**

"Fans of offbeat detective novels will not want to miss this humorous and exciting book, which features witty dialogue, creative writing, and a colorful cast of characters." **Eric Foster. USA**

"A unique detective story with a twist. A must-read for mystery fans - the plot is intriguing, and the characters are complex. Cool thing!' **Marek Kaspar. USA**

"I absolutely loved this book! This quirky murder mystery features a compelling plot and richly developed characters." **Mauro. USA**

"A gripping and beautifully written novel that captures the imagination with its unique story and compelling characters. The narrative is richly layered, blending mystery with a touch of the supernatural in a way that is both haunting and unforgettable. A must-read for those who enjoy novels that are as thought-provoking as they are entertaining!" **Kelly H. USA**

Audiobook read by Billie Fulford-Brown, Audie Fiction Narrator of the Year 2024.

"I loved the narrator! She was super talented and a joy to listen

*to." **Anon-Ymous – USA***

While you're in the mood, why not check out **The Making of Prendergast of The Yard** series of rib-tickling short stories, freely available from most online bookstores. Currently available – **The Curious Case of the Kitnapped Cat.**

*"This unique story is just short yet fun. Adventurous and has a lot of humor which I like about short stories. Sherlock Holmes alike with its own character and plot twists." **Reviewer. USA***

*"A very funny story about a new police officer, Heather Prendergast, and a stolen cat. While reading this very short story, I laughed out loud several times. Fans of short and funny stories will love it." **Piter. USA***

*"I love this story because it's a light hearted and amusing take on the mystery genre. What really made this book interesting to me was how Heather's missteps add a layer of slapstick comedy to the narrative making her a character you can't help but root for. The missing cat case may be small, but it's a perfect start to her quirky, chaotic career." **John Doe. USA***

"I absolutely loved this book! Heather Prendergast is such a fun and quirky character, and her misadventures had me laughing out loud. The mix of humor, mystery, and Heather's determination (despite her lack of skills) made for a thoroughly entertaining read. I enjoyed the witty writing style and how even a simple case of a stolen cat turned into a chaotic adventure. If you love lighthearted detective stories with a comedic twist,

this is the book for you!" **Eetu. USA**

"The protagonist's clumsy attempts at solving a seemingly straightforward case are both amusing and charming. With plenty of laugh-out-loud moments and a quirky take on detective work, this story keeps readers entertained from start to finish. It's a perfect read for anyone who enjoys a blend of humor and mystery in their fiction." **John Perrotta. USA**

"Roll over Nero Wolfe and tell Miss Marple the news! There is a new detective in town! And the place is on fire (literally!) Charismatic, cute and clueless Heather Prendergast is a student at a police college and an aspiring detective. She is also a sociopath. "You seem to think that animals and people are the same" says Heather's teacher, Professor Morrisson. He is wrong. Heather detests humans. However, she is kinder to cats. I will not give away the details. I will just say, that in her search for a missing cat, Ms. Prendergast almost started a nuclear war. Despite the fact that Heather's actions led to robbery, destruction and even deaths, I am sure she will be fine. Her Aunt Elizabeth can afford good lawyers. This is a hilarious and well written book, a perfect vacation or weekend read." **Daniil Rozental. USA**

Next up, The Curious Case of the Prawnographic Nibbles with more due shortly.

Dedicated to Micky Johnson.

Thanks be to Claire, Suzi, Priscilla, Marc, Philippa, Michael, Amelie, Kate, Fiona, Fusscat, Piglet and you.

Also by em thompson

THE PRENDERGAST OF THE YARD SERIES

Elliefant's Graveyard

The Curious Case of The Throatslit Man

Other books

Krill

A political novel for our times

The Stoat Hall Legacy Book Club

Short stories

www.em-thompson.com

www.ingramcontent.com/pod-product-compliance
Ingram Content Group UK Ltd.
Pitfield, Milton Keynes, MK11 3LW, UK
UKHW042359151224
452529UK00004B/102